Teresa Hill lives within sight of the mountains in upstate South Carolina with one husband, very understanding and supportive; one daughter, who's taken up drumming (Earplugs really don't work that well. Neither do sound-muffling drum pads. Don't believe anyone who says they do.); and one son, who's studying the completely incomprehensible subject of chemical engineering (Flow rates, Mom. It's all about flow rates.).

In search of company while she writes away her days in her office, she has so far accumulated two beautiful, spoiled dogs and three cats (the black panther/champion hunter, the giant powder puff and the tiny tiger stripe), all of whom take turns being stretched out, belly-up on the floor beside her, begging for attention as she sits at her computer.

With special thanks to my mother, Rachel McIntosh, who accompanied me to Texas by plane and then on a lovely road trip from Dallas through the Texas Hill Country to San Antonio and Austin. We found San Antonio lush, green and beautiful, ate in a café in Austin with a huge rattlesnake skin on display above our booth and discovered that, for some reason, there are no acceleration lanes on Texas highways! (Really. There aren't. Why? Acceleration lanes are a very good thing.)

Chapter One

Paige McCord lay stretched out on a hilltop about a mile away from Travis Foley's Texas ranch, peering through a pair of high-powered binoculars for the third day in a row of her little surveillance mission.

It was early November, the temperatures warm for that time of year but not oppressively so for this sort of outdoor activity, the fall foliage of the Texas Hill Country at its stunning peak.

But Paige hadn't come to check out the sights or enjoy the weather.

Although there was one particular sight she had to admit she was enjoying.

And there he was.

Paige checked her watch. Nearly three-thirty.

"A tad late today, aren't you?" she asked him, adjusting the binoculars to pick up his image as he headed up the dirt trail toward the old mine entrance.

Paige was twenty-six, born and raised in Texas. She was not the kind of girl to have her head turned easily by some cowboy just because he spent his whole life working outdoors, obviously doing very physical work. Which she admitted tended to make a man lean as could be, and yet beautifully muscled, his skin pleasantly browned by the sun.

There was a certain walk cowboys did, an easy, loose-hipped swagger, in jeans that tended to be worn thin over the years, faithfully following every dip and swell of a man's body.

The look was completed by an expensive pair of boots, scuffed up by hard work over the years and a cowboy hat—not one that was for show—and a little late-afternoon stubble on his face, because he would have gotten up before the sun, and the days were long.

This man had all that, but she'd seen all that before.

And she had things to do, she reminded herself, things that were much more important than admiring a good-looking man.

Everything in her life seemed to be changing, changing too much and too quickly, and it had thrown her harder than any horse that had ever managed to unseat her.

Paige's two older brothers had just gotten engaged, and Paige hoped they knew what they were doing, but wasn't so sure. It had all happened so fast.

Tate, her second-oldest brother, had come home from two tours of duty as an Army surgeon in the Middle East and never been the same. She'd been worried about him for a while. Then he'd dumped his fiancée, Katie, whom Paige really liked, and in no time flat, was engaged to the McCord family's longtime housekeeper's daughter, Tanya. Paige liked Tanya. She did. She'd just always thought Tate would end up with Katie, that Katie would take good care of Tate and finally be a McCord.

Then Blake, her oldest brother, had suddenly decided he wanted Katie for himself, and Katie had just agreed to marry him!

Paige still didn't know exactly how all that had happened, she just hoped neither of her brothers had been hurt, and she didn't want them fighting with each other. The family had enough to worry about without her two older brothers feuding.

Her cousin Gabby, who was practically Italian royalty and the spokesperson for the McCord family's jewelry empire, hadn't settled for just an engagement. Gabby had run off with her bodyguard and married him!

It was enough to make Paige's head spin.

Then, there was her twin sister, Penny, who'd been acting weird all summer, always sneaking off somewhere, keeping all sorts of secrets, and normally Paige and Penny never kept secrets from each other. The last time Paige had talked to Gabby, Gabby had asked all sorts of questions about Penny that Paige couldn't answer. Gabby was sure something was wrong.

Not that any of the McCords were acting like themselves lately and not just because of the flurry of romances.

It was their mother.

And their youngest brother.

And their father, dead for five years now.

None of them were what they seemed to be. Her family wasn't at all what Paige had always believed it to be.

She was still so mad—and so shocked—she hardly let herself think about it, but her mother, Eleanor, had confessed this summer to the entire family that she'd long ago been involved with Rex Foley, the patriarch of a family that had been feuding with the McCords since Civil War days.

Not only been involved with him before she'd ever married Paige's father, but had a child with Rex years later! Paige's adorable youngest brother, Charlie, born after Paige's parents had separated briefly when Paige was a little girl, was actually Rex Foley's son!

Paige remembered, barely, a time when their family's Dallas mansion had been filled with tension. She and her sister, Penny, had hidden together in corners all over the house, trying to avoid the angry voices and all the tears their mother cried, their father gone, supposedly just on a long business trip.

In fact, it was the last time Penny remembered the whole family being so tense until this awful summer.

Back then, her father had eventually come home. Her mother finally stopped crying all the time, and then Charlie was born. Adorable, silly, happy Charlie.

Paige and her sister had been five when he was born, and they thought he was the best present they'd ever received, playing with him as if he was one of their dolls come to life.

She'd thought everything was fine then, and it had seemed that way for so long.

But it had all been a lie.

It was still hard to even comprehend how many lies had been told or what would happen to them all from this point on. It was hard for her to even think about it for too long. She had tried to keep busy and then, thankfully, had found a job to do for her family.

A very important job.

She was happy to have a reason to be out of Dallas right now and away from all the tension at the McCord mansion.

Happy to be lying in the grass on a gorgeous November day, staring through her binoculars at a man who was every bit as gorgeous and distracting.

He climbed off of his chestnut-colored horse, let the horse take a nice, long drink from the stream nearby, then—looked like it was going to be Paige's lucky day—started unbuttoning his chambray shirt.

Oh, my.

He pulled a bandana from his back pocket, then he bent over and dipped the bandana in the stream and turned around to face her.

Paige jerked the binoculars away from her face, as if he had a hope of seeing her from this far away. She'd just been so surprised, looking him in the face, even at a distance.

Although to be honest, she couldn't see his face that well from this distance. Still, it looked like he'd winced at something.

She got the binoculars again, found him and saw him cooling off in the stream, washing off some of the grit from working outside all day.

Looked like he'd landed in the dirt at some point.

Not that she objected.

He lifted his face to the sun and let the water from the bandana run down his face, his neck, run in a line down what looked like a perfectly sculpted set of muscles in his chest and rock-hard abs.

Oh, my.

That water had to be cold, she thought. The days tended to be warm right now in the hill country, but the nights were cooler, dipping into the forties the past few nights.

She knew because she was camping out in the national park that lucky for her was just a few miles west of Travis Foley's ranch. Because there certainly wasn't much of a town anywhere nearby, and a stranger staying in a little town like Llano would be noticed.

And Paige couldn't afford to have anyone—particularly Travis Foley—know she was here.

She went back to watching her cowboy, who'd ridden by this particular spot for the last two days in a row, working hard. She thought he was probably doing grunt work, rounding up strays, checking fences and watching for trespassers, while the boss, Travis Foley, likely sat in his air-conditioned mansion somewhere on the edge of the property, counting all his family's oil money or checking on investments or something cushy like that.

She couldn't imagine a Foley working his ranch day-to-day.

He had men like the one she was watching for that.

He finished cleaning up, put the bandana down and buttoned up his shirt. Then he leaned back against that big rock and lifted his face to the sky, like a man admiring the fall sunshine or the still-warm afternoon breeze.

Or maybe like a man worn-out, whether by his work or his own problems, she didn't know.

Or a man who just really needed to get away from it all, to relax here in the peace and quiet of this empty corner of Travis Foley's ranch.

If Paige had time, she might like to enjoy some peace and quiet with him, maybe even a little time in the dark.

It wasn't the kind of thing Paige did, pick up a stranger for the night.

But the summer had been just awful, and sometimes she got to the point where all the problems, all the changes kept racing around in her head, one after another, piling up in there, the pressure building until she just wanted to scream.

This man, this cowboy…surely he could make her forget.

Even if it was just for a night. Not that she had time for that, either. But a woman could dream, couldn't she?

In the meantime, she had work to do.

Once he left, she'd have a full twenty-four hours before he was back again, if the pattern of the last three days held. She had all her equipment with her in her backpack and was a little uneasy about going into the old silver mine alone—anyone who knew anything about old mines would be—but she'd taken every pre-caution she could.

And she was determined to do this. Her family needed her. She'd promised her brother, Blake, who was CEO of the family's jewelry empire.

Paige stopped thinking about her cowboy. If she did her job right, she'd never even meet him. What a shame.

She put down her binoculars and pulled out her satellite phone. Regular cell coverage was lousy out here in the middle of nowhere.

Blake answered on the second ring, sounding anxious. "Well?" he asked.

"I'm set. I'm going in," she told him. "You know what to do?"

"If I don't hear from you by dawn, I call your friend in the mining department at the university and we come find you," he promised. "Paige, are you sure this is safe? I couldn't stand it if anything happened to you."

"The mine's been there for a hundred years. Travis Foley let a group of archaeologists in there last year to document the petroglyphs on the walls. I got a copy of their report. The place is stable as can be—"

"Still, isn't it dangerous to go in there alone?"

They'd been through this. They'd agreed. No one else could know. Too much was at stake.

Blake merely claimed things were difficult right now financially for the jewelry stores, but that he was handling it. Which is likely what Paige's proud, stubborn, determined oldest brother would say if the world was about to come to an end. He'd be sure he could save it all on his own.

And she was just as determined to help him.

She didn't think the world was coming to an end, just that the problem with the stores was a serious one, and one problem to do with her family that she could actually solve. And she was determined to do just that. Solve it.

"Blake, I'm working on my PhD in geology. I know what I'm doing. Besides, I was in that mine myself weeks ago, just to make sure the reports were right and to make sure I had the equipment I'd need. Trust me. Everything will be fine."

Actually, if her cowboy was the one who caught her, Paige didn't think she'd mind all that much. She was confident she could talk her way out of trouble, if she had to, and she'd be long gone before the news ever got back to Travis Foley that anyone was here.

"I heard the Foleys are having some big family meeting this weekend, which means Travis Foley should be on a plane headed for Dallas by now. So you shouldn't have to worry about him."

"Good." He was one person Paige really didn't want to run into.

"But what about the weather?" Blake asked. "There are some nasty storms predicted from that hurricane in the gulf—"

"Storms that aren't supposed to arrive until tomorrow in the area north of here. I checked the weather radar myself this morning. I'm going in now, and I'll be out before the storm hits tomorrow," Paige told her brother. "You worry too much. I'll be in touch by morning."

Travis Foley got back on his horse and headed up the rise to the rock overhang that hid the entrance to the old mine at the far corner of the 6,500-acre ranch he called home.

It had been his grandfather's before him, his absolute favorite place to be as a child. Out here where he could breathe, where in the quiet he could think and find some peace and do an honest day's work.

The rest of his family, the Foleys, just didn't understand him, and honestly, Travis didn't understand them.

They were oilmen and politicians, big shots out in what they thought was the real world.

This world, to Travis, was real.

It was all the life he wanted, right here.

He wished they'd all just leave him the hell alone and let him enjoy it.

But ever since that old Spanish shipwreck had been found in the Gulf of Mexico, people had gone nuts looking for the Santa Magdalena Diamond, a rock that was supposed to rival the Hope Diamond in size and value.

One of Travis's ancestors, Elwin Foley, had been on that ship when it sank in the 1800s, supposedly along with the diamond and a treasure chest full of old Spanish silver coins.

No one was sure exactly what happened after that. Either the diamond went down with the ship or one of the survivors got away with it. The stone had never been found.

Travis's ancestor survived, bought the ranch on which Travis now lived and started mining for silver. Elwin Foley certainly hadn't lived the life of a man who possessed a fortune in diamonds, working hard on the ranch until he lost his life in a mining accident before ever finding any silver.

His son, Gavin, had even worse luck—raised by his mother alone, barely getting by on the ranch and as a man, developing a gambling problem that led to him losing the ranch and the deed to the old silver mines in the late 1890s in a card game to a man named Harry McCord.

Travis was disgusted just thinking about it and how much the old feud was still alive today between his family and the McCords.

His ancestor, Gavin, had always claimed the poker game was fixed, that Harry McCord was a card cheat. And the McCords had the nerve to strike it rich on the silver mines not long after supposedly winning the deed to the ranch and the mines.

Travis really didn't give a damn. His family had gotten rich in the oil business a few years later. None of them were hurting for money. He didn't begrudge the McCords the fortune they'd built in the jewelry business over the years, a fortune that started with the discovery of silver in the mines.

But he sure begrudged the loss of the ranch.

Because while he lived on the ranch now, as his grandfather had before him, worked it, sweat over it, bled over it, made this place his life, he could never own it.

The McCords did, thanks to a bad hand of poker more than a hundred years ago or a card cheat, depending on which version of the legend a man believed.

Twenty years ago, in an effort to end the bitter feud, Eleanor McCord had offered a long-term lease of the land to the Foleys, which Travis's grandfather had accepted, then come here to make the ranch his own.

Travis had spent the best days of his childhood here and had taken over the ranch when his grandfather died ten years ago. But it wasn't the same as owning the land, and that still had the power to burn a hole in Travis Foley's gut when he let himself think about it too long.

Which was hard not to do when all the hoopla over the stupid diamond and the feud had sprung up again.

Explorers had found the sunken Spanish ship, along with a cache of old Spanish diamonds.

But not the Santa Magdalena.

Which fueled speculation all over again that someone who survived the shipwreck had gotten away with the diamond, and it had long been rumored that person was Elwin Foley, who'd founded the ranch and lived out the rest of his life there.

Which had even more people thinking that the most likely place to find that diamond was right here on Travis's ranch.

Now treasure hunters, gem collectors and even jewel thieves were just showing up here, looking for that cursed diamond. Didn't the damned fools know everyone who'd ever owned it had come to a bad end? Not that it had kept people from looking.

As if Travis didn't have enough to do on a 6,500-acre ranch in November besides keep people from hurting themselves, spooking his cattle, cutting his fences or getting bitten by snakes or something like that.

They'd already kicked five people off the property since the shipwreck was found.

Even worse, Travis's family was convinced the McCords were up to something, something to do with the diamond. Like sending someone to look for it on Travis's ranch.

Had Gavin Foley found it, after he'd supposedly lost the ranch? And hidden it here for one of his ancestors to find later, when one day they might have a hope of owning it free and clear? Finders, keepers?

And had the McCords, after all these years, stumbled upon some clue as to where the diamond might now be?

Travis was highly skeptical of that notion, although his family was not.

He'd finally told them to do what they wanted to figure out what the McCords were up to, that he wanted no part of it. His only concession was agreeing to have someone check each of the mines daily for signs of trouble.

Not just from the McCords but from those damned fool diamond hunters.

Travis had found footprints leading into and away from the Eagle Mine a few weeks ago, had crawled down inside about ten feet and checked things out, but hadn't found anything else.

Still, someone had been there, and it hadn't been him or any of the ranch hands.

So he checked the place himself every afternoon.

Today, everything seemed quiet.

He got off his horse, walked along the long, deep rock overhang, twenty feet wide and at least twenty feet deep, the ceiling sloping downward in the back and at its deepest recess, neatly obscuring the entrance to this particular mine in its dark shadows.

All quiet.

No footprints except his own, which he brushed away with a rake he'd hidden in the brush outside the entrance.

But as he went back outside and stood there, taking a long, cool drink of water from his canteen, he had the oddest feeling.

That someone was out there.

That someone was watching him.

He'd felt the same way at the stream, trying to rinse the dirt off the nasty scratch he'd gotten earlier that day tangling with a barbed wire fence someone had cut.

No one should be out here watching him. From here, it was ranch property for as far as the eye could see, except for that corner of the property that butted up to the national park.

But if someone was watching him, Travis was going to find 'em.

Chapter Two

Paige had to admit, she loved exploring and she didn't get to do as much of it as she liked these days. Too many hours spent at her desk in front of her computer, working on her dissertation.

So she was thrilled in a way to have an excuse to go traipsing through this old mine.

As a highly trained scientist—chief gemologist to her family's worldwide jewelry company, with a master's in geology and hopefully soon a PhD—the idea of discovering a gemstone believed to rival the Hope Diamond was thrilling in a way that had nothing to do with saving the family fortune.

It was the kind of discovery anyone who traveled the world exploring and truly loved the various, extraordinary substances the earth, over time, could yield would have dreamed their entire life about making.

Few scientists ever got to experience the thrill of such a find.

Paige wanted it so bad she could taste it.

Her heart was thrumming so fast it was like a roar in her ears as she stood at the entrance to the mine once her adorable cowboy was gone.

She put down her big backpack, then took out her helmet with her LED light and turned it on, leaving it on the ground to provide some light in the recesses of the overhang that guarded the mine's entrance. From her pack, she pulled out an old pair of coveralls—because exploring was a messy, often cold business. She'd worn her hiking boots in, put one small, spare light around her neck on a cord and another in the smaller pack she'd carry in, along with a small length of rope, spare batteries, power bars and granola, some water, a small notebook and a camera.

Her hair was already in a long braid, which she tucked inside her coveralls. Then she put her helmet on with her LED light wrapped around it. Making sure the light was on, she was ready.

Paige took a breath, let it out slow and off she went into the dark, cool quiet of the old mine.

Travis couldn't believe she went into that mine alone!

He'd hung back, waiting once he'd gotten over the ridge, and there she'd come, a hat tilted low obscuring his view of her face as she hiked over from the ranch's boundary nearest the park.

Looking very efficient, he might add, once he'd crept back close enough and gotten down nearly to ground level so he could watch. She snapped on her light in the deep recesses of the overhang. She suited up, checked her equipment—she'd come prepared, at least—and then seemed to disappear.

He'd been sure there had to be someone else with her, that she wouldn't go inside the mine alone. He'd wanted to catch her companion, too, so he'd waited.

He'd been here when a bunch of archaeologists had explored the mine last year, photographing and documenting the ancient drawings and carvings on the walls called petroglyphs. He had gone inside with them a few times to see what all the fuss was about.

None of the archaeologists had ever gone into that mine alone!

And yet today, there she went!

"Damned, stupid woman!" he growled. His horse gave him an odd look. Travis shook his head. "Not you, Murph," he told the horse.

He climbed into the saddle and headed for the mine, thinking he just might have her arrested for trespassing. Maybe it would make anybody else think twice before trying what she just did.

He needed to put a stop to this nonsense before anyone got hurt.

At the overhang, he tethered Murphy to a small tree and fished in his saddlebags for an oversize flashlight so he'd at least be able to see a bit in front of him, took off his hat, shook his head and swore some more about lost diamonds, family feuds, treasure hunters and women.

He got to the mouth of the mine and headed after her. The entrance was nearly tall enough that he could stand up without hitting his head.

Nearly.

Apparently the miners weren't quite six feet two inches.

If he hunched over a bit, he could stand and walk. The entrance sloped down, but only slightly, nothing too taxing or too dangerous here.

He had the flashlight on but pointed at his feet, not wanting to warn his little trespasser she was about to get caught.

About fifteen feet in, he came to a vertical shaft that went down twenty feet to the next level and another horizontal shaft.

He'd gone this far before, just not alone. The makeshift ladder attached to the mine wall was metal and had been checked and reinforced just last year, had held his weight just fine then.

Travis hoped to hell he caught her somewhere on the horizontal shaft at the twenty-foot level.

He sure didn't want to have to go any farther and allowed himself to mutter some more about stupid legends, ancient curses and women.

He climbed down the shaft, then stood on the horizontal shaft as it opened up both left and right.

Did she know she wasn't alone by now? Had she heard him? She didn't have that much of a head start, and he would hope she was being more careful and moving more slowly than he was, since she hadn't been here before.

At least, he didn't think she'd been here.

Travis stood there, listening, finally hearing a clank and then a muffled curse in the shaft to the left. He hoped she was at least as frustrated as he was and liked the idea that he might scare her half to death, coming upon her this way in an abandoned mine.

If he did, maybe she wouldn't do anything this stupid again.

He crept along, the light out now, going by the feel of the cool, rock wall against his right hand. He caught a glimpse of light, then of what she was studying.

One of the petroglyphs.

An eagle.

He could see it in the light from her helmet, but had only a vague impression of her, sturdy boots, baggy coveralls and a helmet, her nose practically pressed against the rock onto which someone maybe as long as five thousand years ago had carved an eagle.

He was sure she'd come after the diamond.

So why was she studying the drawings?

Travis backed out of the shaft quietly, slowly, wanting to know what she'd do next.

Finally, she started making her way back to the center of the twenty-foot level. From there, it was either explore the passage to the right or descend again.

This time to a hundred feet.

He thought it was downright creepy being that far underground under solid rock.

Surely she wasn't going to do that.

He waited just down the right-hand passageway, peered around the edge of the wall and there she was, checking out the vertical shaft that descended to the next level.

"God almighty!" he muttered, then walked over there and grabbed her around her waist and picked her up as she knelt on the ground peering into a hole, seemingly comfortable as could be, with an eighty-foot drop beneath her.

She screamed so loud he thought she might bring the walls down around them, and he lifted her up in the air and held her there, her body curled up in a ball, mad as hell. She kicked out with her feet and got some leverage against the opposite wall, sent him tumbling back and hitting the wall behind him none too gently.

He held on, one arm around her waist and one managing to get a grip that flattened both arms against her body.

When she finally stopped screaming, he muttered into her ear, "Hush. There's no place to run, and I'm sure as hell not letting you climb down any farther into this mine."

She stopped struggling, finally. She had lost her helmet at some point and its light was now shining down the passageway to the right, so he couldn't see her and she couldn't see him.

He could feel her breathing hard, and didn't feel in the least bit guilty about manhandling her this way, at least not until she calmed down. He wasn't going to let her flounder around and hurt herself or get lost, or God forbid, fall down the eighty-foot vertical shaft in the dark.

"You scared me half to death!" she told him finally, still breathing hard and spitting mad.

Travis eased back just enough to turn her around in his arms, her back against the opposite wall of the mine, then held her there with his own body pressed hard against hers.

"Yeah?" he said, his face so close to hers he could feel the breath coming out of her body. "And you scared me. Do you have any idea how dangerous it is to come into a place like this alone?"

"I know what I'm doing. I'm a grad student in geology at the university," she claimed.

"Do you also know you're trespassing on private property?" he tried, looming over her in the dark, determined to have his say.

"Well…yes," she conceded, finally.

He eased back, still holding her there with his body, but not up in her face, the way he had been.

She was a tiny thing, he'd realized when he'd had her plastered against him just now, slender as could be. Young, too, if she really was a student, like she said.

He didn't think she was going to try to get away any longer, so staying that close to her was more of a distraction than a help at the moment. And he was quickly discovering she had all the necessary attributes to be very distracting to a man.

Travis fought to put those kind of thoughts completely out of his head as he backed away just enough so that he wasn't touching her anymore but could still grab hold of her quickly if he needed to.

"You know if I haul you out of here and call the sheriff, he'd treat you to at least a night in jail," he said.

She sighed. "You don't really want to do that. Do you?"

"If it kept you from trying some damned fool stunt like this again, yeah, I do."

"Look, I'm sorry. I just—"

"Have to find that stupid diamond? Yeah. I've heard it before—"

"Do you have any idea what kind of an opportunity this is?"

"Oh, yeah. Millions of dollars at stake, and you think all you have to do is find it."

"No. Not the money," she claimed. "Finding it. If the Santa Magdalena Diamond is really somewhere on this ranch, it's the find of a lifetime. Scientists spend their whole lives studying and searching, and most of them will never discover anything like this. It's amazing! How could anyone who's serious about a career in science pass up that opportunity?"

Travis frowned, hearing the honest enthusiasm in her voice. Same as with those archaeology students and their supervisors who were on the ranch last summer studying the petroglyphs.

He didn't really understand getting that excited or being so fascinated with those drawings, but he'd seen that kind of enthusiasm and pure joy of discovery before in them.

So she took stupid risks, but that yearning to explore, to discover, he at least understood better than those fools out to make millions by simply getting lucky and stumbling upon a treasure. He believed in hard work much more than luck, so he could understand a bit of what drove her and wasn't quite as annoyed as he was before.

And maybe he even envied her that kind of excitement and yearning. Travis, at thirty, was a man content with his life most days. But every now and then, it felt a little too settled, too predictable.

A little empty.

He didn't remember the last time he was as excited about anything as she was about the chance of discovering the old diamond. A feeling he certainly wasn't going to stand in this old mine and try to analyze.

"Come on," he said, finding her helmet and putting it back on her head, wincing as the light hit him square in the face and quickly turning away. "You're done exploring. We're going up top."

She sighed once again. "Couldn't you just let me look around? I mean, we're already here. What's it going to hurt?"

"The next level is a hundred feet below the surface," he told her.

"I know."

She sounded like the idea thrilled her.

Then he realized something. "You know? What do you mean, you know?"

"From the maps," she said.

"You have maps of this mine?"

"Of course. The people who originally worked the mine kept maps. Not as precise as what we'd make today, but you can find those historical documents if you know where to look. And scientists who've explored the mines over the years kept maps, too. I told you, I'm serious about this. It's not a crazy pipe dream to me. I'm a scientist. And you could help me."

"Why would I want to do that?"

She shrugged. He was close enough that he could feel the movement. "For the money?" she tried. "There's supposed to be a jeweled chest full of old Spanish coins, too. Silver coins. I mean, even a cowboy could appreciate the chance to have that kind of money. This could be the kind of fortune that would let you buy your own ranch someday, if you wanted. And...you wouldn't really even have to help me, if you didn't want to. You could just...not tell anybody I was here? Maybe not tell anyone if I came back and searched some more? I'd pay you, if you wanted, just to...not tell anybody what I was doing."

"You'd go back in here by yourself?" he asked incredulously.

"Yes. And you could stay topside, just to be there in case I did get in trouble. All you'd have to do is call for help. I have friends who'd know what to do to get me out."

Travis swore under his breath. "I think you're nuts to take that kind of risk."

"And I think some people spend their whole lives without ever taking a risk at all, which to me is even worse."

He shook his head. "Well, I think this is a ridiculous conversation to be having while buried under tons of rock. Start climbing."

She hadn't climbed more than two steps on the ladder when a howling, whistling sound swept through the mine.

And then, as the howling died down for a moment, there was a tapping sound, far away and not that loud. Like the beating of a drum. Solid objects hitting other solid objects. And then more howling.

"What the hell is that?" he asked, as they both froze for a moment.

He told himself if it was what he feared—falling rocks—he'd have been hit by something already. Unless it was father down inside the mine or up near the entrance and just hadn't made it to them.

Not yet, anyway.

"Wind," she said.

Okay. Yeah. He felt it, now that he wasn't thinking obsessively of being pelted by rocks. Still, that wasn't all.

"Wind and what else?" he demanded.

"I'm not sure," his gutsy explorer said, not sounding nearly as confident as she had been a moment ago.

He swore, feeling every bit of that distance between him and the surface. "Let's get out of here. Now."

She took off for the top, seeming to know her way in the dark a heck of a lot better than Travis did. He went scrambling after her. When he made it to the horizontal shaft near the surface, she found his hand, grabbed it and pulled him along behind her.

The eerie howling got louder with every step they took and at every moment, Travis still expected to have rocks come hurling down on him, but they never did.

He bashed his head a couple of times on the way out, not able to see that well in the tunnel and moving faster than a man of his size should in a shaft of that size.

Near the entrance, she was sure she smelled rain. But there was no way rain would account for the other sound she heard.

The space around them opened up, but it was still oddly dark, and then Travis realized they'd made it out of the mine, to the long, deep rock overhang that created a covered area sheltered from the elements.

Good thing, too, because outside the sky was nearly black, the world around them a gloomy gray. Out in the open, he saw what looked like miniature, eerily white golf balls bouncing off the ground.

Hail.

It was coming down something fierce, pounding into the ground and then bouncing around until it settled for good. The wind sounded absolutely furious, his horse long gone, no doubt realizing weather was coming long before Travis did and taking off for home.

Travis and the woman backed up against the rock wall as far under the overhang as they could get and still stand up. He was breathing hard, bleeding a bit from the gash he'd just gotten on his head, adrenaline still zinging through his whole body.

Looking at her through the grayish light, he felt a little bit foolish for coming near panic back there, a little bit mad at her for putting them both in that situation and very, very grateful to be out of it and safe.

They weren't buried under tons of rocks.

They weren't dying or already dead.

Just in the middle of a nasty storm. Hail or not, it was just a storm.

He shook his head, trying to clear it, then chuckled, then started laughing.

Maybe because it was the last thing he'd expected to be a part of his day. Descending into an old abandoned silver mine shaft chasing a determined, passionate, half-crazy woman, and then seeing his life flash before his eyes for a moment, only to see a moment later that he wasn't in any danger at all.

He wished he could really see her face. The gloom that had descended was like looking through a thick fog, and she'd clicked off her helmet light, which hadn't shown them anything but rain, and nearly blinded him every time she turned in his direction. He had more of an impression of her than anything else, but he knew she was grinning, too.

A moment later, she was laughing. "It's easy to get spooked down there," she admitted.

"I think I was way past spooked," Travis admitted. "And at the speed you climbed out of that hellhole, I'd say you were, too."

"Well," she shrugged. "Yeah. I guess… I mean, I'm really glad I wasn't down there alone when the storm hit."

"Me, too," he said, thinking, scared or not, it was the most excitement he'd had in his life in months, which was surely a sad commentary on his life right now.

So he couldn't really say he was sorry to have found her sneaking into his mine today, and he wasn't sorry he'd gone in after her, either.

Or even that there was a helluva storm raging around them, lightning crackling loud enough that it seemed like it could split the ground wide open in front of them at any moment.

Storms came big in Texas. He used to love storms on the ranch when he was a kid, so wild and loud, like coming over the top of the biggest hill on a roller coaster and then feeling like he was going to come flying out of his seat at any moment.

Feeling like anything could happen in the next instant, and that no one was really safe.

A man needed to feel like that every now and then, no matter how much he loved the solitude and serenity of his land.

He stared at her, again wishing he could really see her, that he had more than those fleeting moments when he'd watched her climb down the rise and disappear into the mine. Unfortunately, then he'd been concentrating on figuring out what she was up to, not what she looked like. He just remembered noticing a tall, slender body and a dark reddish-brown braid of hair hanging down her back. And he wasn't going to ask her to turn on her helmet light just so he could see her better. They needed to save the batteries, anyway.

She went still, then backed up a bit, and he had to catch her before she went too far.

"You're gonna bump your head if you take another step backward," he said, holding her by the arms, and then putting a hand at the back of her head, between her and the rock overhang. "Right there."

She touched his right temple, her fingers cool and soft against his skin. "You already bumped yours. It's bleeding."

He kept hold of her head and leaned into her touch, too, gentle as could be.

She had on a pair of coveralls that hid every bit of her body. Her dark hair was pulled back from her face and tucked inside the coveralls, her face turned up to his, his body shielding hers from the worst of the wind.

"Do you think it's the hurricane?" she asked.

"I'm not sure."

"Because it's not supposed to be here. It's supposed to stay well north of here—"

"You want to try telling the storm that?" he asked her.

"And it wasn't supposed to get this far inland until tomorrow. I checked."

"Yeah. I did, too. But the weather out here isn't always as predictable as we'd like."

She pouted a bit, and he tried to ignore how cute that little pout looked to him. "I'm just saying…I was careful about everything, and I was watching the weather to make sure it would be okay, and now…well, I guess we're not going anywhere fast in this."

"No, we're not."

He couldn't say he actually regretted that, either.

Chapter Three

Travis tried not to look too eager at the likely prospect of being trapped here all night with her, because he didn't want to scare her, and a woman caught alone for the night with a man she didn't know would have to be a little scared.

So he backed up until the rain blowing in on the wind hit his back in a fine spray, then moved to the side, giving her some space to think things through.

A man who spent his life working the land, often long distances from the ranch house, got caught out in the elements. It was just something that happened. If she'd spent any time in the field as a geologist, she'd probably been caught out in storms, too.

No big deal.

They had shelter from the rain and could likely wait out the storm here just fine, at least until morning light.

He gave up studying her as best as he could through the gloom—it wasn't getting any easier to see—and went with his impressions of her, what he felt she was like. Calm, practical and then...something else.

"You look like you're up to something," he said.

She shrugged. "I'm just thinking that...I'm glad we're out of the rain," she tried.

"Yes." He nodded. "And?"

"And...that...I've been caught in worse weather than this."

"Me, too," he agreed. But that wasn't it, either.

"My Jeep is just over the ridge, maybe a mile away, just across the boundary into the park. I don't suppose—"

Lightning crackled across the sky, then landed with a giant boom.

He could swear he saw her flinch as it hit.

Little Ms. No-Fear was actually afraid of lightning? At least a little bit?

"You really don't want to take a chance on getting hit by lightning," he said.

"I know," she said, like a woman who really knew what a lightning strike could do. "I just thought...the Jeep isn't that far—"

"Even if we didn't have the lightning to contend with, in a downpour like this, the soil out here turns to the consistency of warm mush."

She sighed. "I was afraid of that."

It happened in Texas with its fine, silty soil not accustomed to this kind of rain. It was like trying to walk through quicksand when it suddenly got wet.

"Hey, what happened to your horse?" she asked.

"Long gone. He doesn't like lightning, either, wouldn't leave me for anything but that. Wasn't much around here to tether him to that could actually hold him, if he decided to run, just some scrawny bushes. He would have uprooted the thing by turning his head."

"Oh, okay…. So, for us… What about in the morning? Surely the lightning will have stopped, and we can make it to the Jeep then, can't we?" she said.

"Maybe, although it's still not easy getting any real traction for a while after this kind of storm passes through. Not off-road. You are off-road there, aren't you?"

"By a couple of miles," she admitted.

"Don't worry. If we can't get to your car, there's an old hunting cabin a mile or so from here and high ground between us and it. We'll go at first light, as long as the lightning's through, and hold up there. The ranch hands will be out, checking to make sure everything's okay. Someone from the ranch will find us before long."

"And this spot where we are? It won't flood?"

"Not overnight. If it's still raining like this tomorrow during the day, tomorrow night it might. But don't worry. I've lived on this ranch for the better part of twenty years, know every inch of the place. I know how to keep you safe here, Red, and I'll do it, too."

"Red?"

He grinned. "It is red, isn't it? I can't be sure in this light, but I thought when I watched you walk down to the mine entrance—"

"Yes, my hair is red," she admitted.

"Thought so." He didn't say she had the fiery temperament to go along with it. "So, is this a problem? Spending the night here? Because there really isn't anything else to do—"

"I know. I believe you," she claimed. "So, I guess we should probably…get comfortable. Since we'll be here for the night. Right?"

He nodded. "Are you afraid of me, Red?"

"No." She vehemently denied it.

"Because there's no reason for you to be. I'm not gonna hurt you. Or do anything to you. We're just in this together now, and really, it's a little bit of nothing. One slightly uncomfortable night. That's all. Might as well make the best of it."

He was right. Paige knew he was. No way she could argue the point.

It was just…well, the lightning, for one thing. She hated lightning.

And spending the night with him.

She'd been daydreaming about that very thing when she watched him with his horse by the stream earlier, and she'd felt perfectly safe doing that. Fantasizing about being the kind of woman to just let herself go for a night with a perfect stranger.

She'd never been the kind of woman to let herself do that. A girl growing up with money in a very public way… Well, her father had warned her and her sister early on that there would be boys who wanted her for her money, and she, of course, hadn't listened. It was one lesson she'd learned the hard way, and it had hurt. She'd always been a bit cautious around men since then, a bit distrustful of their motives when they claimed to want her, and she just couldn't be sure they didn't really want a rich woman.

Still, it was a little disconcerting, the way she'd been thinking of him, and to now find herself about to get one night alone with him.

Almost like the world had heard her longing for a man—this man—and delivered him to her.

Paige didn't think the world worked that way.

At least, it never had for her.

She shook her head to clear it of such foolish thoughts, and then started emptying her pockets, taking inventory as she went.

"Let's see what we've got. Extra flashlight, extra batteries for the flashlights, a couple of power bars, some high-energy granola mix, a small bottle of water, a small notebook and a camera. And I hiked in with a backpack, stashed it under the bushes by the…" Her voice trailed off as she saw that he was already headed in that direction. "You were watching me earlier?"

"Yes, I was," he admitted, going right to the spot where she'd left her backpack, finding it with no hesitation at all and bringing it back to her.

She wanted to protest, but how could she? She'd done the same thing, spied on him.

She took the pack from him and started pulling things out. A bigger bottle of water, some more granola, some matches, a survival blanket, which he took and looked over appreciatively.

"That will come in handy tonight."

Then she pulled out her satellite phone.

He shot her a pointed look.

"I'm not stupid. I didn't go in without telling someone what I was doing. If my brother doesn't hear from me by 6:00 a.m., he'll be here soon after that to get me out." She hesitated with the phone, then looked out into the storm. "Do you think—"

"No way," he said. "Not in this."

She tried anyway. "I have to," she told her cowboy. "My brother will go nuts before this storm is over."

Of course, he was right.

No signal.

She put the phone away and hoped she could reach her brother by morning, because he would be frantic otherwise and if the flooding kept him from getting here to her... Well, it would not be pretty.

Her brother thought he could move mountains. And he would to get to her if he thought she was in trouble, and then their whole plan to find the diamond would come out. If the Foleys knew what Paige was up to, she'd have to fight to set foot on this land again.

Yeah, she had to reach Blake by first light, if not sooner.

Paige made herself keep going with her unpacking, until she came to a thick, warm sweater and a fitted pair of sweatpants. She unbuttoned her coveralls and slid out of them, pulling on a second layer of clothes over her jeans and tank top, in favor of the coveralls, which were grimy and dusty from the old mine.

She and Travis shared some granola and water, watched the storm for a bit and then he suggested they might as well bed down for the night. It was early, but the sooner they slept, the sooner they'd wake up and could try to get out of here.

Paige looked over their options. "That spot's the most sheltered, the farthest out of the rain."

He nodded.

She took her coveralls and spread them out on the cold ground right against the back wall of the overhang and motioned for him to make himself comfortable.

As she suspected, he planned to sit up and watch the storm, settling himself with his back to one wall, facing out toward the gloomy night.

"You're sure this area isn't going to flood that quickly?" she asked.

"Reasonably sure, but I'm not taking any chances," he said. "I'm going to watch and make sure."

She sat down beside him, thinking to watch the storm herself.

"There's no reason for both of us to stay up all night," he said. "Or for both of us to be uncomfortable. Come on, Red. I won't bite."

He held out an arm to her and she settled against his side, finding a welcome heat and a body that was hard-muscled, but not as hard as the ground.

He put the survival blanket over her and still had enough left over to cover about half of him, and soon she was toasty warm, her head on his chest, her whole side plastered to his.

She felt his hand at the side of her face, covering her eyes and blocking the lightning, at least a bit.

"Go to sleep," he said. "I won't let anything hurt you."

She tried. Really tried.

But the wind slowly and steadily picked up, the fierceness of the storm growing with every moment. Every bolt of lightning had her struggling more and more to cover her fears, to stay still, to keep breathing easily and deeply, when all she wanted to do was get as close to him as possible and beg him to make it all stop.

It was a foolish thing, being afraid of something as simple as a storm, and yet, there it was. Caught in this eerily dark world, she was afraid.

And there was so little in life she truly feared.

She worked her face deeper into the curve between his shoulder and his neck and closed her eyes. "It is the hurricane, isn't it? The way the winds keep building. It's... That's what hurricane winds do."

"Yeah, it looks like we got the hurricane," he told her, arms holding her tight.

"So we just sit here and see how much worse it gets?" That seemed completely unreasonable.

"Not much else to do, Red."

"I mean, we don't know how much worse it's going to get or when its going to stop—"

"No, we don't."

"Tornadoes spring up from these storms when they're over land—"

"Sometimes," he admitted.

"Tornadoes, lightning, flooding. Perfect night—"

She broke off with a gasp as a huge clap of thunder drowned out her words.

He scooped her up and deposited her sideways on his lap, even closer than she had been to him, draped the blanket around her and grinned as he looked down into her eyes.

"You know, I could make you forget," he said.

"What?"

"The storm. That you're afraid—"

She sputtered, surprised and furious. "I am not afraid!"

"Red, you flinch every time a bolt of lightning strikes. Not a lot, and I know you're fighting it, but you do. And that's fine. I mean, it's no big deal. We're all afraid of something, and I'm just saying, I'm here. I'm happy to be of help, to get you through the night. Whatever it takes."

Paige shook her head, having a hard time thinking, between being on guard about when and where the next bit of lightning might strike and trying to hide her fears and then having this man…this altogether tempting specimen of man make her an offer of…what, exactly?

"Are you saying, you'll…that you'll—"

"Whatever you want," he said smoothly, a hint of amusement and, she thought, sheer wickedness in his tone.

"You think I would be so caught up in you and whatever you were doing to me, that I'd forget all about the storm and being afraid? You think you're that good?"

"I'm saying I'm willing to try, that I'd certainly give it my best shot. I mean…I managed to distract you for the last few moments, didn't I?"

"I—I—I can't believe you—"

"You haven't flinched over the last two lightning strikes, in case you didn't notice. So from where I sit, it seems to be working."

From where he sat!

Well, from where she sat, she was… She was on top of him, all lean muscles and heat and…and…

She had pushed herself upright at one point, wasn't snuggled against him as she had been at first, but she was still sitting on his lap, her hands pressed against his chest for balance and to keep her from getting any closer.

"I don't… I just…I don't do this."

"Do what? Snuggle? Kiss? Play around a little?"

Play around a little?

"That's what you're offering to do?" she asked.

He shrugged easily. "I'm saying I'm open to the possibilities."

He made it sound so innocent, like nothing of consequence at all. Like passing the time in casual conversation or something.

"Actually," he said. "Now that I think about it, not absolutely anything. We couldn't actually have sex. No condoms. I don't generally ride around the ranch prepared in that particular way."

"Not an opportunity that normally presents itself during a normal workday at the ranch?" she quipped.

"No, Red. I have to say, it just doesn't happen. Damned shame, don't you think? I love working this ranch. Something like that happened every now and then… Well, I'd have to say the job would be just about perfect then."

"Get lonely out here, Cowboy?"

He nodded.

She shook her head. "I can't decide what to make of you. If you were half-serious about that or just…just—"

"I was going to kiss you," he admitted, laughing

beautifully, that rich, deep voice of his wrapping around her like a spell in the dark. "Although I am up for just about anything you'd like. I mean…a man needs to take care of a woman. It's just…what a man does."

"Make the sacrifice? Since I'm afraid and everything?"

"Yes, ma'am."

"Is this some cowboy code you live by? You're honor bound to offer your body to a woman in distress—"

"That's just what a man does."

Paige didn't know whether to be embarrassed or charmed.

Both, probably.

"I don't know what to say," she admitted.

"You don't have to say anything. I was just letting you know you had options."

"Oh, well. Options. Okay."

"But really, why don't you just stay here with me, lean down against me." He eased her down against his chest. "There you go. And let your head go right here." Against that warm, inviting curve of his shoulder and his neck. "That's it. Close your eyes."

He spread the blanket over her and him. She could feel him breathing deeply and easily, feel the heat of his body, his heartbeat beneath one of her palms.

He put one of his hands over her ear, and with the other ear buried against his chest, it blocked out a lot of the sound, making a little cocoon of safety for her.

It was nice.

Really nice.

"Go to sleep," he whispered. "You'll be fine."

* * *

She tried.

She really did.

But the storm kept going. She'd be nearly asleep, then find herself jerked out of that half sleep by lightning, feel his arms tighten around her to let her know she wasn't alone, feel the glorious heat of his big, hard body, and then find herself thinking of what he'd offered.

It was just a night.

Just a little comfort in the dark on a big, scary night.

She knew lightning wasn't going to come snaking inside the rock overhang and get her. It wasn't chasing after her.

But an irrational fear was just that—an irrational fear.

And she'd been battling this one since she was a little girl and had gotten caught in her tree house during a big storm. No one had known she was there, and she'd stayed well hidden inside of it, huddled into a little ball, shaking and crying like she never had in her life. Her mother's face had gone absolutely white when she realized her daughter had been in a tree during a lightning storm. To Paige, it had seemed like it had gone on forever, like no one would ever come and save her, that the lightning would surely reach out and get her at any moment.

"I was playing outside when I was five or six, and a storm came, and I took shelter at the closest spot, which turned out to be my tree house," she finally admitted.

"Oooh," her cowboy sympathized.

"Yeah, not the best place to be during a storm. It was awful, and it seemed like forever before anyone found me."

He held her tight as she lay draped over him, bracing for the next boom of thunder. His hands moved gently over her shoulders, trying to soothe and work out some of the tension there. She snuggled closer, her face pressed as far into the curve of his neck as she could get it, the reassuring rise and fall of his chest beneath her, the beat of his heart, steady as could be, thumping against one of her ears.

"I could tell you a story," he whispered.

And she grinned despite her fears. "Thank you, but I'm not five years old anymore. Besides, I never got bedtime stories. I got songs. My mother used to sing us to sleep."

"Okay, I'm definitely not singing. You don't want me to sing."

"Then…I guess there's not much else you could do," she said, thinking it came out sounding like an invitation more than anything else.

Oops.

She didn't mean it that way.

Honestly, she didn't.

So what if he was here? She was here. The storm was here. And it was going to be a long night.

He took her face in his hand, eased back away from her, just enough that he could look her in the eye and said, "Let's just try one kiss, Red. Okay? One. And we'll see how it goes from there."

Well, if he thought she was going to fight him off….

No, he knew she wasn't going to do that.

Just let go, she told herself. *It's just one night, just one kiss.*

He let his mouth settle over hers, firm and sure, insistent and yet moving like a man who had all the time in the world. She opened herself up to the kiss, to him. To the heat and the pleasure, falling into it.

Some men just knew how to touch a woman, when to linger, when to blaze forward, when to tease and when to take.

He knew.

He devoured her, and she let him, helped him as best she could, with long, hungry kisses and hands that roamed restlessly across his chest, his shoulders, his back, into his hair, trying to get even closer.

She wasn't altogether sure how she got there, but she ended up straddling his lap, her hips in his hands, her breasts crushed against his chest, wishing she didn't have a stitch on.

And it all happened as fast as a fire roaring out of control.

"Damn, Red," he said, lifting his mouth from hers long enough to catch a ragged breath.

"I know."

Maybe she'd just been alone too long, gotten too caught up with her work and her family and all of its craziness. Had forgotten to make time for Paige, the woman, with all a woman's needs.

Because this felt very much like need.

He kissed her again, used his hands on her hips to draw her into a rhythm against him that was both arousing and maddening through their clothes.

If he'd laid her down on the hard ground right then and started stripping her clothes off, she didn't think she could have stopped him. She was so aroused already he might not even have to take her clothes off her. If he just kept doing what he was doing, which now included a hand slipping beneath her sweater and her shirt and that little nothing camisole of a bra to her breast, his mouth on her neck…

Her whole body gave a shudder.

The things he was doing to her neck….

He laid her back against that hard ground, settled himself heavily, but still fully clothed, on top of her, pushed up her clothes and took her nipple into his mouth and sucked hard.

"Trust me, Red," he muttered. "Just trust me. Everything will be fine."

Chapter Four

Paige slept like a baby.

Blissfully, heavily, completely unaware of anything, until she woke to the same sound of pounding rain and howling wind of the night before. If anything, it might just be worse.

And she was alone.

She sat up, wiped her hair from her face. It was flying around everywhere this morning, escaping from her braid. Her shirt and her camisole were bunched up under her sweater, and she straightened those, her cheeks filling with heat at just how that had all happened. And her jeans were unbuttoned, unzipped.

And she couldn't say she was sorry at all.

They hadn't actually had sex.

Not quite.

But he certainly had taken care of her.

She'd felt like the whole world exploded quite happily inside of her, with nothing but his mouth and his hands, and felt bad that he hadn't let her do the same for him.

But he'd said he wanted her in a nice, soft, warm bed, in a nice, warm bedroom with all the time in the world to do this right. He didn't want to be rushed. He didn't want to be worried about the storm or a flood, and he kind of liked the idea of her owing him.

So there it was.

She owed him.

And planned on happily making good.

Lord, what a man!

Then she remembered the money thing. Paige's family had serious money. And clout. And history.

Men could get weird about it.

She hoped her cute cowboy didn't get too weird about it. Ranch hands lived simply, most of them on very little, and usually had a healthy disdain for the world in which Paige's family lived.

She just wanted to know the man, enjoy the man, think for a while at least that any and all good things were possible with the man.

How long had it been since she'd felt like that?

She was practically singing as she got to her feet and went to look for him.

It was still very early, not quite five her watch told her, the world still filled with a ghostly white gloom, the rain not retreating in the least. Neither was the wind.

She went from one end of the overhang to the other. It was like searching through thick fog, but he wasn't there.

A moment later he came in out of the rain, a ghostly

image, except she could tell he was dripping wet. He stopped when he spotted her and then through the gloom, she could swear she saw his mouth spread into a big smile.

"Sleep well, Red?"

"Yes, I did," she said. "You?"

"I had really nice dreams and a woman draped all over me. Yeah, I slept just fine."

So that's how she'd slept? Draped all over him?

It must be true, because she'd slept on rock-hard ground before, and the body made its protests known the next day. Hers felt just fine this morning.

"Sorry about that," she said.

"I'm not complaining," he reassured her.

"No, just… You got to sleep on the ground. I definitely got the better end of the deal."

"Well, you can owe me for that, too, Red."

And then she laughed like she hadn't in years.

Yeah, she owed him.

And it felt good to owe him, to think of paying back the favors of last night, leisurely, happily, in a nice warm bed.

"So, where is this nice, warm bed of yours, and how are we going to get to it?"

"My bed is about five miles, as the crow flies. So we're going to have to make do with the hunting cabin I was telling you about. All we have to do is make it through the rain. I'm glad you've got your boots on. And your coveralls are waterproof?"

She nodded.

"Good. You'll be just fine."

"And you'll be soaked," she said, looking at the shirt

plastered to him, his dark hair drenched and slicked back, lying against his head.

"I've been wet before. I'll survive, and we'll get a nice fire going once we get to the cabin and we can dry each other off. Sound like a plan?"

"Yes, it does," she agreed.

A glorious plan.

They gathered up their things. She had her small pack, and he took her larger one. She got into her coveralls and then stared out into the storm.

At least the lightning had stopped.

Still, what a mess.

"The wind's not any worse than it was last night," she said. "Like...the storm's stalled?"

"Right on top of us, I'd say."

Which was not good.

A fast-moving hurricane could drop a lot of rain quickly, but at least it was gone fast, carried along by the forward movement of the storm.

But sometimes a hurricane came ashore and then ran into another front coming the other way, and it was like a standoff in the sky. The two storm systems just sat there, dumping torrential rain carried by the leftovers of the hurricane on the same spot.

The flooding could be devastating, particularly in a place as flat and normally dry as Texas.

"If I thought this was going to get any easier, I'd say we wait it out. But I really don't think this storm is moving, Red. We need to just trudge through it. We'll stick to the side of the ridge, so we'll have high ground. And it probably won't look like a path, but trust me, it's there and I know it. I grew up on this ranch. Cabin's maybe a mile and a half from here. Stick close to me, and if you need help, yell. Okay?"

"Okay," she nodded, trusting him implicitly.

They set off in the cold, soaking rain, so heavy she could barely see him in front of her. He was right about the path. She didn't see one, but he seemed to know exactly where he was going.

At times, off to the left, she could see what she thought was a raging river, where a peaceful stream had been the day before.

The one she'd watched him wash off in, when she'd had all those wonderful fantasies about him.

He lived up to them and more, she decided, and as soon as they got in out of the rain, she was going to peel those wet clothes off of him, dry him off and then heat him up.

It could rain for a week, for all she cared.

They trudged on through the storm. The ground was wet and had the consistency of watery oatmeal under her feet. Even with her work boots, she was sliding all over the place.

Rain dripped off her cowboy hat, blew in at times and rolled down her face, her neck and inside the opening of her coveralls, no matter how tightly she clutched them to her. It soaked through her sweater, her shirt, even her socks.

Yuck!

The sky lightened only marginally as they walked and, presumably, the sun came up somewhere above all the clouds and the rain.

She didn't want to think of what might have happened if he hadn't caught her in the mine. If she'd been inside the mine shaft alone when the storm hit, not knowing for sure what was going on, it would have been a long journey out of there alone. And an even longer night, either huddled alone against the rocks, scared half to death of the lightning or she might have even headed for the Jeep, might not have found it in the gloom, and then what would have happened to her?

Anything.

They trudged on, miserable, cold, wet.

She wondered if the cabin might have a primitive shower or even an old washtub. A bath was highly unlikely, she knew, but a woman could dream, couldn't she?

A bath and then a nice warm bed with him.

That was a fantasy!

In the end, it took more than three hours. Three thoroughly miserable hours, but they made it. Paige didn't see how he found his way, because the world seemed like a wet, foggy, miserable mess to her, but he led them right to a small cabin.

"Come on," he said, opening the door for her.

She wanted nothing more than to get inside, but dug in her pack for her satellite phone instead. It was nearly six, and her brother had to be going crazy.

She huddled under the narrow overhang of the roof, pressed up against the side of the cabin and held up the phone. "I have to try to make a call before my brother shows up with the National Guard or something like that."

He nodded. "I'll start a fire. If you get through, I need to call the ranch, let 'em know I'm okay and to get us when they can."

"Fire!" That was what she heard. "Yes, please. A fire."

He went inside, and she turned on the phone and dialed. There was a ton of static on the line, a couple of seconds when she thought she heard Blake, frantic and calling her name, and then nothing.

Finally, on the fourth try, she could hear him.

"Hey, sorry about that. I got caught in the storm, but I'm fine," she yelled into the phone.

"What?"

"I'm fine!"

"Paige—"

"Out of the mine, taking shelter in a cabin. I'm fine."

"Cabin?"

"Yes. I'm in a cabin. We'll wait out the storm here. I'll call as soon as I can. Don't worry. And don't do anything stupid, like send someone to get me. You'll give our whole plan away. Blake? Blake—"

But he was gone. There was nothing but static now.

Oh, well. *He got the important parts,* she thought. She was safe, out of the mine, out of the storm, and he didn't need to do anything.

Which would be incredibly hard for her big brother, but Paige had to hope that he'd sit tight.

She clicked off the phone and opened the door to the cabin to find no real light, just what she had from her own helmet lamp. Slowly panning the room, she saw a roughly made wooden bed in one corner, a giant fireplace, two chairs, shelves with dry stores of food, a sink and what she really, really hoped was a bathroom behind a door in a corner.

She was still standing on the threshold, literally

dripping wet, when the door opened and out came her cowboy, already out of his wet clothes and into a pair of dry jeans, pulling on a dry flannel shirt.

"I'm afraid there's no electricity, and I was making too much of a mess to do the fire first," he said. "Stay where you are. I'll bring dry clothes to you. Believe me, it's going to be easier this way."

She didn't argue, feeling like a drowned rat and looking away, not wanting anyone, especially him, to see her looking this bad and grateful that there wasn't much light in the cabin yet.

He came back a moment later with a pair of sweatpants and another flannel shirt, even a pair of men's boxers.

"Best I have to offer," he said. "Now, my advice to you would be to get naked right here at the door and drop your clothes where they are. Because there's only one dry towel left, and I imagine you'd rather have it for yourself and not bring all the water and mud into the cabin."

"Did you strip at the door?" she asked.

"No, I just wish I had."

Paige laughed and motioned for him to turn around so she could start stripping. She'd do anything right then to be warm and dry.

He turned to the side and held up the towel between them. She didn't think she'd ever taken her clothes off that quickly. Not that it was easy, since everything was heavy with water and her fingers were practically numb.

But she got them off, leaving them in a sopping pile on the floor in the doorway, then took the towel and wrapped it around herself.

He just grinned and handed her the dry clothes.

"Is that a real bathroom over there?" she asked.

"There's no hot water, if that's what you're asking. But there is running water. Rainwater collection system on the roof, so there's no shortage of water now. Some semblance of a shower, if you could stand the cold. But there is a toilet that flushes and everything."

"That's it. I'm in love with this place," she said, heading across the room for the bathroom. "If there were dry socks somewhere, I'd be in heaven."

"I'll see what I can do," he promised.

"And a fire? Dry socks and a fire? You are my hero!"

"Simple girl, are you? Easy to please?"

"Today I am," she promised, shutting herself into the tiny bathroom.

He'd found a candle in the bathroom and left it burning. The room was tiny, primitive, but clean. She rubbed herself down briskly, dismissed completely the idea of a cold shower right now. Maybe once he got a big fire going, she'd try it. For the moment, she hurried into the boxers, the sweatpants and the flannel shirt.

They felt fabulous. Better than any designer gown she'd ever tried on.

Then she went to work trying to squeeze what water she could out of her hair.

Finally, she wrapped it in the towel and went into the main room.

He had a fire just starting to burn in the giant stone fireplace and she knew they'd soon be warm, given how small the cabin was, once the fire really got going.

She sat down on the raised stone hearth, and her hero presented her with luxuriously thick, warm socks.

"Ahhh!" She moaned in pure ecstasy, then exclaimed, "That's it. It's official. I would do absolutely anything for you!"

"Red, I haven't even made you a cup of hot coffee yet, but I'm about to. What is that gonna get me?"

"I don't know. What do you want?"

"Well, if that fire was going and this place was even halfway warm, I'd have dried you off myself and not given you any clothes to wear. I'd have taken you straight to bed. But I was planning on being gentlemanly about it and warming the place up first, maybe getting some food in you, and then getting you naked. That was my plan."

"That sounds like an absolutely glorious plan."

Okay, just like that.

They had a plan.

A highly satisfying plan.

Travis figured there was only one other thing he absolutely had to do before hauling her off to bed, and that was to try to get hold of someone at the ranch house, just so they'd know he was okay and not waste time trying to find him.

He was sure they had better things to do right now, to make sure everything else on the ranch was okay. He could wait. He might be very happy waiting here with her, letting someone else take care of things for a change.

After all, how many times did he find himself stranded with a gorgeous, willing woman?

It was definitely a first for him. Years of good clean living and hard work were being rewarded right here, he decided. He deserved it and he intended to enjoy it. She would, too. He'd make sure of it.

But first, he took her satellite phone and dialed the ranch. Nothing but static greeted him, despite repeated attempts.

"Try it outside," she suggested, warming herself by the fire, just starting to catch well and throw off some heat and light. "There's just enough of an overhang on the roof to keep you dry, and point the antenna toward the mine. That's where I finally found a signal."

"Okay. Be right back, Red."

He got outside. Lord, it was a miserable day out there, but he was smiling, whistling, even.

He did as she suggested and pointed the antenna toward the mine, and sure enough, there was something of a signal. His housekeeper, a fierce-looking, no-nonsense woman named Marta, answered.

At least, he thought it was her.

The line crackled with static.

"Marta, it's Travis. I'm holed up in the hunting cabin near the Eagle Mine. I'm fine. Tell the men to see to the animals and not to worry about coming to get me until they can."

She said something. He thought she got it. Then asked, "Everything okay there, Marta? Look, tell Jack that the creek near the mine is a roaring river right now, not to be in a hurry to try to cross it to get to me. I'm fine."

He hoped she got that, because the static only got worse. He clicked off the phone and let it be.

He realized he hadn't said anything about his pretty trespasser, but then, what was the point? Nobody there really needed to know, he reasoned.

It was his ranch, and he'd decide for himself what to do with her once they were out of here.

Travis sighed and looked out into the mess of the storm.

He intended to enjoy himself in what time they had here. They'd figure out the rest later.

She sat on the hearth and used the towel to dry her hair as best she could, then finger-combed it to get out the tangles and separate the strands in hopes it might dry faster.

The fire was soon roaring. With that and the light from the half-dozen candles that she found scattered around the room, she could finally see, after hours in the dark and the ghostly gloom. When she had a mug of hot coffee in her hand, her life was nearly complete.

Paige was so busy thinking about what was to come between them that it was only after he'd gone outside and then come back in that she remembered something she should have already discussed with him.

He really had her completely distracted, thinking only of how much she wanted to be curled up in that bed with him naked in his arms.

She looked up as he came back into the cabin, her thoughts warring between him and what she wanted from him, versus her own family and what she'd come here to do.

And she hated asking this of him, bringing this into it, but she had to. She looked up at him and said, "You didn't tell anyone at the ranch what I was doing, did you?"

"No," he said.

But he'd gone still by the doorway, staring at her.

When he stepped closer, into the fall of light from the roaring fire and the candles, she could finally really see him. Not like that glimpse she had through the binoculars when she'd quickly, guiltily looked away. No rain falling between them now, no fog, no storm and no darkness.

He was tall, his body lean and beautifully muscled, hair dark, eyes dark and unfathomable at the moment.

She felt a hint of uneasiness first, a sense that she was missing something, something important that was right in front of her.

"What is it?" she asked, thinking there was something familiar about him. "What's wrong?"

He came close, taking a long strand of her hair in his hand and holding it out in front of the fire.

"It looked so much darker before. But in this light, it's almost like gold," he said. "A golden red."

"Yes." Again, she felt uneasy, and again, she wasn't sure why.

Did he know who she was?

Was that why he was suddenly so wary? Maybe even angry?

Paige's family was Texas's version of royalty, wealthy and often in the spotlight. She and her sister had been in the society pages of the *Dallas Morning News* and all the bigger papers in the state since birth.

And the hair was often what gave her and her sister away.

Not many women had this combination of reddish-gold hair.

"We never got around to introducing ourselves last night, Red," he said.

"No, we didn't." She hadn't wanted to. Hadn't wanted to lie to him and hadn't wanted to tell him her name, just in case it meant something to him. And she'd been happy to think of him simply as her cowboy, a man she'd admired and met by chance. Nothing else. Finally, she found the courage to ask, "You know who I am?"

"Now that I see that hair clearly, oh, yeah," he said. "I'm afraid I know."

Well, if he'd lived on this ranch his whole life, she couldn't be that surprised. The feud was the stuff of Texas legends. Any long-standing family war over good cattle land was enough to make a story last. Throw in priceless jewels and a high-stakes poker game and you got…a good old tall Texas tale.

"One of the twins is a jewelry designer. I'm guessing she wouldn't hold up as well down in a mine. So you must be the scientist," he concluded.

She nodded, really hoping he wouldn't be too mad. "I'm Paige McCord."

She held out her hand.

He didn't.

"That's great. Just great." He swore, shook his head in disgust or maybe fury and finally said, "I'm Travis Foley."

Chapter Five

She laughed despite herself, and said, "No, you're not!"

He nodded, looking like a man not in the mood to be patient with her while she worked this out in her own head.

"You...you were riding around like some ranch hand, checking the fences, checking the livestock. I saw you."

"You were watching me?" he asked incredulously.

"Of course I was. Did you think I'd just show up one day and head down into the mine? With no idea of whether anyone ever came that way? Whether I'd get caught? I watched you for the last three days. Doing the work of a regular ranch hand."

"I'm a rancher. It's what I do. I work the land." He looked furious.

"You're supposed to be in Dallas at some big family meeting," she remembered.

"I didn't feel like going to Dallas for another family meeting," he said bitingly. "And you? You're spying on me? And my ranch?"

"It's not your ranch," she reminded him.

And, *oh, wow*.

That was clearly the wrong thing to say.

He looked like he might strangle her right there where she sat. He was breathing hard, towering over her, looking like he might grab her by her hair and throw her out right then and there.

But he didn't.

He just glowered at her.

"No, it's not my ranch. Believe me, your family would never let mine forget that. You probably wouldn't understand this, but the thing is, a man works a piece of land every day, sweats over it, bleeds over it, takes care of it like it was his, he starts to get ideas he shouldn't have—"

"That's not what I meant," she claimed. "I mean…I know you must…care about the place—"

"Care about it?" He laughed, still furious. "I care about what I have for dinner some nights, whether the Cowboys win a football game, whether it's going to rain or be sunny. What I feel for this ranch is a helluva lot more than care."

"Yes. Okay." She got to her feet, tired of him towering over her, though in truth, he still did even when she was standing. "I'm sorry—"

"So for you to just waltz in here like your family owns the place, which I suppose you think you do, and head down into that mine, like you think you own that, too, to try to find that stupid diamond—"

"Yes. You're right. I'm sorry—"

"To give me that I'm-just-a-grad-student routine? That it's-the-chance-of-a-lifetime routine?" He took her chin in his hand, getting right up in her face and holding her there, glaring at her. "You lie really well, Red."

She shoved him away hard, and then nearly tripped over the stone hearth of the fireplace as she backed away from him.

He swore, reached out to grab her to keep her from falling.

"You really didn't know it was me?" he demanded, his grip on her nearly tight enough to hurt.

"No. Of course not. I told you. I thought you were just a ranch hand. I thought—"

"What?" he demanded.

"Nothing—" She was blushing, just thinking of what she thought. That he was a beautiful man. A beautiful, ordinary man. And of what she'd wanted from him, what she'd let him do.

Oh, Lord, what she'd let him do…

What she'd planned for them to do once they got here…

She swallowed hard, thinking for a moment of all she'd lost in this instant. Glad it hadn't gone any further between them, and yet…

She couldn't believe he was one of the Foleys.

Paige had been introduced to him, of course. A girl didn't move in the upper echelon of Texas society for her whole life without being introduced to the Foleys, even if her family had been feuding with them since the Civil War.

So they'd no doubt exchanged icily polite, icily brief

handshakes at various social functions over the years, charity balls, the governor's mansion, that sort of thing.

There were three brothers, something of a mixed set, all young, wealthy, arrogant and good-looking. In her mind, she could see them standing in a row in black tuxedoes and starched white shirts, looking for all the world like they owned everything they surveyed.

She'd never really been that interested in the feud, in perpetuating it or ending it, had just grown up on tales of how terribly his family had treated hers and been happy to keep her distance from him and the entire clan.

So she'd shook his hand a time or two when forced to do so in the name of good manners and not having any interest in causing a scene.

She really hadn't paid that much attention to the whole brood until her mother's terrible secret had come out this summer.

That her mother had once loved his father, Rex Foley. Her curiosity had driven her to the Internet and the photos she could find. She'd skipped right over the brothers and zeroed in on the father instead.

His father had slept with her mother and fathered a child with her. Paige's little brother, Charlie.

How could that be?

She still couldn't quite believe it, couldn't make sense of it, couldn't...

And all that time she'd been glaring at pictures of Rex Foley, trying to understand, trying to see something of her little brother in him and wondering how it was that they'd managed to keep that secret all these years, how no one had known...

All that time, she should have been looking at the Foley brothers, arming herself, protecting herself against what was to come.

Then she might have known, she might have recognized him from the first. It was just that every time in the past when she'd met him he'd been in a tuxedo, all polished manners and cool, sophisticated charm, dismissive as could be of anyone in her family and disapproving, as well. And while that arrogance might work for some women, Paige had grown up with men like that.

It was old hat to her, a nice-looking man in a tuxedo who acted like he owned the world.

Men like that really didn't do a thing for her.

They just didn't seem real.

That man working the ranch, checking the mine, catching her there… He'd seemed interesting and very real.

So different from any version of Travis Foley she'd ever seen.

Sweaty, a little dirty, in worn jeans and well-worn boots.

A working man.

Real.

Right now he was also furious.

"What?" she asked, lost in her thoughts.

"Before, you said you thought I was a ranch hand, that I was… What? What were you going to say?"

That it would be nice to have someone who looked like you walk right into my life. That I was lonely. That I hadn't had anyone special in my life for a long time and… And…

Oh, God. What did it matter now?

It could never be.

He was Travis Foley.

"I thought you looked like a nice guy," she told him, laughing with as much disgust as she could muster. "How ridiculous is that?"

That seemed to satisfy him for the moment. They retreated to opposite corners of the small room, him leaving her by the fire to get warm while he brooded in the corner by the bed.

A single bed, maybe a single and a half, if there was such a thing.

Paige looked away. She had to forget what happened between them the night before, just completely erase it from her mind. It didn't mean anything, and really, it was nothing. A little flirtation, a little...more than flirting.

Cuddling, kissing, his big, warm body rocking erotically against hers, and all those promises of so much more to come.

Her face burned at the memory.

And then she had a terrible thought.

She got up and glared at him. "You really didn't know?"

"Know what?" he said, his tone biting.

"That it was me? That I was a McCord?"

"No."

She wasn't sure she believed him, although when she thought about it, she honestly wasn't sure how it would have benefited him to lie about it, to pretend. To flirt with her the way he had, and to get her pants off of her and yet still not take it all the way.

Why be a nice guy at that point? If he was looking to just...mess with her head or her body or...

No, it didn't make any sense.

"Red, if I'd wanted you last night, I could have had you a half a dozen times by now, and you know it. So don't go playing the outraged, violated woman with me. It won't fly."

Okay. He could have. And they both knew it.

"Then, I don't understand," she said.

"Understand what?"

Who he was?

Who that man last night had been?

He stared at her from across the room, still angry, but looking more than a little confused now, uneasy, suspicious and maybe even a little vulnerable.

"Nothing. Forget it. I... It doesn't matter now," she said.

He was a Foley. His father had been involved with her mother years ago, fathered a child with her and then walked away. What kind of man was he? What kind of man was the son?

She'd gotten her heart and her ego bruised more than once, and then she'd developed a healthy distrust for men in general, which she'd totally ignored with this man.

What a time to let down that sense of caution.

From outside, the wind came up in a gust that sounded more like a roar. The cabin walls literally shook from the force of it, and the rain kept pounding down.

They ignored each other as best they could for most of the day. He built the fire up until it was roaring. She emptied a few cans of beef stew into a heavy metal pot that hung from a hook over the fire and cooked until it smelled heavenly.

Something about cooking over an open fire and being hungry made it even taste that good.

He was coldly polite, thanking her for the meal, making sure she knew how to hang the pot over the fire and get it off without burning herself, and then keeping to himself on the side of the room farthest from the fire.

Every now and then he went outside, pacing along the side of the cabin under the tiny overhang and staring at the storm.

By nightfall, she'd cleaned the whole place, for lack of anything better to do, fixed another meal of canned ravioli and finished one of only three books she'd found in nooks and crannies in the cabin. A paperback mystery about a wealthy woman whose husband stole every dime she had and ran off, very nearly never to be found again.

It was perfect for her mood right now, when she was thinking you really could never trust a man.

And then she decided she might as well get ready for bed, something she'd been dreading, because there was only one.

She hesitated, not sure what he intended.

From behind her, she heard him say, "Go ahead. Take the bed. I'll sleep by the fire."

"On the floor?"

"We slept on the ground last night, Red, and did just fine."

Yes, they had. Still, she didn't want him to be nice or gentlemanly or anything like that. "You'll get cold," she said.

"Won't be the first time, won't be the last. And tonight we've got a fire."

She nodded, not turning around, not wanting to look at him or to think of what she'd expected this night to be. It was ridiculous, anyway. To think she'd waltz onto the ranch and find this man who did nothing but work the land, an ordinary, hardworking man who wouldn't know about her family's money and power and even if he did, wouldn't care.

Just a man who would get all tangled up in her, practically on sight.

And it was absolutely the last thing she needed to be thinking about right now, with her family absolutely going crazy and their jewelry store empire in some serious financial difficulties, her trapped here with the enemy, caught red-handed trying to steal a priceless diamond right out from under his nose.

Oh, her family would claim ownership if she found it, but it would be a legal fight that could last years, and she'd be painted as a thief by his family. But in the end, she thought her family would prevail, and his would say the diamond was one more thing stolen from the Foleys by the McCords.

All that between them, plus her mother's affair with his father, the child it had produced...

Don't be stupid, Paige. Forget about the man. You have to.

Because he didn't exist anywhere except inside her fantasies anyway.

She climbed into the bed. It was cold but quite comfortable. Either that or she was exhausted, if not from the previous day and night, from the emotions of this whole ordeal.

He knew who she was, and he knew what she'd come here for. Which meant she'd failed in a mission to help her family through a difficult time financially.

It was one problem her family had right now that she'd thought she could actually solve. Not the thing with her mother or Rex Foley or her brother, but the money part. She'd been willing to head into an old, long-abandoned mine alone to do it. She wasn't stupid. She'd known the risks and been willing to take it for the sake of her family.

And she'd failed.

So, the stores were in some trouble, her mother had a thing for Rex Foley, and Charlie…

Poor Charlie.

She feared she'd just made things worse for him.

Travis stretched out in front of the fire and listened to her toss and turn and sigh for as long as he could stand it, then finally turned toward her and barked out, "What is it?"

She gave a start, reminding him of the way she'd done that at each big bolt of lightning.

"Sorry," she said. "I…there's just so much, I don't even know where to start."

"You want back in the mine?" he guessed, because he knew eventually she'd get around to trying to talk him into that.

Even now, caught red-handed, she thought she could somehow charm her way back inside, thinking to steal one more thing from his family?

Unbelievable!

Women!

A man just couldn't trust them.

Just this past summer, Travis's own brother, Zane, had gone nuts over his little girl Olivia's nanny, and Travis had known right away that woman was hiding something. It hadn't taken more than a couple of phone calls to find out Melanie Grandy hadn't always been a nanny. She'd worked as a Las Vegas showgirl. Travis didn't know if Zane knew about that or not, and in the end, he'd decided to leave it alone, thinking they'd work it out. It wasn't like the woman had been a stripper or a call girl.

But now, being reminded himself of just how manipulative women could be, Travis was wondering if he'd done the right thing. He could probably use someone like Zane right now to remind him not to get stupid over a pretty, scheming woman.

"Go ahead," he urged Miss Paige McCord. "Tell me why I should let you back into that mine."

"No, it's not the mine," she insisted. "I mean…yes, I want back in it, but, no, that's not what I was talking about a second ago. It was…I wondered if I could talk to you about just one thing without…well, maybe without this whole lifelong family feud getting in the way of it?"

"Considering the fact that everything between your family and mine started there and is colored by that, I don't see how, Red."

"Yes. I know. You're right. I'm just… None of it's his fault—"

"His fault?"

"Charlie. My little brother… Your… You know about Charlie, right?"

Okay, *that* surprised him.

And *that* particular wound was still raw and festering.

He didn't really know how he felt about having a twenty-one-year-old half brother he'd known nothing about until a few weeks ago.

While he might disagree with his brothers about a lot of things, how they lived their lives, what was important to them, things like that, they were and always would be brothers. They were tight. They were family, and he'd have walked through fire for any of them anytime they needed it.

So to know that there was a fourth Foley brother out there somewhere, who'd never been one of them....

It was just wrong.

Who'd been a McCord instead.

"Yes," he admitted. "My father told us about Charlie."

His father was still reeling from the news himself. His father, steady as a rock, raise-three-boys-alone-after-his-wife-died kind of steady, absolutely reeling.

Travis didn't think anything in this world could have shaken his father like that particular bit of news.

"It's just that...Charlie's special," Paige said. "He's great. He's sweet. He's kind. He's happy. Like a puppy, just kind of silly and goofy. Everybody loves him. And he's so young. I don't...I can't stand the idea of him getting hurt in all this."

Travis got up and came to stand over her, hands on his hips, furious all over again. "And you think my father and my brothers and I are going to hurt him?"

"I don't know." She sat up in the bed, covers falling to her waist, her hair tumbling everywhere. "I have no idea how you're going to treat him or what you think about him. I can still hardly believe it's true. That he's your father's son and not my father's."

Travis frowned. *Okay.* He had to admit what she'd just said was likely true, because he wasn't completely sure how he felt about the whole thing, either. How could anyone be? It was all too strange, too new.

"If I could just…I know you don't owe me anything," she said. "I know I don't have the right to ask anything of you, but you're here and we spent some time together before…before anything about our families got in the way, and… Well, I think you can be a nice man, when you want to be. And I'm asking you, please… Charlie wants to meet your father…his father. I assume at some point he'll want to meet you and your brothers…. Could you just be kind? Please?"

Kind?

What the hell did she think of them? That they were a pack of wolves? That they'd eat him alive?

And yet, he could hear that her concern was genuine and that, for all he could see, she loved her younger brother very much.

"Answer a question for me, Red. How did your father treat him?"

She looked for a minute like…like it had been bad… maybe everything Travis feared. He'd always heard Devon McCord was an ass.

He swore, sat down on the edge of the cot and grabbed her by the arms, holding her there in front of him, not letting her look away. "No. Tell me. He hurt him?" That one question burned a hole in Travis's gut when he let himself think about it.

She looked confused, surprised, hurt herself. "No."

"The guy's always been rumored to have a nasty temper. Ask anybody, and not the people in my family who were taught from birth to hate him. Anybody. They'll tell you he was a big, tough, mean son of a bitch. So tell me. Tell me right now. Did he hit that kid? Did he hit Charlie?"

"No," she said.

"Swear it," he demanded, right up in her face. "Right now. It's... I need to know, Red. I need to know no one hurt him like that when no one in my family even knew he was a Foley, and none of us were there to protect him. Because he's family and we don't leave each other alone to face something like that. It just isn't right."

"No, he didn't hit us."

"Maybe not you or your sister, but what about your brothers? And if he knew Charlie wasn't his—"

"He didn't know," she said. "I'm almost certain he didn't. Charlie was just so easy to like. To love. For my father, too. I don't think there's any way he knew Charlie wasn't his."

"Okay." Then he realized he'd been manhandling her himself, trying to make her sit there and look him in the eye and tell him the truth.

He still had her by the arms in a hold that wouldn't allow any kind of escape from him.

And he'd gotten too close to her again.

He let his hands drop and eased back away from her as she scooted back on the bed to sit up against the headboard, looking wary and surprised and not quite sure what to do with herself or to say to him.

"I'm sorry," he said.

She shrugged off his words, like they didn't really matter, like none of it did and let her head fall until he saw nothing more than a curtain of red-gold curls and all that made him worry even more.

Travis swore and shook his head in disgust. "Did I hurt you, Red?"

"No. It's just…grabbing me like that and acting like you'd shake the truth out of me, if you had to? That was something my father did."

Her father, and now him?

That was perfect.

Just perfect.

"Son of a bitch," he said.

Now he felt like an absolute ass.

"Travis?" She put her hand on his arm. "I'm glad you care enough about Charlie to want to be sure my father didn't hurt him like that. I'm glad you want to look out for him, the way brothers do. That means a lot to me. I want that for Charlie, because I love him. And I'm glad there's at least one bit of family business we agree on. Charlie. That none of this is his fault."

"It's not. I know that," he told her.

"So maybe my family isn't as different from yours as we thought."

He scoffed at that.

Not because he thought it wasn't true, but because he didn't need to be sitting here finding common ground with her, finding reasons to like her. It was the last thing he needed to be doing.

And it didn't help any that he was sitting on her bed,

late at night, the two of them absolutely alone, with him having to keep reminding himself of exactly who she was, to keep from remembering what he'd planned to be doing with her in this cabin, in this bed tonight.

It didn't help either that he'd put his hands on her, even in anger, for a moment. And it was even worse now, when it wasn't anger that was driving him on, but the need to go to her again, this time to make sure she was okay, to comfort her, wishing he could forget everything that stood between them.

Get up, he told himself sternly. *Get up and get out of here, before you make it any worse.*

But he didn't listen.

Chapter Six

He put his hands on her again, same place as before, this time as gentle as he could be, rubbing slowly with his thumbs at the soft flesh of her inner arms. She looked wary, but she let him.

"I'm truly sorry," he said. "I don't treat women that way. It's just that…ever since I heard about Charlie, I couldn't help but worry and wonder…what it was like for him, growing up a McCord."

She gave him a look that just about had him on his knees. A look that said she understood completely and could forgive, not that he felt he deserved it.

"No one in my family wants to hurt him," Travis promised her.

She hung her head. He saw tears falling down one

perfect, pale cheek and a curtain of red-gold hair shielding the rest of her from view. She shivered a bit.

He had to remind himself he didn't get to keep her warm tonight, that the time when he was welcome to do that was long over. "What is it, Red?"

"I don't see how Charlie's ever going to belong anywhere now. Not with the way things are between your family and mine."

Honestly, Travis didn't either.

Paige shivered, and Travis had to get up or he was going to take her in his arms, despite all the reasons he'd told himself he couldn't.

He pulled the covers up around her and eased her back down onto the bed, while she looked up at him, her eyes sad and full of regrets. He let himself touch her in one small way, a hand to her cheek, wiping away those tears, and then she looked even sadder. All sad eyes and tears and that glorious hair spread out on a pillow in a bed in a cabin with him and no one else around for miles.

He wondered what she'd do if he kissed her right then, if she longed for the way it had been between them the night before. If she wished they hadn't been careful or cautious. He could have done anything to her that night, and she would have let him. He knew it.

But it was cold and wet, and the ground was hard, and she was just so soft and feminine, her body yielding completely to his. Not the kind of woman a man had on a bed of solid rock.

He'd wanted something better for her for their first time together, time, a soft bed, a fire and roof over their heads.

But mostly…time.

He'd been sure they'd have it, couldn't foresee anything that would keep them from having that time.

What a fool he'd been.

And now he'd always wonder what it would have been like, despite who she was and who her family was.

"I'm going to build up the fire. Just go to sleep. One of the ranch hands will likely come for us by midday, and we'll go to the ranch house and…I don't know, Paige. I don't know what we'll do from there. Get your Jeep for you and…I don't know."

Let her go? Just like that? No. He didn't want to do that. But what choice did he have? Forget about her? He didn't think he could.

"I just don't know," he said again, then turned back to the fire, made himself lie down and stare at it, not at her, until at some point he finally fell asleep.

Someone walked into the cabin at first light.

Travis got up, sore from a night spent on a floor that was just a tad more comfortable than the rock he'd slept on the first night, and there stood Calvin Waters, a man who'd been working the ranch since Travis was a kid.

"Sorry, Boss," he said. "You said to take care of the animals first, and we did. Just took a little longer than we thought, and then—"

He broke off as Paige rose from the bed on the other side of the room, looking all rumpled and sleepy and gorgeous in the morning light, her hair like pure fire, a curly, sexy mess.

Travis thought he heard Cal swear in utter appreciation and could have done the same himself.

Cal turned to Travis and shot him a look that said, *What the hell are you doing on the floor when you've got someone like her in the bed?*

Travis shot back his own look that said, *Don't say a word.*

Cal nodded. "I didn't bring enough horses. Didn't know you had company."

"We got caught in the storm together," Travis said. "Paige, this is Calvin Waters. He knows more about the history of the ranch than anyone, because he's about a hundred years old and I don't think he's lived a day anywhere but here. Cal, this is Paige."

He deliberately left off the last name, because that would cause a stir throughout the ranch, and he didn't want to answer any questions about her, especially since he had no answers where she was concerned.

"Hello, Mr. Waters," Paige said, giving him a polite smile.

"Oh, ma'am, it's just Cal. Glad to see you two found some shelter. It's a helluva storm out there. Let up a little this morning, but it's still miserable." Then he turned to Travis. "I only have my horse and yours. Want me to go back to the ranch and—"

"No." He wouldn't put Cal or the horses through the extra trip. "Paige and I will be fine on Murph."

He told her to get her things together and put her coveralls on. That would keep some of the rain off of her. He took care of the fire and soon they were outside.

The rain had let up, but had by no means stopped.

They stood under the narrow overhang, and the horse came up to Travis and nudged him in the shoulder.

"I think he missed you," Paige said.

"No, he's reminding me that he was smart enough to know that storm was coming and I wasn't."

Paige laughed and fussed over the horse, rubbing his nose. "Smart and beautiful, then. Good for you."

"We're going to have to ride double, and we're going to get wet one more time," Travis told her. "But at the end of this trip is a real bathtub with a huge hot water tank and it won't matter if we did lose power. We've got a generator. So you'll be warm, and you can have a hot meal, too."

"Sounds heavenly," she told him.

No, not quite, he thought, remembering that first night with her. But it was as good as things were going to get, he feared.

He climbed aboard Murph, eased back as far as he could in the saddle and then reached for her, holding out his right hand and a booted foot.

"I assume you know how to ride?"

She gave him a look of mock outrage.

"Just making sure. Put your foot on top of mine, and don't be afraid to step down hard to lift yourself up. Take my hand with both of yours, and we'll swing you up into the saddle, sideways in front of me."

"I can do it," she said. And ended up making it look easy, or maybe as if she rode double with him all the time.

It meant she was practically in his lap. He eased her against his chest, trying to ignore how that felt, and Cal handed him a blanket from the cabin that he wrapped around her. They were still going to get wet but hopefully it would offer some protection.

Cal mounted his horse and off they went, making slow but steady progress through the rain, the whole world gray and gloomy, Travis feeling that way himself, save for the fact that he had her in his arms.

It was a sad day when a man was grateful to be riding through a cold, driving rain just because it gave him one more chance to hold a woman in his arms.

But that was the shape he was in.

Grateful, despite the cold and the rain, and annoyed as hell at her whole family and his.

Paige huddled against him inside her blanket, rain finding a way to get inside, running cold down into her clothes and finding flesh. Which only made her try to get even closer to him.

She fought it. She really did.

She told herself all the reasons she couldn't have anything else to do with him, and that she really didn't know him and she shouldn't trust him. She planned that she'd be gone from here soon, and then it would be hard to believe she ever even considered…doing anything with him.

Anything else, she reminded herself. She'd already done more than enough.

It was just that, this close to him, when she closed her eyes against the misery of the cold and the rain, she tended to remember only that she was curled up against him, absorbing the heat of him, taking shelter in his arms. And despite knowing better, eventually her thoughts kept turning to that first night with him. How kind he'd been, how gentle, and how those big, hot hands of his had moved so slowly, relentlessly over every inch of her.

Teasing and teasing and teasing, until she just went mad in his arms.

Most men were in such a hurry these days. They'd forgotten how to tease and tempt and take a woman to the point where she was insane to have them.

He'd made her nearly insane with it.

The only thing that had made her wait, in the end, was knowing they would be together and that it would be all the sweeter for the wait.

How was she supposed to ignore that when she was this close to him?

He was the only thing warm in the world, his body swaying against hers, beneath hers, from the motion of the horse, his arm holding her fast, his heartbeat thudding beneath her ear. She was cold, and her whole body ached, and she just wanted to forget all of that. The memory that kept playing through her mind was of him kissing, stroking, teasing her.

"Almost there," he said, his mouth practically pressed against her ear, warm breath leaving her shivering, and not from the cold.

If she reached up and kissed him, took that warm mouth of his with hers, she wondered what he'd do. If he'd push her away or if that would be enough for her to know he was thinking of that night as much as she was, that maybe he had the same regrets, impossible as anything was between them.

She wanted him to have those regrets, she decided, pointless as that was. She just needed to know he felt the same way she did.

It is pointless, she reminded herself. *Absolutely pointless.*

The ride seemed interminable, impossible, and then finally, finally, they came to a stop.

She lifted her head and realized they were at the door to a house, his house, she suspected. He'd ridden right up to the door.

"Let me get down first, okay? And then I'll help you."

She nodded, immediately feeling the cold so much more as he lifted himself up and off the horse.

"Now, just slide down. I've got you."

She did, but her legs were numb from the cold and buckled the moment she hit the ground. The only thing that kept her from landing in a heap in the mud was him.

He caught her hard against him once more, and she couldn't even manage to help hold herself up by hanging on to him.

"It's okay, Red," he said, adjusting his grip and then lifting her into his arms.

He said something to Cal about the horses, and the next thing she knew, she was being carried inside, dripping wet, into a mudroom where a stern-looking older woman, probably his housekeeper, started fussing over her and him.

He put her down in a hard wooden chair, took off her muddy boots and sopping wet socks, took away her big, wet blanket from the cabin, then reached for the zipper on her coveralls.

His housekeeper put a big, fluffy towel into her hands and then helped her dry off her face a bit and get the worst of the moisture from her hair.

Paige's own hands were trembling so badly, she wasn't much help at all.

"Marta," he said. "Why don't you go run a hot bath in my bathroom. I'll bring her up in a minute."

He'd gotten her coveralls unzipped as far as he could with her sitting down, then took a moment to pull off his own boots, wipe the water from his face and the worst of it from his hair.

"Your bathroom?" she asked, even her voice trembling from the cold.

"Biggest bathtub in the house, Red. Looks like a fancy horse trough, but it's made of cast iron, extra long and deep. Trust me. It holds heat like nothing you've ever been in. You're gonna love it. You'll never want to get out."

She gave him a wet, weary smile.

"Come on. Up on your feet." He took her by the hand and drew her up. Her legs were kind of working again as he stripped her of her coveralls, left the rest of her wet clothes on her and lifted her into his arms again.

It wasn't necessary, she thought, fairly certain she could walk as far as his bathroom.

Still, it wasn't like she ever expected to be in his arms again.

She let her head fall to his chest once more, gave herself up to his gentle care. A few moments later, he set her down in a bathroom, big and modern and thoroughly masculine.

"We work hard here, Red," he said, as if he could read her mind. "Muscles get sore, they ache. Warm water helps."

She looked from the tub to him. She went to try to unbutton the flannel shirt she wore and mostly just fumbled with it, her hands still cold and clumsy.

He watched her do it, standing still in front of her, his face growing more and more grim with every passing second. Then he groaned and came to her, his hands replacing hers.

"I won't look," he said.

He turned her around, putting her back to him, reached around her and unbuttoned those buttons with the same no-nonsense kind of approach he might have used to undo his own shirt buttons.

He left the shirt on her, but reached up under it in back to undo her bra, then found the string tie of her borrowed sweatpants and undid them, too, while she stood there, mute, still shaking, not feeling anything but grateful for his tender, very thorough care.

He slid the borrowed pants and her borrowed boxers down a bit, then put an arm around her waist and lifted her against him and up off the floor, while he worked her pants and boxers off. Before she knew it, she was back standing on the floor in a long, flannel shirt that hung at least halfway down her thighs.

"There you go. I didn't see a thing," he said. "Think you can handle it from here?"

She nodded, then turned sideways and said, "Travis?"

He kept his eyes on her face, while she clutched the ends of that shirt together in front of her.

"Thank you."

"I'd say anytime, Red, but...well..."

"I know," she said.

"So, I'm going to walk out this door. Right now. Lock it behind me."

And then he was gone.

She locked the door with a trembling hand, slipped out of her shirt and her bra and into that blissfully warm tub.

Warmth slowly seeped into her cold body—life, heat finally.

She let her head fall back against the tub, her whole body immersed in blessed warmth.

He was right. This was a fabulous tub, about two feet deep and more than long enough for her to stretch out in. She let the tub fill almost to the brim, then cut off the water, rolled up a towel and put it over the rim to cushion her neck. She leaned back in absolute bliss and decided this was the best bath she'd ever had in her life.

She could have thoroughly enjoyed it if she had been able to think of anything but him. How kind he was mostly, how tenderly and gently he'd taken care of her, like she was the most precious thing in the world to him.

Which she wasn't. She knew it.

So that kindness, the tenderness, the care... That was just... Who he was? A part of him?

Travis Foley?

No one would ever believe her if she tried to tell anyone that. At least, no one she knew.

Yet she couldn't imagine anyone taking better care of her.

Paige let her eyes drift closed as her muscles went

slack and soft from the heat. The bathroom smelled faintly of him, a hint of spices and some indefinable thing she'd smelled when she had had her face pressed against his skin.

It was blissfully warm, the first time she'd truly been warm in days.

Her body was slowly coming back to life, her mind was filled with lazy, sensual thoughts of him. Him somewhere in this house, stripping off his wet clothes. He'd be impatient, methodical, almost mechanical, and she thought under the circumstances he'd opt for a quick, hot shower.

She groaned, imagining what he'd look like stepping into a shower, the sight of the water running down his sun-browned skin, all those lovely muscles and that dark hair on his head and his chest.

She could see his hands, lathered with soap, running impatiently up and down his body, and then see him stepping out of the shower, unselfconsciously, gloriously naked.

She wished she could be there to dry him off, taking her time, being as careful with him as he'd been with her and then pressing her body to his.

He'd kiss her hungrily, as he had that night on the ground near the mine with the storm raging, and there wouldn't be any reason to hold back.

They were safe and warm in his house, behind a locked door, and they could shut out the world if they wanted to.

She groaned, her body remembering everything.

How was she going to forget?

* * *

Travis was just outside the door, having taken a quick shower, dressed and come back with some clothes Marta had found that might fit Paige.

He'd been getting ready to knock when he heard a soft, sexy groan from inside that stopped him cold.

"Ah, God," he muttered, leaning his forehead against the closed door, thinking he could happily beat his head against the wall right now to stop thinking the things he was thinking, wanting the things he wanted.

All that subtle sexual tension of the ride here, carrying her inside, undressing without trying to do anything but simply undress her and get her into that tub so she could warm up. Honestly, he'd tried so hard to do nothing but that, to not make her feel uncomfortable in any way. And the whole time, he'd kept fighting the feeling that she was every bit as aware of him as he was of her. He'd thought that, but he hadn't done anything about it.

And now, this one, small, sexy sound from her, and he knew he was right. She felt just the same.

It had been sweet torture, having her in his arms today, having her here in his house now, in his room, in his bathtub.

He'd never be able to use the room again without thinking of her there.

"I brought you some clothes," he said. "I'll leave them in the bedroom."

"Okay," she said softly.

Then he made himself go on. "There's still a lot of work to be done around the ranch, to make sure the cattle are safe. I'm going out with some of the ranch hands. I'll probably be gone all day."

Yes, he'd just run away.

It had to be better than being here with her.

"All right," she said, like she didn't want him to leave her.

Damn.

"Just make yourself at home. There's a library off the den, all kinds of books, a spare computer that Marta uses sometimes hooked up to the Internet by satellite, if it's working right now. There's music, a TV, movies.... Whatever you want. I'll see you tonight."

"You're going to trust me, here in your house? After you caught me trespassing on your property?" she asked.

"I don't see that I have a choice. It's not like I can call the sheriff to come get you. He couldn't get here anyway, and I'm sure he has more important problems to deal with right now."

"Oh. Okay."

"And I'm more worried about the cattle and the ranch than anything you might find in this house. There really isn't anything to find that I think would help your family against mine. Much as you like to think the entire Foley clan is out to get you and your family, always hatching some new plot against you, we're not always doing that. I don't have the time, even if I wanted to. I work a cattle ranch, Red. So I'll see you tonight."

And then he had to think of a way to get rid of her somehow.

He had to get her back to her vehicle and get her off this ranch, before he did something he couldn't take back, something they'd both regret in time.

Chapter Seven

Paige stayed in that tub for a long time, letting the heat settle into her from the outside in and studying the room, all cream-colored and dark gleaming wood. Plain, masculine, yet rich and elegant.

She got out and dried herself off with a giant, fluffy towel and dried her hair as best she could considering there didn't seem to be a blow-dryer anywhere. So she put her hair in a loose braid and went out into the bedroom.

His bedroom.

Again, she found that same color scheme, cream and dark wood, a big comfy leather chair in the corner, that same clean, masculine decor.

She'd planned on trying to simply ignore the bed, not really wanting to know what it looked like, so she couldn't picture him in it. But it was on the bed that she found the clothes.

Very expensive-looking suitcases, open on the bed, all full of women's clothes.

That was interesting.

What kind of man had a house stocked with suitcases of women's clothes?

She looked over the selection in the first big suitcase.

A young woman's clothes. Young and shapely, she decided from the style and size of the clothing.

He didn't have a sister. She knew that much about the family. And none of his brothers were married. Three rich bachelors from an old Texas family did not go unnoticed. She'd have heard if one of them was off the market, although now that she thought about it, hadn't one of them been married briefly? Was it Travis? Was there some brief marriage in his past?

Paige looked through more of the clothes, many of them obviously new, still boasting their price tags. Cowgirl chic? Or someone's idea of cowgirl chic? She finally found a fairly ordinary pair of jeans she thought would fit and a white blouse, a bit frilly with its expansive, ruffled boatneck, but it would do, she decided.

She found a light pink bra she thought would fit and then wondered, if she asked, if she could have more boxers for underwear. She really didn't want to wear another woman's underwear.

But then there it was, a whole overnight case full of undies, including panties of all sorts of bright colors and varying amounts of…material. Okay, not what she would have chosen for herself, but at least they still had the tags on them, too.

She picked a pair in lavender and told herself to be grateful she wouldn't have to run around his house without panties.

There was even a makeup case.

This woman even left her makeup behind?

Paige opened it and there, indeed, was a plethora of cosmetics, scented soaps, lotions....

Had someone left in a hurry? And not bothered to come back for her things?

Paige decided to be grateful for simple things, like a good lotion to put on her face, a bit of gloss for her dry lips and—yes!—a blow-dryer. She could have dry hair.

Dressing quickly, she dried her hair and, bracing herself, opened his bedroom door and went exploring.

His was the only bedroom in this wing of the house, but there was a locked door—probably his office, she guessed—and the library with the spare computer he'd mentioned. She'd be back there as soon as she found something to eat.

The living room was huge, a massive stone fireplace dominating the space, the furniture again oversize, all buttery-soft leather and polished wood. A glance outside the big windows lining the back of the room told her it was still miserable outside.

In the kitchen, she found a pot of soup simmering, smelling wonderful, and a note. The housekeeper, Marta, said she'd left the soup for Paige and Mr. Travis. It could simmer all day and would be fine. That Paige should feel free to help herself to anything else she wanted from the kitchen and to make herself at home in the house. There was a number to call if she needed anything from Marta, who lived in a cottage near the main house, although phone service had been spotty since the storm hit.

Paige happily ate a bowl of soup, along with some homemade bread she found and a glass of orange juice, then decided she really couldn't wait any longer to call her brother, who was likely half out of his mind worrying about her. She only hoped he hadn't done anything foolish, like send someone after her, or decided to come himself.

She eyed the phone in the kitchen, but then thought if she actually got through to Blake, he'd have a million questions, and she really didn't have any answers for him and really didn't want him to know she was sitting in Travis Foley's ranch house, having gotten caught in the mine by Travis.

So she chickened out and sent him a very brief text message from her satellite phone instead.

Safe. Dry. Waiting out storm. Satellite service iffy. Phone battery low. Will call when I can. Paige.

There. She hit the send button and the message seemed to go through.

Her phone rang not five seconds later.

Blake.

Paige felt bad, but she just couldn't do it yet, couldn't tell him she'd gotten caught and that she had no idea if she could salvage anything of their plans to find the Santa Magdalena Diamond, and there was no way she wanted to tell him anything about Travis Foley.

"Sorry," she whispered, and shut off her phone. He'd

obviously gotten her message. He knew she was safe. That would have to be enough for now.

She went into the library to the spare computer, happy to find that the Internet connection, while slow and going in and out with the storm, worked well enough that with some patience she could at least see a few things.

The online weather forecast was grim. The remnants of the hurricane, now mostly just a huge blob of rain, was sitting right on top of them, stalled by a weather system moving in from the west. Massive flooding was possible. No one seemed to be sure when the two big weather fronts would end their standoff over the Texas Hill Country and the rain would move on.

Paige tried not to think about being stuck here for days.

She clicked over to the news. Her cousin Gabby's marriage to her bodyguard was still making the rounds on the gossip sites. The global market for jewelry was still down, gold prices sky high, diamonds and other gems, too. Nothing new there.

Signing into her e-mail account from online, she found multiple messages from Gabby, which she skimmed quickly.

In love. In love. Life is wonderful. In love. Where are you?

Okay, Gabby was fine, just as Paige had left her.

And then a message Paige read word for word: Where did Penny disappear to? I'm telling you, Paige, something is going on with her, and it just doesn't feel right. I think she may have finally gotten serious about a man, if you can believe that, and…well, she's just so darned naive. I'd hate to see her get hurt.

Paige would, too. And she knew her sister was very inexperienced when it came to men. Paige was the adventurous one and by most people's standards, she wasn't very experienced herself. But Penny…she was downright innocent.

Paige shook her head. She typed in a quick message to Gabby, promising to try to find out what she could, then sent one to Penny, as well.

There was a short e-mail from her mother, which Paige dreaded opening but did, just to skim.

Hope you're OK. That work is going well. Miss you. Love you. Please let me try to explain. Mom.

Okay.

More of the same from her mother, trying to explain her affair with Rex Foley.

Paige really wasn't up to that today.

She had her own Foley man to contend with.

Travis didn't think he'd ever spent a colder, wetter, more miserable day on the ranch, and mostly because he couldn't stand the idea of being in his own warm, dry house with a woman. Because he didn't trust himself there alone with her all day.

The ranch hands could have handled things easily. He knew that. They knew that. And they all knew he'd found a woman out in the storm, been stuck with her for an indeterminate amount of time and was, at first, in no hurry to be rescued. And that now she was back at the ranch and he was out here riding around in the cold and the wet with them.

They knew she was young, gorgeous and had fiery

red hair, and anything beyond that was pure speculation. But they were all speculating like mad and having a good old time of it. That he was either an idiot or that he and the woman had already had a spectacular falling-out. One or the other.

"We gonna stay out here all day or find enough sense to come in out of the rain, Boss?" Cal finally asked shortly before dark.

"Just want to make sure everything is okay," he said.

"Everything is just fine. It was fine hours ago."

Travis didn't bother challenging that notion. Just said, "I don't recall asking you to stay out here with me, old man."

"Nope, you didn't. Just hate to lose you again. I promised your grandfather I'd take care of you, and I thought I was doing a fine job keeping that promise. But if you don't even have enough sense to come in out of the rain anymore—"

"Shut up, Cal," he said.

But he turned his horse in the direction of home, and Cal followed him, not saying another word.

By the time they reached the barn and dealt with the horses, Travis was bone tired. Maybe that would be enough.

He walked into the house through the mudroom, stripped out of all of his wet clothes except his jeans, worked a towel through his wet hair as he walked in barefoot through the kitchen, as he usually did when he came in wet or muddy or both.

He nearly made it to his bedroom before he found *her,* curled up in a chair in the library in front of a roaring fire, reading a book, an image that was like a kick in the gut, it looked so…inviting.

Coming in from a long, hard day at the ranch and finding her there waiting for him. All clean and fresh and so pretty, so sexy.

She put the book down and stood up, wearing a pair of jeans and one of his ex-wife's blouses, something he actually found pretty. A creamy white against her flawless, pale skin and all that fiery hair, hanging long and loose around her shoulders. The blouse had big buttons up the front and then stopped in a scooped-out neckline that draped lovingly across the hint of curves at the top of her breasts. Her cheeks glowed from the heat of the fire and her eyes sparkled as she looked up at him like a woman who was glad to see him.

"You must be half-frozen," she said. "I can't believe you went back out into the storm today."

"Ranch work doesn't stop for anything. I have a million dollars worth of livestock out in that storm. I can't ignore that. Not for anything."

Just like he couldn't let himself ignore who she was.

"I know. I just meant…I'm glad you're back and safe."

He nodded. "I'm going to take a hot shower and get dressed."

"Marta left soup on the stove. It's delicious. And some bread I could warm up," she offered.

"Sounds good," he said, then got the hell out of that room.

Yes, she was incredibly pretty and sexy.

A day's hard ride in a cold driving rain and a tiredness that bordered on exhaustion couldn't change that, he'd found.

What was he going to do now?

She warmed up the bread and dished out the soup to him, though he told her he could manage easily himself.

"I haven't done anything all day except read and send a few e-mails, while you were out working," she said. It only seemed fair that she help out a little bit. "You don't have a live-in housekeeper?"

"I don't need a live-in housekeeper. The house isn't that big, and it's just me. It doesn't get that messy or dirty," he said, as he poured himself a big glass of orange juice and sat down in the eat-in kitchen. "Why? You don't think a man is capable of surviving without live-in help?"

"I'm just surprised. That's all," she said, sitting down at the table with him. "You seem quite self-sufficient."

"I'm a rancher—"

"A working rancher. Not some pampered pretend cowboy who lives in a mansion and oversees his property and his livestock from afar."

He frowned. "What the hell kind of rancher is that?"

She laughed. "The kind I thought you would be."

"Okay, first, that is not a rancher. That's a rich wannabe rancher. Real men despise those silly, pampered wannabes."

"Of course," she agreed.

"Just like we don't have much use for spoiled, pampered heiresses—"

"Which I am not!" she insisted.

"No, it doesn't seem like you are."

"So, neither one of us is what the other expected," she said.

"No, we're not," he agreed, not looking too happy about it.

He finished his soup, then stood up and took his empty bowl to the sink to rinse it and put it in the dishwasher, then opened up the refrigerator and said, "Now, let's see what we have for dinner."

"Dinner? You just ate."

"That was a snack to us working men, Red."

Marta had left him a big, thick steak soaking in some kind of marinade, which he grilled himself on the stove in no time, along with a big potato he put in the microwave. When everything was done, he dug into the meal.

She stayed with him, not eating, but enjoying the company, thinking it could get lonely in a place like this, wondering about the woman who'd left all the clothes behind, if it was the isolation of the ranch that had gotten to her.

"So...the clothes? There's practically a whole wardrobe there, a lot of it things that were never even worn," she began, wondering what she could get out of him about this subject. "You just keep things around? In case women this size show up, half-drowned and with no clothes of their own?"

"Ex-wife," he told her. "When she decided she was ready to go, she went."

"Without even taking her clothes?" Paige wasn't a

clotheshorse by any means, but she couldn't imagine just walking out on a whole wardrobe, either.

"She had plenty of clothes. The woman thought shopping was a vocation."

"So, the relationship didn't end well?" she tried.

He laughed, not all that happily. "No, it did not end well."

"And you don't talk about it?" She was altogether curious about the kind of woman he'd marry and the kind who'd walk away from him.

"It wasn't a particularly enjoyable experience," he said. "What do you want to know? I met her. She was young, pretty, flirty and dressed to show off all her curves. Maybe I was blinded a bit by that. We got together fast, way too fast. Let's just say I thought she was something she was not."

And then he stopped talking.

"Something she was not?" Paige tried, hoping he'd keep talking.

"I thought she could be happy here at the ranch. Or she claimed she could, and I believed her. I live here. I work here. This is my life, and I like it. I thought I made that clear to her, but…I don't know." He shrugged. "My family has a lot of money. Women like that—"

"Men, too," she reminded him.

He arched a brow. "You're telling me you have to worry about men chasing you for your family's money?"

She nodded. "I've been fooled a couple of times."

He seemed surprised by that. Did he think women were the only ones who were manipulative enough to come after someone for their money?

"Never married?" he asked.

"No. Thank goodness."

"Well, be careful out there," he told her.

"I'm trying." Right now, she was really trying. "How long were you married?"

"One excruciatingly long year."

"And the wound is still this raw? How long has it been?"

"Three years since she left. You're going to ask if I loved her, right?"

Paige nodded. Yes, she thought she would have had the nerve.

"I think it was more that I loved the idea of her. A woman who could be happy here, share this kind of life with me and be happy. But mostly, I just felt like a damned fool in the end, and I really hate that feeling. That's the part that still burns me up. I trusted her. I believed her completely, and I'm pretty sure she just wanted a rich husband and thought she could get me to give her everything she wanted. Even if it was a life far away from this ranch."

"You don't ever want to leave this place?"

"Not if I had my way." He shrugged, then frowned and swore under his breath. "The thing is, I don't own this land, and I doubt I ever will. Your family owns it. The lease runs out in thirty years. If I ever find another woman I can trust enough to marry, to have a family with, I might be able to raise my children on this ranch, but I could never pass it on to them. I won't even be able to live my whole life here. The lease runs out when I turn sixty."

"Oh."

He said it like he'd rather cut off his right arm than leave this place.

She felt awful. She didn't care a thing about the ranch or that her ancestors and his had been fighting for a hundred and fifty years. But she hadn't thought much about the fact that the long-term lease her mother had offered as a gesture of goodwill would just give someone like Travis a chance to fall in love with the place even more before they had to give it up someday.

And it was one more reason for him to hate her family and her.

"I'm sorry," she said, knowing it was totally inadequate, but needing to say it anyway. "Maybe…maybe my family would extend the lease."

He shrugged, as if he'd absolutely hate even asking for anything from her family.

"Maybe they'd even sell the ranch to your family one day—"

"Don't say that," he told her, a hard edge in his voice that had her nearly flinching. "Not as a joke—"

"I wasn't joking—"

"Not as just an offhand comment—"

"No. I mean…I've never talked to anyone about that, never heard anyone in my family talk about it. I just…it's not like any of us has any interest in working a ranch."

He glared at her, fury in those dark eyes of his. "Just in holding on to this one, if it means keeping me and my family from actually owning it."

"No. I don't… I don't know. I'm just saying… Is this silly feud going to go on forever? Don't we all have better things to do than keep up this fight? I don't care what your grandfather did when he was young. Do you really care what mine did? It's silly—"

"When it means I can work this ranch for most of my life, but never own it, then, yes, I care. I care very, very much."

He got up and walked away, and she let him, not knowing what else she could say. If she could even make him believe she was truly sorry about what this stupid family feud had cost him…. Well, what did it even matter? It didn't change things.

He still loved this ranch and would lose it.

Because of her family.

And she knew, if it weren't for the Santa Magdalena Diamond, none of them would really give a damn about the ranch. Maybe her grandfather or her great-grandfather had, but she didn't. Her mother didn't. Her siblings… had any of them ever even been here? She didn't even know.

So, if and when she found the diamond, could she talk them into foregoing the lease and just selling Travis the ranch?

They'd think she was crazy, first of all, wanting to help Travis Foley that way. She'd never be able to explain in any way that made sense. As far as they knew, she didn't even know the man.

What could she say? He's a nice man. He loves the ranch. He's lived here practically his whole life. Why keep it from him?

And still, they'd all be incredulous and the key question

would be, Why would she want to go out of her way to help Travis Foley?

Because she wanted him.

Paige was ready to cry.

She was trained not to fall for a man who wanted her for her money, and here she was, thinking to bribe a man into falling for her because she might be able to get him his beloved ranch. That was one road to romance she'd never considered going down before. Trying to buy a man's love. What a pathetic comment on her life at the moment.

Contemplating trying to buy a man's love with the gift of a Texas ranch.

Chapter Eight

She decided she just had to get out of the ranch house, even if it was still raining. Thankfully, the horse barn was close.

Finding her boots—cleaned, no doubt by Marta—by the door in the mudroom and a slicker hanging from a hook, she took off through the rain. It had slowed, at least, but showed no signs of actually stopping.

The barn was huge, neat as could be, not ornate by any means but obviously well-appointed and not inexpensive. Travis Foley's horses lived well.

Happily for her, the place was deserted this time of night, save for the horses. She walked from stall to stall, happy to be able to walk, at least. From time to time, one of the horses got curious and stuck his head over a stall. She scratched a few long, broad noses and spoke to a few of the animals.

Travis's horse, Murph, was in the last stall on the right, and he acted as if he remembered her, giving her what for all the world looked like a smile. He tried to slip his nose beneath the hand she laid on the top of the gate to his stall, seemingly begging her to pet him.

"You big, sweet baby," she told him, obliging him with some attention.

She was still fussing over him a few minutes later when Travis walked in.

Paige took a breath, bracing herself for another confrontation with him, but when he walked over to her and the horse, he said, "I'm sorry. I know none of this is your fault."

She shrugged. "And I just wasn't thinking about you having to give up this place one day. I hope it never comes to that, Travis. That our families can come to some agreement, and you don't ever have to go."

"Thank you, but I'm a realist. I'm not holding out much hope for that."

He reached up and stroked the horse, an easy, lazy touch that had her thinking of the way he'd touched her, with a nice, slow hand that seemed to say he would take forever, just touching her. The horse looked as if he'd happily lay down his life for Travis.

She shivered, trying to put the image out of her mind.

"Going stir-crazy?" he asked.

"Just because of the rain and being cooped up inside," she said. "I'm not your ex-wife, Travis. I love the land. It's beautiful. I love being outside, riding, exploring, working the land. I wouldn't go stir-crazy in a place like this."

She would ride every morning as the sun came up, she decided. She'd explore all the old mines, just to see what they were like and imagine what it had been like to mine for silver at the turn of the century. She would know every inch of the ranch, and...

And...

She was dreaming, Paige realized.

About a life she couldn't have.

Paige shook her head and turned away from him and the horse and that life. "So, the weather forecast—"

"It's not good," Travis said.

She nodded. "I looked. I borrowed your computer and that was the first thing I checked. It could rain like this for days?"

He nodded. "We have big trucks with four-wheel drive, and we could try to get you to Llano. But we might just get stuck again—"

"No," she said. Being cooped up inside the ranch house was one thing, but she couldn't get stuck in close quarters with him again, say inside a truck or out at the hunting cabin.

"Okay. So, we'll just wait it out. That's fine. You got ahold of your family? They know you're safe?"

"I e-mailed my cousin Gabby, my sister and my mother. They didn't know I was coming here. They think I'm on an archaeology dig in New Mexico with a friend from grad school. It's just my brother, Blake, who knew. I sent him a text message today to let him know I'm safe and out of the storm, but I didn't tell him I was at your ranch house. He's going to have a million questions, and—"

She broke off and he gave her a sharp look, one that said he was just waiting for something bad to come out of any dealings with her brother, maybe her whole family.

"What is it?" he demanded.

"Blake. He's going to want to know what's going on with the search for the diamond, and I don't know what to tell him—"

"Right. There it is. You want to stay because you think you can talk me into letting you back into the mine, don't you?"

"No," she claimed.

"So, you're just giving up on the search that easily?"

"No… I just… I don't know what to do now. I don't know what to say. I didn't expect to come to your house or even to meet you. I didn't expect to get trapped with you and have some time to get to know you and now… I don't know, Travis. This is my family we're talking about. Our family's business. I told my brother I could do this, that I could find the diamond—"

"Yeah. Thrill of the discovery and all that. I remember you lying to me about it—"

"It wasn't a lie!" she cried. "Granted, it certainly wasn't the whole truth, but it wasn't a lie. I am a scientist. I like to dig in the dirt. I'm fascinated by the things created by the earth, some of them incredibly beautiful things, some of them incredibly old and still here and marvelous. And it's not easy to be taken seriously as a scientist, particularly when you're young and a woman and an heiress to a jewelry fortune. People tend to think you work as some kind of a lark. So, yes, it would be incredible for me to be the one to find this diamond. And yes, that does mean something to me. This is my life, just like this ranch is yours. How about we agree on this one thing. You don't insult my dreams, and I don't insult yours?"

"Fine," he growled. "But don't stand here and try to tell me you aren't trying to figure out how to get me to let you back into that mine, when I know you are."

"I'm telling you the truth. I don't know what to do or what to say, either to him or you. It's all just a big, damned mess, a lot more complicated than that, but that's the bottom line. I don't know what to do."

She was yelling at the end, and the horse whinnied nervously and backed away from the front of the stall, as if the crazy woman was just a little too close, and that's what she felt like. A crazy woman.

He wasn't any better, damned stubborn man.

"This isn't going to go away, just because you caught me and you run me off the ranch. You know that, don't you?" she tried, once she'd calmed down a bit.

He looked coldly furious. "Believe me, I know I'm never getting the McCords out of my life."

And that did it. It was just too much. She was too mad to even say anything. She couldn't even yell at him anymore, and if she stayed there any longer, she was going to start to cry, she feared.

So she turned around and stalked out of the barn. He chased after her.

He caught her just outside in the rain and pulled her back under the slight overhang of the barn roof, barely out of the rain.

"Ah, hell, Red. I'm sorry."

"Of course, you are."

"You just…you make me crazy, okay? You and the whole situation make me mad as hell and a little bit crazy."

"I know."

"It just doesn't seem like we'll ever really solve anything, that even trying is ridiculous, but…I don't want to hurt you, I swear. You asked me to believe you—that you really don't know what to do or say about the stupid diamond. And I do. I'll believe you about that. You believe me about this, okay? I really don't want to hurt you."

"I don't want to hurt you, either," she promised him, looking up at him through the dark with water running off her hair and her face, thinking maybe it would at least keep him from seeing her tears. "And I don't want anybody to take this ranch away from you, and I don't want…anything but good things for you. Only good."

She sniffled and then closed her eyes and shook her head.

"Ah, Red," he said, swearing as he lowered his mouth to hers and all the breath went out of her, right then and there.

That was what she'd wanted all along. Not to fight with him, but to touch him again, to have him touch her, kiss her, take her.

He gave her one, big, devouring kiss, and the current of sexual desire hummed back and forth between them, as strong as it had been that first night and every moment since in her mind.

It was as if they had their own little power source of heat and longing simmering somewhere inside of them, just waiting to be turned on.

She opened herself to him, wrapped herself around him, simply unable to get close enough to his big, hard body.

Her breasts ached. The spot between her legs throbbed. He got his hands under her rain slicker, took her hips in his hands and scooped her up. She wrapped her legs around him. It was dark and raining and no one was here. He could have her against the side of his horse barn, if he wanted. He was hard and ready. What exactly would be the problem?

Everything.

Oh, damn.

Everything that had been the problem before.

He seemed to figure it out just as she did, because he eased her back down to the ground, and his kisses went from frantic and deep and thrusting to soft and slower and slower and then…as if every touch might be the last, should be the last, and he just couldn't stand to stop.

He finally pulled his mouth away from hers, but stayed close, his forehead to hers. "You're killin' me, Red. Just killin' me."

"You're killing me, too," she said softly.

They walked back to the house, and there she was, dripping wet once again, a little cold and alone with him.

"This is a bad habit you've got," he said, taking her slicker, having her sit on a stool by the back door and getting her boots off. Then he pulled a towel out of a cabinet for her hair and refused to give it to her.

"Let me," he said. "It's one thing I think I can do without losing my head over you."

And then he started slowly, painstakingly drying off her hair.

Which made her think of being here before and in his bathroom, and him undressing her without looking at her, taking care of her and trying not to do anything else. Showing a patience and a kind of gentle caring that she had never experienced before.

Men did not take care of her. They flirted with her, they showed off for her, they challenged her, and a lot of them wanted her. But they didn't take kind, tender care of her.

She backed away from him and turned her face to the wall, fresh tears forming in her eyes.

He backed off, too, and handed her a blanket to wrap around her.

"Fire's still going in the library," he said. "Go warm up."

She nodded, then walked through his house thinking she really had to get out of here, that she just didn't know how much more of this she could take.

Wanting him and not wanting to want him. Resisting him as best she could and not wanting to resist him.

She went to the library, sat down on the raised stone hearth right in front of the fire. He came inside a moment later, poured himself a drink of whiskey and then took a seat in one of the big leather chairs nearby. All she wanted to do was crawl into his lap and kiss him silly.

She wondered for a moment if this was how her mother felt about Rex Foley and how long it had gone on—those feelings—and how long Paige could resist Travis.

Years?

Even when she was another man's wife with children of her own?

Her mother had risked everything—even her children—for Rex Foley. And Paige wondered if the son was anything like the father, if the father could possibly be as sexy and appealing.

And she owed her mother an apology, Paige realized. She'd been angry, completely judgmental and cold toward her mother since her mother's big secret had come out, and her mother had shaken her head sadly and said, *You've never really been in love before, Paige. You don't know what it's like.*

And Paige had been horrified.

Her mother hadn't just slept with Rex Foley and had his son. She'd actually *loved* Rex Foley?

So what about Paige's father? Had her mother loved Devon McCord? And if she hadn't, why had she married him and what had their whole life as a family been about? Just Paige's father wanting to keep her mother away from Rex?

What kind of life was that for her mother?

A life of misery and longing and denial. Certainly her mother had experienced a lot more pain than Paige could possibly feel right now, after knowing Travis for only a few days.

So she showed some actual restraint, some intelligence. She got to her feet and told him she was tired and needed to go to sleep, and then she got out of that room and away from him before she could do anything even more foolish than she already had.

* * *

Paige spent a restless night, either awake and thinking about him or asleep and dreaming of him.

She didn't know which was worse.

He'd already left the house by the time she got up the next morning, having slept in a beautifully appointed guest room on the opposite side of the house from his. She showered, dressed in more of his ex-wife's clothes, and found Marta in the kitchen, a hearty breakfast of a spicy Western omelet ready and waiting for her when she appeared.

Marta had been here on the ranch with her husband, Cal, since the Foleys took over the ranch when Travis was ten, and she really didn't like Travis's ex-wife.

Oh, she didn't actually say anything about the woman, but the expression on her face while she avoided Paige's attempts at conversation said everything Marta wouldn't put into words.

Paige could not imagine Travis Foley making a fool of himself over a woman or being so wrong about one. He seemed too intelligent, too controlled to ever do that. Of course, maybe what she was seeing was the man he'd become after his marriage.

Paige, thinking she likely had another long, solitary, rainy day in front of her, went back to the library to check her e-mail.

Gabby had written back, mostly with more of the same from before. In love. In love. Gloriously in love. Where are you? And did you hear anything from Penny?

Paige opened an e-mail to reply, then set it aside,

wanting to see if she actually had heard anything from her twin first.

There it was. Penny wrote, Fine. Busy working on new designs for the stores. Where are you exactly? *Hmm.*

That was odd.

It felt as if Penny was putting Paige off in much the same way Paige was trying to put Penny off, without really telling her anything of what was going on. And they just didn't do that with each other.

Okay, maybe things had been a little crazy since Paige and Blake had hatched their plan for Paige to go diamond hunting in the mine on Travis Foley's ranch, but… Well, Paige had assumed she was the only one with a big secret. She'd been happy thinking Penny was simply busy with her jewelry designs and to leave it at that.

But what if her sister was actually up to something, too?

She could probably find out… Paige could almost always find out what was happening in her twin's life. But twin intuition was a two-way street. While she was trying to read Penny, Penny would be trying to read Paige, too, if her twin caught so much as a hint of Paige trying to keep secrets of her own.

Paige wasn't sure she was ready to risk it. Not just yet.

Maybe when her feelings for Travis Foley weren't such a mess.

Which meant e-mail only for a while with her twin.

So she e-mailed Penny back, asking the same questions she'd asked the day before and gave the same answers. Fine. Working. What is up with you?

That just left her brother, and Paige feared it would

have to be a phone call today. Otherwise, Blake would likely have someone pinging her satellite phone to tri-angulate her position, and if that method proved precise enough to show she was sitting in Travis Foley's ranch house, her brother would have a fit over all the things she hadn't told him.

That she'd gotten caught by Travis Foley himself.

That she liked the man, wanted the man, that it was all she could do to keep from letting herself fall for him completely.

She'd promised her brother she'd find that diamond. But Travis Foley, who already didn't trust a woman as far as he could throw her, would think the worst of Paige if she tried to talk him into letting her go back into the mine to find the diamond. She could just imagine trying to explain to her brother that they had to let the diamond go as a favor to Paige, because she was losing her head over a man, a Foley man.

That would go over really well right now in her family. And yet, foolishly, that's what she wanted to do. To say, just give me this. Let's forget the diamond. I met a man. A really great man.

Right. Like she had any chance of selling her brother on that idea.

She picked up the phone in the library, sitting in that spot by the big stone fireplace she liked so much, and dialed. The line crackled, but the call went through.

Her brother answered, practically roaring, "You're at Travis Foley's house?"

Paige winced. "What?"

"You're at his house!"

"How do you know that?"

"A little thing called caller ID. It says Foley Ranch. How did you end up at his house?"

"Oops." She was so nervous about making the call, she forgot to do it using her own phone. "Blake, I'm sorry, but...he caught me."

Her brother swore.

"The first afternoon, I'm afraid. I thought I was being careful, but he was watching the mine. He saw me go in and came in after me. I didn't have fifteen minutes inside to look around before he was there—"

"Wait, he didn't hurt you, did he?"

"No—"

"Paige? Tell me—"

"No, he didn't hurt me. He's been nothing but kind to me. Not happy that we're snooping around his ranch—"

"It's not his ranch," her brother reminded her.

"Believe me, he's very well aware of that fact. But he's lived and worked here for the better part of twenty years, Blake, and he feels a strong sense of...well, he knows he doesn't own it, but... Oh, what's the point? It doesn't matter. He caught me. He knows we're after the diamond, and he's not really interested in standing by while I go back down in that mine and try to find it."

"Well, that's just too damned bad. He has a temporary lease on the land only. We own it, and if we need a lawyer or even a judge to say we also own everything on the land, I have people who'll do that—"

"Blake?" He was talking to lawyers and lining up sympathetic judges?

What a mess!

"And we never leased him the mineral rights, and my lawyer says if we want to open up the mine, to exploit the mineral rights, we have that right. Travis Foley can't stop us."

She could just see Travis's face when he found out her brother was ready to drag him in front of a judge to force his way onto the ranch and back into the mine.

"Wait," she said. "You need to be straight with me about what's going on. If you're talking to lawyers and looking for a friendly judge… How bad are things, Blake? Because I thought we might be in a tough spot financially. So many companies are these days. But now I'm starting to think it's more than that."

"I can handle it," he insisted.

"Well, I'm the one you're asking to get back into that mine, and I don't want to let you or the family down, but… He caught me, Blake. Travis Foley caught me red-handed and the last thing he wants is a big fuss with people traipsing all over this ranch looking for buried treasure that he thinks doesn't even exist. And he really doesn't want any of the McCords here."

"So talk him into it—"

Right, because she could just do that.

Talk him into it.

"Easier said than done. I mean…if we don't find the diamond, we're not going to lose the company, are we?"

It was unthinkable. McCords was a jewelry empire, respected worldwide. If you truly cared and you wanted to impress, you showed up with a pretty lavender-colored box of sparkling jewels from McCords. The family had worked for decades to build that reputation.

McCords meant flawless, high-quality stones in beautiful, artistic settings.

"Blake?" she said again, when he said nothing. "Tell me it's not that bad."

He sighed, swore once more. "Look, it's... Dad wasn't the greatest businessman. He could be impulsive at times, and he made a few bad decisions, costly decisions. When he was in charge, he was in charge. He kept a lot of information to himself, and when I took over—"

"Things were a mess," she said for him.

"I was sure I could fix it. I was fixing it, and then the whole economy went crazy. Gold and silver prices have soared, and people aren't spending the way they used to. I just... We have to have this, Paige. We have to have that diamond—"

"But even if we find it, its ownership will likely be in dispute for years, maybe decades. Legend has it that Elwin Foley was on that ship when it went down, that he got off with the diamond, and he's the one who first owned the ranch and the silver mine. The Foleys will contend that it's theirs. We'll say it's ours, and we'll be in court for years. And honestly, Blake, if that diamond truly is what legend says it is, the stone is one of a kind, a national treasure. It belongs in a museum."

"I know," he admitted. "We don't need to own the diamond. We just need to be the ones to find it."

"But all that would buy us is a few news cycles with the McCord name coupled in the press with the discovery of a huge diamond. I mean, I'm sure it would capture people's interest, but do you really think that would be enough to save the company?"

"I'm not counting on that saving the company, just making news. Big news. Capturing people's imagination, blowing the market wide open for canary diamonds."

Canaries.

Vivid yellow diamonds.

Diamonds came in all shapes and colors, but in modern times, the most prized ones were white diamonds, colorless ones actually. More recently, there'd been an increase in interest in colored diamonds, pink ones, blue ones, black diamonds. Still, it wasn't a huge market.

But the Santa Magdalena Diamond was rumored to be a huge, vivid yellow diamond, rival in size to the Hope Diamond, with a history as colorful. Some ancient legends even said the Santa Magdalena was part of a pair with the Hope Diamond that first came to fame in India, where they served as the eyes of a giant statue of a goddess. The Hope, the blue eye, the Santa Magdalena, the brilliant yellow eye, and that the people who owned them, who cheated to get them or stole them had been cursed for centuries since the diamonds were separated. In her research, Paige had even found a legend that said the curse would be broken only when the two diamonds were finally together again.

It was a fabulous story.

And her brother was right. If the Santa Magdalena, this great treasure lost for so long, was found after being hidden in the Texas Hill Country all this time, it would be a story that likely fascinated people. It was also sure to bring about a surge in interest in canary diamonds, which for a long time had been nothing but a modest part of the diamond market.

A company that skillfully positioned itself to meet that demand...

"You've been buying up canaries?" she guessed.

"I have vaults full of them," he admitted, sounding very pleased with himself.

"Oh, Blake." It was a huge risk to take, investing all that money at a time when company money was tight. But if he was right, if they found the Santa Magdalena...

"Not just that," her brother said. "Penny's been working for a couple of months on designs, Old Spanish-influenced designs, from the time when the Santa Magdalena was lost. Gabby and the PR people have a campaign that's nearly ready. We can go into production on a whole line using the canary diamonds the instant we find it."

"That's...that's brilliant."

They would own the market. There would be a huge surge in demand for a product that, in the beginning, only McCords would have.

"It had better be brilliant, because honestly, Paige, I'm afraid it's the last hope we have left. We have to find that diamond. Or...we could lose everything."

Chapter Nine

It was sheer torture to be alone with Paige in the house, so Travis went back out riding in the miserable rain, making sure he wasn't losing expensive livestock to the storm.

He was still in the barn, finishing cooling down Murph and getting him settled for the night, when Cal showed up and said his father was on the phone.

Travis swore.

Cal just laughed. "Could be worse."

"Yeah? How?"

"You can take the call in the office here in the barn."

So Travis took the call in the office in the corner of the barn, with Cal laughing at him as he walked in to do it.

"Travis?" his father said. "Glad I finally got through. Everything okay there? The storm looks nasty."

"Yeah. Just a little water, a little mud. We're fine, Dad."

"Good. The flooding on TV looks massive. I'm glad it hasn't been bad this far north."

Travis sighed. "It's big, but we have high ground, too, and we haven't lost any cattle yet. So far, it's just cold and wet and damned annoying."

"I'm sure you're handling the situation just fine, son," he said, sounding tired, Travis thought, maybe even troubled.

"Dad, are you okay?"

"I am. I thought…well, I'm not sure if you want to know this, and I realize it's still a shock. It's still one to me, too, but…Eleanor's son…my son…Charlie decided he was ready to meet me."

"Oh."

"Yeah. I didn't want to rush him. I mean, if I'm fifty-eight and a father three times over already, and I don't know the half of what I feel about this, how's he supposed to know at twenty-one? So I promised Eleanor I'd wait until Charlie was ready, and finally, he was."

Wow. His father actually sounded shaken, vulnerable.

It was something Travis didn't think he'd ever heard in his father's voice or ever would.

"So, you saw him already? How was it?"

"It was—"

His father broke off. Silence came through the line for a moment, and then his voice broke, he sighed painfully.

Was his father in tears?

A man who'd raised three young sons on his own after his wife died? A man Travis had always considered as strong and solid as a rock.

"Dad?"

"Sorry, I... Damn. He's a great-looking kid," his father insisted, laughing and, Travis suspected, doing his best to cover up anything else he was feeling. "I mean, he's my boy. Good-looking, like all my boys, solid as a rock, strong, smart, plays a little football. Great kid. Has no idea what he thinks about me and our whole family, but...just a great kid."

"That's good. I'm glad, Dad."

"Really? You mean that?"

"Yeah, I do. He's a Foley. He's one of us, no matter what else he is," Travis said. Plus, he'd promised Paige he'd smooth the way as best he could for Charlie with the rest of his family, and he was a man who kept his promises.

"Thank you, Travis. It means a lot to me."

"Sure. And...I want to meet him, whenever he's ready." One of the horses started acting up, making a racket, reminding Travis of one thing they could all do together. "Maybe he'd like to come to the ranch one day. You and me, we'll put him on a horse and see what he can do. How about that?"

"That...that sounds great."

"So, you want to tell him? Or do you think I should? I'll do whatever you think is best."

"Well, I'm not sure. I'll let you know," his father said, then hesitated for a moment. "Actually, Travis, what I'll do is ask Eleanor how she thinks we should handle that."

Eleanor?

Travis sat up straight in the office chair, not sure if he liked where this conversation was going. "Okay."

"I'll ask her tonight, when I see her."

Oh.

So, was Travis supposed to ask? Did he really want to know? In the end, he decided he did want to know. "You're seeing her?"

"Yes."

He swallowed a curse. "Dad, I thought you were furious at her for having your son and keeping it from you all these years?"

Travis was, and he knew damned well his father had been in the beginning.

"I was," his father admitted. "But I'm not blameless in this situation—"

"Blameless? You didn't know for twenty-one years that you had a fourth son out there in the world."

"No, but I knew she was married when we were together, and I knew what we were doing was wrong. But I ignored all that because…well, Eleanor and I… There was a time, a long time ago, when I was just crazy in love with her, and she ended up with Devon McCord. But I never forgot her."

Jesus, Travis really didn't want to know this. None of it. Because it brought up a million questions he really didn't want answers to, either.

He hardly had any memories of his mother, but from all he'd heard and what little he did remember, he would have sworn she was a kind, loving, happy woman. Travis really didn't want to hear that his father had never loved her, had spent his whole life in love with Eleanor McCord and wishing he could have her, instead.

What the hell kind of life was that?

"I loved your mother," his father continued, as if reading Travis's mind. "I truly did. She was a wonderful woman, a wonderful mother, and she loved you and your brothers dearly. We were happy together, Travis. I couldn't believe it when I lost her. I felt in some ways I had cheated her, just by having those old feelings for Eleanor, even though I never acted on them while your mother was alive. I promise you that. I hope you believe me. It was only after your mother was gone that…"

"Dad, really, you don't have to—"

"No, I want you to know. I'm sorry. It was wrong, and I knew it. When Devon left Eleanor, she thought their marriage was over, and I thought we were going to get our chance. Then Devon came back and she had to make a choice."

"And she chose him?" How could she choose Devon McCord?

"She chose to protect her children, and that meant going on with the marriage. I know it wasn't easy for her, but…Travis, when you have children, things change. Their needs become more important than yours. You'll have children of your own one day, and maybe then you'll understand what she did."

"And you're going to just forgive her for that? For having your son and keeping him from you all those years?" Because Travis didn't understand that at all.

"Not easily, but I'm damned sick and tired of living without her. I can tell you that. She's here now, and her children are grown and it's time we got to think about ourselves and not anyone else. I'm sorry if that hurts you, or if you don't understand. But Eleanor and I are going to be thinking about ourselves now and what we want."

"Good God, you're still in love with her?"

"I never stopped loving her."

Travis slumped back in the office chair, feeling like the earth had just shifted beneath his feet.

His father was in love with Eleanor McCord? He couldn't even imagine how the ripples of that relationship were going to move through their world. Not easily. That was for sure.

And no easier for the woman inside his house right now.

Paige calmed herself down, thought things through and then decided that one way or another, she had to talk Travis into letting her search for the diamond. She had to. Her family's business depended on it.

And she didn't even think she could tell him that. Which meant...well, she didn't see how she'd make him understand.

So she paced and went over everything she'd figured out about the diamond and its possible location and about the Eagle Mine, and then she paced some more.

The day passed with excruciating slowness, and if the rain didn't stop soon, she was going to scream. By the time she heard Travis come in that evening, she was sitting on the big sofa in the living room trying to scrub her face free of tears that had fallen a while back, hoping it wouldn't show.

He looked surprised to find her where she was, sitting in a dimly lit room, wrapped up in an afghan, seemingly doing nothing at all. But he was wet and tired and no doubt cold, and off he went to shower and change.

She was still sitting there when he came back, and that time, he walked into the room and stopped talking midsentence as he caught sight of her.

Carefully, he came to sit beside her on the sofa, close but not too close, taking her hand in his.

"Let me guess," he said finally. "You talked to your mother?"

That brought her head up to face him. "What's wrong with my mother?"

"Nothing." He looked confused then.

"No. What did you hear?" God, what else could have gone wrong? Her family's business was near to going under, and her mother? What had her mother done?

Travis shrugged. "I figured it had to be a family member. Mother, brother, sister. I took a shot. So, which one was it?"

She hung her head miserably, still trying to figure out exactly how much she could tell him, how she could explain and get him to let her back into the mine without hating her.

"Okay, Red, the thing is, it's hard enough seeing you look this miserable, when I'm just looking for an excuse to touch you. And I'm telling you right now, you start to cry, and that's it. I won't be able to just sit here and do nothing."

"Promise?" she asked.

He nodded.

And she let those tears fall.

He swore softly and scooped her up and onto his lap,

pulling her down against his chest and wrapping her up in those wonderful arms of his.

He didn't even try to tell her to stop or that everything would be okay or that it couldn't be that bad, which she appreciated very much. He just held her and let her cry, tears rolling slowly down her cheeks, misery pouring out of her.

His body was big and hard and warm, and he smelled so good, fresh from the shower. She laid her head on his shoulder and eased into that spot where his shoulder met his neck, one hand pressed flat over his beating heart, letting the comfort and the reassurance of him seep into her.

"Do you ever just want to run away from your whole family and all of its problems and go somewhere where no one can find you?" she whispered.

"Not me. I'd find a way to seal the borders of this ranch and cut it off completely from the outside world. No one would get in without my say-so. That's my idea of paradise when they're all driving me crazy."

Paige grinned. "Okay, do it. That would work."

"Red, the thing is, I just haven't figured out how. But if I did, I'd keep you inside with me, and I wouldn't let anybody from your family in, either."

Which made him her hero.

She let her hand slide up to the side of his face, and snuggled deeper into the curve of his shoulder. How could a man be so comforting and yet so sexy at the same time?

"What do they want you to do, Red?" he asked finally. "Get back into the mine? Is that it? Talk me into it? No matter what it takes?"

She nodded.

"Well, they sure knew the right person to send," he claimed. "If anybody could talk me into it, it's you. You could probably talk me into anything."

"I don't want to do it," she tried to explain. "I want you to understand that. To believe it, if you can. I don't want to do that to you. To use...this thing between us just to get back into that mine."

He took a breath, a slow, deep steadying one, let one of his hands stroke her hair. "But you will anyway?"

"I have to," she said.

He eased her away from him just enough that he could look her in the eye. "No, honey, you don't."

"I promised I'd do whatever it takes to get back into that mine and find the diamond—"

"Whatever it takes?"

She nodded.

"Fine," he said. "Tell your family the price of entrance is you in my bed. See how they like that."

She laughed sarcastically. "I wish it was that easy. You could be the evil Foley man who used me terribly, and I'd be the self-sacrificing heroine of the story who gave up her body to the evil one for the good of her family."

"You make me sound like a complete cad, Red."

"Only to my family. To yours, I'd be the scheming woman who was willing to use her body to seduce you into getting what my family and I wanted."

"Oh, well. In that case...it's a brilliant plan," he agreed.

"It is. Both our families would understand."

He rubbed his cheek, slightly rough with late-day

stubble, against hers. "And we'd get what we want any-way. We'd get each other."

"And our families would have one more reason to hate each other."

"Yes, they would," he said, pulling her closer, his hold one of comfort and admirably restrained desire. "You know, I feel compelled to point out that we don't ever have to tell anyone what we do on this ranch. No one would ever have to know. Have you thought about that?"

"Yes," she admitted.

"And if no one ever knew, who could it possibly hurt?" he reasoned. "Just you and me. If we…came to care enough about each other, or if just one of us cared enough…"

They could get hurt.

She started crying again. He had a hand on the side of her face, pressing her close, and he felt those tears, swore softly and then he was kissing her, slowly, deeply, hungrily.

Nothing more.

Just kissing her like he wanted to devour her right here on the sofa.

She sank into him, into the pleasure, going boneless in his arms, wanting to be nowhere else but there. Her heart started thudding heavily, her body warm and tingly all over, the pleasure centered on the point where his mouth was joined with hers, as if every sensation, every bit of energy, of life sprang from that union.

Take me, she wanted to beg him. *Take me so fast I don't have time to think or to pull away. Just do it, and we'll worry about the consequences later.*

He rolled them in one smooth motion, and she ended

up flat on her back on the sofa with him on top of her, his body all big and hard and ready.

She loved the feel of him there, the weight of him, the heat, the way one of his thighs slipped between hers in an intimate promise of the pleasures in store for them both.

He made short work of the buttons of her shirt, undoing only as many as it took to allow him access to one breast. He pushed her bra aside and there was no teasing this time, just him sucking hard on her nipple, the sensation opening up a line directly to that place between her thighs and setting that spot to throbbing.

She wanted her jeans off, wanted his off, wanted his mouth… She wanted it everywhere, right then, no more waiting.

She'd come right then and there, if he kept sucking on her nipple that way. Just that would be enough.

He slid his thigh high against her, stroking her through her jeans, and she arched up against him, holding his head to her breasts.

The man made her insane.

The whole situation was insane, but he was right.

No one would ever have to know.

It was their lives, their bodies, their secret, their time out of time, right here, right now.

Paige had this crazy impulse to tell him she loved him. It flashed through her head in a second, taking her breath away, leaving her weak and scared and thrilled, all at the same time. Did she love him? She had never really felt that way about anyone before.

He moved from one breast to the other, and she made

a purring sound of pure pleasure, pure need. Now he was messing with her mind as much as her body.

She'd be crazy to even think of loving him.

Still, the idea kept nagging at her, running around in her brain, sneaking through the fog of pleasure he'd created there and making her actually think about it.

What if she loved him?

And then when they finished this, and she had to talk him into letting her go find the diamond...he'd think this was all about that damned diamond.

"Dammit," she muttered.

He lifted his head for an instant, annoyed and breathless and so sexy it hurt. "What?"

"I...I'm sorry, but we can't do this yet!"

He groaned, closed his eyes, hung his head over her chest, the rest of his body still lying heavily on top of hers.

"We just...we have to settle this thing with the stupid diamond first, Travis. I'm sorry, but we do."

"We already did," he complained, but he rolled off of her anyway.

Travis pulled her up on her side with her back against the sofa, and he rolled onto his side, too, facing her. He looked seriously annoyed, seriously aroused.

"You're going to sleep with me, so I'll let you look for the diamond, remember? And I'm going to let you seduce me, and then I'll be so crazy for you, I'll let you do anything, including look for the diamond. It's perfect and both our families will understand, because they expect the worst of each other, anyway."

"I know, but that's for them, if they ever find out and

start being jerks about it. I'm talking about us. We have to settle this first for us because...because..."

"Because why, Red?" He cupped her face with his hand, still breathing hard but giving her a sweet smile.

"Because I couldn't stand it if you thought I was going to sleep with you to get that damned diamond," she said.

He looked completely exasperated. "At the moment, I don't really care why you do it, just that you do."

"I know, but come morning, you will care and I'll care, too. I can't have you hating me, Travis, or thinking I'm just another scheming woman who wants something from you and will use her body to get it."

He sighed, then swore. "I don't think that."

"Maybe not now, but afterward, when I start talking you into letting me back into the mine, you will. So we have to settle this now, and then...we can do whatever we want."

He went still, really looking at her. "Promise? The we-can-do-whatever-we-want part? After we settle this?"

"Yes. And my vote for what happens right after we settle this would be getting naked."

"And you expect me to have a serious conversation with you after hearing that? I hardly have any blood in my brain right now, Red."

"Come on, focus. We have a goal in mind, Travis. We settle this, we can get naked."

He shook his head, trying to clear it. "If this is your idea of negotiating, you're really good at it."

"This is me, sick of everything standing between us and wanting to fix it, so I can take my clothes off and climb into your bed. Come on. Get up. We can't do this horizontally, and I think I have an idea."

Chapter Ten

He sat up, got to his feet, poured himself a shot of whiskey neat and ran a hand through his hair, thinking if she was out to mess with his head, she was succeeding brilliantly.

Maybe he was a fool, but he really didn't care, because he was going to have her. And maybe then he'd be able to think straight and make some sense of this whole thing.

Maybe.

He sat back down, on the far end of the sofa, and she sat at the other end, turned sideways to face him, one leg tucked up under her, her arm stretched out along the back.

God, he loved that wild, crazy hair of hers.

That was his first thought. Not the greatest start to any negotiations, he knew, but still... That hair was magnificent. It made him absolutely crazy. He wanted it spread out over his chest after they made love, could imagine her stroking his entire body with her hair.

"I don't think you're focusing," she said.

Travis rolled his eyes, telling himself she wasn't his ex-wife, and he wasn't about to get stupid over a woman again. The thing was, she was so much smarter than his ex-wife and more beautiful, and he wanted her even more.

Which had the potential to make him even stupider and her even more dangerous, which was a terrifying thought.

God help him.

"Okay, Red," he said. "Tell me why I'm going to let you back into that mine. I'm assuming you have some reason other than the fact that you're gorgeous and sexy, and I want you so bad I can hardly see straight?"

She blinked up at him. "You're not helping. Focus, remember?"

"Okay, tell me why."

"Because my brother is as stubborn as you are, and he won't give up trying to force his way onto the ranch, just because you say no the first time or the first ten times he tries to make it happen. And the whole thing will just turn into one giant hassle that goes on and on, and you'll hate that, Travis. You'll absolutely hate it."

"Yeah, I would, but that's no reason to give him what he wants," he argued, hating her brother right now. "And what the hell is wrong with the guy? Sending his little sister in to do a dangerous job like heading into an abandoned mine? I plan on telling him that, too."

She frowned. "When you have a geologist in the family, someone who actually has experience working in mines, if you're smart, that's who you send to do the job. And you're not staying focused."

"Okay. Fine. But I have to say, the idea of frustrating your brother sounds really good to me."

"Not if that's not what you really want. Think about yourself here and what you want—"

He grinned. "That's easy, Red. I want you."

"Besides me. You want as little hassle as possible with my family, especially over the diamond, which is probably here on this ranch you love. Think about it. No more treasure hunters sneaking onto your ranch, and no McCords taking you to court, if they have to, to get into that mine."

"Court?"

"Stubborn, Travis. Remember, my brother's very stubborn, like you. And, as he's already pointed out, my family owns the mineral rights. We're talking about a mine. He claims we have the right to go in there and mine anytime we want. He'll say we're simply exercising the mineral rights and we can fight in court, if you want, for a long time. But you don't want that. What do you want?"

"Besides you naked? Right?"

"Yes, besides that. Come on. What do you want? You want to never have a hassle over this stupid diamond again, right?"

He blinked once, then again. Absolutely damned right. "Yes. How do I get that?"

"By settling it right now. You and me. We'll do it together. All we have to do is trust each other a little."

He balked at that.

"I know. Not your strong suit. Stay with me here. You

trust me, at least a little bit, right? And I trust you. I want a chance to look for the diamond, and you get a chance to get my brother off your back."

"Only if you find the damned thing. If not we'll be looking forever. There are five old silver mines on this ranch."

"But there's only one that matters. The Eagle Mine. I…I'm trusting you, Travis. We have the original deeds to the silver mines. There's a clue on one of the deeds. A tiny clue on the border to the deed to the Eagle Mine. There's a tiny diamond in one of the eagle's claws. There's nothing else like that on any of the other deeds."

He frowned. "Pretty thin as clues go."

"Your grandfather Elwin Foley was on that ship when it went down. He was the first owner of this ranch. My grandfather Harry McCord is the first one to have a deeded ownership of that silver mine. If Elwin hid the diamond here, and Harry found it after he won the ranch from Elwin, Harry wouldn't have left it there without some kind of clue about where he hid it. He must have been hoping that one of his ancestors would find it later and be able to claim it as his own, with no challenge from Elwin Foley."

Travis was skeptical, but she seemed to believe she knew where that diamond was.

"That mine is full of petroglyphs," she reminded him. "You know that. You let the archaeologists inside the mines last year. I have their final report, cataloging the drawings and carvings. Eight of the petroglyphs in the Eagle Mine are of eagles. Don't you see? The diamond is in the Eagle Mine, the spot marked by one of the eagles."

Damn.

Maybe she would find it.

"And if I don't find the diamond," she continued, "this whole thing will be over in a week or two. I'll go to my brother and tell him the diamond's not there, and he'll believe me. And he'll have no reason to ever bother you with this again. You'll have all the peace and quiet you want."

Travis had to admit, that part sounded good.

"I'll even tell the world we know where Elwin Foley left the diamond, that Harry McCord found it and marked the spot, but it's not there anymore. That we looked, and that someone must have already found it. I'll look exhausted and like I'm ready to cry. I'll trot out all my academic credentials and even show them the clue on the deed. People will believe me, and they'll all leave you alone again."

Travis frowned. Either he was still all caught up in getting her into his bed as quickly as possible, or that made sense. He really did just want the whole mess with the diamond to end. Still, it had been so long since he trusted any woman, and he hated feeling like a fool.

"Travis, this is like the whole thing with the ranch. You don't really care about the diamond. You just don't want my family to have it. And my family doesn't really care about the ranch anymore. They're just too stubborn to want you to own it. Do the right thing here. Do the thing that causes you the least amount of hassles and forget about the rest."

"Forget that your family is getting what it wants," he reminded her.

"Just remember that you're getting what you want. Oh, hell, you think we're all crazy to believe the diamond's even there. I can tell. So if you're convinced we're not going to find anything anyway, then this is just sheer stubbornness on your part, to not want to let any of the McCords look for it."

"Well," he conceded, "the Foleys have been accused of being stubborn before."

"Yeah, I've heard that. Come on. You know everything I just said makes sense."

Damn, it did.

He was almost certain it did.

"I know what you really want is the ranch," she said, "but my brother doesn't own it. I can't get you the ranch from him, but when this is over, I'll talk to my mother. I'll do everything I can—"

"Red—"

"I know. You don't think it will ever happen."

"No," he admitted. "I don't. I accepted that a long time ago."

But he made her want to believe it was possible.

"I'm going to do everything I can," she said.

Like she thought she could do anything in the world.

He shook his head, thinking she was still a McCord, and he was half-blind with wanting her, no doubt not thinking clearly.

"And then, there's the fact that I'd have to stay here until it stops raining," she said, giving him a purely wicked smile. "And it's flooded everywhere. I'd have to wait until the water went down, so I could get to the mine, right? Night after night?"

"Okay, now you're just messing with my head," he said, thinking about nothing but her naked again.

She grinned that super sexy grin of hers. "And…we don't know, but the mine might be flooded underground, too. I'd have to wait for the water to go down there, and then I'd have to have time to search…."

"And you'd spend every night of that time in my bed," he said, not asking her, telling her. "How is this different, exactly, than you sleeping with me to get to the diamond?"

"If I was going to do that, I wouldn't have made you stop a minute ago. This is the two of us having a rational discussion about an issue between us and coming to a rational solution to that problem. So we can put it aside and think now of nothing but ourselves and what we want."

Okay. He supposed he got the distinction.

He still felt fuzzy-headed from wanting her so badly, but he thought she'd made sense in all her arguments.

He just had one reservation. "It's not just stubbornness on my part to want to keep you out of that mine. I worry about you, Red. I can't stand the idea of you getting hurt down there or God forbid, trapped in there. I'd never forgive myself."

"We'll do it together. We'll be careful. I promise. I know how to do this, Travis, and I'll have you with me. I couldn't let anything happen to you, either." She grinned. "So, we've agreed?"

He nodded. "Yes. Now take your clothes off, Red."

"Here?" she whispered tentatively.

He was halfway out of his shirt and kicking off his boots at the same time. When he actually got the shirt over his head and tossed it aside, boots off, he looked over at her, standing hesitantly by the sofa.

"Yes, here," he grinned. "Is that a problem for you?"

The fire was going, and they hadn't turned on the lights as darkness had fallen outside, so the room wasn't brightly lit by any means. And there was a nice, soft rug in front of the fire.

She looked incredible by firelight.

He already knew that from their time in the cabin.

"Anybody could just walk right in here," she protested.

"Has anybody done that in the evenings since you've been here?"

"No," she admitted. "But—"

"Are you nervous, Red?"

"A little."

"Shy?" he tried, wondering if she could possibly be that. He'd had her nearly naked on the ground the first night they'd met, after all.

And what a night that had been.

He'd made her crazy. He'd made sure of it. Absolutely crazy, more than once, enjoying the way she responded so openly, with such honesty and abandon. Wanting her so crazy for him that the minute they got anywhere with a condom, he could be inside of her, no questions asked, no hesitation, no nothing.

And it hadn't quite happened like that, but he'd been carrying a condom in his pocket ever since they got to the cabin, like some damned teenager thinking he might get lucky any minute. Someone had been using the cabin as a love nest. He'd found the condom stash there.

"I'm not..." she began. "Just...I didn't think...."

He took her by the hand, led her to stand in front of him as he sat and told her, "Don't worry. I'll take care of everything."

He started at the bottom button of her blouse, pulling it open, putting his mouth to that spot on her belly near her belly button, his arms wrapping around her, hands cupping her bottom, pulling her to him.

She whimpered, grabbed his shoulders, had her hands in his hair.

"There you go," he muttered against her soft, trembling skin. "It's gonna be just fine. Did you like what I did to you that first night at the mine, Red?"

"Yes," she whispered.

"So we both know that I already know what you like, right?"

"Yes."

"You'll like this even better. Trust me."

She did. She trusted him.

And then his tongue slid around the opening of her belly button and then ever so softly inside.

Her muscles went slack, legs just gone, and it was only his arms holding her tight and the way she draped herself over him that held her up.

That wicked tongue of his...

It felt for all the world like he was inside her, really inside her. Heat blossomed in her pelvis, blood thrumming through her veins, until he dragged her back onto the sofa with him, facing him, straddling him, laughing.

He held her with one hand, undid buttons up her blouse with the other, that wicked mouth following, like he might lick every inch of her with a hot, sensual slowness and make her insane.

He got to her bra, which happened to close in front and flipped it open, nosed the cups aside again, there was that mouth, those little licks of wet heat, under her breast, around it, that ultrasensitive outer curve and then finally he took her nipple in his mouth and sucked hard.

She arched against him, felt him, hard and ready, against her through their clothes. She didn't care anymore that they were in his living room, that anyone could walk in or that it wasn't quite dark in the room.

He went from one breast to the other, and one hand went to the snap of her jeans, the zipper, and then to his own. A moment later, he palmed her hips and stood up, taking her with him. Then he put her on her feet, just long enough for him to strip her of her jeans and panties, then strip off his own, as well.

She didn't think she'd ever felt so naked in her entire life as she did when he sat back down and just gazed at her standing there in front of him, a look in his eyes that dared her to object or to try to cover herself. Her breasts ached with fullness. Her nipples were so tight, and she was absolutely throbbing with desire.

"Red, you're beautiful," he said in that slow, sexy, cowboy drawl of his.

Then he reached out and teased at the patch of red curls between her legs.

"Travis, you can't do that," she objected.

"Do what?" he said, watching as she reacted to his touch.

"Leave me standing here like this."

"But I can see you like this, all of you, and I already told you, you're so beautiful. I love looking at you like this," he said, as his wicked fingers slipped inside those curls.

She grabbed on to his shoulders in an effort to stay upright.

This could not go on. She wouldn't be able to stand it.

Sensation shot through her, wave after wave of it, the touch simply too much to bear. Not that it stopped him. He kept right on going, with her begging him, telling him he just had to stop.

But he didn't.

He kept going until she groaned, then gasped, nearly screamed.

"Now that might actually make someone come inside, if anyone was close enough to hear."

He was laughing as he pulled her onto his lap and wrapped her up in the afghan from the back of the sofa.

She would have yelled at him, but she still couldn't talk, still had waves of pure pleasure shooting through her body. She let her head fall to his shoulder, and with her legs splayed wide this way, she could feel him, throbbing hard against the slick opening of her body, and she rocked against him ever so slightly, because she just couldn't help herself.

Oh, it felt so good.

He felt so good.

"If someone comes in here, I'm going to kill you," she told him.

"You're covered up, and even if they do come inside, they won't stay long."

"Travis!"

He laughed again. "If they were close enough to hear you, they'd have been here by now to make sure everything was okay. So you're safe, Red. And you're not going anywhere."

She arched against him and rocked, using him to please herself now and hoping that would make him a fraction as crazy as he'd made her.

He groaned, a sound she took as encouragement, and then he had his hands palming her hips, finding a rhythm he liked.

She nipped on his ear, teased at it a bit, remembering what he'd done to her belly button, then rubbed against him some more, whispering, "Feel what you did to me. It felt so good. You feel so good."

He growled deep in his throat and pushed her away. She sat back on his lap, puzzled until she realized he had a condom and was putting it on, then pulling her back to him.

She started out high on her legs, fitting her body to his and then let him slowly ease her down around him, letting him slowly open up her body and fill it with him. He was big and hot and throbbing, and she felt her body grip him, squeeze him tight, as if she'd never let him go.

It was too much, too sweet, too hot, too much to control, so she just hung on to him and let him do it, let him set the rhythm with his hands on her bottom, that sexy voice of his urging her on, take him, take more, take him deeper.

She whimpered, protested, buried her face in his hair, and he finally flipped her over onto her back on the sofa and came down hard on top of her, rocking into her in a maddening rhythm, so steady, only so deep, only so hard.

He was trying to kill her, she decided.

Kill her with pleasure.

"What?" she cried. "You want me to beg you to finish it? Is that it?"

"Yes," he said, wicked man. "I think I would like that."

But he didn't make her, he laughed deep in his throat and finally let go of all efforts to control this thing between them or to prolong it.

And then it didn't take anything at all.

She'd been hanging on that edge for what seemed like forever, and he finally pushed her over it. She buried her face in his shoulder, to muffle the sounds she made and felt him surging into her, her body milking every bit of pleasure out of his.

It was amazing. It was beautiful, and it was so much more than she'd ever felt before.

He was a magic man, she decided.

Beautiful, sexy, strong, with a control streak a mile long, but she didn't care. She just gave herself over to the sheer pleasure of finally having him in every way that mattered.

Paige knew that at some point, he rolled heavily off of her, wrapped her in that afghan and carried her to his bed, sliding her between the cool, soft sheets and then covering her up.

She grumbled about the cold.

He laughed. "Give me a minute, Red. I'll be happy to warm you up all over again."

"No," she said. "I need a week, maybe two, to recover from that."

She wasn't sure she could move her own legs or her arms, her whole body was so heavy and so relaxed, it was limp with pleasure.

"A week?"

He was back, standing naked by the bed, condoms in hand.

She looked at him, giving him a slow once-over as he'd given her, except here in his room it was darker.

Still, she could see enough to appreciate the sight.

He pulled back the covers and got in, put on another condom and rolled onto her.

"Travis," she protested, wanting him all over again, just too sated to do anything about it.

"We'll go easy this time, Red. If anything can ever be easy with us," he whispered as he slipped inside her still-aroused body.

Just like that.

Easy as could be.

A million sensations came thundering back, making her whimper and open herself up to him even more.

It was pointless to protest.

She'd give him anything he wanted right now, she realized.

Anything.

Paige woke up to find him looking at her again.

She was in his bed, and it was morning, or nearly morning, judging by the faint light coming in the window.

He was lying stretched out beside her, propped up on his side. He'd pulled the sheet down to the top of her thighs and was stroking her slowly. His hand skimmed just above the surface of her skin, a touch more implied than anything else, and it was as if her body was rising up to meet his hand, begging him in its own way to touch her.

"You are a wicked man," she said, her hand on his cheek, wanting him to kiss her. "And you need to shave. Your skin is rough."

"All the better to rough you up, my dear."

She laughed as he did just that, rubbing his chin against her belly, her breasts, her cheek, taking her back, just like that, to that heated pool of desire between them.

How did he do that?

It was like it was always there, simmering, just ready to boil over.

He kissed her once, then again, then studied her face, touching her cheek, tracing a path around her mouth. "I'm afraid I roughed you up a little bit last night, honey. Your skin is reddish. Is it sore?"

"A little," she admitted.

"What me to shave?"

She shook her head, pulling his mouth down to hers. "I don't want to wait."

"You're gonna be sore in other places, if we're not careful," he said.

"Maybe, but I don't care."

The next time she rolled over, she must have been dreaming. Because something that looked for all the world like morning sunlight was shining in through the bedroom window.

Paige blinked once, then again.

It had been days since she'd seen anything resembling sunlight.

It was like waking up to a completely different world.

So was finding herself naked in Travis Foley's bed.

Paige took a breath, pulling the air in as deep as she could and very, very slowly letting it out.

She'd become his lover, and she wasn't sorry.

She was glad, very, very satisfied and a little bit sore.

The man was insatiable. Wonderfully so. She'd never had a lover so sure of what he wanted and the fact that he was going to get it. It was maddening, and, though she hated admitting it even to herself, really turned on. As if he planned to turn her into his personal love slave, and she'd do it, because he made her feel so good.

She was contemplating actually getting up, maybe soaking in that fancy horse trough of his to get some of the soreness out, when he walked in, dressed this time.

Paige glanced at the clock. It was after nine. He was never home at this hour.

"Back for more?" she asked, thinking this whole love slave thing had gone to his head, too.

He grinned, shook his head and held out the phone she hadn't noticed him carrying to her. "It's your brother."

She gaped at him as he clamped a hand over the earpiece. "No!"

"Afraid so, Red. Sounds like he keeps close tabs on you, didn't like it when he hadn't heard back from you first thing this morning."

Horrified, she looked at the phone like it might jump up and bite her. "You didn't... He doesn't..."

"No. Of course not. And he can't see through the

phone, so he has no way of knowing you're naked in my bed, so try not to look so worried. Or sound so worried. He sounds like he already believes I'd throw you to the wolves if I had the chance."

She took a breath, sat up to lean back against the leather headboard and lost track of the sheet in the progress, having to scramble to cover her breasts once more.

"This is impossible!" she complained.

And then he shoved the phone at her, and she had no choice but to say, "Hello? Blake?"

"What has that man done to you?" her brother practically roared.

Paige fought down a near-hysterical chuckle and motioned for Travis to come back into the room, when he started leaving. She didn't have anything to hide anymore, except bare breasts, at least for the length of this phone call, if she could manage it.

"Travis Foley hasn't done anything," she said, a bold-faced lie, cheeks flaming. "Blake, I'm fine. I promise you. There is absolutely nothing wrong with me."

"You're sure?"

"Of course I'm sure. It even stopped raining this morning. Finally!"

"What about the mine? Did you talk him into letting you back into the mine yet?"

"Actually," she said, looking at Travis, wanting to know it was okay with him, "we've come to an agreement."

Travis nodded. They were still in agreement.

"Really?" Blake sounded astonished. "How did you do that?"

She kept looking at Travis. "He said I was a brilliant

negotiator and that every argument I made, made perfect sense."

Laughter rumbled out of Travis, and he reached out and ticked the side of her breast.

She nearly slapped him away.

Blake fell into a thoroughly insulting silence.

"It's true," she told her brother.

"What did you have to give him?"

"I didn't give him anything." Okay, that was another bold-faced lie, but she thought she made the claim rather well. "What he really wants is for the McCords to leave him alone. I told him if I had a week or so to look for the diamond, and I couldn't find it, that's it. We're done. We won't bother him again. You have to promise me that, Blake. If I can't find it, we drop this."

"I don't get it. What's in it for him?"

"He genuinely loves it here," Paige said. "He likes the peace, the quiet, the privacy. I think you'd have to be a rancher to understand, but that means a lot to him. He hates having fortune hunters invading his space. Now, do we have a deal?"

Paige held the phone out between her and Travis. Her brother's voice came through loud and clear. "Yeah. You tell me the diamond's not there, we're done with the mine."

"With any of the old mines. With searching this ranch."

"Okay. Deal."

"Good. I'll call you as soon as the water goes down and we can get inside the mine."

"You be careful. If that man hurts you—"

She clicked the phone off and handed it back to Travis.

He gave her a long, studying look. "You think I don't trust you, Red? That I needed to hear him say it?"

"I wanted you to hear him say it. I wanted you to know you're doing the right thing by trusting me. I don't want you to have any doubts about that."

She watched him mull that over.

Maybe he had doubts and was fighting them.

Maybe he didn't.

She couldn't be sure, despite the thoroughly satisfying night she'd spent in his arms.

Chapter Eleven

Travis had been kept home by a conference call with his bankers, but he'd left her a present in the library before he headed out to work on his ranch.

Paige couldn't imagine what that might be.

She got up, wondering if Marta was already there. Normally at this time, she would be. Had Travis told her not to go to work in his room? Or maybe she'd gone into Paige's room and found a bed that hadn't been slept in.

Oh, well. Too late to worry about that now.

She put on the robe Travis left for her at the foot of the bed and padded across the hall through the family room and to the wing that held the other bedrooms. In her own room, she showered and dressed quickly, then headed for the library.

What could he have possibly given her?

On the desk in the library, she found a box. A big, old cardboard box.

"How romantic," she muttered to herself.

But inside...inside was an absolute treasure chest of information. All kinds of historical documents about the ranch, diaries of his ancestors and hers, maps, drawings, photos, everything.

She was so happy, she was practically bouncing with joy, couldn't wait to dig into it all.

Best of all, he had what looked like a complete record of the archaeologists' work in the mines with the petroglyphs last year!

She had their published report, but he had...everything!

She was so excited. This was...everything. Everything she needed. If anything could pinpoint the exact location of the diamond, it was the petroglyphs, and the archaeologists had mapped and photographed them all!

She was going to do it! She was going to find that diamond, and Blake would do what it took to save the family diamond empire, and then...

Paige thought of Travis.

And then what?

She pushed the thought out of her mind and settled into a chair with the archaeologists' material to start reading.

Travis caught hell from the ranch hands that day for not only starting the day obscenely late—and no explanations of conference calls with bankers were believed in the least—but also for being ridiculously happy.

Apparently, he'd been a bear to deal with for days.

He found he didn't care.

What he did care about was that there was a gorgeous redhead waiting back at the ranch for him, and he couldn't wait to get back to her, even if it was the first day in forever that it wasn't raining like crazy and there were a million things to be done around the ranch.

But he did his duty, as he always had, and got his work done, despite the temptations of *her.* Then he hurried with almost indecent speed back to the house once the work was done.

Cal offered to take care of Murph for him, and Travis actually agreed, which won him a long, hard look from Cal and a muttered, *Damn, she must be something,* under Cal's breath as Travis walked out of the barn.

For once, he wished a day's work didn't involve him coming home a mess, this time wet and muddy through and through.

He had just gotten his boots off in the mudroom and stood up to take off his shirt when she ran into the room, a beautiful smile on her face and launched herself into his arms, giving him no choice but to catch her.

"I'm filthy," he told her.

"I don't care," she claimed, as she laughed and kissed him.

"Okay, but what happened?" He'd never seen her this happy.

"You! My present! All those old records and the archaeologists' report!"

It was his turn to laugh. She was thrilled with a box of old records about the ranch?

"They're not exactly diamonds," he reminded her.

"No, they're better!" She kissed him again.

He gave her a skeptical look. Better than diamonds?

"You're talking to a geologist, remember? Trust me. They're better."

"Well, in that case…" He'd already gotten her filthy, wrapped around him the way she was, so now they both needed to get cleaned up. "Just how grateful are you, Red?"

She grinned. "You need someone to clean you up?"

He nodded.

"Allow me. Please."

"Only if I get to return the favor, Red."

She nodded. "Done."

They were lying in his bed, much later that night, Travis on his back, Paige curled against his side, him stroking that glorious red hair of hers, when he remembered the conversation he'd had with his father yesterday, about Charlie and Eleanor McCord.

Travis sighed, hating to bring their families into this room, this moment, but he knew she was worried about Charlie meeting the Foleys, and he didn't want to be keeping things from her.

He kept stroking her hair, his touch easy and soothing, he hoped, and said, "I meant to tell you, I talked to my father the other night, and I thought you'd like to know. He met Charlie."

She went to pull away from him, and he let her, only as far as to roll onto her back in the bed beside him, and he followed, up on his side, taking her face in his hand to turn it back toward him.

Because he was determined that they could talk about this and still be two people thoroughly enjoying each other in bed.

"When?" she whispered.

"I'm not sure. Just in the last few days."

She studied his face, obviously worried. "And?"

"And... they met. Listening to my father, it sounds like everybody's feelings are pretty much the same. All mixed up. Charlie is my father's son, except he's not, or he never has been. He doesn't know any of us, and none of us really knows what we feel yet. You should know, my father wanted to meet him all along, but decided to wait until Charlie was ready. Sounded like the whole thing was awkward, but civil. I'm sure they'll see each other again. My father said it's bound to take some time to get over the awkwardness and figure out where they go from here, but... He's a good man, Paige. A good father. And it meant something to him. It meant a lot. I could—"

He broke off.

"What?" she demanded. "Tell me."

"I think he actually started to cry while he was telling me about it," Travis admitted. "I don't remember my father ever shedding a tear over anything. He's a rock. He raised me and my two brothers all by himself after our mother died. The man's a force to be reckoned with, and this brought him to tears, just telling me about it. He'd never be cruel or even unkind to a child of his. You have to believe me about that."

"Okay. I do," she said. "And I'm glad that it meant so much to your father, and that you told me."

"I also told him I'd like to meet Charlie, whenever

Charlie's ready," Travis added. "That maybe he'd like to come to the ranch. Around here we put a man on a horse to see what he's made of."

That won him a smile.

"Red, tell me the kid can at least ride a horse respectably."

"He was born and raised in Texas. Of course, he can handle a horse."

"Good. I don't want to be embarrassed by the kid," he teased, leaning over and kissing her softly, then thinking, *damn,* he had to tell her the rest of it.

"What?" She seemed to have radar when it came to him holding back family news. "It's something bad. I knew it. You told me the good news. Now tell me the bad."

He groaned, closed his eyes and shook his head. "I don't know if it's bad, exactly—"

"If your reaction is any indication, it's bad. Travis, tell me—"

"My father said...he and your mother are...seeing each other."

She frowned. "Seeing... Like my mother is helping him to get to know Charlie?"

Travis shook his head. "No...seeing each other."

Paige looked incredulous. "Seeing as in...dating?"

"Worse," he admitted.

"They're sleeping together?" she cried, looking horrified.

"No! I mean...I don't know. I don't want to know. I didn't ask, and he didn't volunteer any information about that. He just...he said...he really cared about her all those years ago and that...he never stopped."

Paige scrambled to sit up in bed and keep the sheet covering her. Her mouth fell open, and she looked so shocked she couldn't even say anything.

"I know," he said. "I felt the same way when he told me. I just... That's what he said. That they've been apart all these years, and that they're seeing each other and they don't care what anyone in the family thinks about it anymore."

He waited, and she just sat there, looking like a million different questions were rushing through her head every moment, and he wished... He wished everything didn't have to be so damned complicated, with so many ways in which his family was entangled in hers.

"I meant to tell you last night, and we got... Well, you know what we did. But I don't want you to think I'm keeping secrets from you, either, and if you ask me what I think about this, I have no idea what to say. It's just..."

"Unreal," she said.

"Yes, it seems like it can't possibly be happening. But that's what he said. I take it this is not common knowledge in your family or mine, or we'd have heard about it by now from one of our siblings."

"Oh, I'd have heard about it. Blake, this morning, if he had any idea, would have told me all about it." She made a face, like a woman who dreaded what was to come.

"So I shouldn't have told you?" he asked.

She groaned. "I don't know. I don't think I want to know about the two of them. And I certainly don't want them to know about us. I just want to be here with you, without any of the family stuff between us. I know that's impossible, but...that's what I want."

"Well, how about…no more talk about the family while we're in bed?" he proposed, easing back down in the bed and tugging her down after him.

"Oh," she said, letting him pull her to him, those long legs of hers wrapping around his, her pretty breasts once more pressed against his chest. "That sounds like a great idea."

"Okay. Forget I said anything."

"I can do that," she promised. "Kiss me, and I'll forget right now."

He happily complied.

The days that followed, waiting for the floodwaters to recede, were idyllic, among the most joyous of her life, Paige decided.

She studied the historical records from the ranch by day and gave up her nights to Travis, gave herself, her body to him completely, while trying to tamp down any questions about risky emotional attachments, the future or messy family entanglements.

This was like a little present to herself, this time with him, and she meant to enjoy it to the fullest and try not to think about what happened later, once it was time for her to leave the ranch.

Except that she wanted Travis to always have the ranch.

The place had come alive to her after reading the old diaries of the women who'd lived and died here, the record of the struggles they faced, the men they'd loved, and all this life on the ranch had meant to them.

Travis loved it in that same way, and it should be his, she decided.

She wanted to be the one who made sure it was always his.

If she found the diamond, she thought she'd have the leverage to do that. She'd simply tell her family if they wanted her to give them the diamond, he got the ranch, period.

It was, as she'd told him, nothing more than stubborn pride and wanting to best the Foleys that would make anyone in her family hang on to the ranch anyway, and she was sick of the whole feud.

So that would be her parting gift to Travis.

His ranch.

And if, when this was over, he just let her go...she supposed she'd have to find the strength and the pride to go.

She wasn't going to think about it now.

She had a diamond to find.

And his records were going to help her. So far, she hadn't found any reference to the diamond at all, except for the same old speculation that it might be there. No one had put together the clue on the back of the old deed with the petroglyphs. No one said anything about ever searching in that way for the diamond.

So she thought it might still be here, even after all this time.

And with the archaeological records, she had the location of all the petroglyphs. The published report showed eight, but it turned out those were only the most clear, intact images the archaeologists had found. The complete records Travis had showed five more partial eagle images and their locations. With that, Paige had mapped out her own plan to search the mine, once the water went down.

Travis checked the mine every day and said it wouldn't be long now.

Which made her think, it was getting late. He'd be home soon.

She thought about what she might do that she hadn't already done with him, something he would enjoy coming home to....

Having her naked worked for him in a big way. So just waiting for him in his bed was always an option. Or walking into the shower with him, as he got cleaned up after a long day's work. That had proven to be very, very satisfying a few nights ago.

Maybe tonight, she really should wait until after dinner, because the man worked hard and he needed to keep up his strength. She could see that he was fed and then maybe take him into the library and take off her clothes and lie down on the rug in front of the fire.

Paige knew he'd like that. He'd wanted her there that first night, in the light of the fire, and she'd been too shy with him at first to really get into letting him watch while she slowly peeled off her clothes.

But she could do it now.

For him, she would.

She'd do anything for him.

He had that kind of sensual power over her.

It was scary and completely thrilling at the same time.

She'd never met a man like him, one who was so very much a man. A strong, kind, patient, gentle, outrageously sexy man who loved this land, this life with a kind of certainty she found so compelling. It made him seem so much more solid and trustworthy than any man she'd ever known.

Paige had met so many men who seemed to be just playing at life, moving along from this to that with no sense of commitment to anything.

Travis knew what he wanted. He worked hard every day to build the life he wanted, even knowing he might one day lose it to her family. He worked for it anyway.

And he seemed very happy to be sharing it with her. Whether that was simply sexual attraction or convenience…

Oh, please, don't let it be just that.

She didn't think she could stand it if, in the end, it was nothing but that.

Paige shook her head, refusing to think that way. She was here now. That was what mattered. They had this time together, and she intended to make the most of it.

Tonight, she was going to do something she'd never done for any man, because she hadn't ever wanted so much to please a man, to surprise him, to be a little daring, a little outrageous for him.

She was going to strip for Travis Foley.

She'd do it in front of the fire while he watched, if she didn't lose her nerve. Paige planned her wardrobe accordingly, looking for something with lots of buttons she could slowly undo and pretty, tiny, lace underwear. She'd even wear high heels for this. That's how crazy she was for the man.

He knew something was up when he walked in that night and saw her in those shoes.

"Are we going out?" he asked.

"Oh, no. We're staying in." She grinned wickedly.

"Okay," he said meekly. "Is there anything I should… do?"

"No, I'm going to take care of everything. You just do what you normally do. Go get cleaned up so I can feed you and then…you'll see."

"Yes, ma'am," he said, already headed for the shower.

"That was the sexiest thing I have ever seen in my life," he whispered into her ear later that evening as they lay on a blanket in front of the fire. "If it gets any better than that, I don't think my heart could take it."

He'd taken her in a frenzy of blazing heat and need and pleasure so deep and all encompassing, it was as if there was nothing left in the world, like what they shared erased everything else, consumed it.

As if they were the only two people in the world and nothing else even existed, much less mattered.

As if nothing had the power to come between them.

When she was in his arms like this, that's how she felt.

As if nothing could come between them.

Later, pleasantly tired and yet excited by all that she'd found out about the ranch, she wrapped herself up in an afghan, and he did, too, and she showed him some of her favorite old photos of the ranch, read him a few passages from old diaries with speculation about the diamond, and then showed him the deed itself and what she and Blake had found.

There was a scanned copy of it in her e-mail box. She'd had Blake send it to her earlier.

She brought it up on the computer and showed him the image.

"See, right here?" She pointed to the border of the deed, made with hundreds of tiny eagles.

"That's the same image used to mark the Eagle Mine," he said, leaning over her shoulder as she sat at his desk.

"Yes. And look here, this corner. It's hard to see on the scan—and even on the actual map, you have to really be looking to see it—but this one eagle, in his talon is a diamond."

He leaned closer to the computer screen, then shook his head. "I don't see it."

"Well, it's there. I think it's telling us not just that the diamond was hidden in the Eagle Mine, but that the image of the eagle marks the spot where the diamond was buried. The image used on the petroglyphs is the same as the one on the deed, as the eagle holding the diamond in his claw. I know where all those images are because you gave me the archaeologists' report, along with the maps they made. Travis, we can find it! We're going to find that diamond!"

He turned and sat on the edge of the desk, shaking his head.

"You thought I was crazy, didn't you?"

"Maybe. A little."

"But see? It's all here. It all makes sense. The diamond has to be at one of these spots, and there are only thirteen of them. We're going to find it."

"Okay, but can we find it tomorrow? Or two days from now? Or next week?" he asked, trailing kisses from her bare shoulder up to her neck.

She laughed, shivering because it felt so good, and

went to close the image and the e-mail it came in, only then noticing she had six different e-mails from Gabby, all within a two-hour span.

"My cousin Gabby's going nuts about something," she said. "She probably found out my mother's dating your father."

"Uh-huh," he said, teasing her ear with his tongue. "Tomorrow. They'll all be just as crazy tomorrow."

He was right. They would. But just as she was closing the program, she noticed the last subject heading.

Penny in trouble.

A shiver worked its way through her body, this one not of pleasure but of uneasiness, of dread.

"Travis, wait," she said, pulling away from him. "Something's wrong with my sister."

He lifted his head and looked at the screen.

Paige opened the e-mail, scared of what she was going to find.

Gabby wrote:

Wanted to be able to tell you this on the phone, but you never answer your phone. Where are you? Penny's been seeing someone in secret for months now, and I'm terrified for her.

Paige, it's Jason Foley!

She finally admitted that she's in love with Jason Foley, and I can't believe this is all a coincidence. That there's all this stuff going on with the search for the diamond, and Jason Foley just happens to show up and seduce one of the McCords.

Tried to tell Penny, but she wouldn't listen to me.

You have to call her. You have to warn her, before he breaks her heart.

—Gabby

Paige froze.

I can't believe this is all a coincidence.

Jason Foley seducing Penny, at the same time Paige just happens to find herself here with Travis, thinking herself in love with him.

Beside her, reading over her shoulder, Travis backed away and swore long and loud.

One look at his face told her everything she needed to know.

"Both of us?" she asked, clutching the afghan closer to her naked body.

She was sitting here, naked in his library, having just performed a striptease for him, then had sex with him on the rug in front of the fire, crazy to please him.

And he and his brother had...

What?

"Was it some sort of bet?" She threw the words at him. "Which one of you could bed one of the McCord twins first?"

"No!" He looked outraged that she'd even think it.

"And did you win? Or did he?"

"It wasn't a bet! I'm not like that! How can you think I'm like that?"

"Well, there's no way this is a coincidence. Your brother seducing my sister, and you seducing me—"

"I didn't know you were coming here. How could I

possibly know you were going to show up on this ranch—"

"You knew we were looking for the diamond—"

"My brothers thought your family was up to something, but they always think that. They care so much more about this stupid feud than I do. I just want to be here and run this ranch. That's all I want. You know that. I told you that. You've been here. You've seen for yourself how much I love this ranch. Haven't you?"

Paige started to cry then, so mad at herself for giving into that need, so mad that he had to see it. "I saw your face just a minute ago, before you could hide it. You knew what your brother was doing—"

"I never agreed to do anything to you, not hurting you or using you or seducing you. I didn't want anything to do with my family's obsession with your family or that stupid diamond."

"So you're trying to tell me, your brother just happened to seduce my sister at the same time you seduced me—"

"Hey, I don't remember there being a great deal of seduction involved. I remember two people who just flat-out wanted each other and couldn't keep their hands off each other. And I'll remind you, I'm the one who stopped that first night. Not you. I could have done anything I wanted with you that night, and you know it. But I didn't."

Paige felt like all the blood rushed out of her head at that, ashamed and embarrassed and getting even madder.

Just how good was he at this game?

"You need to remember, too," he went on, "that you climbed into my bed knowing exactly who I was, wanting me despite everything that was going on with the diamond and the family feud. You wanted me anyway, just the way I wanted you."

She closed her eyes, hating herself and what she'd done, what she'd let him do to her.

"You and your brother had a plan," she said, glaring at him.

"No, we didn't—"

"I saw your face, Travis! When you first read that e-mail, you knew. I saw the guilt on your face—"

"Over what my brother had done to your sister!" he yelled. "I know you love her, and I knew… I knew—"

Paige gasped. "You knew what he was going to do? He deliberately set out to get close to her? To seduce her? And you knew all along?"

Travis closed his eyes and turned away, swearing under his breath as he did.

Obviously, he'd known.

And that thing she felt deep inside, that was her heart, breaking in two.

She pulled the afghan tighter against her, feeling more naked and humiliated than she'd ever been in her life. Getting to her feet, she tried to shove him out of her way. But he got hold of her and didn't let go, grabbing her by the arms and pulling her close, making her look at him.

Making her let him see just how much he'd hurt her? Why did he have to see that, too? Hadn't he done enough already?

"Listen to me. You've been here with me all this time. You know me. Don't you?"

"I know you knew something about your brother seducing my sister—"

"Okay, yes, I knew. I'm sorry. I didn't even remember what he was going to try to do until right now. But when I saw your cousin's e-mail…. Yes, I knew."

Paige felt like her whole body started to shake at once, like there was no solid ground anywhere, nothing to catch her if she just sank to the floor.

He knew!

"Look, Paige, I got a call from my brothers months ago. They were sure your family was up to something to do with the diamond. They wanted to make all sorts of plans, and I told you already, I didn't want anything to do with the whole mess. I just want to run my ranch and have everybody leave me the hell alone. So it wasn't like I was in on planning this. I was only half listening to them at this point. I do that. My eyes glaze over, and I start thinking about cattle prices or fences that need to be replaced, things like that when they start talking family feud with me. But yes, when I saw your cousin's e-mail, I remembered Jason saying something months ago about needing to get information on what your family was up to, and thinking he could get it from Penny."

"She doesn't know anything!" Paige cried. "She's not like me. She's sweet and innocent. I don't think she's ever even slept with a man before in her life, and now she thinks she's in love with him, Travis. How could he do that to her? How can you play with people's hearts that way?"

He pulled her close, tucked her head against his shoulder and held her while she cried, and she let him.

Dammit, she just let him.

"I'm sorry," he said, again and again. "I'm so sorry. All I agreed to do was watch out for trespassers at the old mines. That's it. I swear to you. And then...there you were."

"I came right to you," she whispered. "I made it so easy for you."

"No," he swore. "It wasn't like that. You know it wasn't."

She pulled away from him, staring him in the face. "Then what was it, exactly? A lucky coincidence?"

"No, it was damned inconvenient. It still is, and you know it. You made me want you despite who you are and how complicated this is, and you want me despite all of that, too."

She wanted to believe him.

Oh, she did.

He was such a dangerous man, because even now, she wanted to believe him.

"These last few days, I haven't been thinking of anything but you," he said.

God, she wanted to believe him.

"Of hurrying back here every night so I can be with you. It's like the whole world is just gone, and I love the rain and even the stupid flood, because it's keeping everybody else away, and it's just you and me. That's all I want. Just you and me."

She gave him a hard look, probably spoiled completely by the tears in her eyes.

"I have to go call my sister," she said with as much outrage and indignation as she could muster against him. "I have to go tell her that the man she thinks she's in love with has been lying to her all along, just to get information about our family."

He took that like a slap in the face, backing away, hands up and off of her, breathing hard, his jaw as hard as granite.

"Fine," he said. "Believe what you want. Make the call."

Chapter Twelve

She cried some more in her room before she could get herself together enough to call her sister, dreading how much what she had to say was going to hurt Penny, whom Paige had always tried to protect from the big, bad world.

Her sweet, dreamy, artsy sister, delicate as a fairy and always seeing men through a kind of filmy, romantic haze.

She hated Travis's brother for this, absolutely hated him.

But she wasn't going to think of Travis himself or anything he'd done to her or how she felt about it. It was too new, too raw. It hurt too much, and she just didn't know what to believe.

Finally, her tears stopped enough that she thought she could do it, she could tell her sister this awful thing. She picked up the phone by her bed, and Penny came on the line, sounding so happy Paige nearly started to cry again.

"Oh, my God! What is it? What's wrong?" Penny cried.

"Nothing. I just... I have to tell you something, and—"

"I have to tell you something, too, but mine is good and it can wait. You go first. What's wrong?"

Oh, this was awful!

Jason Foley should be strung up by his ankles and left to fry in the hot Texas sun. Paige would find the rope and help do it herself, and her brothers would help her.

"Paige, you're scaring me," her sister said.

"I know. I'm sorry. Penny, I'm so sorry about this. I love you. You know that, right? And I'll help you get through this. I promise."

"Get through what?"

"Jason Foley," Paige said.

Silence came from the other end.

"You've been seeing Jason Foley, right?"

"Yes," her sister said. "And I know that no one's going to like that, that no one's going to understand, and I'm so sorry I couldn't bring myself to tell you sooner. It was awful, trying to keep a secret like this from you. I just... All the feelings I have are all so overwhelming, so new that I can still hardly believe it myself, but he's not who you think he is, Paige, I swear. He's not the man any of us think he is. He's wonderful, and sweet and kind, and I'm in love with him. I think he's in love with me, too—"

"He's using you to get information about our family." Paige just blurted it out.

Penny laughed. "No, he's not."

"Yes, he is."

Penny hesitated. "He wouldn't do that. He's not like that."

"Yes, he is. Penny, honey, I'm at the ranch right now. I'm at Travis Foley's ranch, looking for the diamond. Travis was with me when I read Gabby's e-mail telling me you were seeing Jason, and Travis knew…. He knew what his brother was going to do. Jason planned this months ago to try to find out what we were doing to find the diamond."

"No. That's crazy! You're at Travis Foley's ranch?"

"Yes. Honey, listen to me. I'm sorry, but Travis admitted the whole thing. The Foleys were convinced our family was up to something. Jason thought he could get the information from you. By getting to know you, by pretending he was interested in you."

Again, silence.

"I'm so sorry. I could just kill them both with my bare hands, I swear. I will make them pay," Paige promised. "We'll all make them pay for what Jason did to you."

"I thought… I thought I was in love with him."

"I know. Gabby told me. I'm so sorry, honey."

"Paige, I slept with him," she confessed.

Yes, they were going to kill him. String him up and let the ants slowly kill him or maybe buzzards. Texas was full of buzzards.

Jason Foley deserved it all.

"It's…" Penny started laughing, a sad, scary sound. "It's even worse than that, I'm afraid."

Worse?

What could be worse than that?

"Because, I just figured out that… Well, I'm pregnant," Penny confessed. "I'm going to have Jason Foley's baby."

It was a horrible night.

Paige cried. She paced the floor, scrubbed her skin clean in the shower, trying to erase every touch of Travis Foley from her body. She burned with shame the way she'd fallen all over him, practically begging him to take her that first night and then even trying to get all the so-called family business out of the way so they could be together, despite everything else.

And the way she'd given herself to him….

Completely, without reservation, nothing held back.

Not even her heart.

She'd stripped for him in his library and had sex with him on the rug in front of his fireplace, like a woman just crazy-mad for him.

And he…

She had no idea what he felt for her or what she could trust that he'd ever said.

Could a man really just forget that his brother was going to seduce her sister to get information out of her? Was that something anyone could really forget?

Although, she had to admit, her family said a lot of things about his, and there were times when she got sick of the whole thing, too, when she tried her best to tune it all out.

She wanted to believe Travis. And as he'd pointed out, he hadn't seduced her, unless he was even better at it than she imagined and she was just much more gullible and hadn't even realized what he was doing. Because it seemed to her, it was completely mutual, as he claimed.

She buried her face in her pillow and cried herself to sleep.

When she woke the next morning, the sun was high in the sky.

It was nearly eleven.

Her head hurt, and her eyes felt like they'd been rubbed with sandpaper. Her throat ached from crying, and she felt the need to scrub her skin some more, to try to forget every sweet, sexy touch of his body against hers.

She'd have just stayed in bed all day, if it weren't for the fact that her sister was heartbroken and pregnant, and she still had a diamond to find and a family about to go broke if she didn't.

Thank goodness she hadn't told Travis Foley that, at least.

He hadn't had to seduce her to get information out of her. She'd just given it all to him, she realized in horror.

She'd told him exactly where the diamond was!

He could have found it already! He could kick her off this ranch today and take the maps from the archaeology dig and find the diamond himself! He could hold her prisoner here, to keep her quiet and isolated from her family, while he found the diamond!

Paige scrambled up and into her clothes, rushing into the hallway and through the house.

Marta looked at her as if she was nuts when she tried all the doors and found them open, no one trying to stop her from going anywhere.

Of course, she couldn't get off this ranch without Travis. Or at least, without one of his horses or his trucks.

Next, she tried the phones.

All working.

She could call for help right now, if she wanted to. Warn her brother about everything and have him send an army to guard the opening of the mine and the diamond inside.

Paige started to dial and then Travis walked in, looking wary and bone tired and not sure what kind of reception he'd get from her today.

"You need to make a call?" he asked. "I can go into the kitchen, if you want some privacy."

She wasn't sure whether to believe him. "You'll let me make a call?"

He frowned. "Why wouldn't I?"

"Because I could tell my brother what you did and what your brother did, and that I told you exactly where the diamond is."

"I assumed you already had," he said, looking resigned to it all being public knowledge by now.

So, she could just tell her family everything and he'd let her?

Paige thought of her mother then, for the first time. Her mother who was supposedly dating Rex Foley now.

Oh, God!

Her mother!

"Tell me your father seeing my mother has nothing to do with any of this? That at least that part is real."

His jaw went tight with anger. "My father claims he's been crazy about your mother since long before she even met *your* father, and that his feelings haven't changed all these years. You believe that if you want to. I can't stop you if you don't."

Paige wasn't sure. She just couldn't be sure of anything.

And Charlie... What was this all going to do to Charlie and any relationship he might have with the Foleys now?

She didn't know about that, either, and so she decided to try to deal with the situation at hand. Her and Travis, the ranch and the diamond.

"Are you going to keep me here?" she asked him.

"Keep you here? I haven't been keeping you here, Paige. There's a flood that's been keeping you here."

"So you'd just let me leave?" she tried.

"Tell me where you want to go. We'll do our best to get you there."

"Off this ranch?"

"Paige, what the devil are you talking about?" he snapped.

She took a breath, felt like crying again. "I don't know. I thought...you know where the diamond is. I told you. I told you how to find it. I thought—"

"That I'd hold you prisoner here, and go get the diamond for myself and my family?"

He was so loud, so angry, she nearly took a step back from the sheer force of his words.

It sounded crazy when he said it like that, and yet...this whole thing between them had been just crazy.

"It's worth a fortune," she said.

"I already have what most people would consider a fortune. My family struck it rich in oil. I suspect you've heard about it. There's nothing I really want that I can get from that diamond," he said bitterly.

And she wondered exactly what it was Travis Foley might want.

Not her.

Surely not her.

He couldn't have meant that. He was furious with her and probably cursed her whole family right now.

But why was he furious? It was his brother who seduced her sister for information, while Travis... She wasn't sure what Travis had done, exactly, or why he'd done it.

He certainly was the picture of an outraged man, and that just didn't fit.

"So," she began. "The diamond..."

"I assume you still want to find it? And then get the hell off my ranch?"

She nodded.

"That's what I came to tell you. The water's gone down. We can get into the mine today, if you want."

Just like that?

Their previous deal stood?

"You're still going to honor our agreement?"

"Why wouldn't I? Nothing to do with our agreement has changed. Your family's determined to have that diamond, and as long as you believe it's here, one of the McCords is going to be here, bothering me, trying to get it. As I see it, the easiest way to get rid of you all seems to be to let you look your fill, until you either give up or find the damned thing. So go look, please, and let's get this over with. And then you can go."

* * *

Travis took her that afternoon to the mine, insisting that he be the one to watch over her while she looked. He didn't trust anyone but himself to make sure she was safe, and he was at least going to make sure she didn't get hurt on this stupid family quest of hers.

That her family would send a woman, a young, beautiful woman to do something like this still made him a little bit crazy. He didn't care that she was the geologist of the family.

It wasn't the kind of job he thought a man should send a woman to do.

Of course, he came from a family that sent his brother to seduce her sister for information, so it seemed he didn't have much room to talk in the what-your-family-would-do area.

He was still furious with the lot of them.

For the whole, crazy feud.

For the lost diamond.

For her sister getting hurt the way she no doubt had been hurt when she heard the news about Jason.

For Charlie, the brother he never knew about until a few months ago, and the father who'd just admitted to always being in love with a woman other than Travis's mother.

For all of it.

And for the woman who'd shown up on his ranch, him not knowing who she was, for the way she'd bewitched him with need and wanting. For the way he'd do just about anything for her, and she didn't even believe it or care.

For the whole damned mess.

But she just had to find that diamond, so he stood there, watching over her and waiting for her, to make sure she didn't get herself killed over the stupid thing. All so he could stand by and watch her walk away from him when her search was over.

It was all so stupid. And completely infuriating. How was he ever going to let her go? How could he ever convince her to stay?

She finally gave up her search shortly before sunset, coming out of the mine cold and grubby and looking completely worn-out. She'd cried herself to sleep the night before. He'd stood on the other side of her bedroom wall, listening to her, fighting the urge to go to her and beg her to believe him about what he'd known and what he'd done, to beg her to forgive him.

So she had to be exhausted now. But she was still beautiful and he still wanted her, dammit.

"We can come back tomorrow?" she asked.

He nodded.

Fine.

They'd come back tomorrow, and they'd make this thing between them about nothing but the stupid diamond now.

Chapter Thirteen

In the end, Paige didn't tell anyone else in her family anything about Jason Foley or what he'd done.

It was Penny's secret to tell, she decided.

Penny was the one who'd been hurt the most by it, and she had a baby to think about, too.

She called Penny the night after spending a second day searching the mine with no luck, Travis just letting her look, standing so somberly by, not trying to talk her into or out of anything. Just letting her do what she had to do.

Paige didn't understand him any better than she understood herself or her feelings for him, so she mostly tried not to think about any of it.

She had a job to do, and she'd do it.

Part of that was taking care of her poor sister.

It took four tries before her sister would even

answer the phone and when she did, before Paige could even say anything else, Penny just blurted out, "Just don't ask me what I'm going to do, okay? Because I don't know yet."

"Okay," Paige agreed.

"I'm sorry. I just…I don't know."

"That's fine, honey. I know it's all a shock. I just…I wanted to be sure I understand where you are in this. Are you sure you're pregnant?"

"I…well, it looks like it. I'm late, and I took one of those home pregnancy tests. Three, actually. All positive."

"Okay, but you haven't seen a doctor yet?" Paige tried.

"No. Not yet."

"Well, don't you think you should? I mean… Surely sometimes those home tests are wrong—" They could hope.

"Three times in a row?" Penny reminded her.

"Okay, probably not three times in a row. But still, you want to have a doctor check you out, make sure you're healthy and that the baby's okay."

"I guess so," Penny admitted.

"Let me give you my gynecologist's name. She's great. Very gentle, and she'll be completely supportive. I promise." Paige gave her the name, then as gently as she could told her, "I haven't said anything to anyone about this. I'm not going to. It's up to you. If you want me to tell them or be with you when you tell anyone, I will. I'll do whatever you want, whatever I can to help."

"Thank you." Her sister started to cry softly.

"And you didn't ask me, and I probably shouldn't say this, but I think as soon as you've seen the doctor, you should go see that rat Jason Foley and tell him exactly how well his little seduction plan worked—"

"Paige, please—"

"He should know what he did."

"It wasn't just him," she cried. "It was me, too. I wanted him so much."

"And I'm sure he knew just how to make you want him. There's no telling how many women he's seduced over the years, the rat!"

"I can't tell him," she argued. "Not now. It's all too new, too crazy, and I have no idea what I'm going to do about this. No, I can't tell him. You promise you won't tell him, either. That you won't tell anyone."

Oooh, that was a tough promise to make.

True, she'd just promised a moment ago to not do anything her sister didn't want her to do, but she'd never imagined part of that would be letting Jason Foley off the hook completely.

"Paige, promise me. Right now."

"Okay," she said reluctantly. "But you have to tell him eventually."

"Mom kept Charlie's secret for twenty-one years. Do you think we're all better off for knowing?"

"I don't know," Paige admitted.

"Neither do I, so I'm not telling Jason anything right now."

By the end of the fifth day of searching, with no sign of the diamond, Paige was exhausted, frustrated and very, very sad.

Travis had been stonily silent, icily polite, doing what

she needed from him to help with the search but nothing else. Blake sounded more defeated each day when she talked to him and poor Penny still had no idea what she was going to do about Jason Foley or her baby.

How had everything gone so wrong?

Paige sat on the ground just outside the mine entrance, cold, wet, dirty, having no idea what to do next.

She'd never really given up on anything before.

Travis stood just beyond the rock overhang outside the mine, waiting, finally saying, "That was it? The last of the eagle markings? You checked the last ones today?"

She nodded. "Every one mapped by the archaeology team you let explore the mine last year. Unless they missed one or didn't record the location of one—"

"They went over every inch of that place. I thought they were crazy, how excited they were to get inside that mine and then to see how carefully they checked the walls. I went down with them a couple of times to see what all the fuss was about. I have trouble thinking they missed anything."

Paige shook her head. "I knew it was a long shot. I just didn't want to admit it to my brother. I mean, even if Elwin Foley came to the ranch after surviving the shipwreck and hid the diamond in the Eagle Mine, it's been so long. My ancestors worked the mine, bringing out the silver for years. How they could have done that and never found the diamond… I don't know. I hoped it was possible, but… How could they have missed buried treasure when they were mining here all those years?"

"I don't see how they could have," Travis agreed. "And…I'm not trying to be insensitive or to start a fight here, but Paige, why are you letting your family put this on you? This pressure to find the diamond? I mean, it's not like your family needs the money. Can't you just let it go? Tell them to back off? Or to find the damned thing themselves, if it's so important to them?"

Which sounded curiously like he was trying to take care of her. Which was the last thing she'd have expected from him.

And then she was just sick of the whole mess and all the misery it had brought her, all that she felt or thought she'd felt for Travis Foley and how much she missed him, even when he was right here beside her. She couldn't even let herself think of how she dreaded leaving the ranch and never seeing him again, even if she didn't really trust him and was furious at his family.

It was all just such a mess.

She didn't care anymore, so she just told him everything.

"The thing is, we do really need the money," she confessed. "My father…he wasn't the greatest guy in the world, and I guess that didn't just extend toward personal relationships. He wasn't much of a business-man, either. My brother Blake is much better at it, but I guess when he took over the business after our father died, it was in trouble. Serious trouble. Blake's doing everything he can, but I really think it's going to take a miracle to save the family business now, and we were banking on that miracle being the diamond. So, yes, it matters. It matters that much."

She looked at him, knowing she'd told him much more than she needed to, things his family would just love to hear about the McCords. But what did it matter now?

If business was that bad, it wouldn't be a secret much longer.

She couldn't imagine her family without the jewelry stores, without that work to do. It had been much more than a source of income. It had been what they all did together, Blake managing the business, her overseeing the buying of raw stones worldwide and cutting many of them herself, her sister designing settings for the stones, her cousin Gabby the international face and spokeswoman for the stores. It held them altogether, gave them a common goal and a strong sense of pride.

What would they do now?

"I just feel like I let my whole family down," she said.

"Hey, it's not your fault if the diamond isn't there," Travis began.

"I know, but...I just really thought I could find it. Once Blake showed me the deed with that diamond in the eagle's talon, I was so sure. But we've searched every eagle marking in this mine, and it's just not there. Every one—"

But then as she said it, she realized she was wrong.

Oh, they'd searched every one inside the mine.

But right at that moment, she was looking at one spot they hadn't searched.

"Paige?" Travis asked.

She walked over to the big, heavy stone that stood just outside the mine, marking it as the Eagle Mine with an eagle carved into the stone.

"We didn't search here," she said, the idea bouncing

around in her head at warp speed. "It's the same eagle, the same image from the deed. And it's not in the mine! They wouldn't have disturbed this area as they mined for silver, so that's how Elwin could have hidden it at the mine, without worrying about anyone finding it accidentally as they mined the silver! Travis! I think this is it!"

She turned back to him, and he looked skeptical, like she was grasping at straws or just could not admit defeat. But she didn't think so.

This hiding place... This made sense. The diamond would likely be safe here, even if the mine was opened to get the silver out.

She ran over to the rock, tried to move it and found that it wouldn't even budge.

Turning back to Travis, she pleaded with him. "Please? This one last place? If it's not here, I'm done. Promise."

"All right. But quit trying to move that rock. You'll never manage." He pulled a rope off of his saddle. "If we're lucky, Murph can move it."

He looped the rope around the rock, then tied the other end to the saddle horn, and took his place by the horse's head. "Come on, boy. Show us how strong you are."

The horse started backing up, until the line stretched taut and then Murph dug in with his big hind legs and very, very slowly eased back some more until the rock tipped over.

Travis undid the rope, and Paige grabbed a shovel and started digging. A moment later, Travis grabbed another small shovel and started helping her.

They were three feet down when she hit something.

Her heart started racing.

Carefully, they cleared dirt from the top, finding a rectangular-shaped object.

"Tell me it's not a rock," she begged.

"If it is, it's the most perfectly shaped rectangular rock I've ever found," Travis said. "And we won't get it out this way. Start digging on the left side. We need room on at least two sides to pry it loose."

They dug some more.

Finally, Travis could get his hands on two sides of the thing and ease it forward and to the left enough to dislodge it and then lift it to the surface.

Paige gasped.

When the dirt was brushed away, she saw that it was a treasure chest!

An ancient-looking silver chest, if Paige wasn't mistaken, encrusted with precious stones, emeralds, rubies, maybe even diamonds.

"Go ahead," Travis said. "Open it. You've earned the right."

Her hands shook, literally, she was so excited.

The lid came open with a creaking sound and on top was an old, dirty cloth.

She pulled the cloth away and gasped once more.

Coins.

Old silver coins.

Hundreds of them.

"The ship supposedly held a fortune in old Spanish silver," she told him.

She dipped her hands inside the coins, digging in one side of the chest and then the other, finally coming up with a cloth, the ends tied together around something big and heavy.

All the breath went out of her, as she sat the cloth down on top of the coins and just looked at it.

Travis laughed and pulled out his pocketknife, cutting the string that held the cloth together.

"Go ahead. Look," he told her.

"It's huge. I mean, I knew the diamond was supposed to be huge, as big as the Hope Diamond, and I've seen the Hope Diamond before. It was huge, too, but I just don't know if this—"

"Red, just look and see," he said, still sounding amused.

She closed her eyes, took a breath, then opened her eyes and pulled the cloth away.

There inside the old, disintegrating cloth was a stone roughly the size of an egg, primitively cut but glowing yellow and startling in its clarity.

She held it up to the light of the setting sun, watching the stone come to life with light, shimmering all over the different facets of the perfect, flawless stone.

"That's it," she told Travis. "It's the Santa Magdalena Diamond! We found it!"

And then she threw her arms around him, let him pick her up and whirl her around while she laughed like she never had before and cried, and then, when he finally set her back on her feet, kissed him like she'd never let him go.

Paige had to be dreaming.

She had the diamond in her backpack on the way back to the ranch house, and for a moment back there,

Travis had kissed her like a man who never wanted to let her go.

Could he really not want to let her go?

Because it was breaking her heart to think of leaving him. They'd kept things from each other, and hurt each other, and their families had hated each other for years, but he was still the best man she'd ever met. The sexiest, the sweetest, the kindest, the most protective, the most gentle man.

She didn't care if his last name was Foley.

It was hard to accept what his brother had done to her sister, and that was likely to be a sore spot between them for years, not just for the two of them, but for both their families. And there was still all that stuff with their parents dating and Charlie trying to find his own way amidst both families.

Could they ever put all that behind them? Or put it all aside somehow and just be two people who were crazy about each other?

The last few days had been the worst of her life, thinking he'd lied to her and that his whole family was out to hurt hers and that one day soon, she'd be leaving this ranch and never come back.

So it was time to put her heart on the line, to take a leap of faith.

They got back to the ranch near sunset, and he had Cal take care of both their horses. He carried the treasure chest, wrapped in a blanket, into his house, and she had the diamond.

"Why don't you go get cleaned up, Red, and then we'll try to sort this thing out," Travis said.

She was a mess. It seemed the whole time she'd known him, she'd been either dirty or wet or both.

It had been the strangest kind of courtship.

Nerves eating away at her, she ran through the shower, dressed quickly and came to find him in the library, the treasure chest and the diamond on the table in front of the big, leather sofa.

Paige closed her eyes and prayed for strength and a little bit of pride and hopefully some poise, because she had the oddest feeling that the rest of her life depended on the outcome of this conversation, and at the moment, she was scared to say a word.

How did people do this? Get their hearts broken and survive? Because she'd been hurt before, but she'd never cared like this, never risked so much, never been so scared.

"I guess we have a few more things to negotiate, Red," he said, looking so big and strong and gorgeous she could have wept right then and there.

"Negotiate?" They were going to talk business? Now?

Had he forgotten that kiss at the mine after they'd found the diamond? Had it meant nothing to him?

She tried not to let her hurt feelings show. "Okay."

"I guess we're back to your family versus mine," he said.

Oh, God. That was it? She very nearly did cry then.

"I take it you want the diamond, free and clear, no claim of ownership from my family?" he asked.

"Not…ownership, exactly, but no fight. I'd really like to do this without a fight, Travis. Especially not a long battle in court over who owns what. I don't think any of us would benefit from that."

"Okay. I'm not dying for a long, drawn-out fight," he admitted.

"I was hoping we could come to some agreement… you and me…that we could get both our families to agree to."

"So, what do you want?" he asked.

As if it were that easy….

She unwrapped the diamond, picked it up and held it in her open hand, letting it sparkle and shine for him.

"This is… Well, there simply isn't another stone like this in the world. Not of this size and color and clarity. It's a national treasure. International, actually, and, as I see it, the only rightful place for it is in a museum. The Smithsonian in Washington D.C., I would think, where the Hope Diamond is. They were supposed to be a pair, thousands of years ago. It only seems right that they're together again."

He frowned. "That's it? All this fuss over finding it, and all you want is for my family to let yours donate it to a museum?"

"Actually, I was thinking we could do it jointly, my family and yours. Claim joint ownership of it. No fight. You and I found it—"

"You found it, Red. I was just along for the ride to make sure you didn't get hurt going after that thing."

"No." She shook her head. "We found it together, on land that both our families have a claim to, in a mine that both our families can claim, too. But I don't want us to fight anymore. I'm sick of the whole fight, and this… Well, to me, it's simple. The diamond belongs in a museum, where millions of people can see it, and it would be a huge tax write-off for both our families, I'm sure. So it's not without benefit to your family…."

He laughed incredulously. "A tax write-off? That's what you're offering my family?"

"And a chance to do the right thing with the diamond. I mean, you don't want to just keep it? Do you?"

"No, Red. I don't want to keep it. But I thought your family needed it desperately. I thought that's what this was all about? Saving your family?"

"We just need it for a little while. Maybe six months? To display in the jewelry stores. And then, we'll give it to the museum," she tried.

"That's it? Display the diamond for six months, and your family's business is saved?"

He said it like he might actually care and not want her family's business to go under. She took a bit of hope in that.

"Well, no. We're hoping to corner the market on canary diamonds. My brother has everything in place, just waiting for us to find the diamond. It's the publicity from finding the Santa Magdalena, and… You're not going to like this part, Travis. You're probably going to have a lot of people wanting to get onto this ranch, at least for a while, to cover the story and see exactly where we found it and the old mine. I'm sorry, but—"

"Thank God," he said, sounding thoroughly relieved.

"What?"

She didn't get it.

He'd hate having all those people invade his ranch.

"I was counting on having something you wanted really badly, Red. Something to negotiate with, to get what I want," he said, grinning that beautiful grin of his at her.

"What? I don't understand."

"That's the way it works, right? If I have something you want, badly, then you have to give me something I want in return. I'm counting on that."

She stared at him, thinking she was missing something here. Really missing something.

"It's a negotiation, Red," he said, looking so gorgeous, reminding her of him standing in a tuxedo at some party, looking like a man who owned the world, who knew just what he wanted and knew he was going to get it. "Ask me what I want."

And then she started to shake, she was so scared.

What did he want?

"You want the ranch. I know that. I told you I'd do everything I could to get my mother—"

"Aw, baby." He knelt down in front of her as she sat there, trembling and practically unable to speak, took her face in his hand and kissed her softly, sweetly. "Ask me what I want even more than that."

"More than that?" she whispered.

"I want you. And I'll tell you right now, I'm not giving an inch here. No wiggle room. You can have the stupid diamond. You can do anything you want with it. My whole family can have a fit. I don't care. But I get you."

Tears filled her eyes, and spilled over, running down her cheeks. "So…what do you intend to do with me?"

"Keep you. Make you mine. Forever. That's my plan. I should warn you, too, that I don't have a diamond right this minute, and I bet a man who shows up to propose to a woman whose family owns a jewelry empire had better have a really nice diamond. Probably one from her family's stores. So I can't do this properly right this minute, but I can't wait, either. Paige McCord, say you'll marry me."

She nodded, sheer joy spilling over inside of her, as the tears ran down her cheek.

"Say you'll forgive me for everything my family has done to yours over the years," he asked. "I'll forget everything yours has done to mine, and we'll both promise to never let our families' problems with each other come between us. And marry me. I need you to say it, Red. I love you, and I need to hear you say it."

"Yes," she said. "I will. I love you, too. I've never loved any man the way I love you. And I don't care what anyone in either of our families has to say about it. I just don't care."

He got very serious for a moment. "One thing. You have to be honest with me about this. You could be happy? Living here at the ranch?"

She nodded. "I might have to take off a couple of times a year, for the stores. I buy most of the uncut stones we sell in the stores."

"As long as you come back," he said.

"And I like to cut the stones we sell myself. I could... Maybe I could have an office here at the ranch?"

"Anything you need, Red. Anything," he promised.

She smiled so big it was hard to talk. "I love this ranch. I think it's beautiful here."

"And you could spend your life here? Be happy here?"

"As long as you're here with me," she said.

"Well, then. I think we've got ourselves a deal, Red."

* * *

He pulled her into his arms, and it wasn't long before she was naked on that rug in front of his fireplace once again, thoroughly content.

Life was so good, she thought, snuggling beside him, wrapped in an afghan and warmed by the fire. It was unbelievably, amazingly good.

He sighed heavily, let his hands move through her hair. "You know, it's almost Thanksgiving. I think we need to have a big family dinner, right here at the ranch. Your family and mine."

"Oh, Travis. Do you think they're ready for that? For all of us to be in the same room together?"

"I think they're just going to have to get used to it. Because you and I are already together, and our parents might be someday, and there's already Charlie.... I mean, because of him, we're all already family. It's time we started acting like one. I say, we invite my family and yours to Thanksgiving dinner."

"Okay, if you're sure." She wasn't looking forward to sharing him with anyone just yet, but supposed it had to happen sooner or later.

"I'll tell them that you and I are getting married, and that's that. We're not going to ask for permission, because no one's talking us out of it, no matter what. And you can tell them that you and I found the diamond, and that we've decided to donate it in both our families' names to the Smithsonian."

She could handle that. "No arguments. No discussion. Done deal?"

"Done deal," he said.

"I like that," she agreed. "It's the right thing to do. But what about your brother and poor Penny? I mean—"

"Red, I know my brother. He may have started this thing with her for all the wrong reasons, but I finally calmed down enough to talk to him the other night and the guy's a mess right now. He says Penny won't have a thing to do with him, that he has no idea why. I didn't enlighten him. I'll leave that to your sister. But I think he's crazy about her."

Paige's mouth dropped open she was so shocked. "Really?"

Travis nodded. "Just convince her to come for Thanksgiving, and we'll see what happens."

"Did he actually tell you—"

"No, but just wait. I'm looking forward to watching him grovel."

"My brothers may kill him first," she warned.

"Okay, you're going to have to talk them out of that."

"You're right. Because Penny has a little surprise for your brother—"

"What?"

"Just wait. It's going to be a very interesting Thanksgiving. And that reminds me. I found something else in the mine while we were looking for the diamond, something I forgot to ask you about. A reddish crystal. I'd never seen anything like it before."

"A rock? You want to talk to me about a rock right now?"

"I like rocks," she reminded him. "These were really pretty. You know the ones I mean? Like a little bit of red fire trapped in crystal."

"Like you? Red fire?" He gave a soft, teasing kiss. "That's how I think of you. My own little red fire. My sweet red fire."

She laughed, gloriously happy. "This could really be something—"

"I think you're really something," he said, kissing her again.

And she knew, she wasn't going to have any kind of serious discussion with him about this right then.

But that red crystal...

How much could one woman possibly find on a ranch in Texas?

A man to love, a priceless treasure, and...

Well, maybe a brand-new gemstone.

Red fire.

For right now, she was content to be Travis Foley's red fire.

Another day, she'd figure out exactly what else she'd found on his ranch.

Epilogue

One month later

Travis walked in the door and felt like Christmas elves must have been at work in his house while he'd been out on the ranch.

There was a Christmas wreath with a big, red bow on the door, a tree inside beside the fireplace, decorated simply with little red ornaments and tiny, white twinkling lights, greenery spread across the mantle, red and white pillar candles everywhere.

Which could only mean, she was back.

Finally!

"Paige?" he called out.

He heard a little shriek from the direction of the

kitchen, and then she came running toward him, despite her high heels and fancy TV clothes. He caught her in his arms and kissed her like he'd never let her go.

"I didn't think you'd ever get back," he said.

She beamed up at him. "It was only four days."

"Felt like four dozen at least." And it had. It really had. Each time she'd gone, it had felt that way.

The house, the ranch, the entire world seemed empty now without her.

"Tell me you're done with all these press conferences and TV shows and all that," he demanded.

"I'm done! The whole world knows about the Santa Magdalena Diamond, and women everywhere want canary diamonds for themselves, just like Blake thought they would. I don't know how he did it, but he got the diamonds out to the stores this week, and they're selling like crazy. Just in time for Christmas."

"And how do you feel about a nice, quiet Christmas here at the ranch, just you and me?"

"I can't imagine anything better," she said, then made a face. "But I'm afraid—"

"No!" He knew what she was going to say. "Just us. Right here. No more—"

"Yes. We've been invited to a family get-together. Christmas Eve. Mom said everyone's coming."

Travis groaned. "They were just here for Thanksgiving. And it was nice. It was fine. We can do it again next year. How about that?"

"Oh, I think you're going to want to go," she claimed.

"No. I just want to be right here with you."

"But…I think there's something special for you there.

For Christmas. Since you've been so good this year," she said, looking at him in a way that had him thinking he was crazy to be standing here talking to her when he could have carried her off to bed already.

"I have everything I want already," he said, thinking of the engagement ring that had been delivered to the ranch while he was gone, custom made by her sister at his request, which he intended to put on her finger on Christmas Eve. If he had his way, they'd elope and she'd be his wife by New Year's

"No, you don't have everything yet," his red-haired beauty claimed. "There's one more thing. One big thing. A surprise. Just wait. You're going to love it."

* * * * *

THE TEXAS
TYCOON'S
CHRISTMAS BABY

BY
BRENDA HARLEN

First published in Great Britain 2010
Harlequin Mills & Boon Limited,
Eton House, 18-24 Paradise Road, Richmond, Surrey TW9 1SR

© Brenda Harlen 2009

ISBN: 978 0 263 88845 4

23-1210

Harlequin Mills & Boon policy is to use papers that are natural, renewable
and recyclable products and made from wood grown in sustainable forests.
The logging and manufacturing processes conform to the legal environmental
regulations of the country of origin.

Printed and bound in Spain
by Litografia Rosés S.A., Barcelona

Dear Reader,

Since the publication of my first Special Edition novel a little more than four years ago, I've had the pleasure of working on four continuity series. Each time, it's been a privilege to work with a new group of authors, sharing story ideas, discussing character motivations and brainstorming plot problems. During the writing of this series, I also learned a lot of interesting stuff about Texas, mining and jewellery design (which was a *lot* of fun to research, although I had to continually reassure my husband that I wasn't shopping online—just writing).

Anyway, the result of all of this is *The Texas Tycoon's Christmas Baby.* In this book, you'll get to know Jason Foley and Penny McCord, you'll find out what the other members of their families have been up to since last month and you'll also catch a glimpse of what the future may hold for all of them.

Happy reading and happy holidays!

Brenda Harlen

Brenda Harlen grew up in a small town surrounded by books and imaginary friends. Although she always dreamed of being a writer, she chose to follow a more traditional career path first. After two years of practising as an attorney (including an appearance in front of the Supreme Court of Canada), she gave up her "real" job to be a mom and to try her hand at writing books. Three years, five manuscripts and another baby later, she sold her first book, an RWA Golden Heart Winner. Brenda lives in southern Ontario with her real-life husband/hero, two heroes-in-training and two neurotic dogs. She is still surrounded by books ("too many books," according to her children) and imaginary friends, but she also enjoys communicating with "real" people. Readers can contact Brenda by e-mail at brendaharlen@yahoo.com or by post c/o Silhouette Books, 233 Broadway, Suite 1001, New York, NY 10279, USA.

To the wonderful and talented Nicole Foster,
Crystal Green, Teresa Hill, Victoria Pade and
Karen Rose Smith—you proved to me that writing
doesn't have to be a solitary occupation. Thanks for
your help and for making this project so much fun.

Thanks also to Susan Litman, for again thinking of me.

And to Charles Griemsman, because it truly
was a pleasure.

Prologue

Penny McCord was smiling when she hung up the phone after Jason Foley's call confirming their dinner plans. He was in Dallas on business and would stop by after his meetings finished to pick her up for a quiet, romantic evening at his condo. It would give her the perfect opportunity to share the news that had only been confirmed a few hours earlier, and then they could start planning their future together.

She was excited, of course, and just a little apprehensive. She wanted him to be as happy as she was, but as they had never talked about anything long-term, she couldn't be certain.

Still, she believed this was meant to be—fated, as was their meeting at Missy Harcourt's wedding only four short months ago. It was the only explanation she could think of for the fact that, in a room filled with more than five hundred guests, Jason Foley had noticed her.

When her own date for the occasion was called away, leaving Penny stranded, Jason had been there. He'd talked to her, danced with her, taken her home. And then he'd kissed her good night.

A few weeks later, they became lovers. She knew she was fortunate to have fallen in love with the man who'd been her first lover, and if Jason wasn't in love with her yet, she was hopeful it was only a matter of time before his feelings grew and deepened, as hers had done.

When the phone rang again, she assumed it was Jason calling her back—as he sometimes did—just to tell her he couldn't stop thinking about her.

"Miss me already?" she asked teasingly.

There was silence on the other end of the line and Penny mentally berated herself for not checking the call display before grabbing the receiver.

"Penny, it's Paige."

Her sister's voice sounded strained, as if she'd been crying. Not at all like her usual cheerful self.

"What is it? What's wrong?"

"Nothing. I just...I have to tell you something."

Aside from e-mail communications, they'd been out of touch for so long, and Penny had really missed talking to her twin. "I have some news, too, but it can wait. You go first."

But Paige didn't seem to be in any hurry, and as the silence lengthened, Penny's apprehension increased.

"Paige?" she prompted, wondering what could be so horrible that her sister couldn't seem to get the words out. Had she been in an accident? Was she ill? What was going on? "You're scaring me."

"I'm sorry, Penny. I'm so sorry about this. I love you. You know that, right? And I'll help you get through this, I promise."

Now she was even more confused. "Get through what?"

"Jason Foley."

She fell silent.

She and her twin had always been close, but it was only recently that Penny had told anyone she was dating Jason Foley. She didn't usually keep anything from her sister, but she'd justified her silence—at least to herself—on the basis that Paige was too preoccupied with her search for the Santa Magdalena Diamond to focus on anything else. But the truth was, Penny had worried that Paige wouldn't approve, that she would accuse her of being a fool for getting involved with anyone named Foley, and Penny refused to let an old feud get in the way of her relationship with the first man she'd ever loved.

"You have been seeing Jason Foley, right?" Paige asked her.

"Yes, I have," Penny said defiantly. "And I know that no one likes that, that no one understands. I can still hardly believe it myself, but he's not who you think he is, Paige. He's not who any of us thought he is. He's wonderful and sweet and kind, and I'm in love with him. And I think—" she mentally crossed her fingers, desperately hoping it was true "—he's in love with me, too."

"He's using you to get information about our family," Paige told her.

Penny was disappointed. Not in Jason, because she

didn't believe that Jason would do anything like that, but in her sister, for daring to accuse him of such deception.

She laughed to let her sister know that her relationship with Jason was solid and that she wouldn't let unfounded accusations undermine it. "No, he's not."

"Yes, he is," Paige insisted, and the quiet conviction in her voice gave Penny pause.

"He wouldn't do that," she said again. "He's not like that."

"I'm at Travis Foley's ranch right now, looking for the diamond. Travis was with me when I read Gabby's e-mail telling me you were seeing Jason, and Travis knew... He knew what his brother was going to do."

Penny wasn't sure which of her sister's revelations surprised her more. "No," she said, but with less certainty this time. She didn't want to listen to anything else Paige said about Jason. She knew there was a lot of bad history between the McCords and the Foleys, but she really believed Jason cared about her. How could he have said the things he'd said, done the things he'd done, if he didn't care about her?

Penny gnawed on her lip, considering what her sister had just told her. Jason hadn't made any mention of the infamous gem in the past several weeks, but she did recall earlier references, questions subtly slipped into a conversation that might have been intended to elicit information from Penny. Or maybe he'd just been making conversation. She wasn't going to assume the worst just because her sister had done so.

"That's crazy," she said.

"Honey, listen to me. I'm sorry, but Travis admitted the whole thing. Jason told Travis and their other brother, Zane, months ago what he was going to do. He was convinced our family was up to something to do with the diamond, and that the Foleys needed to know what that was. Jason thought he could get the information from you. By getting to know you. By pretending he was interested in you."

Penny didn't want to believe it, but...

"I'm so sorry. I could kill him with my bare hands, I swear. I will make him pay. We'll make all of them pay for what he did to you."

"I thought..." Penny could barely choke out the words now. "I thought I was in love with him."

I thought he loved me, too.

And now all of Penny's hopes and dreams for the future were shattered.

Chapter One

Jason Foley pulled into the long, winding drive that led to his brother's ranch and wondered what the heck he was doing out in the middle of nowhere when he had at least a dozen projects demanding his attention back at his office in Dallas. But Travis didn't ask for much, so Jason found it hard to refuse when his brother did make a request. And for some reason, it was important to his little brother to have the family all together for Thanksgiving this year. And not just to share the traditional meal, but the whole weekend.

Jason might not have minded even that so much except that, for some inexplicable reason, Travis had extended the invitation to include the McCord family, as well. It wasn't so many years ago that the Foleys and McCords would sooner have shot at each other than sat down at a table together, but apparently things had changed.

Unbidden, an image of Penny McCord's smiling face came to mind. Yeah, things had changed. And he felt a pang of loss. He still didn't know what had gone wrong between them, but after weeks of unreturned phone calls and ignored e-mails, he'd finally given up. Obviously, Penny had decided that she was finished with him, and that was fine. The only reason their relationship had lasted as long as it did was that Jason had felt guilty for his deception.

Truth be told, he still felt guilty. It had been his idea to get close to Penny McCord, to find out what she knew about her family's search for the Santa Magdalena Diamond. But it had been a plan born out of desperation, and not one that had sat well with him, even from the beginning.

As he'd grown closer to Penny, his guilt had grown along with his genuine affection for her. So when she stopped taking his calls, he'd almost been as relieved as he was baffled, because he knew that she was better off without him.

And he was better off without her. And if she did decide to show up at his brother's house for the holiday celebration, he would be polite and friendly while maintaining an emotional and physical distance. Maybe she'd meant something to him for a while, but that was over.

Or so he believed, until he walked into the kitchen and found her in his brother's arms.

"Well, isn't this a cozy little scene?"

The words were spoken through a jaw that was clenched as tightly as the fists that hung at Jason's sides.

Travis and Penny sprang apart—and it was then that

Jason saw through the haze of red that had clouded his vision to recognize his mistake.

It wasn't Penny in his brother's embrace, but her twin sister, Paige.

Of course it wasn't Penny. Even before he recognized her sister, he should have recognized that Penny wasn't the type of woman who would move quickly or easily from one man's bed to another's. In fact, she hadn't been in any man's bed until he'd taken her to his own.

And then she tossed him out of her life.

So why should he care if she'd picked up with someone else since then?

He shouldn't. But he did. And it was that realization which annoyed him more than anything else.

"I didn't mean to interrupt," he said now, his fingers slowly uncurling.

"You're early," Travis said, but the admonition was tempered by a smile that assured his brother he didn't really mind.

"I can leave and come back later."

"No need." Travis took Paige's hand and tugged her forward. "You know Paige McCord?"

Jason inclined his head. "It's good to see you again, Paige."

"I wish I could say the same," she responded coolly.

He looked at his brother, his brows lifted in silent inquiry. Travis gave a subtle shake of his head, but Jason wasn't prepared to let her remark pass without comment.

"If you're harboring some kind of grudge on behalf of your sister, you should know that she was the one who ended our relationship," he pointed out.

"And you don't have a clue why, do you?"

Even three weeks later, he didn't—a fact which continued to frustrate him.

"Can we not get into this now?" Travis asked, suggesting to Jason that he knew more than he'd shared with his brother.

"I'd like nothing more than to not get into this," Paige assured him. "In fact, I'd like nothing more than to pretend that your brother was never involved with my sister, but that's not possible now."

And with that, she tossed her hair over her shoulder and exited the room.

"Want to explain that to me?" Jason asked his brother.

Travis just shook his head again. "I'll leave that to Penny, if she's so inclined."

Jason's heart skipped a beat. "Then she is coming?"

"I told you I'd invited all of the McCords."

"But you didn't tell me Penny would be here."

"Would that information have affected your decision to come?"

"No," Jason said. "My decision had nothing to do with Penny McCord."

But even as he spoke the words, he knew that his brother didn't believe them any more than he did.

She shouldn't have come.

As Penny McCord sat wedged between Blake and Tate, her two older brothers, at the long table in Travis Foley's dining room, she wondered why she'd ever let herself be talked into making an appearance at this "family" dinner. Of course, she'd only accepted the invitation because she'd been certain that Travis's brother wouldn't.

Jason Foley was far too busy to take the time for a

long weekend at his brother's ranch. To his mind, business took precedence over family. In fact, business took precedence over everything else, and he would do anything to ensure the company's success. Their sham of a relationship was proof enough of that fact.

When the invitation to share in a Thanksgiving celebration had come through her sister, Penny was anxious to get away from the city, eager to spend some time with her twin, and desperate to cry on the shoulder that had always been there for her. So she'd gratefully said yes, certain that Jason would never take time away from his office to spend the holiday at his brother's isolated Texas ranch.

Apparently she'd been wrong.

Because every single member of the Foley family—Jason included—was in attendance, along with the entire McCord clan. As if the bitterness and animosity that had governed all McCord-Foley interactions of the past century was simply forgotten.

She knew the story—at least as it had been passed down through the McCord family. According to that history, the McCord and the Foley families of Texas had been feuding ever since Civil War, but the feud really heated up in the late 1890s, when Gavin Foley lost his claim to a West Texas silver mine to Harry McCord in a poker game. Gavin Foley swore the game was fixed and that Harry was a card cheat.

At the time, no one paid too much attention to the allegations and everyone thought the claim to be worthless. But there were rumors that the deed, which also served as the map to the mine, contained clues to the location of a buried treasure—including the legendary and supposedly cursed Santa Magdalena Diamond.

No treasure was ever found, though the disputed claim did turn out to be filled with silver ore, which is how the McCords acquired their family fortune. But rumors about the Santa Magdalena Diamond refused to die, especially after the recent discovery of a sunken ship in the Gulf of Mexico—the last known location of the infamous gem. The diamond wasn't on board, and since then, adventurers, gem collectors and jewel thieves from around the world had been searching for the legendary stone.

Penny wasn't sure she even believed that the Santa Magdalena Diamond existed; though, if it did, it was supposedly the world's largest, most perfect canary diamond, reputed to rival the Hope Diamond in beauty and size. But she *was* inclined to believe in the curse— the allegation that the gem had caused misfortune to everyone who had ever possessed it, including an Indian pasha, an Italian Renaissance prince, a seventeenth-century duke and an eighteenth-century Mexican governor—because, although she'd never even set eyes on the jewel, it seemed that her scant knowledge of its rumored existence had led directly to her heartache.

It could be argued that it was her own inexperience and naïveté that had caused her to fall for Jason Foley's seduction routine, and she knew there was some truth to that; but the fact remained that the COO of Foley Industries would never have looked twice in her direction if he wasn't interested in what she knew—or what he thought she knew—about the McCords' search for the diamond.

She determinedly pushed all thoughts of the gem and the Foley-McCord feud from her mind. She wasn't sure how much was fact and how much was fiction, and she didn't really care. She wasn't thinking of old grudges or ancient grievances now. No, her thoughts were on more recent events, more immediate hurts and personal heartaches. And being in the same room with Jason, so close and somehow so far away, scraped the scab off of a wound that had barely begun to heal.

It was the first time she'd seen him, face-to-face, since she'd learned that their entire relationship was a sham.

And the first time since she'd learned that she was going to have his baby.

A baby she had yet to tell him about, despite her sister's urging.

Paige kept telling Penny that Jason had a right to know that he was going to be a father, and Penny knew it was true. She also knew that Paige didn't just want her to share the news with her baby's father, she wanted to ensure that Jason was held responsible for his actions, which meant paying his share.

But Penny wasn't ready to deal with such practical matters. She was hurting too much to put the heartache aside and calmly discuss things like visitation and child support. Besides, she was doing well enough financially that she was confident she could support herself and her child—though the recent difficulties at McCord Jewelers did worry her enough that she tried not to think about them. Her job was as secure as anyone else's at the company, and not just because of her last name but because of the reputation she'd established for herself in the jewelry-design business.

Still, there was no way she was going to ask Jason Foley for anything. Not ever again.

She jolted when she felt an elbow in her ribs and frowned at her brother.

"Gabby asked you to pass the salad," Tate prompted.

"Oh. Sorry." She looked at the dishes on the table before realizing that she held the bowl of salad in her hand, then offered it to her cousin across the table. Glancing down at her plate, she saw that she hadn't taken any for herself. She had, however, put a lot of parmesan cheese on her pasta—and she didn't even like parmesan. She picked up her fork and pushed the noodles around on her plate.

Gabriella nudged Penny's foot under the table to get her attention. "Are you okay?" she whispered quietly.

Penny nodded, though she couldn't meet her cousin's gaze.

"Is it Jason?"

To her credit, Gabby didn't actually say the words aloud so much as she mouthed them across the table, but Penny cast a quick glance toward the man in question, who was seated immediately beside her cousin, and was relieved to find that he was in conversation with his young niece, seated on his other side. Still, the question obliterated any remaining hope that she and Jason had managed to keep their short-lived relationship a secret from anyone.

She shook her head.

But Gabriella obviously didn't believe her, because she leaned a little closer and said, "If you ever want to talk about—"

Penny shook her head again, more decisively this time. The absolute last thing she wanted was to talk about how Jason Foley had used her and how she'd been fool enough to let him, fool enough to believe that a man like him could ever seriously be interested in her.

She felt the sting of tears at the back of her eyes but furiously blinked them away.

Thankfully, Gabriella didn't have the chance to question her further, as Rafael leaned close to whisper something in his wife's ear, and whatever that something was, it brought a luminous smile to Gabby's face.

Penny looked away. That was the thing about national holidays and family gatherings—she was always surrounded by couples, and she was always alone.

This year seemed even worse, because the new faces around her weren't temporary ones that would be replaced next year, as had frequently happened in the past. Because somehow, in the space of six months, everyone around her had miraculously fallen in love.

Gabby and Rafael eloped after a whirlwind courtship, and though many had wondered about a match between the heiress and her bodyguard, it was obvious that they were madly in love with one another. Both of her older brothers were now affianced—and if her brother Tate's involvement with Tanya Kimbrough—daughter of the McCords' longtime housekeeper—had taken everyone aback, that surprise paled in comparison to Blake's engagement to Katie Whitcomb-Salgar, Tate's ex-girlfriend.

More recently, Penny's twin sister had hooked up with Travis Foley. And even her mother had partnered up—with Jason's father, of all people. Of course, Rex Foley was also the father of Penny's youngest brother, Charlie, which revelation had come as a shock to everyone, Charlie included. Apparently the Foley-McCord feud had come to an end twenty-two years earlier, at least so far as Eleanor and Rex were concerned.

The sound of a fork tapping against a wineglass drew Penny's attention back to the present and to Travis Foley at the end of the table. He waited until the various conversations had halted before addressing the group.

"Paige and I have some news that we wanted to share with you, news of something that we can all be thankful for this Thanksgiving."

Paige smiled, her eyes glowing with excitement as she faced the assembled guests. "We found the Santa Magdalena Diamond."

"The Santa Magdalena Diamond," Eleanor echoed, stunned. "All these years...I was never sure it was even real."

"It's real," Paige assured her. "And it's absolutely stunning."

An assessment that was confirmed by the gasps and sighs that sounded when Travis set the spectacular forty-eight-karat diamond on the table for everyone to see.

"I knew it was real," Blake McCord said. "And that it would be the answer to all of our problems, if only we could find it."

"And you knew that it was probably hidden somewhere in the abandoned mines on this land."

"If that's where you found it—on McCord property—then the diamond is rightfully ours," the McCord CEO asserted.

"But Travis is the rightful lessee of the property," Jason interjected. "So the diamond is his."

"Paige and I found it together, so the diamond is ours," Travis said, in a tone that brooked no argument.

"And after much discussion," Paige continued, "we've

decided to donate it—and the chest of ancient silver coins we found along with it—to the Smithsonian."

"But—" Blake began, only to snap his mouth shut in response to the look he got from his sister.

"Of course, we're going to take advantage of all the publicity we can get from the discovery," Paige continued. "And although we've notified the Smithsonian of the find and our intention to donate the stone, we're going to display the diamond at our flagship store in Dallas for a few months prior to making the donation official."

"That will certainly generate traffic to the store," Gabby said approvingly.

"And increase revenues for the business," Rafael affirmed.

"A brilliant PR move," Tate decided.

"Thanks," Paige said dryly.

"I'd hoped the McCords would benefit exclusively from the treasure," Blake unexpectedly admitted to the assembled guests. "But since it's obvious that my sister Paige, found love during her search, an even greater treasure than the Santa Magdalena Diamond…" his gaze drifted from the gem to his fiancée "…I can't say that I'm at all disappointed to have to share the discovery."

"We found something else, too," Paige interjected, smiling at Travis.

"What more could there be?" Tanya wondered aloud, causing laughter to ripple around the table.

"McCordite," Paige said, which announcement elicited various expressions of confusion.

"What's that?" Charlie finally asked.

"This." She set a chunk of another type of rock down on the table beside the diamond.

It wasn't quite as big or as brilliant as the Santa Magdalena Diamond, of course, but it was pretty spectacular in its own right. And, even more impressive, it seemed to change color depending on the angle of the light. From the softest pink to the palest blue to shimmering gold, the gem's smooth, flawless surface seemed to reflect the hopes and dreams of anyone who gazed upon it.

"But what is it?" Charlie asked again.

"That's what Travis and I have been trying to figure out, and after all of our research, what we know is that it is a previously undiscovered gem that seems to be unique to this part of the world. Which is why we're going to trademark it as 'McCordite'—and the mine is filled with it."

"A previously undiscovered gem must be worth a fortune," Blake noted.

"Always thinking of the bottom line," Katie teased her fiancé.

"Someone has to," he retorted, just a little defensively.

"And this will greatly improve our bottom line," Paige assured them all. "After Blake introduces it at the upcoming Tucson Gem Show."

"I'll be happy to," Blake promised.

"Before we move on to dessert," Travis said, his words silencing the renewed murmurs. "I have a request of Penny."

She set down the water glass she'd just picked up, suddenly aware that all eyes were focused in her direction, as she wondered what Jason's brother could possibly want from her.

"I'd like you to design an engagement ring to showcase the new gem," he told her. "Because I've asked Paige to marry me—and she said 'yes'."

Penny swallowed around the lump in her throat and forced her lips to curve into a semblance of a smile. She was happy for her sister—she really was. She just couldn't help but wish that her own relationship hadn't ended so unhappily. "It would be my pleasure."

Suddenly everyone was talking again, offering congratulations and toasts to the newly engaged couple.

And even while Penny's mind was already working through materials and designs for her sister's engagement ring, she felt a pang inside of her chest. She was thrilled for her sister, of course, but in the midst of so many happy couples, she couldn't help wishing that she'd found something more than heartache.

"To the future bride and groom," Melanie, Zane's former nanny, now girlfriend, said.

Travis and Paige both drank from their glasses, then they kissed.

Penny tore her gaze away from the intimacy—and found Jason's gaze locked on her.

Jason had been watching Penny all night, unable to tear his eyes away, subconsciously urging her to glance in his direction. He wanted just one moment of eye contact, certain that one quick look would confirm that the connection they'd shared had fizzled, convinced that was all he needed to be able to put her out of his mind and get on with his life without her.

What he saw in her eyes was surprise and hurt and yearning.

And what he felt was heat that seared all the way to his toes.

The connection had definitely *not* fizzled.

But something had gone wrong, and he needed to know what it was if he had any hope of fixing it.

He let his eyes skim over her face, as if he hadn't memorized every detail during the time they'd spent together. But there were subtle changes since he'd seen her last. Her cheekbones were a little more prominent, her skin a little too pale, and there were dark smudges under her eyes that suggested she hadn't slept any better than he had in the weeks they'd been apart. But most notable—and most damning—were the shadows that lingered in the depths of her beautiful green eyes.

She tore her gaze away, and the all-too-brief moment was lost, leaving Jason with the surreal feeling that she'd somehow reached inside of him and wrenched his heart right out of his chest.

And in that moment, he realized that it was an entirely appropriate analogy, because she did have his heart. Or at least more of it than he'd ever given to any other woman in a very long time.

He'd had a lot of relationships in his thirty-two years. Too many relationships with too many women who never really mattered to him. In fact, since the tragic end of his relationship with Kara, his college girlfriend, he couldn't think of any woman who had mattered…until Penny.

When she'd called and left a message on his voice-mail, canceling their last scheduled date, he'd been more surprised than anything. When she stopped answering his calls and failed to respond to any of his messages, he'd grown concerned. But his worry quickly gave way to annoyance when he realized that she was still going about her usual routine and had simply cut him out of the picture.

He'd tried to convince himself that their break-up was inevitable, that he never intended for it to be long-term. In fact, he'd never really intended to get involved with her at all, not beyond some casual dating and simple flirting to get the information he wanted about her family's search for the legendary Santa Magdalena Diamond.

Yes, it had all started because of the diamond, because his brother had overheard some talk at a party and become convinced that the McCords were in search of the fabled gem. And because Jason had been determined to discover what they knew, to learn how close they were to finding the long-lost treasure.

Then he'd started spending time with Penny, getting to know her, and he'd forgotten that he had an agenda. When he was with Penny, she somehow managed to make him forget about everything but the pleasure of being with her.

His gaze shifted to the diamond at the center of the table, the stunning gem taunting him with the knowledge that what he'd once sought so desperately now meant nothing in comparison to what he'd so briefly had—and lost.

He glanced at Penny again, but she wasn't looking in his direction. She'd been deliberately *not* looking in his direction since she sat down across from him at the table, as if by refusing to acknowledge his presence she could pretend he wasn't there.

She'd been doing that for weeks now, acting as if she didn't know him, as if they'd never meant anything to one another. Now that the fires of the ancient Foley-McCord feud had finally been banked, he didn't want to be the one to add fuel, but he also wasn't going to let Penny's campaign of avoidance continue.

He wasn't going to be ignored any longer.

Chapter Two

Penny stayed at the table only until dessert had been served, then she picked up her dishes and pushed her chair back. She wasn't particularly fond of kitchen duty, but at the moment, it was infinitely preferable to enduring another minute of Jason's scrutiny.

How could he look at her like that? As if he cared. As if he still wanted her, when he'd never really wanted her in the first place.

She exhaled a weary sigh as she scraped the remnants of her dinner into the garbage can and considered how rude it would be to leave the ranch now, without telling anyone.

Inexcusably rude, her conscience—sounding a great deal like her no-nonsense sister—warned.

She sighed again, because she knew it was true.

"Something weighing on your mind?" an achingly familiar voice asked from behind her.

Penny whirled around, and found herself face-to-face with Jason.

Her breath caught in her throat, her heart hammered against her ribs and her knees went as limp as the uneaten spaghetti she'd just dumped. She set her bowl down and gripped the edge of the counter for support. "What are you doing here?"

"I wanted to see you."

"Well, I don't want to see you."

"So you've said to my answering machine and on my voice mail and to my secretary, but you've never said it to me."

"I just did."

"But not without that little catch in your voice that leads me to believe the words aren't really true."

"Go away, Jason."

"I tried," he admitted. "But I can't get you out of my mind."

"The game is over, Jason. Travis and Paige found the Santa Magdalena Diamond—there's no reason to pretend you really care about me anymore."

"You think I was pretending?"

"I *know* you were pretending. I know that from our first dance at Missy Harcourt's wedding to the last night I spent in your bed, it was all about the diamond."

"Everything okay in here?" Gabriella asked, carrying an armful of dishes into the kitchen.

"Fine," Penny said, although her cheeks flamed at the realization that her cousin couldn't have failed to overhear the words she'd spoken.

"Actually," Jason said, "Penny and I would like a few minutes alone, if you don't mind."

Gabby looked at her cousin, as if for confirmation.

Penny refused to give it. "No, we don't."

She knew she was going to have to talk to Jason, that they were going to have to find a way to communicate and make plans for their baby, but not yet. Not when simply being in the same room with him made her heart ache.

"Please, Penny," Jason said.

And her aching heart melted, just a little.

But before she could respond to his plea, Paige came to her rescue. She sailed into the kitchen and, summing up the situation in one quick glance, turned to Jason and said, "Out."

Though Gabby had to know that her cousin wasn't talking to her, she slipped out of the room, obviously not wanting to get caught in any cross fire.

Jason's brows lifted. "I'm simply trying to help with the cleanup."

Paige's smile was forced. "You've done enough. Really."

Penny knew her sister was referring to his relationship with her, rather than the state of the kitchen, and, judging by the way his eyes narrowed, Jason knew it, too.

"I'll catch up with you later," he said to Penny.

She nodded, accepting that it was inevitable, even while she hoped it would be *much* later.

"I can't believe that man is Travis's brother," Paige muttered.

"Which means he's soon going to be your brother-in-law," Penny pointed out. "So maybe you should try being a little less hostile toward him."

"I'm only looking out for you."

"I know. And I appreciate it. But I need to stand on my own two feet."

"Not an easy task when you've had the rug pulled right out from under you."

"I can manage," she assured her sister.

"Manage the dishes all by yourself?" Gabby teased, returning to the kitchen. "Because I'd much rather linger over another glass of wine than tackle the logistical nightmare of loading fourteen place settings into a dishwasher."

"Then you're in luck," Penny said, squirting soap into the stream of hot water that was rapidly filling one of the sinks. "You can scrub the pots instead."

To the sisters' mutual surprise, Gabby didn't balk at the directive, but moved to the sink and immersed her hands into the sudsy water.

"I wish I had a camera," Paige murmured, heading back out to the dining room to finish clearing the tables.

"I know I've been spoiled and pampered most of my life," Gabby said. "But Rafael has been encouraging me to overcome my aversion to domestic chores."

"Still—" Penny handed her cousin a pair of rubber gloves "—the McCord spokesperson can't be caught with dishpan hands."

"Speaking of hands," Gabby said, drying her own in order to don the gloves as Paige returned. "Did either of you notice, when Eleanor and Rex lifted their glasses to toast the new engagement, that they both had gold bands on the third fingers of their left hands?"

"I didn't," Penny admitted, frowning.

She hadn't really been able to concentrate on anything with Jason so near, and she couldn't help but wonder how wrapped up in him she'd been over the past few months, that she'd been so oblivious to the developing relationship between her mother and his father.

"Neither did I," Paige said, then, "Are you sure?"

"Positive."

"Are you actually suggesting that our mother got married without telling her kids?"

Gabby shrugged. "Well, everyone's been so caught up in their own lives and their own agendas lately, and with the volatile history between the two families, she probably just wanted to do it quietly."

It made sense, sort of. "But why didn't they tell us today?"

"Maybe they intended to," Gabby suggested. "But didn't want to steal the spotlight from the news that Paige is engaged to her stepbrother."

"Well, good for Mom, I guess, though the stepbrother thing is a little disconcerting."

"Talk about close family ties," Gabby mused.

"A little too close," Penny said.

"And don't think the media won't figure out the connection," their cousin warned.

A former model, international jetsetter and genuine blueblood heiress, Gabriella had been the target of more than her fair share of media attention and was understandably wary.

Paige just shrugged. "At this point, any publicity for the family is good for the business."

"Even a headline that reads: 'Family Feud Ends with Stepsibling Wedding'?" Gabby asked, determined to ensure that her cousin understood the kind of paparazzi circus she might find herself in the midst of.

"It's better than 'McCord Heiress Gives Birth to Stepbrother's Illegitimate Baby'."

Gabby stared at Paige. "You're pregnant?"

In response to which question Paige automatically shook her head, then winced when she realized the truth that her denial revealed.

Gabby spun around to face Penny.

Penny didn't—couldn't—respond. Nor could she hide the tears that sprang to her eyes.

"Good thing I swore you to secrecy on that," she said to her sister.

Paige winced again. "Oh, honey, I wasn't thinking."

"Apparently, neither was I, or I wouldn't be in this mess."

"Does Jason know?" Gabby asked gently.

"Not unless he was lurking outside the doorway when Paige made her little announcement."

"But you're going to tell him?" her cousin pressed. "Because he seems to me like the type of guy who would step up to do the right thing."

"What is the right thing in this situation?" Penny wondered aloud.

"To get married and give your baby a family."

She shook her head, her throat tight. It was once what she'd wanted, more than anything else. When she'd first learned that she was carrying Jason's baby, she'd foolishly let herself imagine that he would be thrilled by the news, that he would want to marry her and be a father to their child. Then she'd found out that their entire relationship had been a scam from the beginning, and her dream had shattered.

* * *

Maybe it had been a mistake to come.

Jason considered this possibility as he made his way down the hall.

It had definitely been a mistake to think that he could resolve anything with Penny while there were so many other people around, one of whom was her overprotective twin sister. But it was the first opportunity he'd had to see her and talk to her face-to-face since she canceled their dinner plans and stopped taking his calls almost three weeks earlier, and he'd prematurely jumped at the opportunity. And blown it.

Frustrated with himself as much as the situation, he pushed open the door and stepped out onto the porch, nearly tripping over Olivia, his six-year-old niece, in the process. His oldest brother, Livie's father, was waiting for her at the bottom of the stairs.

"Where are you rushing off to?" Zane asked him.

"I was just coming out to get some air," Jason replied.

"We're going to see the kittens," Olivia announced.

"Kittens?"

She nodded enthusiastically. "Uncle Travis said Matilda had a letter of six."

"A litter," Zane corrected his daughter.

"Six kittens," Olivia said, refocusing her attention on the most important piece of information. "They're in the barn."

"Then we should definitely go take a look," Jason agreed, and his response was rewarded with a brilliant smile from his niece.

Olivia skipped ahead. Zane and Jason followed at a more leisurely pace, a few steps behind.

"Good thing it's a clear night," Zane noted. "Living in the city, I forget how dark it can get out here."

"I don't know that I could ever live out in the middle of nowhere, but it seems to suit Travis."

"Hopefully, it will suit Paige, too."

Jason nodded.

"It's kind of funny how things work out, isn't it? I mean, Paige came out here to basically steal the diamond from under our brother's nose, and somehow they ended up falling in love."

"Funny? Seems like falling in love has become an epidemic."

Zane chuckled. "Don't knock it till you try it."

"Thanks, but I'll pass."

"In that case, you must be pleased that Travis and Paige found the diamond."

"What does that have to do with anything?"

"Well, it gets you off the hook, so far as things with Penny McCord are concerned."

"Yeah, it does that," Jason said, with a decided lack of enthusiasm.

"Imagine how awkward it would be for everyone if Eleanor found out you were dating her daughter to get information about the McCords' search for the diamond. Especially now that our father seems to have hooked up with her mother."

"What do you mean—Dad has hooked up with Eleanor?"

Zane stared at him. "You didn't notice that they arrived together?"

Jason shook his head. "I thought they just happened to show up at the same time."

"Did you see the two of them at dinner?"

He shook his head again.

"They could hardly take their eyes off of one another. And they were the first to leave after the meal, as if they couldn't wait to be alone together."

"Please—" Jason held up a hand, halting any further explanation "—there are some things I don't need to know."

"It's funny, isn't it? They apparently fell in love when they were teenagers, but went their separate ways, and have now rediscovered one another so many years later."

"Apparently they rediscovered one another quite a few years ago," Jason said, a not-so-veiled reference to the existence of Charlie McCord, Eleanor's youngest son, who was recently revealed to be their half-brother, the result of a brief affair she had with their father during a period of separation from her husband.

"Still, it's good to see him happy again. To know that he has someone to spend his life with, that he's not alone anymore."

"If that's what makes him happy," Jason agreed.

"Come on," Olivia said impatiently, already at the door of the barn.

"We're coming," her father assured her.

Satisfied with that response, she disappeared inside the building.

"What's it going to take to make you happy?" Zane asked.

Jason followed his brother into the barn. "I am happy."

"Yeah, that's why you've practically been living at the office over the past couple of weeks."

"There's been a lot going on at Foley Industries. Big deals that need a lot of work and personal attention from the COO."

"Is that really it?" his brother pressed. "Or is it that you have no one to go home to?"

"I never wanted anyone to go home to," he said, keeping his voice low, in the hope that his niece wouldn't overhear.

"You should have a kitten," Olivia decided, proving that she had excellent hearing. "That would be someone to go home to."

Jason managed a smile. "A kitten would be very lonely at my apartment, because I'm not there very much."

"Maybe you could take the kitten to work with you."

"She doesn't give up, does she?" Jason asked his brother.

"Never," Zane agreed. "I must have told her a thousand times that we aren't going to take one of Travis's kittens home with us, yet here we are, and you can bet she's already picked out the one she wants."

"There was a time when I knew what I wanted, too," Jason admitted.

"And now?"

"I don't seem to have a clue."

"I think you do," Zane told him. "I think you know exactly what you want—or maybe it would be more appropriate to say *who* you want."

Jason couldn't deny it. "I screwed up, Zane."

"I never really approved of your plan to get close to Penny McCord in order to get information about the Santa Magdalena Diamond—"

"Yes, you made that abundantly clear."

"—but despite that," Zane continued, as if Jason hadn't spoken, "I think the time you spent with her was good for you. I think she was good for you."

Jason couldn't deny that assessment, either. Penny had been good for him, but he hadn't returned the favor. He'd lied to her and used her, and she had every right to be furious with him. Now the only question that remained in his mind was: did he have any right to try to fix things, or should he just let her go?

Penny followed her sister up to the second floor. "Are you sure it's okay that I'm staying here? Because I could get a room at the hotel where the others are staying."

"Of course it's okay. The whole point of you coming for the weekend was so that we could spend some time together."

"I'd think you'd be more anxious to spend the time with your new fiancé." She opened the duffel bag that Travis had earlier taken up to the bedroom for her, and pulled out her nightgown.

"I would rather sleep with him than with you," Paige admitted with a smile. "But that would mean you sharing a room with Jason, which neither of us thought was a good idea, all things considered."

"Thank you for that."

"Although I'm starting to think that we might have been wrong. If you were sharing a room, you'd have the perfect opportunity to tell him about the baby."

"I will tell Jason about the baby," Penny agreed. "When I'm ready, not when you think I should be."

"When will that be?"

"Not now. Not here," Penny said.

"Why not?"

"Because I'm not ready."

"You can't keep your pregnancy a secret forever," her sister pointed out logically.

"I don't want to keep it a secret forever."

"Just for the next seven and a half months?" Paige guessed.

"Why are you so anxious for me to tell him?" Penny countered. "He never even wanted me—what makes you think he'll want this baby?"

"Actually, I might have been wrong about that."

Penny tugged her nightgown over her head. "Wrong about what?"

"That Jason was only using you to get information about the Santa Magdalena Diamond."

Penny stared at her sister.

"He was definitely using you," Paige hastened to explain. "Which still makes him scum of the earth, as far as I'm concerned. But the way he was looking at you all through dinner makes me suspect that his feelings for you might not have been entirely manufactured."

"That possibility makes me feel so much better," Penny said dryly.

"I'm not about to join the Jason Foley fan club," her sister assured her. "But I do believe in admitting when I'm wrong, and it's possible that I was wrong about him."

"It's also possible that your relationship with his brother has clouded your judgment with respect to other members of the family."

"My loyalty is—and will always be—to you."

"You're going to marry Travis Foley."

"You're still going to be my sister."

Penny had to look away, so Paige wouldn't see the tears that had filled her eyes.

Everything was changing—her sister had been lucky enough to find a man she could love and who loved her back. Penny was happy for her—and all too aware that she, too, was embarking on a new phase of her life, but that she would do so alone.

"If he never wanted you, he really is an idiot," Paige said loyally. "But he will want this baby, because it's his child—his heir to the Foley empire."

Her sister's warning lingered in her mind long after they turned out the lights. And though Penny was emotionally and physically exhausted, sleep continued to elude her, the words echoing in her head.

Or maybe it was the rumbling of her tummy that was keeping her awake.

She'd found it difficult to concentrate on the meal with Jason at the same dinner table, and almost impossible to force food into her churning stomach. That same stomach was sounding its protest now.

Penny glanced at the glowing numbers on the alarm clock: 11:47 p.m. Could she hold out until the morning? But if she did, chances were she'd be sitting at a table with Jason again, and not manage to eat anything.

With a silent oath, she pushed back the covers and headed out into the hall.

She hadn't packed a robe, but the quiet house assured her that everyone else was settled in for the night. The growling in her stomach seemed to intensify as she padded down the stairs. The second one from the bottom creaked when she stepped on it, but the rest of the house remained silent, except for the peanut butter sandwich calling her name.

Upstairs, in the guest room that he was sharing with Travis, because his brother had given up the master bedroom to his fiancée, it wasn't silent, though Jason was careful to keep his voice pitched low so as not to disturb the other guests.

"It all makes sense now," Jason said.

"What makes sense?" Travis had long ago settled on the narrow twin bed, on the opposite side of the room from the one his brother had claimed, and was flipping through channels on the television with the remote control.

"Why Penny doesn't even want to talk to me anymore." Jason paced the length of the room. "It was because of you. You told Paige about my plan to get information from Penny and she told her sister."

"I couldn't lie to her." Travis kept his eyes on the television, evading his brother's.

"Did you tell her that you were in agreement with the plan?" Jason challenged.

"The plan was to get information from her," Travis reminded him. "No one told you to seduce her."

"Maybe she seduced me."

His brother snorted his disbelief. "Regardless of who seduced whom—you slept with her, and that wasn't part of the plan."

"Nothing of what happened with Penny was part of the plan," he admitted.

Travis stopped scrolling through channels on the television, to give his brother his full attention. "Then you really do have feelings for her?"

"Why does that seem so unbelievable to you?"

"Because you made it clear from the beginning that your only purpose in getting close to Penny was to best the McCords."

"That was almost five months ago."

"Well, if your reasons for being with Penny changed, you might have let the rest of us in on it," Travis told him.

Which was a valid point, if not one that Jason was in the mood to acknowledge. Because although his reasons for being with Penny had changed, it wasn't something he'd been willing to admit to himself, never mind share with anyone else. So all he said was, "It was none of your damned business."

"But it was," Travis reminded him. "It was Foley business."

"No, it wasn't. What was between Penny and me wasn't business at all," Jason said, and, finally realizing it was true, stormed out of the room.

He resisted the urge to slam the door on his way out. Although the solid smack of wood against wood might be a satisfying reflection of the anger and frustration that were churning inside of him, he was conscious of the fact that his brother's house was filled with guests. The last thing he wanted were witnesses to his suddenly churning emotions, especially when two of those potential witnesses were sisters who were already ticked off at him enough without his temper interrupting their slumber.

So instead of slamming the door, he decided to take a walk, get some air and try not to think about how thoroughly he had destroyed any chance of a relationship with the most amazing woman he'd ever known.

He was on his way down the hall when he heard a

sound from the kitchen and, pausing at the doorway to investigate, found Penny at the counter.

She had her back to him, but this time there was no doubt in his mind as to which twin was standing in his brother's kitchen. The pain that stabbed through his heart and the need that twisted in his belly were proof enough of the fact.

She was wearing a long white nightdress that covered her from throat to ankles. Flannel, he guessed, as the heavy fabric didn't even give a hint of the luscious curves hidden beneath. But he knew the curves were there, he knew how soft her skin was, and he knew how she would quiver in response to his touch.

His hands itched with the need to reach out to her, but he curled them into fists.

"Penny."

She turned so quickly she swayed on her feet, nearly losing her balance.

He instinctively moved forward, reaching out to her.

She knocked his hand away, instead grabbing hold of the edge of the countertop to steady herself.

But she was pale. Too pale. The dark smudges under her eyes seemed even darker now, and he wondered if she was even half as lonely as he'd been since she ended their relationship.

"Are you all right?"

"I'm fine."

"You don't look fine," he said, and felt a twinge of guilt that he might in some way be responsible for that.

"I'm hungry," she said, and picked up half of the peanut butter sandwich she'd just cut.

"You didn't eat much dinner," he noted.

"I wasn't very hungry then."

"You didn't drink your wine, either."

"I wasn't thirsty." But she went to the fridge and poured herself a glass of milk now.

He remembered that her favorite late-night snack was a peanut butter sandwich, and that she always washed it down with a glass of milk. He'd never been particularly fond of peanut butter—until he tasted it on Penny's lips.

"You have every right to be upset with me," he said.

"Yes, I do," she agreed, but she sounded more weary than angry. "But not everything is about you, Jason."

He wanted to make her smile—to see her lips curve and watch some of the clouds lift from her eyes—so he tried to lighten the moment by asking, "Then you didn't skip the wine because you were afraid you wouldn't be able to control yourself around me?"

"No," she said, and looked him straight in the eye. "I skipped the wine because I'm pregnant."

Chapter Three

Penny had imagined a dozen scenarios in which she finally told Jason that she was going to have his child—but blurting out the news in his brother's kitchen wasn't one of them. And it never would have happened that way, except for Paige's nagging and the fact that she couldn't get the pregnancy out of her mind.

"Pregnant?" Jason echoed, confusion—and more than a hint of panic—evident in his deep blue eyes.

"Yes, Jason, I'm going to have a baby."

He swallowed. "You mean, you're going to have *my* baby."

"Yes," she said again.

He leaned back against the counter. "But we were careful."

"Not careful enough, obviously." And she knew that was her fault.

"Are you sure?"

"I took three different home pregnancy tests, and a couple of weeks ago, my doctor confirmed the results." Penny picked up the second half of her sandwich and nibbled. She wasn't feeling very hungry anymore, but she knew that she needed to eat, at least for the baby's sake.

"Come with me."

"What? Where?"

"Outside."

She dropped the rest of her sandwich back onto the plate. "Are you crazy? It's after midnight, I'm in my nightgown, and—"

The rest of the words tumbled back down her throat when Jason picked her up off her feet.

Obviously, he wasn't in a mood to debate the issue any more than she was in a mood to acquiesce to his demands. She wriggled and squirmed, hoping to make him set her down again. But he only tightened his grip on her and moved resolutely toward the back door.

"Put me down right now," she hissed. "Or I'll scream so loud everyone in this house will wake up."

"Is that really how you want our families to learn that you're carrying my child?"

She clamped her lips shut.

"Good answer," he said. "Although you might want to stop wriggling around so much, or I'm going to forget that I'm supposed to be too pissed off to get turned on."

She stopped wriggling. "Why are *you* pissed off at *me?*"

"No one's in the guest cottage," he said, ignoring her question. "We can talk there in private, without anyone else overhearing or interfering with our conversation."

He snagged a key off of a hook by the back door before he pushed it open and stepped out into the darkness.

She shivered as the cold night air hit, and he tightened his arms around her. "You might have just suggested that in the first place—"

"As if you would have meekly followed," he muttered.

"—instead of hauling me off the ground like a bag of laundry," she continued indignantly.

"Honey, no bag of laundry ever felt or smelled as good as you."

"Don't call me 'honey'," she snapped.

"You never objected to it before."

"I didn't object to a lot of things—because I didn't know that I was being played like a pawn in a chess game."

"It wasn't like that."

"Then you didn't get close to me for the sole purpose of finding out what I knew about the search for the Santa Magdalena Diamond?"

She wanted him to deny it, to insist that he cared about her, but his silence said otherwise. And when he finally set her on her feet to insert the key into the lock of the guest cottage, she was tempted to turn on her heel and march back to the main house. But that would be both petty and pointless, as he would only follow her again. And if he was determined to get answers to his questions, well, she had some questions of her own.

He reached inside to flick on the lights, then held open the door for her to enter. She did, and gasped when her bare feet came into contact with the cold, ceramic tile floor.

"I'll light a fire," Jason said, moving toward the stone fireplace on the far side of the room. "It will heat the cabin up quickly."

"Don't bother." Penny sat on the sofa, tucked her feet beneath her. "I don't plan on being here long enough for it to matter."

But once again Jason ignored her. He selected wood and kindling from the box on the hearth and, within minutes, there were flames crackling and blazing.

"How far along are you?"

She shrugged. "Almost fourteen weeks." She folded her arms across her chest. "Do you want a paternity test?"

He scowled at her. "Of course I don't want a paternity test."

She pushed off of the sofa, drawn to the heat of the fire. "You're a wealthy man—I'd be surprised if your lawyer didn't insist on it."

"Do you think maybe we could talk about this without bringing lawyers into it?"

"No matter how much talking we do, if you want to be a part of my baby's life, formal arrangements will have to be made."

"I'd rather see a minister than a lawyer."

It took her a minute to figure out what he was saying and, when she finally did, she couldn't help but laugh. "You're not seriously suggesting marriage?"

He frowned. "Why not?"

"Because we don't even like one another."

"I'd say the baby you're carrying proves otherwise."

"Maybe there was an attraction, for a while," she allowed.

But there was never any real affection. At least not on his part, and that was what—even now—hurt most of all.

"The attraction's still there," he insisted.

Penny shook her head. "Your family must be really

proud of you—to realize the extent to which you were willing to go to get the information you wanted."

"It wasn't supposed to go as far as it did."

"That makes me feel so much better," she said bitterly. "I didn't even make you work for it, did I? I was so willing, so pathetically eager to fall into bed with you."

"You were passionate." He turned her around so that she was facing him. "Incredibly passionate and wonderfully uninhibited."

"Fancy words for '*easy*'." She pulled away from him, moved back to the sofa, partly to give herself some space and partly because she was simply too tired to continue to stand. "Except you never really got what you wanted, did you? I couldn't tell you what you wanted to know because I didn't even know what Paige and Blake were doing. And I'll bet that annoys the hell out of you."

"But I did get what I wanted," he insisted. "Because the more time I spent with you, the less I cared about the damned diamond, the more I wanted you."

As if she was going to believe that now, after he'd dropped out of her life so quickly and completely.

Yeah, she was the one who stopped taking his calls. But if there was one thing she knew about Jason Foley after all the time they'd spent together, it was that he didn't give up on something he wanted. The fact that he gave up on her, and so easily, was just further proof that he'd never really wanted her.

"When I decided to try to get information from you, I didn't know you. I only knew that you were a McCord, and that seemed justification enough for what I was doing."

She didn't manage to hold back the yawn as she

watched him pace and listened to him talk. Now that she'd eaten, even if it was only half of a sandwich, she could no longer fight the exhaustion that had plagued her of late. Or maybe it hadn't been hunger that had been keeping her awake, but worry about how and when she was going to tell Jason about their baby.

Now that hurdle had been knocked down, and she felt her eyes drift shut.

"But as we spent more time together, as I got to know you better, I realized…"

Jason didn't think he'd ever been so open about his thoughts and his feelings, but never had there been so much at stake. He'd hurt Penny with his deception, and while he might have easily dismissed the possibility of such collateral damage as insignificant when he'd begun his campaign, she had become the most significant part of the campaign. And while he might have been willing to let her go, to protect himself from getting too deeply involved, now there was a baby to consider. He didn't really expect that she'd forgive him, but he wanted—no, he *needed*—to convince her to put it behind them so that they could move forward. Together.

He turned back, to gauge her reaction, to hear her response. And realized that none would be immediately forthcoming. Because somewhere along the line, while he'd been pouring out his heart and soul, Penny had fallen asleep.

He stared at her, stunned. He started across the room, determined to wake her so that they could finish their conversation. They were never going to resolve anything if they didn't talk about it.

But his steps faltered as he drew nearer.

She looked so fragile lying there. So pale and beautiful. The flannel gown she wore emphasized the slenderness of her frame. There was no evidence yet of the baby that was growing inside of her. His baby, he amended, and felt a quick spurt of something that might have been excitement or terror.

He definitely hadn't planned for this, wasn't ready for this. It was just another one of those strange curves that fate seemed to enjoy tossing at him, but he would step up to the plate. He *wanted* to step up to the plate. Maybe his mind was still reeling at the revelation of Penny's pregnancy, but he already knew that he wanted the baby. And he wanted his baby's mother.

He lifted her carefully from the sofa. She snuggled into him, her head pillowed against his shoulder. She wasn't protesting now—of course, that was only because she was sleeping, but he couldn't help but cherish the moment. It seemed so long since he'd held her in his arms, and he missed her.

Unable to resist, he dipped his head and dropped a gentle kiss on the side of her mouth. To his surprise, she tilted her head, her lips instinctively seeking—and finding—his. And though he knew he was taking advantage of her sleepy state, he couldn't resist her avid response.

Somehow, her arms found their way around his neck, and she pulled his head down, deepening the kiss. He tasted a hint of peanut butter, and the sweeter, much more seductive flavor that was uniquely her own.

Though she weighed next to nothing, he felt his arms tremble, and he knew it was his hunger for her that made him weak. And instead of carrying her to the door, as he'd intended, he carried her to the neatly made double bed.

He laid her gently on top of the spread, and she pulled him down with her, their mouths still fused together.

Guilt and worry tugged at his conscience, but her hands were on him, sliding up his chest, over his shoulders, and it was impossible to think when all of the blood in his head had drained down to his crotch. And the way she was rubbing against him, she had to know it.

He pressed his mouth to the side of her jaw. Her skin was hot and her pulse was racing. There was no doubt that she was as aroused as he was, that she wanted him as much as he wanted her. But was it real—or had he interrupted some kind of erotic dream?

He lifted his head reluctantly.

"Penny, we really should talk before—"

"I don't want to talk." She was already unbuttoning his shirt, those nimble fingers making quick work of the task.

Then her palms were splayed against his chest, and her touch against his bare skin was almost more than he could stand. Okay, so talking wasn't really what he wanted, either. "But—"

"Shut up, Jason." She captured his mouth again, her teeth sinking into his bottom lip.

Jason shut up and kissed her.

She managed to push his shirt over his shoulders and down his arms, then reached for the button at the front of his pants. He rolled off of the bed and shucked his clothes. Penny propped herself up on her elbows to watch him. Her face was flushed, her eyes dark, her lips swollen from his kisses.

"Your turn," he told her.

Not so very long ago, she would have balked at the request, too shy and self-conscious to comply. But in the time that they'd spent together, he'd helped her to explore and enjoy her own body, and she'd quickly learned how to wield her newly discovered feminine power.

She shifted so that she was kneeling in the center of the bed, then she bunched the bottom of the gown in her fists and slowly slid it upward, revealing just the tiniest glimpse of the pale, smooth skin of her thighs, then a tiny bit more.

He wanted her naked. Now. But he remained standing by the edge of the bed—his hands curled into fists to prevent himself from reaching for her and tearing the gown from her body—and let her tease him.

When the hem of the gown finally reached her hips, he caught a glimpse of cream-colored lace, then more pale skin. Her previously flat belly was now gently curved, and this evidence of their baby growing inside of her made her pregnancy suddenly and shockingly real to him. But as the fabric continued its upward journey, inch by torturous inch, he forgot about the baby and thought only of Penny. Finally, she whisked the gown over her head and tossed it to the floor, on top of the pile of clothes he'd discarded.

She held out her hand to him, and then he was back on the bed with her. Kissing her and touching her. And she was kissing and touching him. He knew how to take things slow, how to draw out a moment and pleasure a woman.

But Penny had her own ideas this time. Her tongue plunged into his mouth, her nails scraped down his back, her body arched against his, urging him on. And, well, what was a guy supposed to do, when he had a warm, willing woman writhing beneath him?

He rose up and plunged into her.

He didn't worry about a condom. What was the point, when she was already carrying his child? But without any kind of barrier between them, she seemed hotter, wetter, tighter than he remembered.

She cried out with shocked pleasure and began to move, pumping her hips in rhythm with his own.

It was rough and fast and just a little bit wild.

She draped her arms over his shoulders, her nails biting into his flesh. He scraped his teeth over her collarbone, nipped at her throat. She locked her legs around his waist, pulling him even deeper inside. His fingers dug into her hips as he drove her closer and closer to the peak.

And then her body convulsed around him, clamping tight like a velvet fist, and dragging him over the edge with her.

Penny lay motionless beneath Jason's warm and familiar weight. Her body was more than satisfied; her mind was spinning. She'd just had incredible, mind-numbing, body-melting sex, which should have been a cause for celebration rather than concern.

But when that mind-numbing, body-melting sex had been with a man whom she'd vowed to cut out of her life, things changed. A lot. When that man also happened to be the father of her baby, the situation got even more complicated.

She'd known exactly what she was doing when she'd kissed him. She'd wanted this to happen, she wanted a chance to say goodbye on her terms. But she'd failed to

fully consider the ramifications of her actions, to anticipate that making love with him again would make it
harder for her to break the emotional ties.

It seemed as if she'd made one mistake after another when it came to Jason Foley, but this was where
it would end.

When he rolled off of her but tried to snuggle her
close against his body, she held herself still. She'd been
surprised, pleasantly so, when she'd first realized that
the tough, implacable businessman was not just an incredibly considerate lover but a cuddler, and almost as
much as she'd loved making love with him, she'd loved
cuddling up with him after making love.

Of course, that was when she believed that they were
making love. The knowledge that he'd only been using
her had tainted all of her memories.

He pressed his lips to the back of her shoulder, and
though she couldn't prevent the goose bumps that rose
up on her skin, she didn't allow herself any other reaction.

"I missed you, Penny."

His voice was husky. The words sounded sincere. But
Penny was no longer the naive virgin who had been
easily duped by this man before. She certainly wasn't
going to be duped again.

She extricated herself from his embrace and retrieved her discarded clothes from the floor. Because
her knees were still trembling, she had to sit on the edge
of the bed to put her panties back on. When he stroked
a hand lazily down her back, his fingertips trailing
down the line of her spine, she felt tears prick the back
of her eyes.

She'd missed him, too. She'd missed the sound of his

voice, the warmth of his laughter and the way his eyes lit up when he saw her, as if her presence had truly brightened his day. She'd missed the sense of companionship, the pleasure she derived just from being with him, whether they were sharing a romantic dinner or watching a late-night movie on television or shopping for groceries. And she'd missed his touch, the casual brushes and seductive caresses, and especially the way he was touching her now.

Their lovemaking had been not just amazing but incredibly varied, and she'd been both awed and overwhelmed to experience the unexpected heights of passion. Whether their coming together had been leisurely and tender or fast and hard, he'd always made her feel wanted. And afterward, when he held her close, he'd made her feel cherished.

Irritated with herself for the self-indulgent trek down memory lane, she yanked her nightgown down over her head, thrust her arms into the sleeves and stood up.

"It was sex," she said, aiming for a dismissive tone to disguise the tightness in her throat. "Don't try to make it into anything bigger than that."

"Just sex?"

She had no trouble hearing the annoyance—and anger—in his question.

She lifted a shoulder, determined to play it casual, to not let him know how much the experience had shaken her. "Apparently, all the hormones that flood a women's system during pregnancy can really jump-start her libido. Obviously, that's what happened."

"So it had nothing to do with the history or attraction between you and me?" The words were bit out between clenched teeth as he dressed. "I was just convenient?"

"Don't go getting all indignant," she warned. "I'm sure, from time to time, you've done it with a woman just because she was there and she was willing."

His gaze narrowed dangerously. "We're not talking about me, though, are we? We're talking about you, and you were a twenty-six-year-old virgin until I took you to my bed a few months ago."

"Did I forget to thank you for that?" she asked. "Because it really was an incredible night."

"I'm not asking for a damn thank you."

"Well, I'm grateful anyway," she said. "And for everything that came after, I'm doubly grateful, because I really don't think I ever would have known what selfish bastards men could be without your experienced tutelage in that regard."

"You're really starting to piss me off," he warned her.

"So it's okay for you to use me for your own purposes, but it's not okay for me to call you on it?"

She saw the muscle in his jaw flex as he clamped it tight, and when he finally spoke, it was in what she referred to as his boardroom voice.

"I think we're getting a little off-topic," he said, his tone both cool and reasonable.

"It was a bad idea to try to talk about this tonight," she responded levelly. "I'm exhausted, which is apparently normal in the first trimester of any pregnancy, but which is unusual for me. I'm also cranky because my whole life is about to change and I haven't quite figured out exactly how I'm going to manage those changes. So if you don't mind, I'd really like to postpone any further conversation until we've both had a chance to think about everything."

"Of course," he agreed solicitously. "But for the record, you mean a lot more to me than you obviously realize."

She wanted to believe him, but she wasn't going to be fooled again. "For the record, I won't ever trust anything you say to me again."

Chapter Four

Jason wasn't in a good mood the next morning.

Of course, being awakened by an urgent call from his secretary after a mostly sleepless night had done nothing to establish a positive outlook for his day. And the cold shoulder he'd been getting from Penny since he crossed paths with her in the kitchen when he went to grab a cup of coffee did nothing to improve things.

How could she have been so hot for him last night and completely oblivious to his presence less than eight hours later?

"All the hormones that flood a women's system during pregnancy can really jump-start her libido. Obviously, that's what happened."

Though her words came back to haunt him, he didn't believe them any more now than he had when she'd thrown them at him the night before.

He did believe that she would spend the whole day pretending he wasn't there, if he let her. But he had no intention of fading into the background just because it was what Penny wanted. And he sure as hell had no intention of denying that it was his baby she was carrying.

Unfortunately, he spent most of the morning on the phone with either his secretary or the assistant VP of an associate office in Denver, but while he went through the motions, his mind was preoccupied with that little bombshell that Penny had dropped on him the previous evening. It occurred to him that he could more quickly and easily deal with the unexpected office crisis if he actually went back to the office, but he had no intention of leaving before he and Penny had come to some kind of agreement with respect to their child.

Of course, she'd actually have to talk to him in order for that to happen, but he remained optimistic. Or maybe it was more accurate to say he was determined.

So, when they were once again all gathered around the big tables set up in Travis's dining room, plates overflowing with slices of turkey and ham and mounds of mashed potatoes and stuffing dripping with gravy, Jason considered his plan.

A plan that got an unexpected boost when his father rose to his feet.

"Since we are all gathered around to celebrate Thanksgiving, I think it's a good time to reflect on the many reasons we are thankful. Throughout my life, I have been blessed with a wonderful family, good health and good fortune. But this year, I have even more reason to be thankful, and that reason is the beautiful bride sitting beside me."

"I don't see a bride." Livie was the first to respond to the announcement.

"I think your grandpa's telling us that he and Mrs. McCord got married," Zane explained to his daughter.

"It's Mrs. Foley now," Rex said proudly. "But you can call her Grandma."

"Or just 'Eleanor'," his wife said, apparently not wanting to push the child to accept her in the unaccustomed role too soon.

"Well, I guess congratulations are in order," Charlie said, though he sounded a little dubious as he lifted his glass.

Not to be outdone, the rest of the McCords and the Foleys followed suit.

"Congratulations."

"May you have a long, happy life together."

"To the bride and groom."

Though toasts rang out amid the clinking of crystal, Jason knew that not everyone was thrilled by the union. Or maybe it would just take a while for both families to accept that the ancient feud was truly at an end, as symbolized by Rex and Eleanor's marriage.

"While we're celebrating good news," Jason began, rising to his feet to address the group crowded around the table. "I have some of my own to share."

The conversations around him slowly died away, the clink of silverware ceased as all eyes focused on him. All eyes including Penny's green ones—which were wide and panicked when they locked on his.

She gave a slight shake of her head, a silent, desperate plea. Apparently she'd finally given up trying to pretend he didn't exist, an illusion that he'd already decided to put an end to in a big way.

"I'm going to be a father." He looked across the table at the expectant mother. "Penny is going to have my baby."

Penny wasn't surprised that Jason's proclamation was met with stunned silence.

Although her sister, her mother and, since last night, Gabby, were aware of her pregnancy, no one else had any idea about the extent of her relationship with Jason.

"Yay, another baby," Livie said, clapping her hands.

She was shushed by her father, who obviously didn't share the child's enthusiasm for the proclamation.

Nor, it seemed, did anyone else around the table.

"I would expect that kind of news to be followed by the announcement of your impending wedding date." Though Rex's comment was directed to his son, Penny was the one who wanted to crawl under the table and hide.

This was exactly why she hadn't wanted to make a public announcement about her pregnancy—because she wasn't prepared to answer all of the questions she knew her well-meaning but interfering family would inevitably have. And obviously Jason's family was no different.

"Penny and I have a lot of plans to make," Jason said, deflecting rather than answering the question implied by his father's statement.

Rex looked as if he was about to say something more, but to Penny's surprise, her mother touched his sleeve and signaled him with a subtle shake of her head.

There were other murmurs and questions, but Penny let Jason respond to them. And then Paige, sensing her sister's quiet desperation, took advantage of a lull and diverted the conversation by asking Blake about his plans for marketing the McCordite.

While there was no further mention of her pregnancy during the meal, she was conscious of the attention focused on her...and the speculation. When dinner was finally over and Penny had started to clear away the dishes again, Blake came into the kitchen and took her by the arm.

"Walk with me," he said.

It wasn't a question but a directive, and though Penny wanted to balk at being ordered around like a recalcitrant child, she welcomed the opportunity to escape the suddenly cloying atmosphere of Travis's home.

"You can save the lecture, Blake," she said, when they were outside. "It's a little too late to warn me about the dangers of unprotected sex."

"If I was going to lecture, it would be about the dangers of Jason Foley," he told her. "But under the circumstances, I won't bother."

"Thanks," she said dryly.

They walked in silence for a few minutes and Penny found the crisp air both refreshing and relaxing. For the first time, she really looked around, and she was pleased with what she saw. Travis obviously took pride in the land and Penny guessed her sister had probably fallen in love with the ranch, as well as the rancher.

"Have you thought about how you're going to handle things?"

Blake's question drew her attention away from the distant horizon and back to more immediate problems.

"I haven't been able to think about anything else," she admitted. "Not that I've come up with any answers."

"Are you going to marry Jason?"

"No," she answered that question quickly, adamantly.

"Have you told him that?"

"What makes you think he wants to marry me? Other than his father wanting him to do so."

"Don't underestimate family pressure," Blake warned her. "But aside from that, he's a successful businessman, a pillar in the community. He'll want to do the right thing, and in his mind, that is marrying the mother of his child."

Something in his tone—or maybe it was her understanding of their family history—made her ask, "You don't think it's the right thing, do you?"

"No, I don't," he told her. "I don't think you'll do yourself or your child any favors by marrying a man you don't love just to give him a father."

She knew, when Blake said "him," he wasn't necessarily referring to her child, but to the child *he* had been, and she knew he'd been badly hurt by their mother's coolness toward him.

It was only in recent years that he realized Eleanor had always resented him, albeit subconsciously, for being the reason she had to marry Devon McCord. And though she'd remained married and had gone on to have three more children with him, the shadows of that initial resentment had never quite faded away.

"I didn't plan on getting pregnant at this point in my life," Penny admitted to Blake. "But I love this baby already, and I promise you that I will never blame him— or her—for the circumstances of conception."

Her brother nodded. "You'll be a good mom, Penny."

Mom. The word created flutters of both excitement and apprehension in her belly. "I hope so."

"And if you ever need anything, just let me know."

She managed a smile. "Like a babysitter?"

"I'm not sure you'd want me to babysit," he warned her. Then, more seriously, "But I mean it, Pen. I don't want you to feel as if you need to count on Jason Foley for anything. Me and Tate and Paige, we're your family. You can depend on us."

"I know," she said, and hugged him tight.

And while she appreciated that her brother had the best of intentions, she knew she couldn't cut Jason Foley out of the equation as easily as Blake had implied.

While Penny was walking with Blake, Jason went outside for some air and was cornered by Gabby on the front porch.

"You do know you didn't earn any points by publicly announcing Penny's pregnancy, don't you?"

He shrugged. "I was making a point."

"That you're too stupid to think about birth control?" She smiled sweetly. "I'm sorry, did I say that out loud?"

"I appreciate that you feel protective of your cousin, but I'm not going to discuss my relationship with Penny with you."

"You're the one who put it on the table—literally. And did you even *think* about the fact that Tanya Kimbrough is a reporter before you decided to make your big announcement?"

He scowled, because he hadn't. "A reporter who happens to be engaged to Penny's brother."

"Do you think that connection is going to make her withhold that kind of news?"

"Okay, I didn't think," he admitted. "I just wanted

Penny to know that I'm accepting responsibility for my child."

"How far are you willing to go to accept that responsibility?"

"Did you hear me say I wasn't going to discuss this with you?"

She waved a hand dismissively, like the blue-blood heiress she was. "I just want to make sure that you've considered all of the angles."

"I'm working on it."

"Including the negative publicity that this news could generate for both the Foley and McCord families?"

"Penny's pregnancy is hardly newsworthy."

"You don't think so?" she challenged.

"She's neither royalty nor a celebrity," he said, but he couldn't deny that Gabby had a lot of experience with the media, and if she was concerned, maybe he should be, too.

"Your brother and Penny's sister found the Santa Magdalena Diamond—that discovery alone is enough to have the press salivating like a pack of mangy dogs over a juicy bone. Not to mention that their appetites have already been whetted by the teaser pieces Tanya did about the Foleys and the McCords and the ancient feud. Now you can add in Travis and Paige's engagement and Rex and Eleanor's marriage, and the paparazzi will be foaming at their mouths to find yet another meaty morsel of gossip to devour."

"I suppose you have some advice on how we should handle it?"

She nodded. "Marry her. Give her—and your baby— legitimacy. Don't let them turn Penny into a dirty little secret and your child into a mistake."

"I mentioned marriage," he admitted. "Penny didn't seem interested."

"You're Chief Operating Officer of Foley Industries. I'm sure you didn't rise to that position without knowing how to overcome opposition, how to make things happen that others thought never would."

She was right. In fact, it was one of the reasons he'd been elected by his siblings to learn what he could about the McCords' search for the Santa Magdalena Diamond. Even if that mission hadn't been a rousing success, at least insofar as finding the diamond was concerned.

But he had found Penny, and he'd lost her without understanding why. Of course, everything was clear to him now, and though he understood her reasons for withdrawing from him, he still wasn't ready to give up on her, on what they'd shared together. And now that he knew she was carrying his child, he was even less willing to let her go.

Gabby was right—he knew how to make things happen.

And he was going to make Penny McCord his wife.

Penny was zipping up her duffel bag when the knock sounded on the door.

"Come in," she said, because she assumed it was her sister. Because she assumed that Jason wouldn't have the nerve to come looking for her after what he'd done.

Then he stepped through the door, and she realized she'd assumed incorrectly.

He looked at the bag, then at her. "You're leaving?"

"Your powers of deductive reasoning are amazing."

"Because of me?"

"Believe it or not, Jason, the world doesn't revolve around you."

She reached for her bag, but he grabbed the handle first.

"I'd like you to stay," he said. "Just through the weekend, so that we can figure some things out."

"Tomorrow is the busiest shopping day of the year, and I need to be at the store."

"You work on the design end, and you can sketch anywhere. At least, that's what you used to say when you spent weekends at my penthouse in Houston," he reminded her.

She used to say a lot of things—and so did he. But she refused to go down that road with him. "There are times when I need to be available for customer consultations. This is one of those times."

He didn't look happy with her response, but he was in no position to refute her argument. "I could come to the city for the weekend," he offered instead.

"I appreciate that you're making an effort, but the fact is, I'm going to be busy all weekend, and it would be a waste of your time to come to Dallas if your only purpose is to badger me."

He ran a hand through his hair, a rare gesture of impatience. "I have to go out of town on Monday."

"You don't have to account for your whereabouts to me," she told him.

He ignored the edge in her voice. "I'll be gone most of next week, but when I get back, we'll make plans to talk."

"Talk? As in discuss? Because as far as I can tell, you don't discuss anything. You make decisions and act upon them, regardless of the impact on anyone else."

"You're annoyed that I announced your pregnancy to

our families," Jason guessed. And maybe he had over-played his hand there, but he wouldn't make the same mistake again.

"It wasn't your announcement to make."

"It's my baby, too."

"As if I could forget," she muttered.

"How many times do I have to say I'm sorry?"

"You can say it as many times as you want, but those two little words can't undo what you did."

"You're right," he agreed. "So why don't we put the past behind us and move forward?"

"I am moving forward," she told him. "And I'm doing it without you."

"Come on, Penny. Have you never made a mistake? Done something you regretted?"

She met his gaze evenly. "Yes, I have."

He forced himself to remember that he knew how to overcome opposition, even if he wasn't accustomed to that opposition being presented in such a maddeningly attractive package.

"I know you're angry with me," he said reasonably. "And you have every right to be. But I'm not going to let you cut me out of our baby's life."

"You don't want this baby, Jason. Why are you pretending otherwise?"

"How do you know what I want?" he challenged.

"Okay, maybe I should have said that you didn't plan this baby."

"Neither of us did."

"And if I wasn't pregnant, you wouldn't be here right now."

"But you are pregnant," he pointed out.

"Maybe you should put it on a billboard," she said, yanking the handle of her bag from his hand and slinging it over her shoulder. "Because it's possible there are still some people in the great state of Texas who haven't actually heard you shout out the news yet."

He realized that both of their voices had risen and he deliberately lowered his when he responded.

"Obviously, we both need some time to think about things. We'll continue this discussion when I get back next week. But while I'm gone," he continued, in what he thought was a perfectly calm and reasonable tone, "I want you to think about a wedding date."

"You don't want to marry me, you want the baby. And Jason Foley doesn't give up on anything he wants."

"You'd be wise to remember that," he told her.

"How could I forget, when that's what got me into this situation?"

"Maybe there's something else you've forgotten," he said, and crushed his mouth to hers in a hard, punishing kiss.

Penny kept her lips tightly clamped together. No way was she going to respond to such Neanderthal tactics.

But then his lips softened, moving more persuasively than persistently now, and it was just like the first time he kissed her...

Chapter Five

Penny hadn't really wanted to attend Missy Harcourt's wedding. Though they'd attended the same private schools and moved in the same social circles throughout the years, she and the bride had never been particularly close. But it was important, her mother said, for there to be a representative of the McCord family at the wedding, since the Harcourts were old friends of the family. Since Penny was the only one who didn't already have plans for the day in question, she was nominated.

When she complained about attending the event alone, Tate had mentioned that he had a colleague who was interested in going out with her. It turned out that Doctor Edmond Lang had actually been hoping to score a date with Paige, but, as Penny's outgoing twin never had any trouble lining up her own escorts, had been persuaded to settle for Penny. Not that either Tate or Edmond admitted as much, but her date calling her Paige—not once but three times—was a pretty big clue.

In any event, when Dr. Lang was paged by the hospital just as dessert was being cleared away, Penny wasn't overly disappointed. And she figured losing her date was a valid excuse for her to cut out early, too. In fact, she was on her way to the hotel concierge desk to request a taxi when she saw him across the hotel lobby.

Jason Foley. Of the infamous Foleys, sworn enemies of the McCord family since the Civil War. While the Foleys and the McCords were unlikely to issue challenges of pistols at dawn to one another in the current day, they were just as unlikely to cross a room to say hello to a member of the other family. But that knowledge had never prevented Penny from admiring any of the very handsome Foley brothers from afar. And Jason Foley—the second of Rex Foley's three sons—was the one she'd admired the most. All six-foot-two, Colin-Farrell-look-alike yumminess of him.

Her heart gave a little bump against her ribs.

It wasn't fair that a mortal enemy should look so darn good, or that she should be so attracted to a man who would never look twice in her direction.

She'd seen him at various society events over the years, but never had he given her more than a passing glance. This time, however, his eyes locked on hers—and held.

Penny's heart gave another, harder bump.

Then he crossed the room, actually going out of his way to approach her. Had there been anyone else in the vicinity, she would never have made such an assumption, but all of the other guests were still inside the main ballroom.

"You're not trying to duck out already, are you, Penny?"

The deep baritone voice skimmed over her skin like a caress, raising goose bumps on her flesh. But it was his use of her name that nearly made her knees buckle. Not even her own date had remembered she wasn't her sister—or maybe he hadn't wanted to remember. But Jason had somehow known who she was and had sought her out anyway...

Her pulse was racing now, but she lifted one shoulder, deliberately casual, determined not to let him see how much he'd flustered her. "My date had an emergency and—"

"I didn't come with a date," he interrupted smoothly. "So I would be incredibly grateful if you'd take a turn with me on the dance floor."

He wanted to dance...with her?

"I appreciate the invitation, Mr. Foley, but—"

"Jason," he said, interrupting her again. "And the way to show your appreciation would be to accept the invitation."

Penny took his proffered hand and hoped he didn't notice that her fingers trembled.

It was, after all, only a dance.

But even when the dance was over, he didn't leave her side. It was only when the bride and groom had departed that she realized they'd been talking for a long time, and while she was reluctant for the evening to end, she knew that she should be getting home.

Jason seemed equally reluctant to say good-night, and when she politely declined his offer to go somewhere for coffee, he insisted on at least giving her a ride

*home. That offer she accepted, simply because it was
more expedient than waiting for a taxi.*

*And then he insisted on seeing her to the door. Jason
Foley walked her right up to the front door of her
parents' house and lightning didn't strike.*

*And then he kissed her. And she thought maybe she'd
been wrong about the lightning, because the moment his
lips touched hers, something jolted through her system
and singed her right down to her toes.*

And with that first kiss, he'd completely swept her
off her feet.

Of course, Penny still hadn't believed anything more
would ever come of it. Or maybe it was more accurate
to say she hadn't dared let herself hope anything would
come of it. Because although his kiss had awakened
every hormone in her body, it was still just a kiss. Sure,
no one had ever kissed her with such tenderness and
passion before, but she was certain Jason Foley had
kissed a thousand women in just the same way.

Okay, maybe not a *thousand,* but the man did have
something of a reputation. And he'd dated a *lot* of
women. Glamorous and sophisticated women. And
while Penny knew she wasn't the ugly stepsister—how
could she be when she looked exactly like her twin?—
her innate shyness frequently relegated her to the shadows behind her fabulous and outgoing sister.

When she didn't hear from Jason the next day, she
wasn't surprised. Obviously, he'd been bored at the
wedding and was simply toying with her.

But the day after that he *did* call, and he invited her
to grab a cup of coffee. She had been as excited as she

was surprised by the invitation, and happily agreed. Somehow, coffee had led to dinner. And during that first dinner, all of her preconceived notions about him—and about herself—went flying out the window.

And so began their relationship.

She'd had boyfriends before—she wasn't a complete neophyte when it came to dating. But she'd never had a relationship that made her feel so good about who she was, and so optimistic about the future. She had never felt anything like she felt when she was with Jason.

With every date, every touch and every kiss, she fell a little bit deeper and harder for the handsome executive. It wasn't just flattering to have a man like Jason Foley interested in her, it was mind-boggling. But Penny had been too thrilled that he was, to question why.

For the first time in her life, she hadn't been the "youngest daughter" or someone's "sister" or "Paige's twin"—she'd been her own person. She'd been the woman Jason Foley chose to be with.

The only factor that took some of the shine off her happy glow was that she couldn't tell anyone they were dating. She didn't dare.

Growing up in Devon McCord's home meant that "Foley" was a taboo F-word, so she'd kept their relationship a secret.

Until one night at dinner, frustrated by the patronizing attitudes of her family, she blurted out the truth. Even then, she wasn't sure anyone believed her relationship with Jason was serious, and—in retrospect—the doubts had been well founded.

But Penny had romanticized the obstacles she and Jason faced, believing they were star-crossed lovers, like Romeo and Juliet. But she'd trusted that their attraction was stronger than the influence of their respective families, stronger than a silly old feud.

Then she learned that their entire relationship had been fuelled by that feud, by Jason's determination to ensure that the Foleys finally bested the McCords. She'd been falling in love and he'd been digging for information.

And still, it seemed as if she'd learned nothing from the experience. Because all it took was a look, a touch, a kiss, and she was like putty in his hands, willing to forget everything he'd done and give him another chance.

But another chance for what? To break her heart? Or to be a father to their baby? Because if he wanted to be part of their baby's life, then he would inevitably be part of her life, too. And how the heck was she supposed to deal with that?

She should hate him. She *wanted* to hate him.

But in her heart, she couldn't forget how wonderful he'd been.

Maybe it had all been an act, but her heart wasn't entirely convinced. Deep inside, she clung to the belief that if all he'd wanted from her was information, he could have found out what she knew—which was actually nothing—over the occasional cup of coffee. But the first cup of coffee had led to an invitation to dinner, and dinner had led to more kissing, and maybe she was guilty of having her head in the clouds, but she was pretty sure she would have remembered if he'd been asking about diamonds and querying her on the McCord finances while they were naked together.

And that was what she kept coming back to, the hope

that refused to die, the belief that, regardless of Jason's motives, he had grown to care about her.

Or maybe she *was* as pathetically naive as everyone believed her to be.

Although Jason had cursed—loudly and creatively—while he'd been making plans to go to Denver to untangle a mess that had been left behind by the now-departed VP, he realized that a few days away would give him the time and distance he needed to really think about Penny's pregnancy and make plans for their future.

If he wasn't quite ready to be a father, he knew he had no one but himself to blame, and that he obviously should have given the matter some thought before he got naked with Penny. Not that he'd simply disregarded the use of birth control. No way—he was smarter than that.

Unfortunately, he was *not* smart enough to realize that when a woman with decidedly less experience assured him that she was "safe," they might be thinking different things. And he was *not* smart enough to have known that when she hesitated before saying she didn't sleep around, what she really meant was that she'd never been with a man before.

And despite this miscommunication, he was the villain because he'd seduced sweet, innocent Penny McCord.

Okay, so she was sweet—probably the sweetest woman he'd ever known.

And she had been innocent.

She'd also been willing and eager, sexy and seductive, and incredibly and passionately responsive…

After weeks of long late-night telephone conversations and occasional stolen moments when Jason was in Dallas, he'd finally convinced Penny to come to Houston for a weekend. He told her about a new dance club that had opened up and that he was anxious to check out, and how he really hoped she would go with him. When she'd hesitated, he hastened to assure her that he had a guest room in his penthouse, and she'd finally agreed.

It was nearly eight o'clock when the doorman called to tell him that he had a guest. While Penny was riding the elevator to the twenty-second floor, Jason uncorked the chardonnay he'd chilled and poured two glasses. They would have a drink, nibble on the fruit and cheese he'd set out, share some conversation, then head out around ten.

His plan flew out the door when he opened it and saw her standing there.

He'd always known she was attractive. Though she had a tendency to downplay her natural prettiness, there was no disguising the luster of her long red-gold hair or the sparkle in her deep green eyes. But in the little black dress that was more little than dress, with her hair spilling down her back in wildly spiraling curls, she wasn't downplaying anything tonight. In fact, her mile-long legs were shown to full advantage in the short skirt and sexy heels that brought her five-foot-eight-inch frame to a height that nearly matched his own, putting that slick, glossy mouth in direct line with his.

"I opened a bottle of wine," he said, finally recovering enough to speak. "But you look as if you're ready to go."

"Wine would be nice." She took the glass from his hand, lifted it to her lips. She sipped, then traced her tongue over her lower lip. "Yes, very nice."

He swallowed hard as two thoughts battled for su-

premacy inside his addled brain: "what happened to sweet Penny McCord?" and "how soon could he get her naked?"

"Are you hungry?" he asked. "Because we could go out for a bite before we head to the club."

He hadn't forgotten about the fruit and cheese, he just figured it would be smarter to go out to eat, to leave the penthouse. Now. Or they might not leave at all.

He didn't know if she read his mind or if she simply wanted the same thing he did, because she said, "Actually, I was thinking that maybe we could stay in."

"Oh. Well." He sounded like an idiot, but he found it difficult to form words with his tongue tied in knots. "I thought you wanted to go to the club."

"I thought you could give me a tour of your place...including the guest room I have no intention of sleeping in."

Well, he didn't need to be hit over the head. Not more than once, anyway.

He took the forgotten glass of wine from her hand and set it aside, then he reached for her.

They came together, hearts pounding, mouths fusing, bodies straining.

It was crazy. Even while it was happening, he knew it was crazy. He hadn't been so desperately aroused since...he didn't even know since when. Probably since he was in tenth grade and Nadia Sinclair let him unfasten her bra, beginning a lifelong fascination with female breasts.

As his mouth fastened over Penny's tight nipple through the fabric of her dress, he couldn't help but think that Nadia had nothing on Penny McCord. And then he wasn't thinking about anything but Penny.

Somehow, they made it down the hall to his bedroom. Her dress was on the floor, along with a couple of pieces of skimpy satin and lace that probably deserved more attention than he'd paid to them in the few seconds it took him to strip them away. But he paid a great deal of attention to the long, lean, completely naked and very sexy body that was stretched out across his king-size mattress.

They'd been moving toward this moment for weeks. But even so, he hadn't expected to be so frantic and needy. And if her moans and sighs were any indication, she was as desperate for their joining as he was. He shed the last of his clothes and joined her on the bed. Her arms came around him, drawing him close, closer.

He was teetering on the edge of no return when he pulled back. His breathing was harsh and ragged, his body screaming for release inside of her.

Her eyes flickered, opened, revealing that deep green, dark with desire, clouded with confusion.

"What's wrong?"

What was wrong was that he wanted to plunge inside her hot, wet body more than he wanted to take his next breath, but caution—or maybe it was a finely honed self-protection instinct—had managed to pierce the sexual haze that clouded his brain.

"I wasn't prepared for this," he admitted, inwardly cursing himself for the oversight. But he'd never expected things to go so far so fast. Yeah, he had plans for the weekend, and he'd hoped those plans would lead to this moment. But not before he had a chance

to stop at the pharmacy, which he was going to do on the way home from the club. Except that they'd never gone out to the club, and he'd never expected to want her so much.

"Please tell me you have some protection?" It was a plea, heartfelt and desperate.

She blinked, uncomprehending.

"Condoms," he clarified.

She shook her head, then ventured, hesitantly. "I don't...sleep around, Jason. I'm...safe."

Which he'd assumed to mean that she was on the pill or using the patch or some other form of birth control. And since he hadn't had unprotected sex in more than a decade because he cared more about his long-term health than short-term gratification, he trusted that he wasn't putting her at risk....

Obviously, he'd been wrong. And while the details had yet to be determined, the one thing Jason knew for certain was that the baby Penny carried meant they were now bound together in ways he never intended.

He'd always expected that he would marry and become a father someday, and though he hadn't expected it to happen so soon, he wasn't bothered by the acceleration of his plans. After all, it wasn't as if he'd been waiting to fall in love. No, he'd been there, done that, and had no intention of repeating that painful experience again. But he did care about Penny, and he was confident they could have a good life together.

Of course, the biggest challenge would be in convincing Penny to marry him. He'd seen the look on her face when his father mentioned a wedding date, and he knew she wouldn't want to get married simply because she was pregnant.

But a baby needed two parents—he didn't think that belief was old-fashioned so much as it was practical. And he wanted to be involved in every aspect of his child's life, which meant being there when his child went to bed at night and when he or she woke up in the morning. He was a little less enthused about the prospect of midnight feedings and dirty diapers, but he was willing to share those responsibilities, too.

In fact, he was willing to do almost anything to make Penny his bride.

Anything but open up his heart to a woman who already meant more to him than he'd ever intended.

Chapter Six

Penny picked up the raw piece of McCordite and turned it over in her hand, watching the subtle shift of shimmery colors. It was a truly unique gem, and she was thrilled to have the chance to play with it, to experiment with designs and metals to show it to full advantage.

Images swirled through her mind like pictures on a carousel. Her pieces would be the latest rage, worn by the wealthiest women with the most discriminating tastes: the wives of old fortunes and new entrepreneurs, the mistresses of European royalty, the names that topped Hollywood's A-list.

She never lacked for inspiration in her designs, and she could already picture elegant pendants and jewel-studded chokers, dangling earrings and thick, chunky bracelets. There was so much she could and would do with the stone, but her first task—and undoubtedly the most difficult one—was her sister's engagement ring.

It was part of her usual process to meet with a customer prior to the design of a custom piece. She believed it was important for a gift of jewelry to reflect something of the person who would wear it, of the relationship between the gift giver and the recipient.

She shouldn't have to interview her sister or have her sister's fiancé complete a questionnaire, but she couldn't deny that she was…well, *blocked* seemed the most appropriate word for what she was feeling. She was trying—really she was—but every time she closed her eyes and envisioned Travis sliding the ring on Paige's finger, her own eyes filled with tears, blurring the image, so that the inspiration she sought remained elusive.

It was shamefully obvious to Penny that she was envious of her sister. She was genuinely happy for Paige, thrilled that her dreams were coming true. And though she didn't know Travis well, it was readily apparent that he adored Paige. Yes, Penny was happy for them—even if, right now, she was feeling absolutely miserable, because she so desperately wanted what they had found.

She set the rock back on her desk and wiped at the tears that had overflowed and slid down her cheeks. She wasn't a crier, not usually, but lately it seemed as if the littlest thing could set off the waterworks. She knew it was the pregnancy that was responsible for her hormones being so completely out of whack, but that knowledge didn't assuage the ache in her heart.

The ring of the phone jolted her back to the present,

and she grabbed for the receiver, grateful for the reprieve from the dangerously seductive memories—until she heard Jason's voice on the other end.

"I just wanted to give you the number of my hotel in Denver," he told her. "In case you needed to get in touch with me while I'm away."

She waved a hand in front of her face, trying to cool her suddenly heated skin. Yeah, those pregnancy hormones were definitely running rampant, when just the sound of his voice made everything inside her quiver.

"I'm not going to need to get in touch with you," she assured him, her tone carefully neutral. "And if I did, I have your cell number."

"Oh. Right."

"So why did you really call, Jason?"

"Would you believe I just wanted to hear the sound of your voice?"

"No."

His voice dropped, the low, intimate tone sending shivers down her spine. "I have missed you, Penny."

She steeled herself against the weakness that washed through her. She didn't know what game he was playing now, but she wasn't playing it with him. Not this time. "You saw me yesterday."

"I wish you were here with me now," he said. "Just the two of us."

She closed her eyes and tried to ignore the seductive words, reminding herself that it had never really been just the two of them—that Jason's hidden agenda had always been with them. "I have to go."

"Wait, Penny. Please—"

She couldn't wait, because she didn't trust herself not to respond to the plea in his voice.

Instead, she hung up on him.

Jason stared at the buzzing receiver in his hand.

She'd actually hung up on him.

His first response was disbelief, then annoyance, which was ultimately followed by relief. Because he knew that Penny wouldn't have disconnected so abruptly unless she was feeling confused and uncertain, unless she was worried that he might talk her into something she didn't want to be talked into. Something like…*marriage?*

Not that she was a pushover by any stretch of the imagination, and not that he'd ever had to talk her into anything. In fact, looking back on their brief relationship, he was hard-pressed to determine who'd been the pursuer and who'd been pursued. Yes, he'd been the one to approach her at the Harcourt-Ellsworth wedding, and he'd been the one to initiate the follow-up contact a couple of days later. But ultimately, she was the one who had seduced him.

Not that he'd resisted her seduction. Why would he, when he'd wanted her as much as she'd obviously wanted him? But the forthrightness and the passion she'd demonstrated that first night in Houston had created a sensual fog around his brain that kept him in the dark about a couple of key points—most notably that she was a virgin and that when she'd assured him she was "safe," she hadn't been referring to birth control.

That was the night their baby was conceived. He was certain of it, because he'd made a trip to the pharmacy the next morning. And though he'd resented the barrier he'd purposely put between them every time they made love thereafter, he'd never balked at doing so, because he didn't want to put her at risk.

Obviously, his precautions had been too little too late. And now…

He blew out a breath as he pulled out a suitcase and began to pack for his trip.

Now he couldn't blame her for being angry and wary.

He was the one who should have known better. He should have taken more care. And he should have let her know how much he cared, before everything blew up in his face.

Penny ignored the ringing phone. She didn't want to talk to Jason or about Jason or her baby, and she just wished everyone would leave her alone until she figured out what she was going to do.

If she had a choice, she would cut all ties with Jason Foley. But while she recognized that might give her a certain amount of satisfaction in the short term, it was hardly a viable solution for the long term. Because, as hurt and angry as she was over his treatment of her, there was a much more important consideration: her baby.

Jason's baby.

Her hand automatically went to her tummy, to the slight swelling that was already evident there, proof of the tiny life growing inside of her.

All of the pregnancy info she'd read on the Internet claimed that first pregnancies usually didn't start showing until the second trimester. Of course, most women lost a few pounds in the early months as a result of morning sickness, but Penny hadn't experienced any nausea, except when she was hungry.

So it seemed that she'd been eating almost constantly, and instead of the three to five pounds she should have put on by this stage of her pregnancy, she'd put on three *plus* five pounds. It was enough that she might have wondered if she was farther along in her pregnancy than the fourteen weeks she'd assumed, except that she'd been a virgin until fourteen weeks ago.

Because Penny was healthy and in good physical condition, the doctor had been surprised but not overly concerned, though she did warn the expectant mother to be careful as to how she satisfied her hunger. Apparently, chocolate chip cookie dough ice cream wasn't a pregnancy-approved breakfast food.

And now, here she was, eight pounds heavier, twenty-six years old, unmarried and pregnant.

Well, she could change the "unmarried" part if she wanted to. But Penny didn't want to marry a man who only wanted to marry her because he felt responsible. Maybe she'd been naive and idealistic to dream of falling in love and being loved in return, but she wasn't ready to give up on those dreams yet.

She felt the tears well up again and tried to blink them away. She'd never cried so much as she'd cried since the phone call from Paige that had decimated all of her hopes for a future with Jason. Because the future he was offering her now wasn't the one she wanted.

This time, when the phone started to ring, she glanced at the call display, frowning at the unfamiliar number. Even the area code wasn't one that she recognized. Out of state, she assumed, and the pieces clicked into place. Jason was in Denver. He called three times already from his cell phone—a number that she recogized—and she'd opted not to answer any of those calls. She just wasn't ready to talk to him, and she wasn't going to let him badger her into doing what he wanted when she still didn't have a clue what she wanted.

The phone finally stopped ringing when the answering machine picked up, and Penny held her breath, waiting. There was a pause, then a click, as the caller hung up without leaving a message.

She left her room and made her way to the kitchen.

Though she still lived at home and still slept in the same room she'd occupied while growing up, she'd never felt the urge to move out on her own, the need to experience greater freedom and independence. Maybe because her mother had always seemed to respect her space and never imposed unreasonable rules or curfews. Or maybe because the house was big enough that ten people could coexist peacefully without tripping over one another.

It occurred to her that she might have to rethink her living arrangements now that she was going to have a baby of her own. But right now she wasn't going to worry about anything, except what to have for dinner.

The phone in the kitchen was ringing when she made her way there, the same number showing on the display. Either Jason was trying to reach his father now or hoping to catch her on the main line. She waited for the ringing to stop, then took the receiver off the hook so she could have her dinner in peace.

She took a moment to study the contents of the refrigerator. As always, it was well stocked, but nothing really appealed to her. She opened the freezer, hoping for better prospects there, and found a tub of her favorite chocolate chip cookie dough ice cream.

She'd had the strangest cravings since she'd gotten pregnant—most notably, wanting ice cream at eight o'clock in the morning, every morning, salt and vinegar chips during a morning coffee break, oatmeal raisin cookies in the afternoon. Spinach salad was another new favorite, and while that was at least healthy, she didn't seem to be eating enough of it to counteract the effects of all the junk food. In fact, her pants were already feeling a little snug around the waist.

After only a few spoonfuls of the ice cream, she forced herself to put the tub back in the freezer and take out a box of fettuccine Alfredo with chicken and broccoli. Though JoBeth, the McCords longtime housekeeper, frowned on prepackaged meals of any kind, she did keep a stock of them in the freezer for Paige and Penny, for the nights she was off, of which tonight was one. It wasn't that the sisters couldn't cook, it was just that they rarely bothered to do so.

Penny nuked the pasta in its box, then dumped it into a bowl and sat down at the table. She was just finishing up her dinner when she heard footsteps in the hall. Since Eleanor had gone on a business trip with her new husband, and Paige had been staying with Travis at the ranch, Penny figured she had the house to herself.

She was surprised—but also grateful—when Paige came through the door. She could always count on her twin to distract her from her worries; and right now, she desperately needed a distraction from thoughts of Jason.

"I didn't really believe you were unconscious on the kitchen floor or trapped under a heavy piece of furniture," Paige said to her.

"Sorry to disappoint you," Penny said.

"Of course, I wouldn't have had to come all the way over here to prove it if you'd answered the phone."

"Did you call?"

"I tried, but the line was busy—" Paige arched a brow as she replaced the receiver on the wall "—and your cell went right to voice mail."

"I didn't want to talk to anyone," Penny said, feeling more than a little guilty at the thought that her sister had left her fiancé to check on her. "Did you come from the ranch?"

"I should let you think that I did," Paige said. "But I was coming into town anyway for an early meeting tomorrow."

"So why are you giving me such a hard time?"

"Because Jason has been trying to get in touch with you all day," her sister told her. "He was worried."

"Worried that I won't fall into line with what he wants," Penny muttered.

"You're pregnant," Paige said, as if Penny needed to be reminded of the fact. "You weren't answering your phone. Mom and Rex are out of town and JoBeth's not here. Is it so unbelievable that the father of your child might be concerned about you?"

"Is it so unbelievable that I might have been busy? Maybe I had errands to run—or went to see a movie."

"For five hours?"

Penny felt another twinge of guilt as she realized the

first call she'd ignored had come more than five hours earlier, but her willingness to talk to Jason hadn't changed in the time that had passed since then. "Maybe I had errands and then went to a movie."

Paige's cell rang and she flipped it open. "Yeah, I found her," she spoke into the phone. "Relatively unscathed. So far."

Penny deliberately tuned her out and dumped her empty pasta bowl in the sink. "If you only came over here to nag me, you can go now," she said, when Paige had ended her call.

Her sister sighed. "I know you're dealing with a lot of stuff right now—"

"Not really a lot," Penny denied. "Just one really big thing."

"I can't imagine what you're going through," her sister admitted. "But if there's anything I can do, or even if you just want to talk, you know I'm here for you."

"I do know, but there isn't anything. Unless you want to run interference and keep Jason out of my life while I figure things out?"

"Honey, I'm not sure even a bulldozer could keep Jason out of your life—or that it's a good idea."

"You never liked the idea of me dating him in the first place."

"That was before you got pregnant."

"You like him better now that you know he knocked me up?"

Paige rolled her eyes. "I'm just acknowledging that he is the father of your baby. And since he doesn't seem to be running from that responsibility, maybe you should give him a chance."

"A chance to do what? Stomp all over my heart again?"

"A chance to make things right."

"As if."

"You have every right to be angry and upset," Paige said. "But you're going to have to get past what he did for the sake of your child."

"I know," Penny agreed. "But it's not just that he used me or lied about his reasons for being with me."

"There's more?"

Penny nodded and went back to the freezer for the ice cream. She'd had the pasta, and there were even vegetables in it, and now the baby wanted ice cream. But she did get two spoons and gave one to her sister.

"I don't have a lot of experience with such situations, obviously, but when I told Jason that I was pregnant, I expected that he would try to deny it, or run from the room in a panic."

"Those would be typical male responses to news of an unplanned pregnancy," her sister agreed, dipping her own spoon into the tub.

"But not Jason's response," she told Paige. "As soon as I told him I was going to have his baby, he was immediately and completely focused on that. Okay, there was a moment—a flash of panic, or maybe it was horror in his eyes—but then it was gone and he was wanting to discuss options and make plans. I mean, I've had almost five weeks to accept it and my head is still reeling, but after five *minutes,* he's ready to calmly and rationally discuss our options."

"You're thinking he's a control freak like Dad," Paige guessed.

Penny nodded again.

"I can see why you'd be wary," her sister said. "We saw firsthand how Dad tried to control everyone. Not just Mom, but all of us. He was as ruthless in his personal relationships as he was in his business dealings, willing to do anything and everything to get what he wanted."

"Jason slept with me to get information about our family."

"I'm not going to deny that's true—how can I, when I was the one who found out what he was doing? But I am going to add a proviso to that."

"A proviso?" Penny managed to smile.

"Honey, whatever his reasons for taking you to his bed, he couldn't have faked what happened in that bed. And the fact that a man who is usually so cool and controlled overlooked something as basic as birth control—even on one occasion—tells me that he got a little carried away. And I assure you, that had nothing to do with the Santa Magdalena Diamond."

"The sex was good," Penny admitted, deciding it wasn't the time to enlighten her sister that she might have misled him on the subject of birth control, albeit inadvertently. Then she sighed. "Really good."

Paige grinned. "Then I'd have to say that some things do run in the family."

"Is that why you're marrying Travis?"

"I'm marrying Travis because he's the most incredible man I've ever known. But good sex is certainly a factor in that."

"Except that good sex is all Jason and I had," Penny reminded her. "Everything else was a lie."

"I'm not telling you to give the guy another chance," Paige said. "Only you can decide if you want to do that.

But I am going to remind you that there's more at stake now than just you and Jason."

She nodded. "Believe me, I'm thinking about the baby. I've hardly been able to think about anything else. But I didn't think that Jason might be worried, and I'm sorry you had to come all the way over here to check on me."

"I was planning on coming back anyway," her sister admitted. "I'm meeting with Blake in the morning to talk about the unveiling of the diamond."

Penny latched on to the change of topic gratefully. "Do you think that showcasing the diamond will be enough to turn things around for the McCords?"

"I know it will get customers in the door," Paige said. "After that, it's your designs that will do the rest."

"Speaking of designs, I have an engagement ring to work on in the morning, so I should get some sleep."

"Since I'm very excited to see what you come up with for that engagement ring, I'll let you." Paige kissed her cheek. "Sweet dreams, Penny."

But as she left her sister in the kitchen with the ice cream, Penny hoped she wouldn't dream at all. Because lately, all of her dreams seemed to focus on Jason.

Chapter Seven

Foley Industries had a corporate jet, and Jason had always felt that one of the biggest perks of being COO of the company was being able to avoid the usual headaches and hassles of commercial travel. Unfortunately, it was only one jet, and on rare occasions when it was in use elsewhere, he was forced to fly with a public carrier. First class, of course, but still…

His trip to Denver was one of those times. Thankfully, it wasn't a very long flight, and he had his Black-Berry and his laptop so he could work throughout the journey. Or at least pretend to work, while his thoughts were on Penny and the baby they were going to have.

Now that he was on his way home, he was anxious to see her, to plead his case in person and make plans for their future.

It took a few minutes before the baby's cries penetrated his thoughts, but once he became aware of them, nothing seemed to block them out.

He'd seen the mother in line at the check-in counter. She'd had a rolling suitcase in one hand, a three- or four-year-old child holding the other and a baby who couldn't have been more than a few months old in a sling across her chest. And he'd said a silent prayer of thanks that she wasn't waiting for the executive check-in.

But the curtain that separated first class from coach wasn't much of a sound barrier, and once he'd tuned into the baby's crying, he couldn't tune it out. In fact, after a few minutes it seemed to be growing louder, as if the baby was coming nearer.

Probably just his own impending parenthood playing games with his imagination, or so he thought, until the flight attendant moved briskly past him. He heard her, a few rows behind him, ask in a slightly impatient tone, "Can I help you?"

"My son needs to use the bathroom," a decidedly harried female voice replied.

"There are two lavatories at the rear of the plane," the attendant informed her, standing guard against any intrusion.

"I'm aware of that," the frazzled mother said through gritted teeth. "But they're both occupied, and a three-and-a-half year-old doesn't have fabulous bladder control, so unless you want to deal with that kind of mess, you'll please let me come through…"

With a resigned sigh, the attendant held back the curtain for the woman and her children to pass.

"Isn't there anything you can do to settle her down?" the flight attendant wanted to know.

Her question almost made Jason smile. The young woman clearly had even less experience with babies than he did, which was saying something. Because, aside from his niece, Olivia, who was now six years old, and whose diaper he'd changed exactly once way back when she was still wearing diapers, his experience was nonexistent.

"The switch is inside her diaper. As soon as I can get to it, I'll turn her off."

The flight attendant's mouth tightened, even as Jason's lips curved.

But the mother's troubles were not over, as she couldn't maneuver into the narrow bathroom with the baby.

"Mommy." The little boy's urgency was apparent.

She glanced around, anxiously searching for an answer to her dilemma. Most of the seats in executive class were occupied on this flight, and most of the occupants were busy with their laptops or their newspapers, or otherwise pretending they didn't even see the woman who had dared venture into their midst.

Her eyes locked on Jason's. He should have looked away, but she was obviously desperate and the flight attendant wasn't going to be any help, and while he wouldn't say he had a sudden paternal urge, he did hear himself say, "Do you need a hand?"

"Yeah. For just a minute. If you don't mind." And with that, she dropped the squawking red-faced baby in his lap and ducked into the bathroom behind the little boy.

"Well."

Jason looked down at the infant, who looked back at him with the biggest, bluest, tear-drenched eyes he had ever seen. Of course, the baby didn't respond to his comment. In fact, he guessed she didn't even hear it as she hadn't stopped screaming, except for the briefest fraction of a second and only then to draw more air into her lungs.

She squirmed, kicking her chubby little legs and flailing her pudgy arms and generally letting him know that she wasn't comfortable being held at arms' length on a stranger's knee. So Jason lifted her up against his shoulder, awkwardly patting her back with his free hand as he vaguely recalled having done with Olivia.

The baby stopped squirming, hiccupped twice, then let out an enormous belch, and spewed a gallon of something disgusting and smelly all over his suit jacket.

On the plus side, she did stop crying.

As much as Penny wanted to believe she could make her own decisions and figure out her plans, she didn't think it would hurt to talk to someone who had been in the same position she found herself in now.

Eleanor and Rex had returned late the night before, and Penny tracked her mother down in the library, where she was lounging on the sofa with a new book by her favorite author.

Eleanor looked up and, seeing her daughter hovering in the doorway, immediately put her book aside.

"How was your trip?" Penny asked.

"Fabulous," Eleanor said. "I've always loved San Francisco, and seeing a favorite city with someone you love…well, it just makes the experience even better."

"Where's Rex today?"

Her mother pouted. "He had to go to Houston for a meeting. Apparently being independently wealthy hasn't eradicated his desire to work every day—to feel useful, he says. Not that I really mind, it's just that after so many years apart, I don't want to miss out on another, single moment together."

Penny didn't know what to say to that. She had no experience with that type of all-consuming emotion, and circumstances being what they were, she wasn't likely to get any.

"But now you're here," Eleanor said, "which is just as good, because we haven't had a chance to chat, just the two of us, in a long time."

"I did want to talk to you," Penny admitted. "And then I wasn't sure if I should."

"Talk about Jason, you mean."

She nodded. "I know it must be awkward for you, since you're married to his father now."

"I was your mother first," Eleanor said. "And I'll always be your mother."

"It's a little strange, isn't it, that there was such distance between the two families for so long, and now you and Rex are married, Paige and Travis are engaged and I'm having Jason's baby."

"There have been a lot of big changes, but I'm happy that the feud is finally at an end."

Penny plucked at an imaginary thread on her sweater. "I'm worried that this…situation…with Jason and me might stir things up again."

"Don't," her mother said. "The situation with you and Jason has nothing to do with anyone but you and Jason. Although I am curious to know if you've decided what you're going to tell him when he gets back from Denver?"

"Tell him about what?"

"His proposal."

Penny frowned. "If you could call it a proposal. And how did you know about that anyway?"

"Rex, of course."

Penny should have guessed that Jason would tell his father, and that Jason's father would tell his wife. But when Penny and Jason had first gotten involved, there weren't so many family ties, and now she couldn't help but feel as if all the connections were tying her hands.

"So," Eleanor prompted, "are you going to say 'yes'?"

"No."

Her mother frowned, obviously disappointed.

"We're going to have a baby," Penny said gently. "But we were never really 'together'—you know Jason was only using me to get information on our search for the diamond."

Eleanor's frown deepened. "He may have had ulterior motives in the beginning, but I'm sure that once he got to know you, his intentions changed."

"Why are you sure of that? Because Rex said so?"

"Because the man who subjected himself to the wrath of two families by announcing your pregnancy at Thanksgiving dinner wouldn't have done so if he didn't intend to stick around for the fallout."

"I don't know what he intended," Penny admitted. "And even if he told me his intentions, how could I believe him? I was dating him for the better part of two months, and the whole time I honestly thought we had something special, that he cared. Now I know it was all a lie."

"I think he does care. And if you worked at building a life together, that caring would grow."

"I can't believe you're suggesting that I even think about marrying him," Penny said. "Especially after you spent thirty years trapped in a marriage to a man you didn't love."

"There's a big difference in the two situations."

"How do you figure that?"

"I was in love with someone else when I married your father," her mother reminded her gently.

"With Rex," Penny said.

Eleanor nodded. "I fell in love with him when I was sixteen years old and I never stopped loving him."

Penny was pleased that her mother had found happiness with her new husband, but there was still a question nagging at the back of her mind, one that had been there ever since she'd learned that Eleanor and Rex were teenage sweethearts finally reunited. "Did you never love Daddy?"

Her mother thought about the question for a long moment before answering.

"Devon had a lot of wonderful qualities," she finally said. "And I often thought that I might have fallen in love with him if I'd known him first. But later I was too busy resenting him for the circumstances that forced me into a marriage I didn't want and wasn't ready to appreciate the man that he was."

"And yet, you want to force me into a marriage with Jason."

Eleanor shook her head. "I don't want to force you into anything," she denied. "In fact, I want you to do what I didn't—to follow your heart."

Jason saw the mother from the plane again at baggage claim. Lindsay Conners she'd told him her name was, in the midst of her embarrassed and profuse apologies and offers to give him money for dry cleaning. Jason had declined, of course, simply removing the jacket and, folding it to cover the milky vomit, tucking it into his carry-on bag.

The baby was back in the sling over the mother's shoulder and, if not asleep, at least quiet. She found her suitcase and dragged it off of the luggage carousel, and when she turned, her eyes went wide, darting around the crowd of bodies and bags, frantically looking for something else. Or someone else, Jason realized, spotting the little boy over by the luggage carts where he'd set himself up with his coloring books and crayons.

In two quick strides, Jason was by her side, pointing her toward her son. "Over there."

"Oh, thank God." Her breath shuddered out, her eyes immediately filling with tears of gratitude and relief.

"Actually, my name's Jason," he told her.

She managed a laugh. "Thank you, Jason. I told him to stay put, but, well, I tell him a lot of things he doesn't seem to hear these days."

Jason lifted his bag off of the carousel and followed her over to where the little boy was coloring.

"Do you have kids?" she asked him.

"No," he said. "Not yet. But that will change in about six months."

"That would explain the I-want-to-help-but-don't-have-a-clue look on your face on the plane."

He winced. "Was I that transparent?"

"Yes, but you were still my savior," she told him.

"Any words of advice for a first-time dad-to-be?"

"Yeah, don't leave your wife at home with the kids

you claimed meant the world to you while you take off to Cozumel with your twenty-two-year-old secretary."

"I'm guessing it wasn't a business trip."

"The only business he ever thinks about these days is avoidance of family responsibilities. Now I'm scrambling to get back into the workplace after he urged me to give up my job to stay at home with the children." She sighed as she finished packing away the thick crayons. "I'm sorry. I didn't mean to go off on you. You just picked a bad time to be nice."

"I don't believe there's ever a bad time to be nice."

She managed to smile in response to that. "Well, thank you again for your help, Jason."

"Foley," he said. "Jason Foley."

"I thought you looked familiar," she said. "I used to work for your brother, Zane. It feels like a lifetime ago." She glanced pointedly at the little boy and then her baby. "Actually two lifetimes ago."

"How long did you work for Zane?"

"I was his executive assistant for four years. But like I said, it was a long time ago."

He handed her a business card. "When you get settled, give me a call."

"I appreciate the offer, Mr. Foley, but I don't need your charity."

"I'm not offering you charity, I'm offering you a job. You wouldn't have lasted four years as my brother's executive assistant if you couldn't manage people or handle pressure."

"Well, when you put it that way." She took the card. "I may be proud, but I'm not stupid."

That should have been the end of it, but Jason found

himself thinking about her long after he left the airport—or not Lindsay Conners so much as her situation. He didn't know how she managed on her own, or how Penny would manage on her own if she insisted on doing it that way. He knew that single mothers were hardly an anomaly in the current day and age, but he wondered why a woman would choose to go it alone if she didn't have to.

He could understand a wife booting her cheating husband to the curb, but he would never be unfaithful to the woman he chose to marry. He believed strongly in the sanctity of marriage and would neither commit nor forgive any infidelity. Of course, Penny didn't know him well enough to be sure of that, and recent revelations hadn't painted him in the most favorable light, but he figured he could prove himself over the next fifty or sixty years of their marriage.

Except that he still hadn't quite figured out how to get her to agree to the marriage.

When she left her mother in the library, Penny was feeling more confused than ever.

Follow her heart?

That's exactly what she'd thought she was doing when she made the decision to have her baby on her own. She didn't need a husband, and she sure as heck didn't need Jason Foley.

Except that Jason wanted to be a father to their baby, and she knew she couldn't refuse that. Still, there was a lot of ground between coparenting and cohabiting with legal ties.

But now even Paige was pressuring her to get back

together with Jason, so they could raise their child together. Of course, her sister was blissfully in love and wanted everyone else to be, too.

At least Blake seemed to be firmly ensconced in her corner, insisting that Penny shouldn't feel pressured to get married simply because she was pregnant. Of course, he had his own reasons for taking that position.

Only Tate had seemed neutral on the subject of her pregnancy. On the other hand, Penny hadn't really had an opportunity to talk to him about it, either.

But Penny wouldn't let herself be swayed by anyone else's thoughts and opinions. She already loved the child growing inside of her and would ultimately make a decision based on what was best for that child. And even though her relationship with Jason hadn't been everything she'd wanted it to be, she would never regret a single moment of the time she spent with him, because he had given her the greatest gift she could ever imagine in the baby growing inside her womb.

Jason was tired when he got home, and not particularly happy to find his father waiting in his living room.

"What are you doing here?"

"Your doorman let me in," Rex told him.

"I didn't mean my living room," he clarified. "I meant Houston."

"I had a meeting that went late, so I thought I would crash here tonight and drive back to Dallas in the morning."

Jason didn't mind his father dropping by or planning to stay. What he minded was the third degree he knew he was going to get.

"I brought a six-pack and ordered pizza," Rex said.

"I ate on the plane." But he went to the fridge, grabbed a bottle of beer he didn't particularly want and twisted off the cap. "Why are you really here, Dad? Because if it's to tell me that I screwed up, I don't need that pointed out to me."

"You did screw up," Rex agreed. "But you can still fix it."

"I'm working on it."

"Then you do plan to marry Penny?"

Jason took a long swallow from his bottle. "Yes," he said. "As soon as I can convince the bride."

"Then you should be busy planning a wedding, because I've seen you work impossible business deals, and I know that if you want this badly enough, you'll find a way to make it happen."

"Penny seems a little…resistant…to the idea."

Rex frowned, as if that possibility had never occurred to him. "She was happy enough to date you for the past couple of months. Why wouldn't she be jumping at the chance to marry you?"

"Maybe because she knows she was manipulated and she's determined not to be manipulated any longer."

"There's a difference between manipulation and finesse."

Jason set his half-empty bottle on the counter and scrubbed a hand over his jaw. "I'm not going to manipulate or finesse her into doing something she doesn't want to do."

"Then make her see that it's something she wants."

"I hope it is," he told his father. "But I had a lot of time to think while I was in Denver, and the one thing I realized is that no one has the right to decide what's right for Penny except Penny—not you, not her mother or her sister and especially not me."

"Well, I'll be damned," Rex said softly. "You have real feelings for her, don't you?"

Jason scowled. "Of course I have feelings for her."

"Do you love her?"

"Why do I have to put a label on my feelings?"

Rex shook his head. "I would have expected all of your experience with women to have taught you a few things."

"What things?" Jason asked warily.

"That women are romantics. They like candlelight dinners and flowers and wine—okay, maybe skip the wine because of the baby. But make an effort, show her how you feel, tell her how you feel. Women like words, too."

"I'm not going to lie to her."

"Of course not," his father agreed. "After all, lying's what got you into this mess."

Jason would have said that having unprotected sex was what had gotten him into this mess, but then he realized his father was right. The "mess" wasn't Penny's unexpected pregnancy but their separation, and Jason was determined to fix it.

Chapter Eight

"Penny, hi."

She heard the surprise in Jason's voice and knew he'd expected her to ignore the call, as she'd ignored so many of his calls and e-mails and text messages over the past few weeks.

"Hello, Jason."

"I just wanted to touch base to let you know that I'm back from Denver."

"Did you have a good trip?" she asked politely, because she'd promised herself she would make an effort to have a civil conversation with him. She was still hurt and angry, but she knew she had to get over those feelings if they were going to work together for the sake of their baby.

"It was successful, at least from a business stand-point," he told her. "But it took longer than I expected, so now I have to go in to the office tomorrow."

"I work in retail," she reminded him. "I have no sympathy for anyone who complains about having to work an occasional Saturday."

"Are you working tomorrow?" he asked her.

"No," she admitted.

"Good, because I should be finished at the office by noon and I thought I might make the trip into Dallas after that, so that we could talk."

"Actually, I have plans for tomorrow," she told him.

"Oh." He managed to express both disappointment and skepticism in the single syllable.

She couldn't blame him for being skeptical, not after the way she'd been dodging him over the past several weeks. But she did have legitimate plans this time, as she explained, "Someone was considerate enough to give me a spa day, and I've booked it for tomorrow."

"Then I guess I shouldn't complain," he said.

"And I should say 'thank you'."

"You thought it was considerate, huh?"

She'd thought it was thoughtful and sweet, and she still remembered the note he sent via e-mail to her. The subject line had read simply *SPA-tacular,* and Penny had nearly deleted the message, assuming it was an unsolicited advertisement. Then she recognized Jason's e-mail address and curiosity had prompted her to read further.

Please contact Gina at SPA-tacular to schedule a day of pampering for yourself and a friend. My treat. Because I know I've been the cause of far too much stress in your life recently.

Enjoy,

Jason

"I did think it was considerate," she said now. "But that doesn't mean I forgive you."

"I know. And I don't blame you. I just wish—"

"Don't."

"Don't what?"

"Don't push," she said. "Let's just both be satisfied that we've managed to have a fairly civil conversation tonight."

"Okay," he agreed. "I won't push. But what would you say if I invited you to go for dinner tomorrow night after your spa day?"

"I'd say you were pushing."

"I take it that's a no?"

"That's a no," she confirmed.

"Then I'll say good night now, and maybe I'll talk to you tomorrow."

"Maybe," she agreed, but she was smiling a little when she said it.

Penny had never felt so pampered.

She knew what Jason was doing—softening her up so that she would be more amenable to his plans, which apparently included getting married so they could raise their baby together. And at the moment, she definitely felt like she was softening. She'd been buffed and polished and massaged and oiled so that her skin was like silk and her muscles were completely lax. But while she was definitely feeling appreciative of his efforts, she still had no intention of giving up her dreams and settling for a marriage of convenience.

"It's occurred to me," Paige said, lounging in a cushy leather chair identical to her sister's as they waited for the polish on their toenails to dry, "that maybe I was wrong about Jason."

Penny's brows lifted. "Or maybe being slathered in warm mud made you mellow."

"Maybe," Paige agreed. "I did like the mud. And the massage. But you have to give the guy points for thinking of it. I mean, what woman wouldn't want a man who is willing to pamper her like this?"

"*This* woman," Penny said firmly. "Because he didn't do it to be thoughtful and generous, although he can be both. He did it to score points."

Her sister raised her arms over her head. "Touchdown."

Penny picked up her glass of mineral water, sipped. "You're so juvenile."

"Youthful," Paige corrected, with a saucy grin.

"Juvenile," Penny said again.

Her twin stuck out her tongue, then she asked, "Have you given any more thought to his proposal?"

"How can you think I would even consider it, after everything he did?"

Paige was silent for a minute, no doubt remembering how furious and indignant she'd been when she'd learned about Jason's plans—and she wasn't the one he'd been sleeping with.

"Okay, I can understand why you'd be reluctant," she allowed.

"I'm not reluctant, I'm firmly opposed."

"Then you're stronger and braver than I am, because I'd find the idea of having a baby on my own a little daunting."

"Believe me, I'm daunted," Penny told her sister.

"I'm just not convinced that getting married for the sake of a baby would be anything less than a disaster."

"If the baby was the only reason you were getting married," Paige agreed. "But you and Jason had something good going. You were happy with him."

"I was oblivious."

"You were in love."

"I think my toes are dry," Penny said.

Paige reached over and covered her hand so that she couldn't get up and flee. "I know you, Penny. And you never would have slept with him unless you had pretty strong feelings for him. Those feelings don't just disappear because you want them to."

"I want *him* to disappear," she grumbled.

"I don't see that happening, either," her sister warned.

"I want…" Penny sighed, then finally admitted, "I want what you have with Travis."

"Why do you think you can't have that with Jason?"

"Because he doesn't love me."

"Did he say that he doesn't?"

"No, but he didn't say that he did, either."

"And even if he did, you wouldn't trust his motives at this point," Paige guessed.

She nodded.

"Well, no one would disagree that you have reason to be wary. On the other hand, without risk there is no reward."

But for Penny's bruised and battered heart, the risks were just too great.

When Jason went into work Saturday morning, his secretary was already at her desk. Since Barb rarely worked overtime and never worked weekends, he couldn't help but wonder why she was there.

"Coffee's on in your office, there's a fax on your desk from EDI Drilling and a pile of correspondence to be reviewed and signed so that I can get it into the mail before the post office closes today."

"Thank you," he said cautiously.

But his surprise must have been evident, because she said, "You can thank me with a bonus in my next paycheck."

Jason made a mental note to do that.

First things first, though. He poured himself a cup of coffee and glanced at the fax. It wasn't anything urgent, so he set it aside and directed his attention to the correspondence.

An hour later, he took the stack of letters out to Barb's desk. She was busy at the computer, and he took a moment to glance around at the assortment of photos that were taped around her work station. It was like a family history in pictures.

In a place of honor beside her computer was the photo of Barb and her husband, Ted, on their thirty-fifth wedding anniversary. Then there were photos of each of the three sons they had together: the eldest with his wife on their wedding day; the middle one in his military uniform; and the youngest in his cap and gown at his college graduation. Then there were the photos—at least half a dozen—of her new grandbaby.

Jason had no photos on his desk. Of course, there were no macaroni pencil holders or floppy stuffed elephants hanging over his computer monitor, either.

But as he moved closer to drop the papers on her

desk, he found his gaze again drawn to the anniversary photo.

"Thirty-five years," he mused, realizing—probably for the first time—that his secretary had been married for more years than he'd been alive.

Though Barb looked up from her computer screen, her fingers never stopped moving on the keys. "Did you say something, Mr. Foley?"

"I was just remarking on the fact that you've been married thirty-five years."

Her eyes moved automatically to the photo and her lips curved. "Actually, it's almost thirty-eight now."

Thirty-eight. His dad and his mom had barely shared half that number of years together before she died. He'd never known anyone who had been married—and apparently happily—for so long.

"Thirty-eight years ago, when you were exchanging your vows, did you know it would last?"

She stopped typing and swiveled in her chair to give him her full attention. "Of course," she said, then chuckled. "But I was nineteen years old and incredibly naive. I had no idea how hard it would be at times to make our marriage work.

"Had I known then what I know now…" She shook her head. "Let's just say I probably wouldn't have been so eager to rush down the aisle. On the other hand, I also wouldn't give up a single day that we've had together. I couldn't imagine my life without him."

"You're lucky," he said, "that your marriage succeeded when so many fail these days."

"Lucky?" The scorn in her voice left him in no doubt as to her opinion about that. "Luck has nothing to do with it. It's hard work and commitment that get you through the tough times. The reason so many marriages fail is that young people nowadays don't know what it means to stick it out through the tough times."

He was no stranger to hard work or commitment, and if he managed to convince Penny to marry him, he would stick it out. He had never walked away from his responsibilities and he sure as heck wouldn't walk away from his child.

"Why the sudden interest in my marriage?" Barb's gaze narrowed. "Did you meet a special lady who has you thinking about forever?"

Jason wasn't in the habit of talking to his secretary about his private life. In fact, he wasn't in the habit of talking to anyone about his private life. On the other hand, it seemed as if everyone had an opinion these days on what he should do—and a vested interested in his plans. It would be interesting to get the opinion of someone who had nothing to gain, and Barb was nothing if not discreet.

"Someone very special," he said, because that part, at least, was true.

"And you love her?" she prompted.

Jason hesitated, and she huffed out an impatient breath.

"If you have to think about that, then you have no business thinking about marriage.

"Hard work and commitment may be the building blocks of a solid marriage, but love is the mortar that holds it all together. Without love, any wind of discontent or distrust—and believe me, there will be storms—will have the blocks tumbling down."

It was hard to argue with thirty-eight-years' experience, but Jason wasn't discouraged. Because he would love the baby, and he knew Penny would love the baby, and he just had to trust that would be enough. Because he wouldn't risk anything more.

Penny called Jason when she got home from her spa day with Paige. It was the first time since their breakup that she'd initiated contact, and she was more than a little nervous about doing so. Especially when he didn't immediately answer.

Not that she'd expected he would be waiting by the phone, but she was a little disappointed that he didn't seem to be home. And then she wondered, it being a Saturday night, if he had a date.

The thought came to her out of the blue, but it wasn't an unreasonable one. Yeah, he'd proposed to her, but only because he knew she was carrying his baby. In reality, they'd broken up weeks before, and there was no reason that he couldn't be dating someone else by now.

Just when Penny had resigned herself to leaving a message—or not leaving one—he picked up.

"Hello?"

"Oh, uh, hi. Jason. It's Penny."

"I recognized your voice," he said, and sounded pleased to hear from her. "How was your spa day?"

"Fabulous," she said. "Actually, one of the reasons I was calling was to thank you."

"You already thanked me."

"Not as profusely as I would have if I'd known how truly wonderful the experience was going to be."

"Did your sister enjoy it, too?"

"So much that she's ready to join the Jason Foley fan club."

"I have a fan club?"

She laughed. "Not really, no. At least not that I'm aware of."

"Well, you're welcome anyway. But you said that was one of your reasons for calling."

"Yeah. I also wanted to let you know that I have a doctor's appointment Tuesday."

"Is something wrong? Are you feeling okay?"

"Nothing's wrong," she assured him. "I'm fine. It's just a checkup."

"Oh. Okay. What time is it?"

"Two o'clock."

"Are you just keeping me informed, or are you asking me to go with you?"

She knew he expected her to balk, and maybe there was a part of her that wanted to, that wanted to keep this baby all to herself. But she knew that wouldn't be fair, that this was too important for her to shut him out.

"That's up to you," she said.

"I'll pick you up at the store," he told her.

"I can meet you—"

"I'll pick you up," he repeated.

She sighed. "You're pushing again."

"I'm being environmentally conscious—saving you gas, since we're both going in the same direction," he countered.

"You have an answer for everything, don't you?"

"Not yet," he said. "But I'm working on it."

And that was precisely why she was worried.

* * *

When Jason arrived at McCord Jewelers Tuesday afternoon, the first thing he noticed was that the Santa Magdalena Diamond had been given a place of honor at the center of the showroom floor. Set atop a pedestal inside a glass case and spotlighted, it was shown to full advantage. Certainly, anyone gazing upon the gem would be attracted by its beauty, and alarmed to learn of its history.

Originally mined in India, the Santa Magdalena Diamond had apparently caused misfortune to everyone who had ever owned it, so maybe it wasn't so surprising that Paige and Travis had decided to donate the diamond to the Smithsonian rather than risk being subjected to its reputed curse. But using it on an interim basis to generate traffic through the store was another brilliant idea. And apparently a successful one, as the sales staff were all busy with customers, while still others were avidly browsing.

"It seems busy for a Tuesday afternoon," he commented to Penny when she joined him.

"Business has been good. Partly, it's the season—we're always busy between Thanksgiving and Christmas. But busier this year, I think, because of the diamond. We haven't had a quiet moment in the store since it was put on display."

"That was the point, wasn't it?"

"Yes, as much as I'm sure it disappoints you, the McCord fortunes seem to be turning around."

"Believe it or not, I'm not disappointed at all," he told her.

Penny didn't know what to believe, especially when

she herself had mixed feelings about the gem. She was happy it had been found, grateful it was helping to resolve the family's financial woes, and still a little resentful that it had meant so much to Jason that he'd used her to try to get information about the search for it.

The Santa Magdalena Diamond was a status symbol to him, and finding it—especially if he'd been able find it before the McCords did—would have been quite the coup. There were times she couldn't help but wonder if he thought of their baby in the same way. If it was all about the acquisition to him. And if, as soon as she gave in to his demands, he wouldn't want her or their child anymore.

"And in case you didn't hear," he continued, "the Foley-McCord feud is over."

Jason's comment snapped her out of her reverie.

"I thought that was just a rumor," she said lightly.

"You don't believe it?"

"I'm reserving judgment."

"In that case, I will do everything I can to prove it to you."

Penny knew he would, and what worried her was how much she already wanted to believe him.

The doctor's surprise upon seeing Jason come into the examining room with Penny was obvious.

"I'm Jason Foley," he said, introducing himself before Penny could—or maybe because he suspected that Penny wouldn't. "The baby's father."

Dr. Brennan looked askance at the mother-to-be. Apparently, she remembered Penny telling her that the baby's father wasn't around and wouldn't be involved in the pregnancy or birth. Which had obviously been wishful thinking on her part.

She put her regrets aside as the doctor went through the usual checkup routine, including the measuring of her blood pressure and her weight. Penny kicked off her shoes before stepping on the scale, as if that would make a difference. And while the doctor didn't comment on her action, her raised brows told Penny that it hadn't gone unnoticed.

After noting an additional three-pound gain on her chart, Dr. Brennan excused herself for a moment. That wasn't a usual part of the routine, which of course made Penny wonder about it.

"We usually do an ultrasound at twenty weeks," the doctor told Penny and Jason when she returned. "But we have a room and a machine available, so I'd like to take a look at your baby today."

Penny swallowed. "You think something's wrong with the baby?"

Jason moved closer and took her hand.

For a minute, she'd almost forgotten he was there. But now she was glad of his presence and his support. If there was something wrong, if she'd done something—

"I don't think anything's wrong," the doctor's assurance interrupted her panicked thoughts. "But I have some questions that an ultrasound may be able to answer."

"Can I stay for the test?" Jason asked.

"As long as it's okay with Penny," Dr. Brennan said.

Making it impossible for Penny to refuse.

But she really was grateful he was there with her. The doctor didn't seem overly concerned, but she'd probably done hundreds of ultrasounds and delivered hundreds of babies. This was Penny's first, and she was terrified. She'd been doing everything the doctor and the pregnancy books said—okay, ice cream intake excluded—but what if she'd done something wrong before she knew she was pregnant? What if she was somehow responsible for harming their baby?

As if cognizant of her thoughts, Jason squeezed her hand reassuringly as they followed the doctor to another room.

The bed had been prepped and Penny was given a sheet to cover up her lower body.

"Do you want me to wait outside?" Jason asked.

"You're not going to see anything you haven't seen before," she reminded him, even as she wished she could forget that he'd seen it all as recently as a week and a half earlier.

She wriggled out of her skirt and draped it neatly over the back of the chair. Then she hopped up on the bed and unfolded the sheet she'd been given. All the while, Jason pretended to be engrossed in a series of posters depicting the stages of a baby's development through pregnancy. Or maybe he wasn't pretending. Maybe he really was interested in what their baby looked like right now.

When the doctor came back in, she took the chair near the bed and directed Jason to stand on the other side, so that he could see the image that would be visible on the screen. Then she folded down the sheet and squirted some warm gel on Penny's tummy, spreading it around with a plastic probe—a transducer she called it, and explained that it transmitted the echoes of the sound waves into a picture on the monitor.

"Well, that explains it," Dr. Brennan said.

"What?" Penny stared at the screen but couldn't really decipher anything other than a dark, elongated oval with two lighter colored shapes inside.

Two?

She blinked.

Maybe the doctor's equipment was out of whack. That was the only explanation she could think of for there to be two images, almost like mirrors of one another. Unless—

Dr. Brennan smiled. "You're going to have twins."

Penny stared at the monitor, but she refused to believe what she could see with her own eyes. She'd barely had a chance to adjust to the idea of one baby and now the doctor was suggesting there were *two* babies?

"What do you mean? How can there be twins?"

Dr. Brennan pointed at the screen. "As you can clearly see, there are two babies in there. And the presence of those two babies explains your excessive tiredness and unusual weight gain."

"I can't have two babies," Penny protested. "I don't know what to do with one."

"That's a common concern of first-time mothers who learn they're carrying twins," the doctor said, as if that might reassure her. "Having a baby requires some major lifestyle changes, so having two babies requires even more.

"But you're fortunate," Dr. Brennan continued, "in that you have an interested partner willing to share both the joys and trials of pregnancy and parenthood with you."

Penny managed a weak smile, though she thought the doctor was being rather presumptuous considering that Jason had, so far, been present at one appointment.

A thought which made her realize that Jason hadn't said a single word since he'd come into the room, and she wondered if he was feeling as shell-shocked as she was. But when she glanced over at him, she saw that he didn't look stunned or panicked, he looked…awed. As if he had never seen anything more amazing than the sight of those two tiny little hearts beating on the screen. And in that moment, something inside her own heart softened.

Chapter Nine

When Jason suggested picking up something for dinner, Penny didn't object. Of course, he probably could have suggested they go straight to the airport and catch the next flight to Vegas and she would have nodded, still with that deer-in-the-headlights look in her eyes. And he couldn't deny that the thought did cross his mind, but he'd meant what he'd said to his father. He didn't want to manipulate her, and that's what it would be if he took advantage of her current state of shock to pursue his own agenda.

He stopped at the supermarket near his condo to pick up a few groceries, and it was only when he parked the car that Penny seemed to register where they were. She got out when he did and followed him into the store. He grabbed a basket and started toward the produce section. He picked out some red and yellow peppers, a head of broccoli, a bunch of carrots, a zucchini, some spring onions and a handful of shiitake mushrooms. Penny didn't say a word, even though he knew broccoli wasn't one of her favorite vegetables.

He led the way toward meat and poultry, where he picked out a nice lean steak, because the doctor had said that red meat was a good source of iron. Again, Penny followed wordlessly behind him. Her unusual silence was really starting to worry him, so when they cut down the aisle with baby essentials on their way to the checkout and they were walking past a tower of diapers, Jason couldn't resist teasing, "Think we should start stocking up on those now?"

And Penny burst into tears.

He put the basket down in the middle of the floor and pulled her into his arms. She came willingly, burying her face in his shoulder to muffle her sobs.

If he was surprised that she turned to him rather than away, he didn't waste too much time thinking about it. He was too busy enjoying the feel of her soft curves pressed against him. He rubbed her back gently, murmured reassuringly, although he wasn't exactly sure what he was reassuring her about.

After a few minutes—and more than a few curious glances from passers by—the flood of tears had reduced to a trickle.

She said something then, but her words were muffled against his shirt. So he dipped his head toward her and, inhaling the familiar fresh citrus scent of her shampoo, realized it was just one of the many things he'd missed about her.

"What did you say?" he asked gently.

She drew back, just a little. "I said, I d-don't even know how t-to change a d-diaper."

"Well, we've got some time to figure that out."

"I d-don't know how t-to do anything."

"We'll figure it all out," he said. "Everything will be okay."

She tipped her head back to look up at him. Her green eyes were red-rimmed and shimmering with tears, her nose was red, and her cheeks were streaked, but she was still beautiful. And still wary. "How do you know?"

"Because we're going to take it one step at a time," he told her. "Together."

After her meltdown in the middle of the grocery store, Penny just wanted to go home and hide under the covers of her bed forever—or at least until after her baby was born.

Babies, she mentally amended, and nearly melted down again.

Clearly, her pregnancy hormones were out of control, and while hiding under the covers still seemed like a good idea, she knew that she had to talk to Jason first. But not until after dinner. She tended to avoid confrontation at the best of times, and an empty stomach was definitely not the best of times.

Even though Jason ate out so often during office hours—whether with business associates or just grabbing a bite on the run—he'd learned to cook so that he could enjoy a homemade meal every once in a while. Penny used to think she was a decent cook, but his abilities in the kitchen put her efforts to shame. And even after a long day at the office, he never complained about putting in some extra time in the kitchen. And his cooking was one of the perks she'd enjoyed while they were dating.

While Jason chopped and diced, Penny sat back and watched. His movements were easy and sure, and without a cookbook in sight. When the veggies were prepared, he dumped them into a large glass bowl and set it aside. A new knife, a new cutting board and the steak was cut into long thin slices.

Watching him reminded her of being at one of those Japanese restaurants where the chef does all the cooking in front of the customers. Except that she'd been intimately involved with this chef, and watching Jason's hands chop and mix and stir with such effortless mastery brought to mind memories of those hands moving with the same effortless mastery over all the erogenous zones of her body.

He drizzled olive oil into the deep frying pan, then tossed in the garlic cloves he'd crushed, and the sizzle and scent made her mouth water. Or maybe it was the delicious man in front of the stove who really made her mouth water.

"What are you thinking?" Jason asked her.

She couldn't very well tell him the truth, so she went for the next thought that popped into her mind.

"I was thinking that two babies mean I have twice as many reasons to be terrified." And it was absolutely true, even if it hadn't been what she was thinking in the moment.

"I thought I was the only one who was scared."

She stole a slice of pepper from the bowl while he wasn't looking. "And I didn't think anything scared you."

"Neither did I, until you told me that you were pregnant."

"You didn't show any signs of panic."

He shrugged as he stirred the meat. "I wouldn't be a very effective negotiator in the boardroom if I didn't know how to hide my feelings."

"And your motives." The words were out before she could stop them, or maybe she didn't even try.

"You're right," he admitted. "Although I'm usually more forthright in my personal life than in my business dealings, the line got a little blurred when we were together."

"For you, maybe. I didn't even know there was a line."

"I think we're getting a little off-topic here." He dumped the veggies into the pan, added the stir-fry sauce he'd already whisked together—again without a recipe.

"You're right. I'm sorry. But I honestly don't see how we can come to any agreement about anything when I can't trust that you mean what you say."

"I never told you anything that wasn't true," he told her.

"You just never told me the whole truth."

"I'm telling you the whole truth now. I want to be with you, Penny, and to be a father to our babies."

He dished up the stir-fry, setting one bowl in front of Penny and one on the other side of the table. She picked up her fork, though she suddenly wasn't feeling very hungry.

"I also think," Jason continued, "that two babies need two parents on hand."

She wasn't fooled by his easy tone—she wasn't going to be fooled by anything he said again. So she didn't want to admit that she was feeling more than a little unnerved by the thought of handling twins on her own, especially remembering that her mother had often said two babies were about ten times as much work as one. On the other hand, her meltdown in the supermarket had probably given him at least a hint of her feelings.

"Maybe I could hire a nanny," she suggested.

He sighed. "You're right. There are other options. But I want to be involved, Penny. Let me help. Please."

Maybe it was that he'd asked instead of demanded. Maybe it was just that she was feeling more than a little panicked. But whatever the reason, she found herself actually considering his offer.

"Okay," she finally said. "*You* can hire the nanny. You can more easily afford it, anyway."

"I don't want to hire someone." He stabbed a piece of steak with his fork. "I want to marry you."

She shook her head, but not as vigorously as she might have three days—or even three hours—earlier. "Don't you think a wedding would cause more problems than it solves?" she asked him.

"No, I don't," he replied, and sounded as if he really meant it.

She pushed her empty bowl away. Obviously, she'd been hungrier than she'd realized, or the babies were, anyway. And just thinking *babies* nearly sent her into a tailspin again.

"Are you proposing a business relationship or a personal one?"

"What do you want?"

"I want to go back five months and take a cab home from Missy Harcourt's wedding."

"I screwed up, Penny. I know that. But I can honestly say that I don't regret a single moment that I spent with you."

"Even though you didn't get the information you needed to find the Santa Magdalena Diamond first?"

"Maybe I wasn't honest with you at the beginning, but the truth is, what happened between us stopped being about the diamond long before I ever took you to my bed."

She didn't believe him. Because if she did, she might let herself hope that their relationship actually meant something to him. And if she started to believe that, then she might be willing to open up her heart to him again. And that was something she couldn't let happen.

She didn't want to marry him, and yet… "I don't want to deprive my babies of a father."

"I'll be there for them," Jason assured her. "And for you, however and whenever you need me."

She took a deep breath. "Well, it's starting to look like I might need a husband."

Husband.

The word echoed in Jason's mind.

"Are you saying…that you'll marry me?"

She nodded. "It seems like the most reasonable thing to do, under the circumstances."

He shouldn't complain about the reason when it was getting him what he wanted, but it didn't seem like an enthusiastic endorsement for marriage. But he knew she was still shaken by the revelation that she was carrying twins, and despite his earlier assertion that he wouldn't use that info to sway her, he wasn't going to try to talk her out of it, either.

"How's Friday?" he asked.

"For what?"

"The wedding."

She blinked. "*This* Friday?"

"Why not?"

She was silent for a moment, as if trying to think of a reason, but in the end, she only shrugged. "I guess if we're going to do it, there's no reason to wait."

Unfortunately she was only talking about marriage and not any one of the numerous other things he wanted to do with her. He pushed the thought aside, to focus on more immediate matters.

"Is Vegas okay, or did you want to go to one of the islands?"

"I was thinking city hall," she admitted.

"We'll go with Vegas," he decided. "Then we don't have to worry about any waiting periods."

"How did we go from a doctor's appointment to dinner to a wedding date?" she wondered aloud.

Jason felt a slight twinge of guilt but reminded himself that the ends justified the means. Maybe they hadn't planned this pregnancy, but he wouldn't ever be sorry, because the babies she carried had given him the second chance he hadn't even known he wanted.

Now it was up to him to make the most of it.

But Penny started to doubt her decision almost as soon as Jason dropped her off at home. By the time Friday morning came around, she was still wavering. Was she really going to do this? What had changed her mind? Was she foolish enough to hope that a marriage of convenience could lead to real, long-lasting happiness?

Because she wasn't sure of the answers to any of those questions, she didn't advise anyone of her plans. Instead, she told Paige that she was going to work from home on Friday, finishing up some design work. And she waited until her mother had gone out to run some errands, then left a note in the library for her, saying only that she would be away for the weekend.

She still wasn't sure she would go through with the wedding.

But her bag was packed and her passport was in her purse, so she played around with some sketches while she waited for him to show up. That way her working-from-home story wasn't really a lie, and she wasn't watching the clock and worrying that Jason might have changed *his* mind.

But as she finished up the sketch of a bracelet to be made of twisted strands of copper studded with numerous gems, she worried about her deception. She'd never had secrets from her sister before. Not until she started dating Jason the first time, and now she'd fallen back into the same pattern. Then again, Paige had obviously been keeping secrets from her, most notably her search for the Santa Magdalena Diamond and her romance with Travis Foley.

The knock at the door had her pencil slipping from her fingers, then JoBeth peeked into the room and announced that Penny had a guest. Her tone of disapproval revealed Jason's identity more clearly than if she'd announced his name. She'd been Devon McCord's housekeeper for more than thirty years, and his dislike of all things Foley had apparently seeped into her blood. Which made Penny wonder how Rex—now married to Devon's widower and living in the McCord mansion—was settling in. But she didn't wonder long, having her own greater worries at the moment.

And one of those worries was that she still didn't know what she should do. But she grabbed her bag, pointedly ignored the housekeeper's raised eyebrows and went to meet Jason.

He was waiting in the foyer, and her heart gave one of those funny little bumps against her ribs, proving that whatever else she felt, she was still attracted to him. As for the rest of those feelings, well, if he was willing to marry her and be a father to their babies, why wouldn't she say yes and figure it out later?

"Are you ready?" Jason asked.

"I'm ready," she said, and hoped it was true.

Penny always thought she'd like to visit Vegas. Everything she'd seen of the city on television shows or in the movies was glamorous and exciting, but as the private plane began its descent, her stomach was a mass of knots and nerves.

Again, Jason seemed to be attuned to her mood and her concerns, as he reached over to take her hand, linking their fingers together.

"We're doing the right thing," he said.

She nodded, though she wasn't entirely convinced.

"I'll do my best to be a good father to our babies," he told her.

She just nodded.

"And I'll do my best to be a good husband, too."

"We're getting married for the babies," she said. "I don't want or expect it to mean anything more than that."

"I can't blame you for being wary," he said. "But I hope that in time you'll learn to trust me again."

"Speaking of time," she said, because she didn't want

to talk about their past and she dared not look too far into the future, "how soon can we get married?"

His smile was wry. "I'd like to think you're anxious to wear my ring, but I'm guessing you just want it over and done with."

"Ring?" She felt a tiny surge of panic. "I didn't even think about the rings."

"Don't worry," he said. "It's taken care of."

And he pulled a box out of his pocket to prove it. The lavender color of the packaging was unmistakably McCord's, so she had to give him credit for both tact and taste. But when he opened the lid, she was stunned.

It was a three-carat, brilliant-cut canary diamond set in a wide band that had been formed by forging together eight narrow ribbons of yellow gold, symbolizing the linking of two hands together.

"Where did you get that?"

"At McCord's, of course." He smiled. "Did you really think I would dare shop for your ring anywhere else?"

"But why that ring?"

His smile faltered. "You don't like it?"

"I'm just…surprised. It's not a traditional design."

"Maybe that's why it appealed to me. Because nothing about our relationship has been traditional." But something in her voice must have clued him in, because he said, "It's one of yours, isn't it?"

She nodded. "You really didn't know?"

"I didn't think about it," he admitted. "But now that I do, I should have guessed."

It wasn't just one of her designs, but designed while she was dating Jason and inspired by her relationship with him—not that she was going to admit as much.

"I'm guessing, then, that you like it?" he prompted.

"It's one of my favorite pieces," she said. "But...what about your ring? Or didn't you—"

He handed her another lavender box. Inside it was a masculine version of the same design—a little bit wider and heavier, and minus the diamond, but clearly designed to match, like two parts of a whole.

As they were going to be two parts joined together when they exchanged the rings.

The thought sent funny little quivers through her belly, more excitement than apprehension now. Or maybe it was just the plane touching down.

Penny was in awe as they drove down the strip toward their hotel. It was so much bigger and brighter, more than she'd imagined.

"Where are we getting married?" she asked Jason.

"We're scheduled for a two o'clock ceremony in the Starlight Chapel."

She tore her gaze away from the window. "You booked a ceremony?"

"Is that a problem?"

"No," she said, though she was surprised that he'd obviously paid a lot more attention to all the little details of their wedding than she had. "I just figured we'd find some little chapel on the strip and have a quick ceremony officiated by a second-rate Elvis impersonator."

"Just because it's Vegas doesn't mean it has to be tacky."

"I'm beginning to realize that."

"You've never been to Vegas before," he guessed.

She shook her head. "It's nothing like I expected. I mean, the strip is exactly what you see in all the movies and on television, but there's so much more than just the neon lights and flashy cars.

"Oh," she exclaimed, as something else caught her eye. "The Venetian."

The name was barely more than a reverent whisper, as her hand lifted to the window, as if she could reach through it and touch the majestic hotel.

"Is it true that you can actually ride a gondola and eat in St. Mark's Square inside?"

"It's true," he assured her. "And it is pretty spectacular, but on a much smaller scale than Venice itself."

"I've never been to Italy, either," she admitted.

He frowned at that. "Don't you have family in Italy?"

"Gabby's mother is Italian," she confirmed. "And she invited Paige and me to go over for a visit the summer we were sixteen, but my dad wouldn't allow it."

"Why not?"

"Because Gabby's beauty and celebrity had already put her in the spotlight and he worried that she would be a negative influence on us."

The more Jason knew about Devon McCord, the more he agreed that the man had been a selfish sonofabitch. While he kept his wife and children safely ensconced at home, he was traveling the world and frittering away their fortune. No wonder Penny had been so eager for a little attention and excitement, so eager to experience life.

"Vegas isn't Italy," he said again. "But we'll take a few days and I'll show you around."

"Really?" She seemed surprised—and unexpectedly pleased—by his offer.

"Sure," he said. "Although a few days isn't really long

enough to see and do everything, it will at least give you a preview of what you might want to see on another visit."

"I think I'd like to come back sometime," she admitted.

"How about for our first anniversary?"

"That would be nice," she said, but the light in her eyes faded and he inwardly cursed himself for mentioning their impending marriage, because now she was thinking about the reasons for it. And he knew it wasn't the babies she carried that dimmed the spark of excitement, but her distrust of him. He'd done that to her, taken her innocence, destroyed her naïveté.

He would give anything to go back in time and tell her the truth before she heard it from her sister, because the whole truth was more than Paige had known. The truth was, he'd grown to care a great deal for Penny— more than he was even ready to admit to himself.

Jason had made reservations at the Celestial Resort and Casino, and after he'd taken care of the check-in, they rode up to the thirty-fifth floor—just the two of them, a bellboy with their bags and the elevator attendant, in an elevator that could easily hold fifty people and was as lavishly decorated as everything else she'd seen in the short walk through the lobby.

Their hotel suite was even more spectacular.

Penny was a McCord, so she was hardly a stranger to wealth or extravagance, but she had never seen anything that compared to the stunning opulence of the rooms.

Jason tipped the bellboy and sent him on his way while Penny checked out the view from the wall of floor-to-ceiling windows, and found herself looking down at a lake-size swimming pool.

"They don't do anything by half measures here, do they?"

"Not at any of the places I'll be taking you," he assured her.

"I have to admit, whenever I thought about getting married someday, I never thought it would happen like this," she told him.

"In Vegas?"

She managed to smile. "Actually, I'm okay with the Vegas part. It's the whole getting-married-because-I'm-pregnant-and-too-damn-scared-to-go-it-alone part that's bothering me. And the why-am-I-doing-this-when-I-know-he's-going-to-wake-up-one-morning-and-realize-he's-trapped-in-a-life-he-never-wanted part."

"This wasn't what either of us planned, obviously, but I'm not unhappy about the babies or our marriage."

"You're not?"

"It wasn't as if I never planned to get married and have a family someday, I just hadn't yet gotten to that part of my plans."

"Really?"

"I'm a thirty-two-year-old, financially secure man with a stable job, so I don't have any concerns about what this marriage means for me."

"You have concerns about me?"

He shrugged. "You're only twenty-six and you've led a fairly sheltered life. After today, you're going to be a wife, and in less than six months the mother of two babies."

"Are you trying to get me to change my mind about this?"

"No," he said, then paused. "But maybe I'm a little worried that I pushed you too quickly in this direction."

He sounded as if he meant it, as if he really was concerned about her wants and her needs, and the knowledge stirred feelings she'd been trying to ignore.

"I know how to push back," she assured him.

He studied her for a long moment, and finally nodded. "In that case, we'd better get ready for the wedding."

As much as she thought she was ready, Penny experienced another moment of uncertainty when the ceremony began. Standing beside Jason and listening to the dark-suited minister recite the traditional words, she felt a pang of regret that this wasn't, except in the most technical sense, a real wedding.

She'd never been a gambler, but this was Vegas, and she knew she was taking a very big gamble in agreeing to marry Jason. But despite her nerves and apprehension, she wasn't going into it against her will. Even knowing what he'd done and why he'd done it, she wanted to marry him. She wanted to be with him, to raise her babies with him, to build a family together.

She wanted him to love her as much as she loved him.

There. She'd admitted it. She was in love with Jason Foley. Maybe she was stupid, maybe she was naive, maybe she was setting herself up to have her heart broken again—she didn't know. She only knew she could no longer deny her feelings.

Follow your heart, her mother had said, and that was what she intended to do.

Maybe it was a gamble, but she was ready to ante up. Because she was in love with the man she was going to marry and she was betting everything she had on a long and happy future together.

She'd felt a twinge of regret as she walked toward the front of the chapel past the empty chairs that lined the aisle. Whenever she'd let herself dream of her wedding day, she'd always envisioned her family celebrating the occasion with her. But she'd deliberately kept silent about her plans to marry Jason, not just because she hadn't been certain it would happen but because she was even less certain of their support.

Then she'd looked up and met Jason's gaze, and the easy warmth and obvious appreciation she saw pushed aside any regrets about the haste and secrecy of their wedding.

His eyes skimmed over her slowly, from head to toe and back again. The heat of his gaze was as tangible as a caress, making her skin heat and tingle in anticipation. Desire swept through her, sweeping away the last of her nervousness. Suddenly she was anxious to get through the ceremony and move on to the wedding night—even if it was still the afternoon.

Jason's lips curved, as if he knew exactly what she was thinking, and as if he was thinking the same thing. And she felt a surge of renewed confidence that everything would work out. Because certainly a man who looked at her the way he was looking at her, who wanted her as he had proven he wanted her, had to have real feelings for her. And that gave her hope that, in time, he might grow to love her as she loved him.

Jason spoke his vows clearly and confidently. Penny's voice wasn't nearly as clear or confident, but the words came from her heart as much as her lips. And as she recited her lines she silently prayed that this marriage would last, not just until their babies were born, but "so long as we both shall live."

Then the minister pronounced them husband and wife and told Jason that he could kiss his bride, and Penny braced herself for the perfunctory touch of his mouth against hers.

Except there was nothing at all perfunctory about his kiss.

His lips came down on hers, soft but firm, possessive and persuasive. She had no intention of revealing the feelings she'd only just acknowledged to herself. But the stirring in her blood was all too real, and despite her intentions, her eyelids drifted shut, her arms went around him and she kissed him back.

Chapter Ten

After the ceremony was concluded, Penny and Jason were ushered to a private dining room with a single table set with pristine white linens and sparkling crystal and gleaming silver. There was soft music piped into the room from unseen speakers, audible enough to add to the romanticism of the scene, but not so loud as to interfere with conversation.

The candle inside the hurricane lantern at the center of the table had been lit and there was a tuxedo-clad waiter at the ready with a bottle of nonalcoholic Champagne. He introduced himself as Gabriel, then presented the label for their approval, before popping the cork and pouring the golden liquid into two tall flutes.

In the background, the photographer who had taken pictures during the ceremony continued to snap away, making Penny feel self-conscious about everything she did and said.

Gabriel recited the dinner specials, took their orders, then excused himself to check on the meal preparations in the kitchen.

"Have I mentioned how spectacular you look tonight?" Jason asked, when the waiter had gone.

"Yes, you did," she said, and tried not to remember how her body had heated in response to the obvious appreciation in his eyes when she'd stepped out of the sumptuous dressing room in their suite.

It had been something of a last-minute decision to buy a new dress for the occasion, but in the end she'd decided that a woman's wedding—regardless of the circumstances behind it—warranted a shopping trip. The simple, ivory-colored sheath she'd found was elegant without being fussy, and seemed well-suited to the occasion.

And part of the wedding package Jason had booked was a bouquet for the bride. Hers was a bunch of creamy roses tied with a wide satin ribbon that happened to match the wide ribbon trim on the square neckline and knee-length hem of her dress.

But it was the jewelry she wore that had seemed to catch Jason's eye, for probably the same reason she had hesitated to put it on. Both the earrings that dangled from her lobes and the pendant that sat at the base of her throat held canary diamonds.

For the past six months, Blake had been buying up all of the canary diamonds he could find, trusting that their popularity, and thus their value, would soar when the Santa Magdalena Diamond was found. It had been a gamble, but one that had already started to pay off.

And while Blake brought home the diamonds, Penny was entrusted with the task of designing a series of pieces to spotlight the gems. The resulting collection, traditional Spanish designs reflecting the history of the Santa Magdalena, had recently been spotted on the cover of *Vogue* and on the red carpet in Hollywood.

The earrings she wore—elongated gold filigrees with tiny canary diamonds sprinkled along the bottom like fairy dust—had been a thank-you gift from her brother for the extra hours she'd put in on the project. The necklace—a solid rope-style chain, on which sat a similarly styled pendant—she'd bought for herself, simply because she'd been unable to resist.

Of course, she couldn't have known when she'd chosen her jewelry for this occasion that Jason had also chosen a canary diamond for her, and she couldn't help but wonder if that was just a coincidence...or fate.

"Well, I'll say it again." Jason's words drew her attention back to the moment, as he lifted his glass. "And offer a toast to my beautiful bride."

He, of course looked fabulous in a charcoal-colored suit, pewter shirt and burgundy tie. She'd always thought he looked as if he'd walked off of the cover of *GQ* magazine, but she didn't think she needed to tell him as much. Instead, she said, "And to the quintessential groom," and tapped her glass to his.

The photographer moved a little closer, recording the clinking of crystal and the sipping of wine.

"Is he going to hover around all night?"

Jason shook his head. "Pictures of the wedding night were an additional fee, and while I didn't object to the cost, I wasn't sure you wanted that kind of photographic record."

"I appreciate your discretion," she said, knowing he was only teasing.

But his words also made her think about something she'd been trying not to think about since she agreed to this marriage—the wedding night and every night thereafter. They hadn't really talked about what they each wanted or expected from this marriage, whether it was to be a union in name only or a real husband-and-wife-sleeping-together-in-one-bed relationship. And how the heck was she supposed to ask that kind of question now?

"I think, once he has pictures of us dancing and cutting the cake, he'll leave us alone," Jason said now.

"Dancing and cutting the cake?"

"It's all part of the Ultimate Wedding Package."

"It's been pretty impressive," she admitted. But while she'd been pleased with the details, her attention had mostly been focused on the groom.

"I wanted you to be able to look back on our wedding day and have memories of something better than a ceremony performed by a second-rate Elvis impersonator."

"I'd say you definitely succeeded."

"Then you're not sorry you agreed to this?"

She circled the base of her wineglass with a fingernail as she considered her response. "I think it's too early to tell."

"Not quite the answer I was hoping for," Jason admitted.

She sighed. "We both know that you never would

have proposed—and I would never have considered accepting—if I wasn't pregnant."

"Are you forgetting how you got pregnant?"

"I do remember my sex ed classes," she said, keeping her tone light and trying not to focus on any specific memories of making love with Jason.

"I wasn't actually talking about the logistics, but the attraction that was there from the beginning, the desire that was undeniable, the intensity of the connection between us." His voice was low and seductive. "We were good together, Penny. You know we were."

She lifted a shoulder. "How would I know? I had nothing to compare it to."

"Then you'll have to defer to my knowledge and experience," he said, as he drew her out of her seat and into his arms.

In the low-heeled pumps she wore, she was almost at eye level with Jason. While they'd been dating, she'd appreciated that one of the advantages of going out with a man who was more than six feet tall was that she could wear heels and not tower over him. But not only did she not tower over him, he had a way of making her feel distinctly feminine and completely cherished when she was in his arms.

"In fact," Jason continued, "we were *very* good together."

"What are you doing?"

"We're dancing," he said. "It's a tradition at a lot of weddings."

Yes, at traditional weddings. But this one was anything but traditional. It was certainly nothing like the wedding she'd dreamed of when she was a little girl.

And though it was definitely more than she'd expected, she wasn't going to forget and forgive everything else just because he'd gone out of his way to make the day special.

"I remember dancing with you at Missy Harcourt's wedding," she said now, to remind herself as much as him of his reasons for pursuing her and how all of this had begun.

But Jason wasn't the least deterred by her observation. "That was the first night I held you in my arms. The night I realized I wanted a lot more from you than I was supposed to."

As she swayed in his embrace and listened to his voice skim over her, as sensual as a caress, she knew—despite all of her efforts to the contrary—she was falling under his spell all over again.

"So, if you think this—you and me, here and now—isn't what I wanted, you're wrong," he told her. "It might not be how I planned for things to happen, but I'm not disappointed, and I believe we can make our marriage work."

"This is Vegas, Jason. Where fortunes are won and lost on the flip of a card or the role of the dice. Our marriage vows are as much a gamble as what's happening at all those tables downstairs, and the odds are stacked against us."

His hand skimmed up her back, and even through the fabric of her dress, she felt the heat of his touch—and then the answering fire in her blood.

"I used to think you were a dreamer, not a defeatist." The words were little more than a whisper, as his lips cruised close to her ear.

"I'm a realist," she told him, desperately trying to re-member what was real and what was nothing more than a temptingly seductive illusion.

"If you were a realist, you wouldn't be so intent on denying the attraction between us."

"You want to hear that I still want you? Okay—I still want you," she admitted. "I don't want to want you. But apparently my body and my mind are in disagreement on the matter.

"But I also know that having sex with you isn't going to change anything between us. Sure, it might make me feel good for a while, but it won't actually change any-thing. It certainly won't make me forget that you lied to me or that you dated and slept with me only because you wanted information about Paige's search for the Santa Magdalena Diamond."

"Are you ever going to get over that?"

"Probably not."

"Then you should know that I'm not a martyr."

"Meaning?"

"If all I wanted was information, I would have taken you out a few times and been done with it. I took you to my bed because you were fun and smart and sexy." He drew her closer, forcing her to tip her head back to maintain eye contact. "And because you turned me on like no other woman has in a very long time."

He dipped his head toward her, and Penny knew he was going to kiss her again.

As his mouth inched ever closer to hers, her throat went as dry as the Nevada desert.

Then his cell phone rang.

Jason froze…then swore under his breath when the ring sounded again.

Penny moistened her lips with her tongue, not certain whether she was grateful or annoyed by the interruption. "Don't you think you should answer that?"

"I don't want to answer that," he admitted. "But I left some loose ends hanging at the office, and—"

Another phone began to ring.

She frowned, realizing it was her own.

Jason dropped his arms from around her to reach for his cell, while Penny moved back to the table to get her purse and the phone that was inside.

CALL FROM PAIGE was showing on the display, and the uneasiness that had stirred in her belly when her phone started ringing only moments after his solidified into a nasty ball of fear.

She connected the call. "Paige—what's wrong?"

"Where are you?" her sister demanded, almost frantically. "And how did you know something was wrong?"

"I'm with Jason," Penny admitted, skipping over the details of their secret wedding for the moment.

"Well, I guess that's good then," Paige said. "You can come with him."

"Come with him where?"

"Memorial Hospital."

Penny swallowed. "What happened?"

"It's Mom. I'm not sure what happened. Rex was a little sketchy on the details—and frantic—when he called me. Travis and I are on our way now."

Penny had no idea how long it would take them to get a flight back to Dallas, and then to the hospital from the airport, but she responded, "We'll see you there."

* * *

Jason knew how to make things happen, but even with his guidance and connections, it took more than three hours to get from the hotel in Vegas to the hospital in Dallas. By that time, Eleanor had been in and out of surgery and moved from recovery to a private room.

"Appendicitis," Blake explained to Penny and Jason when they finally arrived. "It was a close call, but the doctors managed to remove the organ before it ruptured."

Penny's eyes filled with tears of relief. "Thank God."

Her brother smiled. "Yeah, we've been doing a lot of that."

Jason squeezed her hand, then asked, "Where's my dad?"

"He's with my mom. Charlie's in there, too. They're only letting her have two visitors at a time right now, so we've been taking turns."

"Where are Tate and Tanya?" Penny asked.

"They were here earlier," Blake told her. "They waited until she was out of surgery, but then they had to take off because Tanya has some kind of big project deadline coming up."

"Gabby and Rafe were here, too," Katie said.

"And Zane and Melanie and Olivia," Paige added. "In fact, you were probably coming up in one elevator while they were going down in another."

Which she knew was her sister's somewhat subtle way of prompting Penny to explain why she was so late in arriving.

"I got here as soon as I could. I mean, *we* got here as soon as we could," she said, including Jason in her explanation. "We were out of town. In Las Vegas, actually."

"Las Vegas?" Blake frowned.

"What were you…" Katie's question trailed off, the answer obviously coming to her as her gaze dropped to Penny's left hand and her eyes widened. "Oh."

It wasn't quite how she'd planned to share the news, but she felt guilty for showing up after all the waiting and worrying had been done by her siblings, and she wanted to explain the reason for her delay.

"Penny and I got married," Jason confirmed, for anyone who hadn't jumped to that conclusion as quickly as Katie.

"You always had to be the first at everything," Travis teased his brother. "I got engaged, so you jumped ahead and got married."

"Expediency seemed prudent under the circumstances," Jason replied easily.

"Well, congratulations." Travis hugged his brother, then his new sister-in-law. "And welcome to the family. Again."

"Thanks." Penny hugged him back, then hugged her sister.

"I can't believe you really did it," Paige said. "And without telling me."

Penny wasn't sure how to respond to that, and was grateful that Charlie's arrival shifted the topic of conversation to Eleanor.

"Rex just wanted a few minutes alone with Mom," he said. "But she's awake and lucid and everything's fine."

When Jason excused himself to step outside of the waiting room to keep an eye out for his father, Blake took the opportunity to shift closer to his youngest sister.

"Are you okay?" Blake asked her. "Is this marriage really what you want?"

Penny nodded. "It surprised me to realize it," she admitted. "But, yes, this is what I want."

"Then I'll say congratulations," Blake said, and kissed both of her cheeks. "And good luck."

She smiled. "You could try to sound a little less cynical when you say that."

"I'm sorry. I really do wish you the best. I'm still just a little wary when it comes to the Foleys, I guess."

"I can understand that," she said. "But I really think Jason and I can make this work."

"If he makes you unhappy, you let me know."

She smiled again. "I love you, Blake."

He hugged her tight. "Right back atcha, sis."

When Rex finally made his way down the hall from Eleanor's room, Jason couldn't help but notice that his father—always the epitome of calm—was a wreck. His eyes were shadowed, his face was pale and drawn, and his hair was in disarray, as if he'd been repeatedly running his hands through it.

Jason could understand why his father had been so worried. He had known a guy in college who had an emergency appendectomy to remove the inflamed organ before it could rupture, so he knew how dangerous a ruptured appendix could be. Thankfully, Eleanor's surgery had been successful, but that didn't help Jason know what to say to his father.

In fact, he felt as helpless now as he did when his mother had died. Of course, Jason had been ten when Olivia Marie passed away, and Eleanor wasn't going to die; but clearly Rex had worried that she might, that he might lose her as he'd lost his first wife.

He saw the lingering fear in his father's eyes, and it was, in his opinion, just one more reason not to fall in love, one more reason not to give away his heart completely, as he'd given it to his college girlfriend, Kara, so many years before. Because he knew that if he did, he would be left with nothing when the woman he gave it to was gone. He'd learned that lesson when Kara died while there was still so much unresolved between them. The tragic end of her young life had left him feeling guilty and confused and unhappy. And that was something Jason wasn't ever going to risk again.

Penny and Paige slipped out of the waiting room to steal a quick moment with their mother, so Jason asked his dad if he wanted to go down to the cafeteria to grab a cup of coffee. But Rex declined the invitation, not wanting to be too far away from his wife.

It was only about ten minutes later that Penny and Paige came back.

"Mom kicked us out," Penny said.

"Apparently, she didn't need all of her kids to come running over something as insignificant as appendicitis," Paige added.

"Insignificant?" Rex was on his feet again, too agitated and worried to sit. "Her appendix nearly ruptured inside of her. She could have died."

The raw anguish in his voice left no one in any doubt about the depth of his feelings for the woman he'd married.

Jason wondered what it would be like to love so deeply, to risk so much, and thanked his lucky stars that his union with Penny was based on practical considerations, and that neither of them wanted or expected a relationship characterized by that kind of all-consuming emotion.

Instinctively Penny reached out, touching Rex's arm, reassuring him. "But she didn't. Because you got her here in time."

"Yeah," he agreed, though he didn't sound mollified. "But it was too damned close for comfort."

Paige kissed his cheek. "Well, thanks. For being there for her. For everything."

"I wouldn't be anywhere else," he assured them.

Jason knew it was true. His father had always been devoted to his family. And now his family included Eleanor, and Eleanor's children were part of the family, as well—including the new daughter-in-law he didn't yet know was his daughter-in-law, because he'd been with his new wife when Penny made the announcement to the rest of the family.

"Mom was asking for you," Penny told Rex.

"Is it okay?" His gaze moved from Eleanor's daughters to her eldest son. "Do you mind?"

"Go ahead," Blake said. "You're the one she wants right now."

There was no bitterness in the words, and Jason knew there could have been, as the rekindling of Rex's romance with Eleanor would have inevitably reminded Blake that his mother had only married Devon McCord because she was pregnant with him.

"Thanks," Rex said, already on his way back to his wife's room.

Jason wasn't clear on all of the details of those past relationships, but he knew enough to be grateful that neither he nor Penny had been involved with anyone else immediately prior to hooking up. If their relationship didn't work out, they would have no one to blame but themselves.

Maybe Penny was right—maybe the odds were stacked against them. But Jason never backed down from a challenge, and he never saw failure as an option.

Penny held back a smile as she watched her new stepfather practically race down the hall to his wife's side. She'd had some reservations when she realized her mother and Rex had married so hastily, but after her conversation with Eleanor in the library—was it really only eight days ago?—she accepted that her mother was truly happy with her new husband, probably happier than she'd ever been before. And while she was happy for her mother, she was also a little envious because she didn't know if she would ever love anyone the way her mother loved Rex, or if she would ever be loved the same way.

Jason had married her, but she had no illusions about his feelings for her. All she had were hopes and dreams. Hope that he would someday grow to love her as much as she loved him, and the dream that they would live happily together as a family.

"She's going to be okay." Jason, obviously misinterpreting the reason for her silence, slid an arm across her shoulders.

Penny nodded. "I know. I just didn't expect that it would shake me up this much. I mean, it was just appendicitis, but maybe it's because it came so close on the heels of her breast cancer scare that I'm being forced to accept that she won't be here forever."

"But you're not going to lose her anytime soon," he said.

"No, thank God." And then she remembered, and she winced. "I'm sorry."

"For what?"

"For being insensitive. I didn't even think about the fact that you've already lost your mom."

"A long time ago."

"I don't imagine that makes it any easier."

Jason shrugged, not wanting to think back, to admit how big a hole had been left in his life when his mother was gone. It had been his first real experience with death and with grief.

Yeah, he'd only been a kid when his mom died, and he'd been devastated. But he'd been wise enough to see the effect that her death had on his father, to realize that the day they buried his mother he'd lost a part of Rex, too. And he realized that loving someone meant giving them a piece of your heart, and that once that piece had been given, you could never get it back. He'd vowed then that he would always protect himself from loving and losing so much.

A valiant objective for a ten-year-old boy, but as the years passed and his grief faded, so did his resolve. He started dating in high school, had some minor flirtations and more serious crushes, but he still didn't know what it meant to really love someone. Then he met Kara Richardson in college.

Loving—and losing—Kara had renewed his determination. Since her tragic death, he never let anyone else get too close, never let himself fall in love again.

Not that he'd ever been tempted, really. At least not until Penny.

Now—well, it was a little late to be having second thoughts about making Penny his wife, and soon she would be the mother of his children. It was almost too easy to imagine a future with her, living side-by-side with her, raising their children together, growing old together, maybe even loving one another.

No, he wasn't going to go down that road again.

No way.

His brother nudged him with an elbow, forcing his thoughts back to the present.

"I think it's time to take your wife home," Travis said, nodding toward Penny.

She was nestled in a vinyl chair by the door and struggling to keep her eyes open. He knew she tired easily these days because of the pregnancy, and today had been a long and emotionally draining day for her, something he should have realized without his brother pointing it out to him.

He went to her and took her hand to draw her out of the chair. She came without protest, a testament to how truly exhausted she was.

"We'll check back in tomorrow," Jason announced to her family. "But for now, I'm taking Penny home."

Except that after they'd said their goodbyes and left the hospital, one important question remained unanswered: where was home?

Penny woke up when the car stopped moving and the engine shut off. It took her a moment after that to realize she was in Jason's car and that his car was parked in her mother's driveway.

As he'd already climbed out of the driver's seat and was coming around to open her door. She had to wait until he'd done so before she could ask "What are we doing here?"

He shrugged. "I just thought, with everything that's happened today, you might feel more comfortable staying here tonight."

"Oh. Yeah. Thanks." She wasn't sure if she sounded grateful or disappointed or just tired. Because she wasn't sure if she was grateful or disappointed, but there was no doubt about the tired.

"We never talked about where we were going to live," Jason said, as he walked with her up to the door.

"We never talked about a lot of things."

"I'd like you to move into my place."

She was tempted to argue, maybe because she'd gotten so used to arguing about everything, but when she thought about it, she realized it made sense. She was going to have a baby of her own, she needed a home of her own; she couldn't expect to continue living at her parents', especially now that she was married. And now that Eleanor had married Rex.

Besides, Jason's downtown condo, though not as big or fancy as his penthouse in Houston, had a spare bedroom that could be converted into a nursery, and it was conveniently located near Foley Industries' Dallas office and McCords' flagship store.

But even while they'd been dating, when she asked why he didn't come to Dallas more, so they could spend more time together, he'd insisted that his base of operations was in Houston. More importantly, Barb, his secretary-slash-assistant, was in Houston, and he couldn't manage without her.

Of course, that might have been just his excuse to keep things from getting too serious between them, because while she'd had illusions of a relationship, he'd only been on a fact-finding mission. Now that they were married, he must have reconsidered.

"You're going to move to Dallas?" she asked, seeking clarification on that point.

Jason frowned. "No. I was referring to my place in Houston."

Her heart sank. "I can't move to Houston."

"Well, you can't expect that I would move to Dallas."

"Why not?"

"Because my office is in Houston."

"You have an office in Dallas, too," she reminded him.

"My base of operations is Houston."

"Mine is Dallas."

He let out a long-suffering sigh. "It's been a long day, Penny, do you think maybe we could argue about this tomorrow?"

"I don't want to argue about this at all."

"Could have fooled me," he muttered.

She narrowed her gaze. "If you think you can just issue orders and I'm going to blindly obey, think again. I'm your wife, not your puppet."

"I don't want a puppet," Jason assured her. "What I want is to have a rational conversation."

"Are you suggesting that I'm being irrational?"

"I'm suggesting that we should table this discussion until we've both had some sleep."

"Fine," she said, because to argue such a logical point might be construed as irrational.

"Thank you." He leaned over to brush his lips against her cheek. "Good night, Penny."

The man she'd married only a few hours earlier, who had given every indication of being interested in a real wedding night while they were in Vegas, had just walked away after kissing her cheek.

Her *cheek*.

"Good night," she replied, more baffled now than tired.

But he was already gone.

Chapter Eleven

Jason picked her up in the morning to take her back to the hospital. Penny claimed that she didn't need him to drive her, reminding him that she had both a license and a car of her own, but he felt strongly that—less than twenty-four hours after they'd exchanged wedding vows—they should at least give the appearance of a united couple. Throughout the drive, though he was sure they were both thinking about their unfinished discussion from the night before, neither of them mentioned it.

He popped into Eleanor's room to say hi to his new mother-in-law, who congratulated him enthusiastically on having the good sense to marry her daughter; then he claimed that he had some things to do at the office, promising to come back to get Penny in a couple of hours.

There wasn't anything urgent going on at Foley Industries. After all, it was Saturday, and he'd expected to still be in Vegas with his bride. Obviously, his father's call had come at the right time, because if they hadn't been interrupted, he would have made love with Penny. And although he knew he would have enjoyed every minute of it, in the bright light of day—without her subtle scent fogging his brain—he realized that intimacy between them might not be the best way to keep their emotions out of the mix.

When he returned to the hospital later, it was with a renewed determination to keep their relationship within clearly established boundaries.

As they were leaving the hospital, Penny said, "Paige invited us to meet her and Travis for dinner tonight."

"I'm not feeling very sociable," he told her.

"I suggested we have dinner at your condo instead of meeting at a restaurant somewhere."

"Well, call her and tell her that something came up."

"What something?" she demanded.

"I don't care what you tell her, but I'm not in the mood for another interrogation by your sister."

"Who is now your sister-in-law," she pointed out. "And who is also engaged to your brother."

"Fine," he said, though it was anything but. "We'll have Travis and Paige over for dinner."

"*I* intended to anyway," she told him.

He scowled. "You would really have gone ahead with your plans without me?"

"I'm not going to fall in line with whatever you want whenever you want, like—" she snapped her jaw shut, leaving the rest of the statement unfinished.

"Like what?" he asked. "Or should I say—like whom?"

"Dinner's at six."

Clearly, she wasn't going to answer his question. Of course, he didn't need to be a rocket scientist to figure it out. She only had one sister, and Paige wasn't the type to be told anything by anyone. Which meant that Penny had to be talking about her mother.

Eleanor didn't strike Jason as a doormat, either, and he knew his father would never have fallen for a woman who didn't have her own ideas and opinion. But he'd heard stories about Devon McCord ruling everything in his domain—business and family included—with an iron fist. Not that he actually used his fists, at least as far as Jason knew, but there were a lot of ways to manipulate and control, and he sensed that Penny had witnessed enough to vow that she wouldn't let herself be subjected to the same.

In fact, two of the things he'd most admired about Penny while they were dating were the sharpness of her mind and the strength of her convictions. Maybe not as much as he'd admired her sexy body, but any man who claimed to be more attracted to a woman's mind than her body was either a liar or not getting any.

He sighed and resigned himself to admiring her mind, because he didn't think he was going to be in a position to admire anything else, anytime in the near future.

Jason grilled steaks for dinner, which he served with baked potatoes, green salad and warm, crusty rolls. Conversation flowed easily around the table, and Penny gradually relaxed, accepting that it was unlikely her sister and her husband would come to blows. In fact, they weren't just civil to one another but almost friendly. When Paige went to the kitchen to dish up the cheesecake she brought for dessert, Penny automatically followed to help her.

"You're worried about something," she noted, as her sister carefully lifted the chocolate-caramel-pecan confection out of the box.

"Nope, just thinking about how much I've been dying to taste this."

"Come on, Paige. I know you better than that."

Paige took the knife her sister handed her. "Okay, I guess I was thinking—and maybe worrying a little—about the fact that you're actually married."

"You said I should get married."

Paige sliced through the cake. "I said you should *think* about it."

"I did think about it," Penny said. "And then I did it."

"What changed your mind?"

"It wasn't any one thing, really." She resisted the urge to tell her sister it had been two things, because she and Jason had decided they would keep the news of the twins to themselves, at least for a while. "I guess I just finally decided that if he was so determined to be there for me and our baby, I would let him."

"I think there's more to it than that," Paige said.

Penny handed her a stack of plates. "What else could it be?"

"I think you're still in love with him."

Her sister always had had a sixth sense when it came to knowing what was on Penny's mind—and in her heart. "I don't know what my feelings are right now," she said, unwilling to admit to anyone else the feelings she'd just recently acknowledged to herself.

"Are you happy?" Paige asked gently.

Penny sighed. "I don't know if it's the pregnancy hormones or our history or my own insecurities, but one minute I'm excited and optimistic, confident that we can make this work. The next I feel this overwhelming sense of disappointment and doom, as if I've just made the biggest mistake of my life." She added forks to the plates. "He wants me to move in with him."

"Your husband?" Paige feigned shock. "What is he thinking?"

Penny smiled. "Okay, I know I sound ridiculous, but it's just another one of those things we never talked about before we got married."

"Well, you'll have lots of time to talk now."

"His penthouse is in Houston. I work in Dallas."

"It's the age of technology—you can work anywhere you want, without being tied to a specific office," her sister reminded her.

"But my doctor's in Dallas, too."

"So you'll come back for your appointments or you'll find a doctor in Houston," Paige pointed out reasonably.

"You're right," Penny admitted. "I guess I'm worried that this is one more thing that Jason is getting his way about."

"It's not a contest."

"I know," she said again.

"And Jason's not Dad," Paige said gently.

"I know that, too. I mean, when I'm thinking logically and rationally, I know. And then I have moments of panic, when I think I've given up my identity to be his wife. And then I have moments of doubt and self-pity, when I'm sure this marriage will never last and then I won't be his wife anymore."

"Honey, you are seriously messed up."

Penny managed to laugh through her tears.

"So, when are you moving?"

"I have no idea."

"Well, if you need any help, let me know."

"A lot of help you'll be, since you're mostly living at Travis's ranch now."

"Can you blame me for not wanting to spend a minute apart from the man I love?"

No, Penny couldn't blame her. She could only hope that someday the man she loved would love her even half as much as Travis obviously loved her sister.

After dessert, Penny decided that Jason should help Paige with the dishes, because she needed to talk to Travis.

"What happened to the one who cooks being exempt from cleanup?" Jason grumbled.

"You grilled steaks, you didn't make coq au vin," Penny said. "Though I'm sure you could, if you wanted to."

Her husband didn't look appeased as he carried the dessert dishes into the kitchen.

Paige picked up the wineglasses. "And since I'm guessing they want to talk about my engagement ring, I'm more than happy to let your wife sneak off with my fiancé for a few minutes." Then she turned from Jason to Penny and warned her sister, "But only a few."

"I'll bring him right back," she promised, nudging Travis toward the French doors that opened onto the patio.

"You've finished the design?" he asked, as soon as she closed the doors, so as not to be overheard by those still inside.

"Last week," she told him. "And I know I should have

sent you the sketch, but—" she pulled the ring out of her pocket and handed it to him "—I thought I'd let you see it in 3-D instead.

"I don't always have a specific customer or inspiration for my designs," she told him. "But I wanted this one to mean something to both of you, something more than just a means of showing off the new gem you discovered together."

"There are a lot of stones," he noted, turning the platinum band to examine it from every angle.

She nodded. "The big one at the center represents the Santa Magdalena Diamond, because it was the search for that which brought the two of you together. The slightly smaller ones on either side represent you and Paige, and the even smaller stones, graduated in size until they're almost just jewel chips at the back of the band, are for all of the little treasures that your future together will bring."

Travis was silent, still studying the ring.

Penny was unaccustomedly nervous as she waited for his verdict. She'd created designs for rich and famous customers around the globe, but no project had mattered to her as much as this one, the ring that would be given to her sister by the man she loved and worn by her forever.

"I know you asked for a design, not a finished product, but I was really excited to see what it would look like, and Edmond had the time to put it together, but—"

"No buts," he finally interrupted to say. "I think it's absolutely perfect."

She exhaled. "Really?"

"Really. And I'm so glad I asked you to do this."

Her personal relief gave way to professional indignation. "You had doubts that I was up to the challenge?"

He shook his head. "But I did wonder if I should have put you on the spot with my request. Because I realized after the fact, that it was a little insensitive to ask you to design an engagement ring for your sister, in light of everything that was going on between you and my brother.

"And for what it's worth," he continued, "I'm really glad things have worked out between you and Jason."

"I wouldn't say they're worked out, but we're working on them."

Travis nodded. "Fair enough."

"Now we should get back inside, so that you can take your fiancée somewhere more private to make your engagement official."

"And so you can be alone with your husband?"

She ducked back into the condo rather than attempt to find an answer to his teasing question.

While Penny and Travis were out on the balcony, Jason was trapped in the close confines of the kitchen with his new sister-in-law. Paige didn't seem nearly as uncomfortable as he felt, but maybe that was because she hadn't seduced his virginal sister. She had, however, been caught sneaking around his brother's ranch—a somewhat lesser violation, perhaps, but a violation nonetheless.

Still, she was the first to break the silence.

"I think I'd like to try your coq au vin sometime," Paige said, offering the proverbial olive branch.

"Because you enjoyed your meal so much, or because getting together for dinner again will give you an opportunity to keep an eye on your sister?"

"You're perceptive," she noted. "And maybe I'm feeling a little guilty, too."

"About ratting me out to your sister?"

"Hardly." She put the salad dressings back in the refrigerator. "About telling her she should marry you."

He smiled at that. "You think you talked her into it?"

"Maybe."

"Penny doesn't do anything she doesn't want to do," he reminded her sister. "Ever. She may look sweet and docile, but she has a spine of steel and a mind to match."

"Hmm." Paige considered him as she wrapped up the leftover cake. "You might understand her better than I gave you credit for."

"I didn't think you'd given me any credit."

"I'm trying," she said. "But that doesn't mean I'm willing to wipe the slate clean."

"I wouldn't dare hope that you would."

"You hurt her, Jason."

He didn't reply to that, because he knew that no glib response could refute the truth of her statement any more than it could reflect how truly regretful he felt.

"She may have a sharp mind and a strong will," Paige said. "But she also has a soft and generous heart, and you took advantage of that."

He finished loading the cutlery and closed the dishwasher door. "I know."

Her brows lifted. "You're not going to offer any explanations or excuses?"

"Not to you."

Paige seemed taken aback by his response at first, but then she nodded. "Take care of my sister."

"I will," Jason promised, then smiled. "If she'll let me."

* * *

After Travis and Paige had gone, Penny felt awkward and uncomfortable being alone with Jason. She'd watched her sister and his brother throughout the evening, and had envied the casual intimacies of two people who were obviously connected on so many levels.

It was ironic, really, because Paige hadn't been with Travis even half as long as Penny had dated Jason, but they were so at ease with one another, so obviously in love.

Penny, on the other hand, was pregnant and married to the father of her babies, but love had never been part of the package.

She felt a pang of longing deep in her heart, and the empty feeling wasn't at all assuaged by Jason's next words.

"I want to head back to Houston tomorrow," he told her.

"You've been away from the office a lot recently," she acknowledged.

He nodded. "But if you need to stay until your mom comes home from the hospital, or—"

"I don't need to stay," she interrupted. "She has Rex, and I'd probably just end up feeling like I was in the way."

"You want to come with me?"

He sounded not just surprised but wary, and she wondered if, despite his invitation the night before, he didn't want her with him in Houston.

"It will be kind of difficult for both of us to be there for our babies, if we're not living together," she said.

"We have some time before the babies come," he reminded her.

"What are you suggesting—that we continue to live apart until after I give birth?"

"No, of course not. I'm just suggesting that, if you need some time, you should take it."

"I don't need time, Jason." She waited a beat. "Do you?"

"No."

His response was both immediate and adamant, and eased the nerves in her tummy a little. The nerves eased a little bit more when he reached for her hand and tugged her down beside him on the couch.

She leaned back, but couldn't quite relax. She didn't have the first clue about being a wife or simply being with the man who was suddenly her husband.

"Did you know that Travis is four years younger than me?" he asked.

She frowned at the question that seemed to come out of the blue. "What does that have to do with anything?"

"He's four years younger than me but two years older than your sister, and you're the same age as Paige, which means that I'm six years older than you."

She'd never thought about the age difference before and she certainly wasn't going to worry about it now. But apparently, he was, so she responded lightly, "That just makes it less likely that you'll throw me away for a younger model in ten years, because I'll still be the younger model."

"There is that," he agreed with a smile.

Then his gaze locked with hers, and his smile slowly faded. His eyes darkened and his head dipped closer. Penny felt her breath catch and her heart pound.

But then he drew back and abruptly pushed himself off of the sofa.

"Come on."

She blinked, confusion and disappointment tangling inside of her. "Where are we going?"

"I'm getting you home so that you can get packed," he said. "It's moving day tomorrow."

Chapter Twelve

Penny awoke early the next morning, filled with both apprehension and excitement. It was, as Jason had called it, moving day. But she knew it was more significant than just moving her clothes from the McCord mansion in Dallas to his penthouse in Houston. It was the day they were finally going to start moving forward with their life together.

Rex brought Eleanor home from the hospital just before lunch, allowing Jason and Penny to share a quick visit with their respective parents before heading out. Penny was pleased to see that her mother was doing so well. In fact, she didn't just look good, she looked radiant, though Penny suspected that had more to do with the care of her husband than the doctors at the hospital.

But after a quick lunch, they said their goodbyes and

headed out. Because she wanted to have access to her own vehicle in Houston, Penny drove her car and Jason drove his. And she realized that four hours alone on the road was a lot of time to think.

Mostly, she thought about Jason and their marriage. She wanted them to get settled and feel comfortable with one another before the babies came along and created further chaos in their lives, but she suspected that wouldn't happen easily. Even though he'd been the one to suggest getting married, she wondered if he felt trapped by the circumstances that had triggered his proposal. But then she remembered the look on his face when he'd seen their babies on the sonogram, and she discarded that thought.

Her mind was still filled with unanswered questions when she followed his car into the parking garage. Or maybe it was the not knowing what Jason wanted from their marriage that had her feeling as nervous as a virginal bride. Ironic, considering that she'd lost her virginity months earlier and her status as a bride two days previously.

Technically, she and Jason were newlyweds, but she didn't feel like a newlywed. In fact, she didn't feel wed at all because, aside from the ring on her finger, absolutely nothing had changed in their relationship since they'd spoken their vows.

In all fairness, they'd been both busy and preoccupied since their quick trip to and from Las Vegas. Now that they were alone together, she was sure that things would change.

Wouldn't they?

* * *

When Lucas, the doorman she remembered from previous visits to the penthouse, came in with her luggage, Jason was on the phone in the den.

"Where would you like your bags, Miss?"

"In the spare bedroom, please, Lucas."

He smiled, pleased that she remembered his name, and went to do her bidding.

He didn't know, obviously, that she and Jason were married, and since she wasn't feeling very married, she didn't bother informing him of the fact. Or maybe she didn't tell him because she didn't want him to wonder why Mr. Foley's wife wouldn't be moving into his bedroom.

By the time he came back to the foyer after delivering her bags, Jason had finished his call.

"Thank you, Lucas," he said, and slipped a no doubt very generous tip into the man's hand.

"Thank *you,* Mr. Foley," Lucas replied, then nodded to Penny and walked out, leaving Jason and Penny alone with a whole lot of tension.

She felt awkward and tongue-tied, like a woman on a blind date, certainly not like a woman who was finally alone with the man she'd married two days earlier.

"Are you hungry?" Jason asked, breaking the silence.

"I'm always hungry these days."

"I've got some pasta sauce in the freezer."

"Sounds good to me."

"I'll put the water on to boil, if you want to unpack."

"Sure," she agreed.

They escaped the awkwardness of the moment by moving in different directions—Jason into the kitchen and Penny down the hall.

She looked around the room she'd claimed as her

own, at least temporarily, and decided it was more than suitable. The dark mission-style furniture contrasted with the natural bamboo flooring and combined with the copper and bronze colors in the bedding and drapes to provide an overall effect that was both attractive and warm. It could use a few feminine touches, perhaps, but Penny hoped she wouldn't be sleeping there long enough for it to matter.

But for now, she unzipped her duffel and began transferring her clothes from the bag to the dresser.

She was nearly finished the task when she heard footsteps in the hall. Glancing up, she saw Jason in the doorway.

His brow furrowed when he realized what she was doing. "Did you forget where the master bedroom was?"

"No," she said. "I just thought we might both need some space. For a while."

His frown deepened. "I thought we'd make this room into a nursery."

She noticed that he didn't actually say he wanted her to share his room and his bed, only that he had other plans for this one.

"We've got almost six months before the babies are due," she reminded him.

He shrugged. "Yeah, I guess that's true."

It seemed to Penny that he was almost relieved by her decision, a belief that was supported when he made no further protest about the sleeping arrangements but only said, "Dinner's ready."

After they'd eaten, Jason said he wanted to catch up on some e-mails, so Penny claimed exhaustion and went to bed.

She thought it was ironic that her first time in Jason's penthouse as his wife was the first time she would be sleeping in the guest room. Not that she expected to get much sleep. How could she, when there were so many questions swirling through her mind? Most notably—how had things gone so wrong so quickly?

Everything had been good when they were in Las Vegas. Better than good. Jason had obviously made an effort to give her a wedding with all of the trimmings, an effort that reminded her of the wonderful man he was, the man she'd started falling for when he crossed a wide hotel lobby to say hello.

Unfortunately, their celebration had been cut short by her mother's emergency surgery, but she didn't understand how or why that would change anything between her and Jason. Because something had definitely changed.

He hadn't kissed her since their wedding. There had been some casually affectionate gestures—a touch of his hand to her arm, a brush of his lips against her cheek—but nothing more than that.

It was as she'd feared: now that Jason's ring was on her finger, the challenge was gone. He had what he wanted, a marriage to the mother of his children, and he wasn't interested in anything more.

But what about what she wanted? Because a marriage in name only wasn't exactly her dream come true.

The problem was, she didn't have the first clue how to go about getting what she *did* want.

By the end of the week, Penny still didn't have any answers.

It wasn't as if Jason ignored her so much as he always

seemed to have excuses for keeping a careful distance between them. If she was cooking dinner, he was on the phone. If she was watching television in the living room, he had work in the den. If she wanted to go for a walk, he had any one of a dozen excuses that rolled easily off of his tongue.

And though Penny was usually a cheerful person, she found herself falling into a funk. She felt so far away from everything that was familiar, everyone she knew. She missed her sister, her mother, even her overprotective brothers, though everyone seemed to be so busy with their own lives she wasn't sure she'd have seen much of them, even if she was still in Dallas. But she wasn't in Dallas, so it wasn't even an option.

Apparently, her dark mood wasn't something she could or did hide very well, because even Jason commented on it when he found her nibbling on a slice of toast in the kitchen Saturday morning.

"Are you okay?" he asked her, pouring himself a mug of coffee from the pot she'd brewed. "You look a little out of sorts."

She shrugged. "I'm just feeling a little lonely, I guess."

"Ouch."

She managed a smile. "Maybe homesick is more accurate."

"You miss your family," he guessed.

"I know you're my family now, too," she said, "but you're hardly ever here. And when you are, you treat me more like a roommate than your wife."

"Because I don't demand dinner when I walk in the door?"

He was joking, but Penny wasn't amused. She was

trying to adjust to all of the recent changes in her life, and he wasn't helping.

"Because you don't demand anything," she told him. "Because you rarely come home before eight o'clock at night, and even when you do come home, I'm not sure you realize I'm here."

"I'm sorry if you've been feeling neglected," he said. "But we have some big projects going on at work, and—"

"I'm not asking you to change your schedule to accommodate me. I don't need to be entertained, just acknowledged. Until they get my office renovated at the Houston store, I'm working from here. Day in and day out, these walls are the only thing I'm seeing."

"You want a change," he guessed.

Which was both a true and wholly inadequate generalization of what she was feeling, and she wondered if he really didn't get it or if he was deliberately misunderstanding her.

"I want to spend some time with you."

"Okay," he said. "Let's go shopping."

Shopping?

Jason almost couldn't believe it when he heard the word come out of his mouth. But truth be told, anything—even shopping—was preferable to being alone with her in his apartment all day. Sure, he could hide out in his den, but it seemed as if he'd been doing a lot of that, and sooner or later, Penny would figure out that he was deliberately distancing himself from her. What she wouldn't know was that he was doing so because it was the only way he could be sure to resist the temptation of her.

But if he couldn't maintain a safe physical distance between them, he could at least add the buffer of a crowd and a public venue. As explicit and prurient as his fantasies might be, it was highly unlikely he would be overcome by lust in the middle of a shopping center on a Saturday afternoon.

They started at a major home décor center, and he willingly followed her around, looking at window coverings and throw pillows and lamp shades.

"What do you think of that rug?" she asked, pointing to a carpet on display against a wall.

He shrugged, deciding it was inoffensive, if not particularly appealing. "Where would you put it?"

"In the dining room."

"Sure," he agreed.

"You didn't even look at the price."

He shrugged again. "If you want it, the price is irrelevant."

She shook her head. "What I want *isn't* a dining room rug."

"What is it?" he asked, aware that he might not want to hear her answer.

But she only shook her head again. "You had a professional decorate your home. Who am I to change anything?"

"You're my wife," he reminded her. "And it's your home now, too."

She didn't say anything, and he couldn't begin to guess what she was thinking. He always thought she was one of the most open and honest people he'd ever known, but lately he hadn't been able to get a read on her at all. On the other hand, maybe it wasn't Penny who was making the reading difficult but the distance he was deliberately keeping between them.

"And there is one room that definitely needs some work," he prompted her.

"The nursery?" she guessed, and seemed to brighten a little.

And that was how they ended up at Baby World.

If Jason was to make a list of his top-ten favorite things to do on a Saturday, Penny couldn't imagine that shopping would make the cut. That he was happily browsing the aisles of Baby World left her speechless.

It was Jason who pointed out, logically, that they needed to get some things so they would be ready for the babies' arrivals. Although they still had several more months before then, Penny agreed. Besides, she thought it might be fun to shop with him, to pick out cribs and playpens and high chairs, and it was—but Jason wasn't ready to stop there.

He picked up an enormous stuffed dog with big floppy ears and a ridiculous bowtie in place of a collar.

Penny shook her head. "We have to fit two cribs, a change table, and probably a rocking chair in that room. There is no room for that ridiculous dog."

Jason frowned at her disapproval but put the dog back on the shelf.

As they browsed through the clothing aisles, a little sleeper caught Penny's eye. It was white velour with tiny yellow ducklings marching across the front, and it was absolutely the sweetest thing she'd ever seen.

Unable to resist the impulse, she lifted the hanger off the rack and touched a fingertip to one of the fuzzy little tails.

"Is a baby really supposed to fit into that?" Jason asked. "It's tiny."

"Babies are tiny," she told him, and, with a last glance, replaced the hanger on the rack.

"Why did you put it back?" Jason asked her.

"It's too early to be buying outfits," she said, though she couldn't deny that she was tempted. "Besides, we don't know if we're having girls or boys or one of each."

"It's white and yellow," he pointed out, taking not just one but two of the sleepers off the rack again and tossing them into the cart. "Do you want to find out?"

"Find out what?" she asked, her attention on the sleepers he'd added to the rapidly growing pile of items in the cart.

"If the babies are girls or boys or one of each."

"I don't know." She'd been thinking about it, considering the pros and cons, but was still undecided. "Do you?"

"Yeah," he answered without hesitation, obviously having given the matter some thought himself. "I think it would be more fun to plan and prepare. And it would definitely be easier to pick out names."

"Do you have a preference?"

"For names?"

She shook her head. "Gender."

He considered. "I know I'm supposed to say I don't, that so long as the babies are healthy nothing else matters. And that is the most important thing," he agreed. "But if I could choose, I think I'd really like at least one girl."

"You want a girl?"

"Why does that surprise you?"

She shrugged. "I just figured...I mean, most men want boys to continue the line and carry the family name."

"A lot of women keep their family names when they marry. You did."

There was something in his tone—disappointment, maybe—that caught her off guard. "Does that bother you?"

"It shouldn't," he admitted. "But in some ways, it seems as if it's not legal, not real. I'm still Jason Foley and you're still Penny McCord."

"You could change your name."

"Yeah, that would go over big with my family."

She didn't know what to say. She wasn't sure why she hadn't changed her name when they married, unless it was for the reason that he'd guessed—because their marriage didn't feel real.

Or maybe because she hadn't been sure it would last.

She was an optimist by nature, but only a week after their exchange of vows, she was already wondering how long they could go on with the way things were between them—and she was slowly driving herself crazy trying to figure him out.

She knew he was still attracted to her. Maybe if she'd been farther along in her pregnancy, she might have doubted that, but though the changes in her body were obvious to her, she had barely begun to show. And she'd caught that look in his eyes—the heat, the desire, the need—when he thought she didn't see him looking.

For goodness' sake, they were married. She was his wife, soon to be the mother of his children, and all those pregnancy hormones racing through her body—not to mention the effect of his proximity—were combining to drive her insane with wanting.

So why was he holding back? Why was he so determined to maintain this charade of friendship? What was going on with him?

What was going on with him was that Jason had figured out the only way to keep Penny from mattering too much was to compartmentalize their relationship and his feelings for her.

First she'd been his lover, then she'd become his wife, and somewhere in between, they started to be friends. In just a few more months, she would also be the mother of his children. And the more time they spent together, the more the lines between the titles and roles became blurred. But there was still one line that he had not crossed.

And if he crossed that line, if he gave in to the urge to make love to her—and there was no doubt about those urges—there would be no compartments. She would be his wife, his friend, his lover. His everything.

And if he lost her, he would lose everything. Just as he'd lost everything when Kara died.

That was a risk he wouldn't take again.

So he ignored her signals. The way she touched him, or brushed against him, or looked at him. It wasn't easy, but he managed.

He was in the den Tuesday night, not really working so much as avoiding his wife, when she tracked him down. He focused on the e-mail that was open in front of him, without really seeing the words, all too conscious of Penny hovering in the doorway, waiting for him to look up, to acknowledge her.

He'd always thought his penthouse was a little too big, that there was too much space. Since Penny had moved in, he felt as if the walls were closing in on him.

It wasn't really as bad as that, and it wasn't her fault. It's just that he couldn't go anywhere in the whole damn apartment without stumbling across some sign of her presence—a bouquet of fresh flowers in an old milk bottle in the kitchen, a glass vase filled with river rocks in the dining room, some scented leaves and flowers in a bowl in the bathroom. Everywhere he turned, he saw her, smelled her, wanted her.

The only rooms that bore no evidence of her presence were those she hadn't stepped foot into since moving in: the master bedroom and bath. But they weren't devoid of memories. Every night when he crawled into his king-size bed, he pictured her there, naked and rumpled and tangled in the sheets, a sleepy smile curving her lips. And every time he stepped into the shower, he remembered her there—her long, lean limbs slick with the soap he'd rubbed over her body.

He forced the tempting memories aside and glanced up from the computer screen.

"I don't want to disturb you, if you're in the middle of something," she said.

"Nothing that can't wait," he said, unwilling to admit exactly how much she disturbed him—every minute of every day.

"I was just wondering if you knew where our marriage certificate was."

"It's in the filing cabinet. Why?"

"I need a notarized copy to register my change of

name," she told him. "I didn't think too much about it before, or I would have done it automatically when we got married."

"Why are you doing it now?" he asked.

"Because I want to prove to you that I'm committed to this marriage."

Boundaries, he reminded himself.

He might have been a little annoyed, maybe even disappointed, that she'd remained Penny McCord after their exchange of vows. But then he'd realized that the name was a symbolic barrier, a confirmation that their marriage hadn't blurred all of the lines, and he needed that barrier now.

"You don't have to prove anything to me."

"I'm not doing it for you. I'm doing it for us."

That was what he was afraid of—that she was thinking in terms of "us" while he was still trying to keep their lives separate and apart as much as possible.

"Do you have a problem with that?" she asked, when he didn't say anything.

"I'm just concerned that I pushed for too much too soon."

"You're not just talking about the name change," she guessed.

"No, I'm not," he admitted.

"It's a little late to be having second thoughts, isn't it?"

Much too late, he admitted to himself.

But what he said was, "We haven't consummated our marriage."

Penny glanced away, but not before he caught a glimpse of the wounded confusion that clouded her eyes, and he mentally cursed himself. He was doing this so as not to hurt her again, so that neither of them could hurt the other.

"So what happened today?" she finally asked, turning back to him again. "Did you run into an old girlfriend? Or a new prospect?"

"This has nothing to do with anyone else."

"Two weeks ago, you didn't want anything as much as you wanted to marry me and be a father to our babies, and now you want an annulment?"

"I don't want an annulment," he told her, though he wondered if it might have been better for both of them if he did. If he could cut all ties and let her go, to live her life with someone who could give her everything she wanted and deserved in a relationship. Someone whose heart wasn't beyond reach. "But I thought you might."

"I agreed to marry you of my own free will."

"You agreed to marry me because you're pregnant."

She lifted her chin, met his gaze evenly. "And the action that led to that was also of my own free will."

"You were a virgin."

"So? My lack of sexual experience didn't interfere with the working of my brain."

"I took advantage of your inexperience."

She actually laughed at that. "Do you remember our first night together?"

He did, in achingly vivid detail.

"I seduced you," she reminded him.

"You think so?"

"I know I did." Her lips curved in a smile of pure feminine satisfaction. "You didn't even know what hit you."

"Is there a point to this trek down memory lane?"

"I'm getting to it," she assured him, but seemed to go completely off-track with her next question. "Why did you want to marry me, Jason?"

"I thought that was obvious."

"So your decision was based on nothing more than the fact that I'm pregnant?"

"I want to be there for you," he said. "And to be a father to our babies."

"When we got married, when we were dancing at the hotel in Las Vegas, you said that we were good together. You talked about desire and attraction."

"A man will say almost anything to get a woman into his bed."

"And yet, you haven't made any attempt to get me there since that night."

"It didn't seem right to take advantage of the situation."

"You might have talked to me about it," she said, reasonably. "Instead of making me feel as if you didn't want me anymore."

"I didn't want to complicate things."

"And a husband and wife sharing a bed, sharing affection, is a 'complication'?"

"You were the one who wanted to sleep in the guest room," he reminded her.

"Because I didn't want you to assume I'd sleep with you just because we were married."

"Yeah, I got that."

"But it wasn't that I didn't want to sleep with you."

"Huh?"

She huffed out a breath. "Apparently, you didn't get that."

"Penny, it's been a really long day and I don't have

the time or the energy to decipher some complex female code. If there's something you want to say, just say it."

"I love you," she said. "Is that simple and straight-forward enough for you?"

He shook his head, battled against the instinctive panic that rose up inside of him upon hearing those words. He didn't want her to love him, and he sure as hell didn't want to love her.

"You don't love me," he said. "You're just romanti-cizing the situation."

"For goodness' sake, do you think I wanted this to happen? Do you think I wanted to fall in love with a man who obviously doesn't want to love me?"

"Then what do you want?"

"I want a real marriage."

He didn't need her to spell it out any more explicitly. And he wouldn't admit that he wanted the same thing. He wouldn't risk blurring the boundaries he'd so care-fully maintained.

"I care about you, Penny. You know that I do. But you want more than I can give you."

"Maybe that's true," she said softly. "But why won't you at least try?"

"I can't."

Even if he'd guessed that she wouldn't accept such a vague answer, he still wouldn't have anticipated her response.

"Tell me about her," she said.

He frowned. "About who?"

"Whoever made you afraid to open up your heart again."

"You have quite an imagination," he said, but he didn't quite meet her gaze when he spoke the words.

"And you built up those walls for a reason."

She moved closer, deliberately invading his personal space, as if to push right up against those walls she mentioned and tear them down. But he was more determined not to let her.

"I'll be a good father to our babies and a faithful husband," he said. "But I can't promise you more than that."

"Faithful?" she challenged, taking another step until she was so close her breasts brushed against his chest. So close that when she tipped her head back, her lips— full and soft and tempting—were only inches from his own. "You'd have to actually be sleeping with me to be faithful to me."

The challenge was in her eyes as much as her words, and if there was a man alive who could deny himself the one thing he wanted more than anything else when it was so blatantly offered, that man was much stronger than Jason.

"Is that what you want? Is that what will make it real for you, Penny? If I take you to bed, will that be enough?"

"I don't know." She met his gaze evenly. "But at least it would be a start."

All the warnings of his brain were drowned out by the much louder and more insistent demands of his thoroughly aroused body. He grabbed her wrist. "Let's go, then."

Chapter Thirteen

Penny knew that Jason was trying to shock her into protesting, and that if she pulled back, he would only be too willing to let her go. But she had no intention of pulling away when he needed her so much. Because she'd finally figured out that he did, that he'd been so intent on pushing her away because he was afraid to hold on, afraid to admit his feelings for her. She still didn't understand what was behind that fear, but now that she recognized it, she was determined to help him overcome it.

Once they were in his bedroom, he turned to face her, his eyes dark and unreadable. "You're sure this is what you want?"

"Positive," she said, giving no hint of the knots in her belly as she calmly began stripping her clothes away.

His eyes followed the movement of her fingers, as

she unfastened the row of buttons that ran down the front of her blouse, and the knots intensified.

What if this wasn't what he wanted?

What if she'd been wrong?

But she'd come too far to back down now. She wouldn't give up on their marriage without a fight.

As the silk top floated to the floor, his eyes dropped to her breasts, covered only by whisper-thin black lace. She hesitated only a fraction of a second before unfastening the clip at the front, and then, even that scrap of lace slipped away. His eyes flared, dark and hot.

The intensity of his gaze, the naked heat in his eyes, had her fingers fumbling as they worked the button at the back of her skirt, then the zipper. She pushed the skirt over her hips, let it pool at her feet.

Gone were the days when she worried that she didn't have a model-perfect body. At fourteen weeks into her pregnancy, gone were any hopes of having a model-perfect body. But Jason had never seemed to mind that she was imperfect. In fact, he'd shown her time and again while they were dating that he loved her body—even if he didn't love her. And since it was one of few weapons she had in her arsenal, she was prepared to use it.

As she stripped away the final scrap of lace, she knew she was baring not just her body but her soul.

"Now the question is…is this what you want?" she asked him.

He swallowed. "If you're asking do I want to have sex with you, I'd have to respond with a very enthusiastic 'Yes!'"

But he was still holding back, refusing to give her what she wanted, what they both needed. It was as if he'd dug in his heels so deep, he didn't know how to take that first step.

So she lowered herself onto the edge of the mattress and prompted him with a smile and a crook of her finger. "Then why don't you bring some of that enthusiasm over here?"

He stripped away his clothes, then came to join her on the wide bed. He curled his hand over her shoulder, and the warmth of his palm against her bare skin sent shivers of excitement dancing through her veins. His gaze dropped to her mouth, and her lips parted, anticipating, wanting.

But he didn't kiss her, and though she was disappointed, she wasn't surprised. Kissing was an intimacy he wouldn't allow himself, not now, when he was so intent on making a point. This wasn't about feeling close and connected. It was about sex—raw and uncensored. He wasn't going to pretty it up with soft words or gentle touches.

But she didn't need it to be anything more than what it was: primitive, elemental, real.

He tangled his hand in her hair, pulling her head back. Then he feasted on her throat, using his lips and tongue and teeth to drive her to distraction. She fell back on the mattress, dragged him with her, arching in response to the fast and impatient stroke of his hands over her quivering flesh.

His teeth scraped over her collarbone, his tongue swirled around one peaked nipple, then the other. Her breath was coming in short, fast bursts now, as she fought to draw air into her lungs while the world spun around her.

She cried out in shocked pleasure as the fierce suckling of her breast sent her tumbling off the edge of the first sharp peak of pleasure. Then finally, his mouth came down on hers, hot and hungry, giving nothing while demanding everything.

She let him take and take, and she gave, freely and openly. She held nothing back and offered up everything that was in her heart.

He drove into her, hard and deep and she cried out again, as fresh waves of pleasure crashed over her. She wrapped herself around him, arms and legs holding on to him through the storm of dizzying pleasure.

And then, unexpectedly, his kiss softened, his hands gentled, his strokes slowed. There was no more taking or giving, but sharing. Two bodies joined together, moving together, loving together. And it felt so right, so good, so perfect.

The physical aspect of their relationship had always been spectacular. True, her experience was limited, but she'd heard enough complaints from other women to know she'd been fortunate in choosing a first lover who was so considerate of her needs, who ensured her pleasure before taking his own.

But this…this was beyond spectacular. It was beyond anything she'd ever imagined.

Penny closed her eyes so that he wouldn't see the tears of joy that filled them. Yes, this was what she'd wanted: to truly join together with him—to make love with the man she loved.

She gasped and shuddered and clung while her body tightened around him, and gloried in the pulsing release of his body into hers.

Penny lay motionless beneath him for a long while,

afraid to move, afraid to burst the fragile bubble of happiness that surrounded her. Making love with Jason had been an experience that transcended all others. And she didn't believe for one minute that he could make love to her the way he'd just made love to her unless he was in love with her, at least a little.

Of course, that didn't mean he was comfortable with his feelings, or willing to admit them, as he proved when he rolled away from her and off of the bed. She blinked back a rush of tears as he picked his clothes up off of the floor and began putting them back on. She didn't know why he was fighting so hard to deny what was between them—or how long she could continue to bang her head against the walls he kept building to keep her out.

"At least that puts your annulment argument to rest," she said, keeping her tone light.

He paused in the buttoning of his shirt to glance over at her. "Is that what this was really about?"

"You know what this was really about."

He didn't say anything as he fastened his belt, then turned to face the mirror to straighten the collar of his shirt.

Apparently, she was going to have to bang her head once more.

"I love you, Jason."

He stood for a moment with his back to her, though she caught his gaze in the mirror, and the anguish in his eyes tore at her heart.

But all he said was, "Damn you."

Then he stormed out of the room.

Penny stared at the empty doorway for a long time, as if she could will him to come back. But a few minutes later, she heard the click of the lock and knew he'd not just left the bedroom and the apartment, he'd left her.

She pulled her knees up and hugged them tight against her chest, where her heart was breaking wide-open.

When Jason left Penny in his bed, he didn't know where he planned to go, he only knew he couldn't stay. He wouldn't let himself be sucked into her fantasy. Because that's what love was—an illusion at best, and usually only a temporary one.

"I love you, Jason."

Well, he hadn't asked her to love him. And he sure as hell hadn't wanted to love her.

And he didn't.

She was his wife, the woman carrying his babies, and he fully intended to make a home with her and live together as a family. But he absolutely was not going to fall in love with her.

Too late.

He ignored the taunting voice in the back of his mind, refused to believe it. Nothing had changed between them. Making love with her didn't change anything. Because he'd fallen in love with her long before he'd made love with her again.

And while falling in love sounded easy, like a leisurely descent through the clouds in a hot-air balloon, the reality, at least for Jason, was different. More like a jump from a plane at fifteen thousand feet without a parachute, the realization of his feelings slamming into him with the force of hitting the ground.

He had no idea how or when it had happened. Obviously sometime between their meeting at the Harcourt-

Ellsworth wedding and their own. But it had taken the physical act of lovemaking for him to realize it. The shared intimacy had broken through all that remained of the barriers around his heart. He simply couldn't continue to hold out against her. She was so soft and warm and giving, and he was helpless to resist her.

But old habits die hard, and he wasn't ready to admit that he could or did need anyone else to make his life complete. After all, he was perfectly happy with his life before Penny came along, and he could be just as happy again without her.

So why was he feeling so miserable? And how was he going to be a father to their babies if he walked out on their marriage before they were even born?

They were questions he didn't know how to answer, or maybe he didn't want to accept the answers. At least not yet.

Until he figured it out, he opted to stay at the office where he had a spare shirt in the closet and a couch almost long enough to stretch out on. He had everything he needed—except the softhearted, green-eyed woman who had somehow stolen his heart.

What he didn't think he had—and certainly hadn't expected—was a secretary who returned at ten o'clock that night and caught him trying to stretch out on the couch in his office.

"Don't you have a bed at home?" Barb asked him.

Jason glared at her. "What are you doing back here?"

"I forgot to water the plants."

"That's not in your job description."

"Neither is dispensing marital advice, but apparently I have to do that, too."

"Thanks, but I don't need any advice."

"If that was true, you wouldn't be sleeping on a couch in your office."

"Okay, what's your advice?" Jason asked, figuring, the sooner she said what she wanted to, the sooner she would be gone.

"Take your sorry ass home."

He frowned. "That's your advice?"

"I never claimed to be Dr. Phil."

"And what makes you think I have anything to be sorry for?"

"You're the one who got kicked out of your home."

"She didn't kick me out." Of course, he hadn't stuck around long enough to give her the chance. Instead, he'd run away like the coward he was.

"Then there's no reason you can't go back," Barb said, logically.

No reason, except that he'd done exactly what he'd promised himself he wouldn't do—he'd fallen in love with the woman he married.

He wasn't a man who was easily fazed. He knew how to keep his cool in the face of a crisis. He'd handled the news of Penny's pregnancy; he'd coped with the surprise that she was carrying twins. Yet the realization that he'd fallen in love had sent him into a complete tailspin.

But Jason knew it wasn't really the loving that scared him—it was the possibility that he could lose Penny as he'd lost Kara so many years before.

He didn't come home that night or the next.

Penny could have called Jason on his cell or at the

office, but she didn't think there was any point. She'd said everything she needed to say, and so had he.

Once again she'd been a fool.

The first night he was gone, she cried. She cried for herself, for Jason, for everything they might have had together. She cried until she was sure there were no tears left inside of her. The next day she wallowed in misery and self-pity until a question began to tug at her mind.

If Jason didn't care about her, if her feelings meant nothing to him, why was he running scared? Because, after two days, she realized that was exactly what he was doing.

Well, she wasn't going to chase after him. She'd given him her heart, she was determined to at least hold on to her pride.

She felt a flutter of something in her tummy, like the brush of butterfly wings. Then it came again, and she sucked in a breath as realization stirred along with the babies inside her. Her hand moved instinctively to her belly, her palm splayed protectively over the tiny lives growing in her womb.

Okay, so there were bigger things at stake than her pride.

But the way she figured it, he had to come home sometime, and she would be there when he did. Beyond that, she didn't really have a plan.

Having Devon McCord as a father taught her that the path of least resistance was unquestioning obedience. As a child, she'd done what she was told to do when she was told to do it. As an adult, she'd had to make a conscious effort to break that pattern.

Jason had never tried to tell her what to do. He'd

never made her feel as if she was incapable of making her own decisions. The only doubts she had came from within herself. Doubts that had been planted by her father's criticisms and were nurtured by her own efforts to avoid conflict.

But this time, she wasn't going to sit back and accept whatever came her way. She was going to take control of her life and her future.

The first step was moving out of the guest room. Because she wasn't a guest—this was her home, too, and it was past time she started acting as if she was living there instead of just visiting.

For the most part, she did like Jason's penthouse the way it was. The room she was least fond of, however, was the master bedroom. The walls were a dark green, the furniture was teak, the bedding and window coverings a deep burgundy. While everything coordinated nicely, it was a little dark for her tastes. And if she was going to be sleeping in there—and she planned on it— she would need to make some changes.

She bought a can of sage-colored paint and painted only one wall—the longest one behind the bed. Of course, she had to call building maintenance to get someone to move the bed for her—she wouldn't attempt to move a king-size bed on her own, even if she wasn't pregnant. Then she added new bedding and window coverings in a light tan color, keeping the burgundy and green throw pillows for color, and hung some sepia-tone prints in oversize frames on the dark walls.

When it was done, she fell into bed, exhausted.

Her last thought before she fell asleep was that she would tackle the nursery tomorrow.

* * *

Jason was staring bleary-eyed at the quarterly report on his computer screen when the phone buzzed, not realizing that he was half-asleep until the noise jolted him awake. Three days had passed since he'd walked out on Penny—and so had three endless, sleepless nights.

He reached for the receiver with one hand and his coffee mug with the other. "Yeah."

"Lindsay Conners is on line two."

"Who?" He lifted the mug to his lips, grimaced when he swallowed a mouthful of cold coffee. He must have been dozing longer than he'd realized for his coffee to have chilled so much.

"She said if you didn't recognize the name to tell you that she's the mother of the baby who spit up on your suit."

The fog around his brain cleared. "Oh. Right. Thanks, Barb."

She disconnected and he picked up line two.

Five minutes later, he was sitting across from Lindsay in the café in the lobby.

She was, he noted with surprise, alone. "No kids today?"

She smiled, looking a lot more relaxed than the last time he'd seen her. "No. They're being taken care of by…a friend."

"Are you here about a job? Because I can contact Margaret in HR and…" His words trailed off as she shook her head.

"No, I'm not looking for a job. I just wanted to stop by and thank you for being so kind to me that day on the plane, and for making me remember that there are still some nice guys in the world."

"You didn't need to come over here for that."

"I did," she insisted. "Because when I finally got home that day, and finally got the kids settled, I started thinking about another nice guy, one I hadn't spoken to in a lot of years. Long story short—I'm moving to Alaska."

He wasn't sure if she'd omitted a lot of information or if his sleep-deprived brain was failing to make a logical connection. "You're moving to Alaska…because I held your baby on the plane?"

She laughed. "Because you made me remember Ethan—the man I should have married. Except that I was twenty years old when he proposed and afraid of everything I would miss out on if I tied myself down at that point in my life. So, instead of taking everything that he offered, I turned away.

"Six years later, when I was a little more mature and experienced, I met Brian. Maybe he wasn't the love of my life, but he was the man I was with at the time I was ready to get married and have a family. By the time I realized I never loved him the way I'd loved Ethan— and that he never loved me, either—we had one baby and another on the way.

"I don't regret the years we had together," she said. "Because despite everything else, I ended up with two wonderful kids. But when Brian left, I went through the whole gamut of emotions. I was stunned, hurt, angry, sad. But mostly I was afraid. Afraid that I would never stop hurting, and never have the courage to open up my heart again.

"And then I called Ethan and we talked. I hadn't seen or heard from him in almost fifteen years, but our conversation wasn't in any way awkward or uncomfortable. We talked again the next night, and the night after that, and finally he said, 'Lindsay, are you going to come to me or do I have to come down to Texas to get you?' And I knew that he would do it, because even after fifteen years, he still loves me. And I still love him.

"So that's why I'm taking my kids and moving to Alaska, which is a heck of a lot scarier than anything I faced when I was twenty," she admitted. "But I've finally realized that not everyone gets second chances, and I'm not going to let this one pass me by."

"Well then, I'll wish you luck," Jason said to her.

Lindsay laughed. "I don't need luck, because this time I've got love on my side."

He pondered that comment long after she'd gone, long after he'd let another cup of coffee grow cold, and he marveled at the courage of a woman who had lost so much and was willing to risk it all again. For love.

He'd been in love before. His feelings for Kara had been real—certainly more real than anything he'd ever experienced to that point in his life—but they weren't nearly as deep or as strong as what he felt for Penny.

And after three days away from her, he realized that he'd been using his grief over Kara's death as a shield against loving Penny—and not very effectively. Maybe loving Penny was a risk, but it wasn't as if he had a choice in the matter. Not telling her how he felt certainly hadn't stopped the feelings from growing.

He went back up to his office, marched past his secretary's desk without saying a word, grabbed his coat and his briefcase and walked back out again.

"It's the middle of the day," Barb said. "Where are you going?"

"Home," he said simply, and felt as if an enormous weight had lifted off of his chest.

She huffed out a breath. "Well, it's about time."

Jason followed the pulsing beat of a Van Halen song toward the spare bedroom, and with every step he took, his heart pounded harder against his ribs. He didn't know if Penny was even speaking to him, but at least she was still here. It wasn't until he opened the door of his penthouse and heard the music that he acknowledged the fear, buried deep inside his heart, that he might already be too late, that she might already be gone.

Instead, she was standing on a stepladder, painting the trim around the window, and he just stood for a moment, watching her. She turned to dip her brush in the can of paint and spotted him there.

The paintbrush slipped out of her hand, bounced off a step on the ladder, then against her thigh, before landing on the ground. Jason crossed the room to pick it up carefully by the handle and set it on the tray.

"Good thing you put down drop cloths," he said.

Penny didn't seem to know what to say. She just stared at him with a mixture of hope and wariness in her beautiful green eyes.

He reached for the rag she'd been using, found a clean corner, and started to rub the streak of butter yellow paint on her leg.

She swallowed. "You'll get, uh, paint on your suit."

"I'm not worried," he said, and continued with the task. Then, "I thought you'd be at the store."

"Is that why you came home in the middle of the day—so you could sneak out again without seeing me?"

"No." He put the rag down, looked up at her. "I wanted to see you. I just thought I'd have to wait until you got home to do so."

She started down the ladder, and he stepped back, out of her way. "I decided to take a couple of days off."

"Why?"

"It occurred to me that I needed to make some changes around here if I wanted to feel like it was my home, too."

"Then...you're staying?"

She lifted her chin, almost defiantly. "I'm staying."

He'd been prepared to plead, to beg, to do whatever he needed to do to keep her in his life. And while he didn't think she'd made her decision to make things easier for him, he was both relieved and grateful. "I'm glad."

"Are you?"

He nodded. "I've missed you."

"No one told you to go," she said, silencing an exuberant David Lee Roth with the press of a button. "Or to stay away."

"I know. I just needed some time." And though she didn't ask, he told her, "I've been sleeping at the office. Or maybe it would be more accurate to say I've been trying to sleep at the office."

"Your choice," she reminded him.

"Yes, it was," he agreed. "And not one of the smartest choices I ever made."

"And now?" she prompted.

"Now I want to come home," he said. "To be with you, to start our life together. But I understand, if that's going to happen, I need to be honest with you about some things. I need to tell you about Kara."

Penny sat on the edge of the bed that was covered by an old sheet to protect it from paint splatter. He sat on the blanket chest so that he was facing her, so close that their knees almost touched.

"We met when I was in my second year of college, she was a drama major—bright and fun and beautiful. And I was completely infatuated.

"It wasn't all smooth sailing," he told Penny. "In fact, it wasn't smooth at all. She started to demand more and more of my time, she was clingy when we were out in public, and when we weren't together, she accused me of being with other girls. Of course, the more possessive she got, the less I wanted to be with her. We broke up. We got back together.

"She seemed to thrive on the constant drama, but it made me crazy. So, at the end of the year, after we both finished our exams and were going our separate ways for the summer, I suggested that we take a break.

"She cried and pleaded, but she'd been crying and pleading for months, and I couldn't deal with it anymore. I came home for the summer and went to work at Foley Industries. With every day that passed, I half-expected she would show up—it was the kind of thing she would do—but she never even called. A few weeks later I learned, through a mutual friend, that she'd got a minor part in a stage production in some little town not far from where she lived.

"I went up one weekend to check out the play, and we had a great couple of days together. She seemed happier, more secure about who she was and what she was doing, and we talked about getting back together when we returned to school in September. She called me a few weeks later to invite me to come up for the year-end cast party. I had responsibilities at my job and couldn't get away, and she got ticked. She accused me of caring more about my job than her, and then she hung up on me.

"I should have called her back, tried to make her understand. Or maybe I should have taken the time off of work because I knew it meant a lot to her. But I didn't—and as it turned out, that was the last conversation we ever had.

"She went to the cast party with her friends, and I don't know if there was alcohol or drugs or both—Kara was always game to try anything at least once—but she ended up falling off of a bridge into the river below and drowning."

"Oh, Jason." There were tears of empathy in Penny's eyes as she reached out to take both of his hands in hers. "I'm so sorry."

"I felt so lost and so guilty. My experience with Kara taught me to be wary, to never let myself get too deeply involved. I didn't want anyone to matter that much again. I certainly had no intention of ever falling in love again." He leaned forward and kissed her. Softly, gently. "You blew all my plans to pieces by making me fall in love with you."

Her breath caught, the fingers that were linked with his gripped tighter. "What did you just say?"

He smiled. "I love you, Penny. Maybe it took me a while to realize it, but I finally did. Kara was my past. You are my present and my future. And I know that there are no guarantees in life, but I want a life with you. For now and forever."

"Well, that works out pretty good," she said. "Because that's what I want, too."

Then she wrapped her arms around him, pressed her mouth to his, and as Jason sank into the kiss, engulfed in the warmth of her embrace, he knew that he was finally home.

Chapter Fourteen

Penny was awakened by a kiss on Christmas morning. She lifted her arms without opening her eyes, winding them around Jason's neck to pull him closer.

"You're going to make me forget that I'm holding a breakfast tray," he warned against her lips.

Her eyes flickered open. "You brought me breakfast in bed?"

"Just some cinnamon rolls I heated up, and some fresh fruit and yogurt."

She shifted into a seated position so that he could set the tray across her lap.

"This is so sweet."

He shrugged. "Well, everyone does the decorating of the tree and hanging of stockings, but I thought we should start some Christmas traditions of our own."

"I like this one," she said, stabbing a plump ripe strawberry with her fork and popping it into her mouth.

"Well, hurry up with it," he said, "because we have to check under the tree to see what Santa brought."

"Santa only delivers presents to good girls and boys," she teased.

"Wasn't I good last night?"

Her lips curved. "Very good," she agreed. "Though I'm not sure the jolly old elf concerns himself with the type of behavior you're referring to."

But she dutifully finished her breakfast, sharing bites and nibbles and kisses with Jason, then got out of bed and slipped her robe on over her nightshirt.

There was a veritable mountain of presents under the huge balsam fir that was propped up in the corner of the living room. Certainly a lot more than had been there when she'd gone to bed the night before. And more than half of them were "from Santa," according to their labels.

When opened, she found a ton of baby things— rattles and bibs, board books and teddy bears, and two impossibly small Texas Rangers baseball jerseys.

"Obviously, Santa enjoyed shopping at Baby World as much as you did," she teased her husband.

Jason just smiled as he tore at the paper on one of his presents.

She'd struggled, trying to pick out gifts for her new husband. But she'd found the complete series of one of his favorite television shows, a luxurious cashmere sweater that matched the blue of his eyes, a new putter he'd coveted when they were shopping together for a gift for his father, and—after much debate—she'd gone back to Baby World and bought the big floppy dog that he'd been so disappointed about having to put back.

For Penny, Jason had the babies' sonogram picture framed and he gave her a coffee-table book about Venice. When she flipped open the cover, a pair of plane tickets fell out.

"Because I want to take you for dinner at the real St. Mark's Square," he told her. "And I figured we better go sooner rather than later, because you won't be able to travel in a few months."

"The time seems to be flying by so fast," she admitted. "I can hardly believe that by this time next year, we'll have two babies crawling around."

"Probably trying to pull down the Christmas tree," Jason warned.

"Ripping bows off of presents," Penny added.

"Wanting to eat the ornaments."

"And generally running both of us ragged."

But she smiled after she said it, and he couldn't help but smile back.

"Are you still scared?" she asked.

He wrapped his arms around her, pulling her close. "Terrified."

She leaned her head back against his shoulder. "Me, too."

"But I figure we can handle anything together."

"I hope— Oh."

Jason turned her around, so that she was facing him. "What is it? What's wrong?"

But Penny only smiled as she took his hand and laid it on the curve of her belly.

"What…it moved. He moved. They moved. One of them moved."

She laughed. "Yeah."

"Have you felt it—him—them—before?"

"A couple of times," she said. "But never as strong as that."

The flutter came again, and Jason's eyes went wide. "Wow."

"It's pretty amazing, isn't it?"

"You're amazing," he told her, pulling her into his arms. "Thank you."

She tipped her head back. "For what?"

"For not giving up on me."

"I love you," she said simply.

"Well, that's good," he said. "Because it so happens that I love you, too."

And then he kissed her.

And as he was kissing her, he steered her toward the couch, swearing against her lips when he banged his shin on the coffee table.

Penny giggled.

Jason pulled back and looked around. "There really isn't a lot of room for two rug rats to run around here."

"I'm sure they'll manage."

He considered that for a minute. "And there's no backyard."

"We'll visit Uncle Travis's ranch to give them a real taste of the outdoors," she suggested.

"That's another thing."

"What is?"

"We're quite a distance from grandparents and aunts

and uncles who might otherwise be talked into babysitting every once in a while."

"Is there a point to all of this, or are you just thinking out loud?"

"I'm thinking that we need more space," he said again. "Yeah, maybe we could manage here with the twins, but what happens when we have another baby?"

"Another baby?"

"Or two."

"Could we get through *this* pregnancy first?"

"Of course," he agreed. "I'm just suggesting that we might want to rethink our living arrangements."

"You want to move?"

"Not right away. After all, it will take a while to decide on a plan, then find a builder, not to mention the time line for the actual construction."

"You want to *build* a house?"

He shrugged. "I figure, now that we've got a solid foundation, we can start building our future. And I want a house with a wide porch, where we can sit together when we're old and gray, and reminisce about where each of our children took his or her first steps. What do you think?"

He glanced down at her, saw that her eyes were all misty and soft. "I think it sounds wonderful."

"Good," he said. "Because I got a really good deal on some vacant land just outside of Dallas."

"But you work in Houston."

"Foley Industries has offices in Dallas, too," he reminded her.

"But what about your assistant? You always said you couldn't manage without her."

"Well, her husband is retired now, and, as it turns out, Dallas is actually closer to her new granddaughter, so Barb is quite happy to make the transition whenever we do."

"Is that really what *you* want?"

"I really want to be with you, and I can do that in Dallas as easily as anywhere else," he said.

"Speaking of which, we have to be there for dinner in less than six hours, so we'd better start getting ready, if we don't want to be late."

Jason tugged on the belt of her robe and the knot came undone. "Who says we don't want to be late?"

They made it on time…barely.

Of course, everyone else was already there when Jason and Penny arrived at the McCords' Dallas mansion. The house had been decorated to the nines, as it was for every holiday, but this year there was something extra—love was in the air, as tangible as the scent of pine and as intoxicating as the wine that was being poured at the table.

It had been a busy year for both families, and though there had been some trials and tribulations, everyone was looking forward to continuing to build the new relationships they'd established and to strengthen the bonds between the families.

"Grandma Eleanor," Olivia said, fairly bouncing up and down in her seat at the table. "I have something to tell you."

"What is it, sweetie?"

"You're going to be a grandma again."

"That's true," Eleanor said. "Because Auntie Penny's going to have a baby in June."

"And my new mommy's going to have a baby, too," the little girl proclaimed.

Unlike when Jason had announced Penny's pregnancy exactly one month earlier, the response to Zane and Melanie's news was overwhelmingly positive.

"And before you say anything, Dad," Zane announced, "yes, we are planning to get married."

"And definitely before the baby comes," Melanie assured everyone.

"Speaking of weddings," Eleanor said, shifting her attention to Tate and Tanya. "I just want to express our pleasure and gratitude that you were able to be here to celebrate with us today, despite your wedding being only a week away."

"Christmas is about family," Tanya said easily. "And I'm thrilled to be joining this one."

"And how are plans for your wedding coming?" Paige asked Katie.

"I've learned that a wedding is like a snowball," the bride-to-be responded. "The more you try to keep things rolling, the bigger and more unwieldy it seems to get."

"You wanted the big, formal wedding," Blake reminded her. "I just wanted to make you happy."

And it was obvious that they were.

"I have an announcement to make, too," Charlie said. "No, I'm not getting married or going to be a father," he hastened to assure them. "But it has to do with my father." He looked toward the head of the table, where Rex was seated, where Devon—the man he'd always believed was his father—used to preside. "I've decided to legally change my name to Charles McCord Foley."

Rex's hand shook slightly as he put his glass down,

and his eyes shimmered with an unfamiliar moisture. "Is this really what you want to do?"

"Yes, it's really what I want, so long as it's okay with you." He paused. "Dad."

Eleanor didn't try to hide the tears that spilled onto her cheeks.

"It's more than okay," Rex said gruffly. "It's the best Christmas present you could give me."

Olivia, bless her, lightened the moment by announcing, "I'd rather have a puppy."

Everyone laughed, but her father shook his head firmly. "You already have a kitten, and you have a baby brother or sister on the way, definitely no puppy."

As she pouted, Jason leaned closer to whisper in his wife's ear.

"I'll bet you she has a puppy before she has the baby brother or sister."

Penny shook her head. She'd seen, firsthand, how easily the little girl wrapped her daddy around her finger. "I'm not taking that bet."

Eleanor wiped her cheeks with her napkin, then lifted her glass. "To the Foleys and the McCords—a merging and ever-growing family."

Penny lifted her glass of nonalcoholic wine. "It's growing even more than you realize."

Paige, somehow instinctively guessing what her sister was going to say before she made the announcement, gasped. "Really?"

Penny nodded.

"Really what?" Tanya demanded.

It was Jason who answered the question. "Penny and I are expecting twin boys in early April."

"Twins?"

"Boys?"

"I think you're going to need a bigger place," Travis said.

Jason nodded. "We're hopefully going to start building early in the new year, not just because of the twins, but because I hope to have more babies with my incredible wife."

"Speaking of houses," Rex said, nudging his wife.

"I was going to wait until we were opening presents," she told him, but the excitement in her voice revealed her eagerness to share more news. "Since Travis has finally put a ring on Paige's finger—"

"I had to wait for my sister-in-law to create the perfect design," he told them, raising Paige's hand for everyone to see, then bringing it to his lips and brushing a kiss over her knuckles.

"As I was saying," Eleanor continued, "since the engagement is now official, I wanted to give you a special gift to commemorate the occasion."

But it was Paige who held up the envelope that had been hidden beneath her plate.

Travis's smile was quizzical as he lifted the flap and pulled out the folded papers. His eyes grew wide when he opened the document and realized what it was. His gaze went to Paige, who smiled and nodded, then to Eleanor, who also nodded.

"It's the deed to Travis's ranch," Paige announced to everyone, since her fiancé seemed too stunned to say anything.

"That's quite an engagement gift," he finally said.

"I wish I could say that I'd thought of it," Eleanor

said. "But it was Paige's idea. She thought it appropriate that the land you've worked for so long should finally be yours."

"Ours," he said, squeezing Paige's hand.

"Yours," she said, and leaned over to brush his lips with a quick kiss. "Until we're married, then it will be ours."

Everyone laughed.

Beneath the table, Jason linked his hand with Penny's.

She looked up and smiled at him, marveling at how much had changed in the four weeks that had passed since Thanksgiving. At that time, she'd been so hurt by Jason's deceptions and so filled with distrust, she didn't even know how to tell him that she was carrying his baby. Certainly she couldn't have imagined that, only a few weeks later, so much would have changed.

Now, there were no secrets between them and the promise of a beautiful future ahead.

* * * * *

On sale from 7th January 2011
Don't miss out!

Available at WHSmith, Tesco, ASDA, Eason
and all good bookshops

www.millsandboon.co.uk

PRESCRIPTION FOR ROMANCE
by Marie Ferrarella

Paul had a funny feeling about his new PR manager Ramona. Was she a
spy trying to uncover his secrets...or a well-intentioned ingénue trying
to steal his heart?

LOVE AND THE SINGLE DAD
by Susan Crosby

Donovan's just discovered he's father to a young son. But the newly
minted single dad won't be single for long if old flame Laura has
anything to say about it.

WEALTHY AUSTRALIAN, SECRET SON
by Margaret Way

Charlotte is shocked when Rohan walks back into her life. Her heart still
beats his name. But can she tell him her secret after all the heartbreak
of the past?

3-22·72 88   15

2 FREE BOOKS
AND A SURPRISE GIFT

We would like to take this opportunity to thank you for reading this Mills & Boon® book by offering you the chance to take TWO more specially selected books from the Cherish™ series absolutely FREE! We're also making this offer to introduce you to the benefits of the Mills & Boon® Book Club™—

- **FREE home delivery**
- **FREE gifts and competitions**
- **FREE monthly Newsletter**
- **Exclusive Mills & Boon Book Club offers**
- **Books available before they're in the shops**

Accepting these FREE books and gift places you under no obligation to buy, you may cancel at any time, even after receiving your free books. Simply complete your details below and return the entire page to the address below. You don't even need a stamp!

YES Please send me 2 free Cherish books and a surprise gift. I understand that unless you hear from me, I will receive 5 superb new stories every month, including two 2-in-1 books priced at £5.30 each, and a single book priced at £3.30, postage and packing free. I am under no obligation to purchase any books and may cancel my subscription at any time. The free books and gift will be mine to keep in any case.

Ms/Mrs/Miss/Mr _____ Initials _____

Surname _____

Address _____

_____

_____ Postcode _____

E-mail _____

Send this whole page to: Mills & Boon Book Club, Free Book Offer, FREEPOST NAT 10298, Richmond, TW9 1BR